UP CLOSE AND PERSONAL

AUCKLAND MED. 3

JAY HOGAN

SOUTHERN LIGHTS PUBLISHING

Published by Southern Lights Publishing

To request permission and all other enquiries contact the author through the website

https://www.jayhoganauthor.com

Trade Paperback ISBN:978-0-9951324-7-4

Digital ISBN: 978-0-9951324-8-1

Digital Edition published March 2020

Trade Paperback Published March 2020

First Edition

Cover Art Copyright © 2020 Kanaxa

Cover content is for illustrative purposes only and any person depicted on the cover is a model.

Editing by Alicia Z. Ramos

Proofread by Lissa Given Proofing

Printed in the United States of America and Australia

For my family who read everything I write and keep saying they love it all, blushes included.

ACKNOWLEDGMENTS

As always, I thank my husband for his patience and for keeping the dog walked and out of my hair when I needed to work. And my daughter for all her support.

Getting a book finessed for release is a huge challenge that includes beta readers, editing, proofing and cover artists and a tireless PA. It's a team effort, and includes all those author support networks and reader fans who rally around when you're ready to pull your hair out and throw away every first draft. Thanks to all of you.

CHAPTER ONE

RAIN LASHED AT THE FLIMSY WINDBREAKER ED HAD GRABBED BY mistake, pissing through the material like it was a semipermeable membrane, soaking him through to his irritated skin in under thirty seconds flat. *Fucking Auckland's, fucking subtropical, fucking weather.* Late summer in his beloved Christchurch had never involved a week of torrential rain like this—rain with a hard-on to make the Guinness world record for the ten best ways to fuck with a crime scene.

He grabbed his crime scene case and a pair of gumboots from his go-bag and pulled his head out from the BMW's open trunk, which had just earned a big fat zero for shelter. Juggling everything under one arm, he reached up to close the trunk and took a step back—ankle deep in a mud sucking puddle. *Oh, for fuck's sake.*

A constable rushed over with an open golf umbrella and received a withering glare for his effort. "I'd work on your timing," Ed deadpanned.

The constable grinned in a good-natured way. "Sorry, sir. I'll get right on that. Cats and dogs, right?"

Ed cocked a brow. "Freaking elephants and rhinos, kid. Now,

have you got anywhere I can change without risk of being washed away to fucking Australia?"

"You can use that van." The constable indicated one of the half-dozen police vehicles lined up along the muddy strip of coastal scrub bordering the beach. A few sheltered officers were busy on their radios and computers, while their unlucky colleagues could be seen combing the surrounding area in the milky evening light, rain pelting down from above.

"At least it's still daylight, sir. And there's a tent over the body."

"Thank Christ for that." Ed took a step and sank into another pool of muddy sludge. "Goddammit." He drew a breath, gathered the frayed threads of his patience, and shook the mud off his shoe, ignoring the constable's half-swallowed chuckle.

"Where the hell are we, exactly?" His gaze swept the bleak headland. "My satnav gave up talking to me about ten kilometres back, and that last couple were a damn goat track."

"On a farm just south of the Manukau Heads," the man answered, chirpily enough to have Ed wanting to slap some cynicism into him. That much youthful cheer had no place in this weather. "The dirt road acts as a private local access to the beach," the constable continued. "Detective Knight figures the body was dropped offshore somewhere and the big swells dumped it here. Without the cyclone it might never have made land. Lucky for us, right?" The kid practically beamed, and Ed wondered if he'd ever been that fresh and optimistic.

"Yeah, real lucky." He reached the van and hauled himself inside to change into his coveralls. "Don't you dare move a muscle," he called through the closed door. "If I have to find my way to the body unprotected in this rain, there'll be two homicide inquiries, understand?"

"Yes, *sir*." Followed by another cheerful laugh.

God help me. Ed was done in a couple of minutes, after which he followed the constable down to the beach, past a couple of crime scene techs doing their best to see anything in the murk, and on to check in with another waterlogged constable standing guard over a smallish green tent whose sides heaved with the impact of the bucketing rain. The shore was a pattern of flattened sand ribs, the thundering waves at its back damn near deafening.

He dipped his head to avoid the clots of wet sand being whipped up and thrown his direction by the unforgiving westerly and rolled his eyes at the constable on guard. "'*Come to Auckland,*' they said, '*the weather is so much better,*'" he practically shouted.

The man grinned as water dripped from his chin. "If you think this is fun, sir, just wait till the humidity hits."

Ed winced. "Don't even start with me." Then he turned to the first constable, who was trying—and failing dismally—to fix the umbrella, which had promptly turned itself inside out as soon as they'd hit the beach. "You may as well head back," he said. "I'm as wet as I can possibly get."

The perky constable grinned, gave a jaunty wave, and hoofed it.

Jesus Christ. Whatever that kid was on, someone needed to bottle it—they'd make a bloody fortune. Because if there was a word for beyond fucking saturated, the state of Ed encapsulated it, and cheerful he was not.

He ducked his head and pushed through the tent flap, straight into Mark Knight, and nearly bowled him over. He sighed. *Nope. Not even close to cheerful.*

Knight reflexively grabbed on to Ed's arm to steady himself, and heat radiated from that single point of contact straight to Ed's groin, managing to bypass everything in between—including that small particle of common sense Ed had been trying so hard to nurture.

Goddammit. For some unknown reason, Mark Knight rattled every brick in Ed's fastidiously built walls. It had been that way from the first time he'd run into the detective while giving evidence in a case Knight had come to observe. That was less than a week after he'd shifted from Christchurch to take the forensic pathologist's role at Auckland Med, and he'd nearly lost his tongue in the damn witness box, pinned by Knight's unrelenting scrutiny from the public gallery.

Since then, they'd worked a few cases together, and every minute spent in the man's proximity had been... unsettling.

Mark Knight was... well, gorgeous, to put it plainly. And at least six feet six of solid muscle to Ed's not-inconsequential six. With a wide, inviting mouth and medium-length chestnut hair worn in an unruly yet somehow flattering style that framed a pair of laughing hazel eyes, Knight was friendly, flirtatious... and gay—something he'd made clear from the get-go. The appreciative once-over he'd given Ed, along with an accompanying wink, said it all. So, yeah, pretty much everything Ed didn't need in his life right then—or ever, actually. Though how Knight had known Ed wasn't straight remained a goddamn mystery. Or maybe he just didn't care. Knight was... disarming, to say the least.

"Sorry." He waited for Knight to regain his footing, then stepped sideways, well clear of the man.

Knight tracked the move with a slow smirk. "Evening, Doctor. Sorry to interrupt your Wednesday night. Wet enough for you?"

Ed jumped as the tent snapped beside him with a sudden gust. "Evening, Detective. And I refuse to answer the question due to an insufficient supply of suitable adjectives, none of them complimentary."

Knight laughed, and the sound sent a wave of something warm skittering through Ed's chest. Then he indicated his partner, busy leaning over a body half covered with sand. "You remember Liam?"

The tent did little to muffle the roaring of the wind outside, making even loud conversation tricky and forcing Ed to lean in to catch Knight's words. The move brought with it a hint of pleasing citrus cologne that did nothing to subdue Ed's reaction to him one iota.

"Of course," he said as the younger detective looked his way.

In his late twenties, with a buzz cut and stunning green eyes, Liam Crowley appeared to be everything Mark Knight wasn't: a sober young man, forever on the verge of a yawn, who maybe needed to smile a little more. Still, he'd heard Liam had two kids under three

—enough to suck every last thread of vitality from any working parent. He did, however, offer a thoughtful contrast to Knight's irreverent, effervescent personality, and Ed figured they made a good team.

He nodded at the young man. "Detective Crowley. Now, I know you're not thinking of touching my work, right?"

Liam held up his hands. "Not a chance, Doc. I value my balls just the way they are."

Ed gave a chuckle. "Good call." He glanced over and caught Knight's appreciative gaze. They locked eyes.

Knight grinned. "Sorry to get you out in this shit."

Heat rose in Ed's cheeks. "I'm thinking you're really not."

Knight chuckled. "And you'd be right. Misery loves company, and you're good company." He threw Ed a hand towel. "Wouldn't want you to drip all over the evidence."

Ed snorted. "I suspect that's the least of our worries." He dried his face and handed the towel back, careful not to catch Knight's eye again. Then he turned to study the body. "Anything I should know before I start?"

Knight moved alongside, his proximity throwing off enough combustible energy to power a small sun. "Not much. Farmer found him about six thirty p.m. and called it in."

Ed checked his watch. Eight thirty. Not too bad, considering how far out they were. He started to walk around the body, taking mental notes.

Knight continued, "The farmer had been here earlier this morning and it was clear, so the body's washed up in the last ten hours, give or take. No obvious ID..."

Ed lifted his eyes, wearing a scowl of disapproval.

Knight held his gaze with just the flicker of a smile. "We were careful. Used gloves. Just checked his pockets. Found nothing. But there *was* a guy reported missing yesterday. Family hasn't heard from him since Sunday. The description and clothing fit. And this one doesn't seem to have been in the water long, not that I'm an expert... of course." He gave a wry smile.

Ed rolled his eyes and refocused on the body. "Okay, I'll give you a strong maybe on the timing, based on first impressions, but we'll see. In the meantime, you go do whatever it is you need to do, Detective. I'll get the preliminaries sorted and let you know when I'm done."

Knight grinned in that oh-so-charming-shark way he had and bumped Ed lightly on the shoulder. "You got it, Doc. I'm sending junior number one out for some coffees. Warm us all up. It'll be a thirty-minute round trip. You want?"

Hell, yeah. "Thanks. Black, two sugars."

"A pleasure."

And that right there was Ed's problem. Two innocent words from the man's mouth, and a flurry of goose bumps ran over his skin. *Ugh.*

He shooed everyone out and took a deep breath, following it with a few moments' silence. Not that Ed was overly religious, but he did believe that all life, whether lived well or not, was due acknowledgement as its energy passed. If this body's owner hadn't been a respectful host, well, maybe the next one would be. It really wasn't a lot to ask, and it had always grounded him in the gravity of his work. His job mattered, both to the living and the dead, and Ed would be damned if he'd let either one down.

That done, he got to work with an initial catalogue of the body, ensuring any potential evidence would be protected during transport to Auckland Med for the full autopsy the next day. The crime scene techs would take hundreds of photos, but Ed liked to take a few of his own so he got exactly the images he needed. Once the body was moved, there was no going back. As he worked, he tried once again to understand the puzzling sense of disequilibrium that always plagued him in the presence of Mark Knight.

Ed wasn't *that* guy, had never been *that* guy. Never been one to crush or lust over *anyone*, especially if he barely knew them.

He scanned the body under his ministrations, taking a mental inventory and recording his thoughts on his phone as he worked.

He'd never reacted so immediately and so viscerally to a man, or a woman. In fact, he'd been told more than once that he was likely a demisexual bisexual. *Whatever.* He wasn't convinced, and didn't much care either way. He was just himself, Ed. And Ed needed time with pretty much *everything* he did in life, romance included. He didn't fluster over a few ridiculous appreciative looks sent his way. Shit like that meant nothing. He took things slow, and he liked it that way—the word hookup wasn't anywhere in his vocab, ever. He'd stuck with mostly women partners, not because he leaned more that way, but because women usually appreciated a slower burn, whereas men—or at least the ones Ed had been attracted to—seemed to expect sex pretty much up front after little more than a "Hello, nice to meet ya."

He wasn't a prude—far from it. He enjoyed sex, on the whole. And he didn't judge others for chasing no-strings-attached quickies— more power to them—he just didn't see the attraction himself. Like everything else in Ed's life, sex was something to be savoured, and the concept of a slow burn had pretty much dominated Ed's romantic playbook for over twenty-four years—ever since fifteen-year-old Ed had glanced at Vicki Stanton's pillowy breasts and then, an hour later, at Mitch Ellington's epically glorious arse in the boy's change room and thought, huh, Houston, we might have a problem.

His insta-reaction to the sexy detective therefore made no sense, and Ed would've gladly consigned the minicrush—or whatever the hell it was—to the trash, but for the immensely irritating fact that it just wouldn't fucking go away. Not to mention there was nothing about Mark Knight to indicate he was any different from all the other sex-obsessed men Ed had steered clear of for years. It had only taken a week on the job to learn via the grapevine that Knight had a reputation for enjoying life, and men: certainly not relationship material. Especially not the style Ed preferred. So his unexpected reaction to Knight was, to say the least... troubling.

But, enough. Ed shoved his personal disquiet aside and focused on his job.

The body in his hands was that of a Pakeha man, likely in his early forties, give or take. The farmer must have rolled the body onto its back to take a look, since indentations in the sand and discolouration from blood pooling suggested it had lain on its side for at least a few hours. The wash of the waves could also have been responsible.

The body was clothed in a filthy, tattered short-sleeved shirt of indeterminate colour and a pair of trousers, ripped around the knees and the right hip. No watch or ring, although there was a small tattooed band around the left ring finger.

There was no immediate indication of cause of death, but there was obvious bruising on the exposed skin of the arms and legs, and the face was peppered with contusions and lacerations—one eye swollen closed and both lips knocked about. And when Ed turned the head to check the back of the skull, his gloved fingers detected the telltale seesaw of bone on bone from a skull fracture, and then another. *Well, okay then.* Barring damage post-mortem, the likely possibility of blunt force trauma made its stage debut. Only the autopsy would determine whether the victim had been dead before entering the water or not.

The body wasn't overly bloated, and there was little evidence of any creature feeding, so it likely hadn't spent a lot of time in the ocean. Whoever dumped the body in all likelihood hadn't counted on the cyclonic storm surge depositing it onshore within hours. One to the good guys.

Removing the tangled seaweed from the lower arms exposed further evidence of unnatural death. A series of round burns on the underside of each forearm added an unwelcome element to the overall impression of assault, and Ed groaned. The deliberate infliction of cruelty always left him floundering to maintain a foothold of optimism about humanity, and his gut rolled at the thought of what the victim might have endured. Blessed with a cast-iron stomach, he unfortunately also possessed a good imagination, both a boon and curse. It helped him think outside the box, but it also came with the ability to conjure graphic imagery he could usually do without.

He finished the rest of his examination, stopping only to enjoy the mediocre but thankfully warm coffee delivered as promised, before spending a little time checking the immediate area. Finding nothing further, he left the tent and deposited his gloves into the bin provided, only mildly surprised at the stark glare of spotlights that sliced through the darkness to light up the tent and the proximate stretch of beach. He checked his watch. Ten p.m. One hour thirty. Not bad. And at least the rain had stopped and the wind had eased a notch or two.

He nodded in sympathy at the sodden constable still standing guard with his shoulders hunched against the chilly air, then stepped around a couple of crime scene workers on their hands and knees in the spiky tussock. Keeping to the access marked with police tape, he slogged his way back to the huddle of police vehicles framing the scene while mentally reviewing how he was going to pitch his verbal report. The detectives would latch on to the smallest clue and run with it, and that meant Ed had to show restraint. Nothing was solid until the full autopsy was done, but he could give them some direction at least.

Mark Knight spotted him straight away—of course he did—and headed over with Liam Crowley at his side. Ed's hands shot up to ward off the imminent barrage of questions.

"I'll tell you what I can, but it's all conjecture at this stage, got it?"

Knight and Crowley nodded.

He continued, "Long as we're clear. Well, on first impression it certainly supports the possibility of wrongful death, so I'd suggest you work it as a homicide, for now. There's significant trauma at the base of the skull, though I won't be able to confirm anything in detail till autopsy—nor whether it was cause of death. There's plenty of lacerations and bruising, although some of those may be the result of churning around in the ocean for a few hours. I'll be able to tell you more tomorrow. And the undersides of both forearms have evidence of burn marks consistent with the application of something like a cigarette—"

The detectives exchanged a look, and two sets of raised eyebrows landed back on Ed.

"Yeah, I thought that might be of interest," he said.

Knight blew out a sigh. "Anything else?"

"I take it you saw the tattoo on the guy's ring finger, since that hand was exposed?"

"Yeah. And while you were doing your thing, we got hold of our recently missing man's wife. Apparently, he had a custom tattoo instead of a wedding ring, due to all the lab work he did. The wife is going to send us a photo so we can compare. If they match it'll be enough to work with for now. Someone will bring her to Auckland Med for an official ID tomorrow."

"Good. Well, I'm off to get some sleep. I'll see you two bright and early."

"Exactly how bright and early?" Liam ventured. "I doubt we'll get out of here anytime soon."

Ed smiled. "I'll be opening him up at eight a.m. Be there or be square, Detectives."

Both men groaned.

In the police van, Ed managed to peel himself out of his jumpsuit, not that the coverall had done much to keep him dry. He felt like a wet banana, sodden to his skin, and was thankful for the change of clothes always ready in his go-bag. He'd have to live with his water-laden shoes a little longer.

Sloshing his way back to his car, he felt the heat of eyes on him and turned to lock gazes with Mark Knight once again. He was standing under a battered golf umbrella talking animatedly with two other officers. He gave Ed a quick nod, which Ed duly ignored. The last thing he wanted was to encourage Knight.

Back in the driver's seat, he cranked the engine to warm the car up and took a minute to breathe in the relative peace. He kicked off his shoes, ran his hands around the well-cared-for leather steering wheel, then flicked through his music till he found his favourite Whiskeytown album. He sang along with the first verse as he bumped his way down the goat track before finally hitting tarmac.

On the drive home he tried very hard not to think about the frustrating detective who crowded his thoughts, but it was easier said than done. Mark Knight was a large and very annoying wrinkle in Ed's carefully groomed life. The move to Auckland had provided a timely job promotion and a much-needed change of scenery after the Christchurch terrorist attack and the deluge of horrific autopsies the atrocity had sent his way. But it hadn't come without its stresses, and Ed didn't need any more added to the mix.

He called up his contact list and his sister answered on the second ring.

"Hey, Sis."

"Ed? What the hell? It's nearly midnight, you arsehole. I have to be in court at eight am."

An employment relations lawyer, Grace fought for the little guys. She was smart as a whip—lethal in a courtroom—and Ed was just so damn proud of her.

"What's happened? Are you okay?" Worry loomed large in her voice.

Shit. He should've known she'd leap to the worst possible conclusion. Sarah had ensured all his family were well primed for that.

"I'm fine," he reassured her. "Just been to a body, that's all. Wanted to hear a friendly voice. I didn't think, sorry."

She sighed heavily. "No, it's me who's sorry. I shouldn't have jumped down your throat like that, it's just..."

"I scared you. I know."

Nothing was said for a few seconds, and he could picture the wistful look on his sister's face. Of the three remaining, Grace had been the closest to Sarah. "Yeah. Bad habit, right?"

He nodded to himself. "Me too. You said you're in court tomorrow? What's this one about?"

"Local construction firm. Thought they could cut loose an employee with no redundancy package on some trumped-up reason, when really it was because the person had newly come out as gay. I'm gonna nail their damn balls to the wall."

And she would. He had no doubt. Grace was a pit bull wrapped up in a Gucci suit, and Ed would've given his right testicle to have been able to watch her in court the following morning. It was something he'd tried to manage as often as possible when he was living down there.

"So, what's up?" Perceptive as usual.

"Nothing."

Silence.

"As I said, I just wanted to hear your voice. It's been... harder... than I imagined. The move, I mean. I miss having you guys close."

Her voice was quiet. "It was time, Ed. Past time, in fact. And you know that. We've loved having you close all this while, but you need to spread your wings a bit. You're too—"

"Stuck in my ways?"

"—careful."

"Nothing wrong with careful," he grunted.

"No. But we don't need you to look after us any more, sweetheart. Love you, but don't need you. And you need to find what you want in life—and I'm not talking about work."

It stung, just a little, hearing the words, even though Ed knew he was being ridiculous. He and his other siblings had already been adults when they lost Sarah, the youngest. And yet he'd still felt an impossible responsibility to be there for them all—even for his parents, who'd often joked that Ed had been born with not only his, but all of his sisters' genetic quotas of duty and organisation as well. They in turn had gotten any ounce of extroversion he might have possessed.

So he liked things orderly and predictable and quiet. Nothing wrong with that.

"We're fine," she reassured him. "We're big girls now. Let us be here for Mum and Dad for a change... and for you too. Do us all a favour and try to live a little. Let the rest of the world see all those wonderful sides of you that we love."

"No one's interested."

"No one knows. Find a girlfriend—or a boyfriend. Just... try."

An image of Mark Knight sprang to Ed's mind. "Men are... messy."

Grace laughed. "Then find a woman."

He hesitated. "Maybe." But he hadn't been quick enough.

"Wait. Are you interested in someone? Is that what this is about?"

"*Pfft—*"

"Holy shit, you are. Who is it?"

"I'm *not* interested in anyone." *Liar.*

"Don't lie to me, Edward Newton. Now spit it out."

"I'm... attracted, *not* interested, per se. There's a difference."

"Barely. So... a name?"

"In your dreams. You're not getting a name, sugarplum, but he's a detective." Ed smiled at the sharp intake of breath at the other end.

"*He?* Holy crap, big brother. I can't remember the last time you were interested in a guy."

"Attracted to, remember, *not* interested."

"Whatever."

"Put the ticker tape away. Nothing's gonna happen, because apart from being a work colleague—which has all kinds of complications written all over it—he's also so *not* what I need."

"How come? Does he like you?"

"I... think so, yes."

"Does he breathe?"

Ed snorted.

"So, then?"

Had he mentioned pit bull? "He's... nice looking... and he's funny and intelligent—"

"So far I'm not hearing a downside."

"—and he's *also* not relationship material. He flirts all the time, and not just with me, and he has a... reputation. And you know how I hate the casual sex thing."

"Yes, Edward. Believe me, we *all* know how much you hate the casual sex thing. I think the poor schmucks who overwinter at Scott Base in Antarctica know how much you hate the casual sex thing."

"Shut up."

"But you like him, right?"

"No. He's irritating and—"

"So you like him." Statement.

"Maybe. But that's neither here nor there. Nothing's gonna happen."

"Maybe it should."

A swell of something uncomfortably like anticipation bloomed in Ed's chest before he squashed it. "No, I don't think that's a good idea. In fact, I think it's the worst."

Grace was quiet for a minute, then said, "So tell me the last time any of the *good* dating ideas actually worked for you?"

She had a point. Ed's dating history was hardly wrapped in accolades. "But that's the thing. Mark doesn't *date*. Everyone says that about him. He flirts and fucks. And I'm too damn old for all that."

She stifled a laugh. "Sounds *horrifying*. He should obviously be arrested at once. And you were always too old for that." Then she really did laugh. "But so what? If he doesn't date, then change his mind. I'm not saying you should fuck him and walk away—that's not you, I know that. But for Christ's sake, Ed, you can be as responsive as a dead fish when you dig your toes in. Respond a little, maybe give him a reason to *want* more than a one-night stand. Yes, you could get hurt. Yes, you might have to shake up that pristine little world you've built for yourself, but you also might get the chance to live a little. Sarah would want that for you."

Shit. "Low blow, Sis."

"Shit. I know. I'm sorry. But it doesn't make it any less true. She was the biggest risk-taker of all of us, you know that."

Also true. "I'll think about it. And thanks. Now I'll let you get some sleep. And leave the poor construction company with one or two organs in place tomorrow, yeah?"

She laughed. "Yeah, nah. Where's the fun in that. Love you, Bro."

An hour later he pulled into his drive, switched off the engine, and sat for a minute, relishing the blessed silence. Then he grabbed his wet gear from the trunk and fought his way through another band of rain to his front door. After sliding the key into the lock, he pushed the door open and called down the hall.

"Honey, I'm home."

CHAPTER TWO

MARK CHATTED WITH LIAM ABOUT THE CASE AS THEY MADE their way through the endless snaking corridors in the underbelly of Auckland Med towards the autopsy and pathology suite. The old subterranean maze connected the sprawling jumble of above-ground structures and offered a less crowded option for staff moving between them—even if it was creepy as hell. Hospital Architecture 101 had to include the mandatory section, 'Find the spookiest site for a morgue and build it right fucking there.'

To be fair, Mark could've parked a lot closer, gone in the sparkly new entrance, and avoided the dungeon tunnel maze altogether. The forensic pathology suite had undergone a recent facelift and been modernised to boast the highest specs in the country, and it was, in fact, the antithesis of spooky. But the original tunnel approach left a lot to be desired—lined with ceiling pipes and access hatches, it was painted a dismal grey, lit with flickering fluorescents, and stank like a dodgy thrift shop.

Feeling like he'd fallen into an episode of *The Addams Family*, Mark shivered. Liam was close enough to notice, and his bright green eyes danced with amusement. Partners for eight months, they'd taken a while to gel—complete opposites in lots of ways. The younger man was far more serious than Mark and prone to long periods of quiet reflection that Mark had struggled to not take as a personal indictment. It was a far cry from Kevin Banner, his last partner, now retired. That man was a veritable chatterbox and, if Mark were truly honest, more than a little lazy. But over the last couple of months, he and Liam had finally found their groove, even if the younger man was still a little too hard to read for Mark's liking.

"You all right there, boss?" Liam bit back a smile.

"Shut up. Bad enough having to watch a body being turned inside out at this hour of the morning without having to arrive through what could pass for the hallway to Uncle Fester's bedroom."

"Who?"

He gave Liam a playful shove into the wall. "You're an embarrassment to nerds everywhere."

Liam chuckled. "I still think this case is gonna be about drugs. I mean, the cigarette burns, the dumping of the body? It just reeks of gang-related shit."

Mark shrugged. "Maybe. Seems a bit too much effort, if you ask me. A gang's all about territory, theft, or the breaking of some fucked-up code. That leads to a beating or a quick death followed by the body being easily found. Kind of hard to check others back into line if the punishment isn't on display, right? What I *wouldn't* expect are cigarette burns and a dump at sea. Not saying you're wrong, just that it doesn't sit well."

Liam's expression said he wasn't convinced. "Ten bucks says I'm right."

Mark grinned. "You're on."

A pair of nurses in green scrubs passed them by, the young blonde sending a winning smile Mark's way.

Liam grunted in amusement. "You're clogging up the heterosexual airspace, my man. The least you could do is wear a sign or something, send them our way."

Mark nearly choked on his tongue and made a slow turn to his partner. "A sign?"

"Yeah. Or a badge. You know, something. Level the playing field for us poor slobs."

"You're married, Liam." Mark rolled his eyes. "You don't need a level playing field."

"I don't want to get in the ring. But it would be nice to be at least seen as a possible contender once in a while."

Mark shook his head. "Remind me to sign you up for the next diversity and inclusion in-service course. A fucking sign? Arsehole."

Liam laughed. "So, tell me again why we didn't come in the new entrance?"

Mark ignored him, keeping his gaze straight ahead.

Liam smiled sweetly. "Oh, *that's* right. *You* wanted to grab a coffee for our new pathologist. Don't remember you ever getting one for Tom Spencer... let me see..." He looked thoughtful. "Nope, never."

"Tom Spencer was seven hundred years old," Mark fired back. "Besides, the coffee was for us. The doc was a mere afterthought."

Liam gave him the side-eye. "Of course he was."

"And parking's easier up the top. It's still raining, in case you hadn't noticed."

"Would you like a bigger spade for that hole you're digging?"

Mark thought he was doing just fine with the one he had.

"Have to say I wouldn't have pegged Ed as your style," Liam continued to tease. "Just saying."

They pressed themselves to the wall to allow a pair of orderlies to push a steel body box past, and Mark took the moment to study Liam. "We've been partners... what, eight months?"

Liam nodded warily. "Seven months three weeks, to be precise."

"Right. And I think we've talked about my sex life all of... hmm, let me see... *never* in all that time. So forgive me, but I wouldn't have thought you'd have any idea, let alone an *opinion*, on my *style*, Detective. Please, do enlighten me."

Liam's neck reddened. "Well, I haven't, not really. But I'm not immune to the grapevine gossip either. And if you go through *young* gay dudes at the rate they say you do"— Liam's eyes glittered with mischief— "well, I just wanted to say that I'm seriously impressed. I honestly don't know how you find the energy. By the time I get home and get the kids to bed, I can barely lift my toothbrush, let alone any parts south of that. But on that note and in answer to your question, I just meant the doc is hardly in the same category as your usual pickings."

No. No, he isn't. And that was Mark's problem in a nutshell. He let Liam chatter away about the sad state of his own married sex life while Mark pondered the implications of Liam's belief about Mark's. It wasn't like the office chatter about Mark was new, or even inaccurate. That people thought he was a flirt and a lightweight had never bothered him before. So why did it all of a sudden sting, just a little bit? It was a question he suspected he knew the answer to if only he was brave enough to stop running long enough to consider it—which he wasn't.

"I wouldn't believe everything you hear," he said, interrupting Liam's inventory of sleep deprivation and its effects on the male refractory rate. "And why the hell are we even having this conversation?"

"Because I'm your partner?" Liam returned Mark's playful punch.

"*Hmmph.* You've never shown any interest before."

Liam shrugged. "Maybe I should have. Besides, you know in intimate detail all the highs and lows of my own childrearing disasters and the effects of newborn-baby cock-blocking syndrome."

Mark snorted. "True. Not that I couldn't have done without all the straight monkey sex imagery. I'm fucking scarred for life, man. Never had to deal with that shit from my last partner."

"Kevin Banner was old," Liam scoffed. "His dick probably had more wrinkles than a Shar Pei. He'd have been lucky to even remember what sex was."

Mark barked out a laugh and nearly dropped the coffee carry crate, scrambling to recover just in time. "I'll tell him you said that. Kevin was fifty-five, you arse. He just wasn't comfortable with the whole gay thing. Figured if we didn't talk about me having sex, he could pretend it didn't happen. The logistics simply blew his small mind apart."

Liam fired him a concerned look. "He cause you problems?"

"Nah. He was okay. Just a bit precious about his perceived place in the world. I think he struggled with the fact that he liked me, but then there was this thing where I took it up the arse. I was the first gay guy he'd really had anything to do with on a daily basis, and it rattled his whole world view. We got on great, as long as we didn't go there."

Liam went quiet for a minute before responding, "It had to be hard, though, playing that game."

Mark shrugged. "It was what it was. He was the senior of the two of us, and we rubbed along just fine, most of the time."

They reached the oversized elevator at the end of the corridor, and Liam pushed the call button. "Still, I don't envy you that revolving door on your bedroom, just saying."

Mark sighed. "Sure you don't. And who says I let them in my bed?"

That earned him a frustrated side-eye.

"Okay." Mark sighed. "I know I'm gonna regret asking this, but why don't you envy me?"

A nest of wrinkles appeared at the corners of Liam's eyes. "Because that whole dating scene is fucking exhausting, that's why. I don't judge you, man—"

Liam paused as the elevator arrived and they waited for an X-ray technician to wheel her portable machine out before they could board for the one-floor journey up. Alone again, Liam continued, "Variety is exciting, I get it. But don't think us poor married guys are slumming it. Sex with someone you really care about doesn't have to grow old."

"I think I like the old Liam better," Mark grumbled. "The one that kept his opinions to himself and his nose out of my business. Less buddy-buddy, more... *silent junior* partner. You're starting to sound like Josh—"

"The dog handler? Nice guy."

Hah. Now it makes sense. The doors opened on the next floor and they took a left, sun filtering through the large windows that formed one side of the corridor on to the endless beige linoleum floors. "Yeah, I just bet you two get on like a house on fire." His gaze narrowed. "Holy shit. Did he put you up to this? He did, didn't he?"

Liam's cheeks pinked. "He didn't... well, not much."

"I *knew* it. Just wait till I see that smarmy-faced, self-righteous—"

Liam smirked. "He married that doc here, right? They seem pretty happy, from what I hear."

They were. Something Mark tried hard not to think too much about. "Don't even go there. But just so you understand, your first mistake was in using the *d* word about what I do. I *don't* date, not any more. I learned my lesson. I fuck. There's a big difference. Dating *is* exhausting. Fucking a guy's brains out? Well, that's just plain fun. And love? Shit. All props to the guys it works for, man, but I'd as soon cut my right nut off. I get shivers just thinking about it."

The words rolled off Mark's tongue as effortlessly as they had done for years. That the truth of them was no longer sitting quite as easily was no one's business but his own. The sooner this conversation finished the better, and he made a mental note to corner his so-called best friend for a few words on minding his own damn business.

They arrived at the pathology suite, which still carried that new-paint aroma, and Liam immediately veered towards the autopsy room.

"Hang on." Mark stopped outside a door with the brass name-plate reading, "Edward R Newton, MD," affixed. It had been bugging him for months what the R stood for. "Let's try in here first. Not sure I want my coffee with a side of formaldehyde." Mark pushed open the door, took a step inside, and... froze. *What the hell?*

Liam barrelled into him from behind, pitching them both forward into the small room. Edward's coffee lid jolted loose and a third of its contents sloshed to the floor.

"Bugger." Mark pressed the lid back in place and glared at Liam. "Jesus Liam, watch where you're going."

But his partner was too busy walking in a slow circle around the room. "Whoa. Check this out."

Whoa, indeed. It had been over three months since Mark had been in the small pathologist's waiting room—since before the old pathologist had retired. He usually bypassed it on his way to the autopsy suite itself, and the change was striking. Country-pop cross-over wafted through the speakers... and since when had there been speakers? The grotesquely uncomfortable couch Mark had spent many restless hours on—even slept on once—had been swapped out for two oversized pillowy chairs and an elegant coffee table stacked with *Architectural Digest* and photography magazines. Edward had good taste.

"We're not in Kansas anymore, Toto," Mark commented.

Gone were the sterile hospital-grey walls, replaced by warm blush and accented with three sizeable photographs that were, frankly, stunning. One looked to be Venice: a line of picture-perfect pastel villas bordering a canal, with a group of local children dangling their feet over the edge. Another captured a night-time landscape: the Northern Lights caught mid-dance, misty jade rolling through a thinly painted ink sky with a single illuminated farmhouse as a foot-light. And in the last frame, an ageing drag queen: blood-red lips on a craggy face, thick foundation, and laughing painted eyes that spoke of a hard-earned soulful peace.

"Wow." Liam stepped in for a closer look at the latter.

"Yeah." Mark could do nothing but stare, unsure a week in the room would be enough time to digest everything the photographer had captured through that lens. Dragging his eyes away, he took a few seconds to study the rest of the room.

A water filter and coffee maker stood in one corner with a sign reading, "Drink Me" on the wall next to them. A dish of candy sat on the coffee table with "Eat Me" next to it. And on the wall beside the door leading into the pathologist's office, a brand-new call button with the words "Push Me" pinned above. He grinned. So the doctor *did* have a sense of humour. *Good to know.*

Apart from their professional exchanges, all of Mark's personal interactions with the sexy new pathologist had elicited responses that ranged from wary disapproval to blatant irritation—nothing that would have indicated Edward possessed this charming lighter side. It was an insight into the man Mark could've done without. Keeping Edward Newton in the purely lustful column was hard enough as it was without the man being amusing as well.

Mark kept to a steady diet of twinks for a very good reason: they didn't tempt him beyond a simple hookup. He wasn't looking for deep conversation or a meaningful relationship, so conversational skills weren't high on his agenda either. All in all, hot, young and willing pretty much summed up his "style" to anyone looking on. Or it had, up until recently, when stubborn, mysterious, and impossible had begun trending hard. The fact that even Liam had picked up on the change was... concerning.

Because Mark very definitely *did* have a type—it was just that Liam and pretty much everyone else was dead wrong about *what* that type actually was. Mature, steady, self-contained, and generally not very interested in Mark were in fact the ingredients of his personal kryptonite, and the sultry pathologist had all those in spades, making him dangerous to Mark in so many, many ways.

To that end, he'd dealt with his inconvenient and burgeoning attraction in his usual manner: flip comments and outrageous flirting to push every one of the man's tight little buttons and ensure Edward kept himself at a distance and out of Mark's reach. Mark would lay bets that his attraction to Edward was returned, but it was also patently clear Edward wasn't about to go anywhere with it, and that suited Mark just fine—or it had.

Because the problem was, Mark's strategy was beginning to fail, big time. Sure, he'd succeeded in pissing Edward off most times they met, and to be fair, that came with its own brand of warped and amusing satisfaction, but it had done zero to quench his growing interest in actually *getting to know* Edward Newton—three words that rarely entered his head about *anyone, ever.*

And if anything, the prickly response he'd consistently received had done nothing but add fuel to those southern fires. Feisty-and-hot-under-the-collar Edward had a lot going for him in the sexy department, leaving Mark speculating what Edward would be like unbuttoned and let loose in his natural habitat. Fucking spectacular, he suspected. It was a subject he was beginning to spend an inordinate amount of time pondering, and it was doing his head in. He just didn't know how to stop.

He rang the man's bell, thinking how very much he'd like to do just that to the sexy pathologist in different circumstances.

Edward Newton opened the door between his office and the small waiting room wearing a frown and immediately checked his watch. "You're early."

Had he mentioned pedantic? Mark grinned at the terse welcome and pushed the remains of the man's coffee his way. "Black and two sugars, right? Sorry, we lost a bit on the floor there. You can thank Liam for that—"

"Hey, you're the one who just stopped midwalk," Liam protested.

Mark ignored him, his eyes fixed on Edward's icy blues. The man's eyes were as changeable as the weather: steel grey to baby blue, depending on his mood and his level of irritation with Mark's flirting. "I thought you could use the boost, Edward."

Edward's cheeks pinked unexpectedly, and he worried his bottom lip as he glanced to the spill on the floor and then back to the coffee. "It's Ed. And, um, thanks." He took the cup and waved them both into his office.

Liam sauntered past while Mark wiped the floor with one of the coffee shop napkins he'd been carrying, then followed. Edward pointed to a bin under his wash basin and Mark disposed of the soggy paper which earned him a nod of approval.

"I was just about to head on in," Edward informed them. "We can go through this way." He took a sip of his coffee and studied the cup with apparent surprise. "It's, um... good," he said, taking a much larger swallow.

"Glad you like it. The hospital coffee shop does a better job than the cafeteria."

"I'll have to remember that." Edward studied him with softer eyes. "It's much appreciated." He took another sip and set about gathering some files into the crook of his arm.

Mark warmed at the approval, feeling more than a little ridiculous that he gave any kind of shit about what Edward thought about his damn coffee. But of course he did. This was Edward, after all: destroyer of common sense, sent to Earth with the sole purpose of fucking with Mark's life.

Something of all that must have shown in Mark's expression, because Liam caught his eye and smirked. *Bastard.*

While the doctor finished collecting what he needed, Mark scoped out his office. The soft, comfortable furnishings and warm colours from the waiting room continued here. The doctor had good taste and apparently liked his workspace to be... cosy—something that seemed at odds with his usually cool demeanour.

Not to say Mark had expected the man's office to be all hard-edged utilitarian and caustically professional, but he wouldn't have been surprised. There was evidence of Edward's fastidiousness, for sure: things lined up on his desk just so, no piles of books on his shelves—all stood and arranged by size, jacket hung on an honest-to-God coat hanger rather than just the hook, outdoor shoes set neatly by the door. But nothing... cold. Everything ordered but just short of obsessive.

So maybe it was only Mark that Edward was icy with? And, as Edward balanced his files and coffee and made his way out a second door, Mark pondered why that idea suddenly didn't sit so well, especially since he'd gone out of his way to ensure that was exactly what happened. *Huh. Like you don't already know the answer.* Because the reality was, Mark very much *wanted* to know this other side of the man. The soft-furnishings, photographs, quirky-humour side. He wanted to know what welcoming, relaxed, and happy-to-see-you Edward looked like. An image of spooning and lazy mornings in bed rattled into focus, and... *what the fuck?* Maybe he needed a holiday. Or maybe he just needed to pull his head out of his butt and get to know Edward R Newton.

He shoved that itchy thought back under its rock and trailed Edward and Liam into a clean, bright corridor and along to the autopsy suite itself—because he'd pretty much ensured the chance of Edward *ever* letting Mark get to know him rated approximately zero.

He needed to get his head on straight.

Liam and Edward waited at the door to the autopsy suite for Mark to catch up. Although autopsies were part and parcel of the job, it didn't mean Mark liked them—though he'd long ago gotten over being queasy. Liam... hadn't, and Mark grinned at the sudden influx of nervous energy apparent in the younger man and the way he binned the remains of his coffee as though it were noxious. Mark threw his empty one on top.

"Lost your thirst, partner?"

Liam regarded him with a scowl. "Shut up. I didn't want to spill anything in there, is all."

He snorted. "Of course you didn't. Can I entrust you with the note-taking today, or do you think you might have to make a sudden exit?"

Liam answered with a grumbled "Dickhead" and a spiky flash of those gorgeous emerald eyes, and Jesus, Mark hoped his wife appreciated what she had there.

"Grab a gown." Ed waved them towards the small visitors' change room. "I'll meet you inside." His eyes shifted directly to Mark. "And thanks again, for the coffee."

"My absolute pleasure." Mark's choice of words and their slow delivery was deliberate. He hadn't missed the flushed look on Edward's face when he'd said a similar thing the night before. And sure enough, Edward frowned, ducked his head, and disappeared into the autopsy room wearing another rosy tint. *Gotcha.* Mark grabbed a gown and followed him in, Liam trailing behind. Then he set about watching Edward do his thing.

Covered head to toe, with his face protected by a plastic shield, Edward still managed to provide ample eye candy for Mark to feast on. Especially with the appearance of a pair of sexy-as-fuck nerdy black-rimmed glasses. And just where the hell had they come from? Mark couldn't recall Edward ever having worn them in the past... and he definitely, *definitely* would have remembered. Not least because they apparently came with their own set of library fantasies. Who knew?

Watching Edward in his element was a lesson in appreciating the man's understated manner and evident skill. He was shorter than Mark by a fair number of inches and leaner. Tight, bunched muscle, lithe and strong, moved Edward's body where he needed it with minimum effort. Mark had observed more than his fair share of autopsies in his career and at least a half-dozen of Edward's since the pathologist had arrived at Auckland Med—enough to know Edward was no slouch when it came to his job. He worked in a meticulous manner, with refined grace and a fluid, economical style that reminded Mark more of an intimate dance than an autopsy. And when the saws and spreaders and big-arse interventions came out, Edward remained remarkably serene, conversing with his attentive assistant in a casual, warm manner.

As with every autopsy, Edward started with a careful overall inspection, recording notes for himself and issuing instructions to his assistant, Sandy, who took photos as they worked. The man's clothes were removed or cut off with care, every scrap investigated before being sampled and bagged as evidence. Long, gloved fingers glided over the dead man's anatomy, lifting, calculating, taking stock, gentle but intent, and Mark found himself transfixed. Scars, tattoos, injuries were all noted, described, and sampled where necessary—in particular, the burns on the underside of the dead man's forearms. Once all the externals were completed, Edward opened the body up with a large Y incision and set about the internal examination.

Inoffensive country music of the same ilk as in the waiting room —some band Mark had never heard of—filled the cavernous clinical space, which had been decked out in predictable white and stainless steel. The only pop of colour came from a further four oversized photographs, as intriguing as the ones in the waiting room, and which Mark couldn't remember seeing there before. Edward's gaze wandered their way whenever he was thinking, and Mark had the sudden notion that maybe Edward was the photographer. If so, it was another interesting piece in the delectable puzzle that was Edward R Newton.

"Are these your work, Edward?" he asked as Edward handed Sandy the victim's lungs to weigh.

Edward glanced up, confusion showing on his face, but before he could answer, Sandy called out the lung weight, and even Mark knew that was too light if the lungs had been filled with water.

"Looks like he was dead before he hit the water," Edward commented. "Though you'll have to wait till I open them up before confirming. Homicide is looking more and more on the cards." His mouth set in a grim line, as if he was personally affronted.

Mark glanced at Liam to make sure he was taking notes. "Hardly a surprise, all things considered."

Edward grunted and went back to his work.

"So, about the photos?" Mark pressed.

Edward raised a wary eye.

"I wondered if you were the photographer. If so, you've got a great eye."

Edward's gaze ran to the prints, and his cheeks brightened ever so slightly. "Ah, yes, I am... thanks. I only just unpacked them." His head ducked back down to his work.

"He's good, right?" Sandy chimed in. "They've made this cold space feel way more inviting."

Edward threw his assistant a sharp glance. "I'm just an amateur. Can you get some extra tissue samples from those burns, please?"

Sandy set about the task he'd been given while Edward fumbled as if trying to remember what he was up to. And *oh, boy.* Things didn't get much better than a flustered Edward Newton, and Mark appreciated the hell out of it.

"I think that's my favourite." He indicated a rugged Alaskan forest landscape on the far wall above the stainless counters. It had been taken from the forest floor perspective looking up and was all angled shadows and glimmering ice amid a towering canopy of green fir, all cut with the soft orange rays of an evening sun.

Edward's gaze tracked to it and softened. "It's mine too. I took it on a camping trip last summer with a... friend..." Edward's gaze flicked his way just for a second, and Mark felt something slither uncomfortably in his gut, something he was at pains to ignore. *A friend?*

"It's just a hobby," Edward faltered, clearly uncomfortable with the direction of the conversation.

Did he really not know how good they were? Mark couldn't, wouldn't let that stand. "They're stunning, Edward. You're really talented. Honestly, I love them. What about you, Liam?" He turned in time to see Liam's head jerk up in surprise.

"Huh? Oh, right." Liam glanced at the images. "Yeah. Um, nice shots."

Mark shot him a narrow-eyed glare, to which Liam bugged his eyes pointedly and mouthed, "What?"

He spun back around to find Edward looking at him sideways, a wrinkle in his brow as if he didn't quite trust what he was hearing—perhaps expecting Mark's usual sarcasm to make a reappearance any moment. And yeah, Mark really couldn't blame him for that.

Sandy watched the exchange with interest. Mark didn't know much about the long-limbed guy other than that if he wasn't queer, he'd eat his damn detective's badge, and the young man was way, way too casual and handsy with his boss. Nothing overtly flirtatious, just touchy in that kind of natural, unconscious way some people had. Regardless of the reason, it was beginning to get on Mark's nerves. Mostly because Edward didn't seem to have any objection to it. This, when Mark knew, just *knew*, he'd have been all kinds of pissed off if Mark had even looked like trying it. And no, he didn't want to examine those feelings either.

When Mark didn't add anything further to his comments about the photos, Edward seemed to relax and answered, "I wouldn't use the word talented. I just... like them. Especially here. They remind me of life, beauty... hope, maybe? This job can get depressing if you let it. It gives a jaundiced view of life: dead bodies, sad stories, and all too frequently a reminder of just what cruelty and violence people are capable of. You'd know all about that too, Detective. The land-scapes give me... perspective, anchor me in something beautiful, help me think. Stop me from losing my mind, quite possibly."

They stared at each other for a long minute as Edward's words sank into Mark's consciousness and set off all kinds of warning bells along with a hunger he didn't want to look at too closely. Then Liam cleared his throat from somewhere behind and broke the spell, and Edward went back to his work, calling Sandy to his side.

A few more seconds of silence passed before Mark found his tongue again. "You're a complicated man, Edward," he said, causing Edward's wary gaze to flick his way. "And I get the feeling I'm only just scratching the surface. Makes me wonder what other surprises lurk beneath that cool exterior."

Edward's shoulders tensed, and he snorted. "I can assure you, Detective, there's nothing interesting about me whatsoever. I expect you'd find my life predictable and boring, just how I like it. What you see is what you get."

A slow grin slid over Mark's face. "Somehow I very much doubt that," he said softly, holding Edward's appraising gaze. The man's dour expression cracked for just a second, revealing something shockingly close to predatory in those glimmering eyes. Then, as quickly as it appeared, it was gone, and Edward broke off eye contact and went back to his work. But the damage was done. That single glimpse of an unfettered, rapacious Edward had seared itself into Mark's brain, and the saying *be careful what you ask for* sprang to mind. Still, when had Mark ever let common sense get in the way of foolishness?

Oh, no. Edward R Newton was anything *but* the boring, simple man he touted himself to be. In fact, Mark suspected Edward was more like a Russian doll, with a wealth of surprises locked into every layer. Maybe he was a screamer? Maybe he liked to be tied up? Craved to be topped hard? A smile tugged at Mark's mouth. *Yeah.* All that cool control? He could see Edward needing to hand that shit over, and... *fuck...* that thought had rapidly gone nuclear.

An electric saw fired up and dragged Mark back into reality, reminding him they'd reached his least favourite part of the autopsy, the opening of the skull. A strangled groan from behind gave a good indication Liam was of a similar mind. He turned to where the other detective was scratching away in his notebook. So far Edward hadn't given them much more to work with, but Mark knew better than to press for any details. Edward would summarise when he was good and ready—Mark had learned that the hard way.

Liam's determined expression now had a decidedly nauseated tinge to it.

"You okay?" Mark mouthed silently.

"Fine," Liam replied in a similar manner, although clearly, he wasn't. But he went back to his note-taking and refused to meet Mark's eyes.

So be it. They all coped in their own ways. Mark thought of Edward, and yeah, they each needed to find their own anchor to a brighter world, their own set of internal landscape photographs. For Liam he suspected those were his family, his children. But for the life of him, Mark wasn't sure of his own. Not his family, that was for certain.

An unruly lock of hair fell over Edward's face shield, partially obstructing his vision as he worked to open the skull. With both hands occupied, he kept flicking his head to clear it, but to no avail, and Mark wanted desperately to reach across and tuck it behind the man's ear. He stopped himself in the nick of time, sidetracked by the swipe of tongue across a pair of full lips as Edward finally managed to flip the offending hair out of the way.

The shiver of desire that surged through Mark was... unexpected. After all, he wasn't some naïve virgin. He didn't indulge in flustered teenage half-chubs... at least, not usually. As if reading his mind, Edward's gaze flicked up for a second, and Mark responded with an innocent grin—a child caught with his hand in the candy jar. Edward's groomed brows dipped into a full-on scowl, but Mark wasn't about to feel embarrassed at being busted ogling the eminently droolworthy pathologist.

Your serve, Edward. You can't fool me. You're feeling it too.

Edward dismissed the attention with a frustrated shake of his head.

It had become an exhausting dance between them, but Mark didn't know what else to do. For three months he'd been unable to ignore the man's baffling effect on him, yet he hadn't been willing to let it become more than that either. Josh's voice yammered in his head about what the hell he was doing with his life. Did he really want to just keep fucking his way through men? Did he want to grow old alone? *Did he?*

He'd thought he knew the answer to that, thought he'd made his peace with it. Now he wasn't so sure. Regardless, he suspected it was too late to change anything with this *particular* man. Edward's impression of Mark, based on precisely what Mark wanted him to see, was full of holes, more lie than truth, and earned zero points in his favour—something Mark found himself regretting for the first time in a long while. Was it too late to change that? Probably.

Liam nudged him, and he realised he'd missed something... again. A quick glance found Edward beckoning both of them for a closer look at the skull and tissue damage, and also a good look at those cigarette burns.

It sure as shit looked like the victim had been tortured.

Liam tapped his elbow, looking distinctly green around the gills.

"Go on." Mark shooed him out of the room. "I've got this."

Edward looked up as the door closed and gave a half smile.

Mark shrugged. "Kids these days."

Edward snorted, and when Mark was done getting his look at the injuries, Edward handed over to Sandy to finish up and close. Then he pulled his face shield off his head and disposed of it and his gloves into the bin before crossing to where Mark leaned against the freezing tile wall, stifling a yawn.

"Keeping you up, Detective?"

Mark grinned wolfishly. "You wouldn't catch me complaining about that."

Edward's brows dipped. "Detective—"

"Sorry, I don't know what came over me." Mark bit back a smile. "And it's Mark."

"*Detective.*" Edward wore a long-suffering expression, as though Mark were little more than a toddler. "I get that you're an unrepentant flirt—I imagine half the population of Auckland is aware of that."

Ouch.

"Irritating but not to be taken seriously, right?" He stepped directly into Mark's space and eyeballed him from a few inches away. "But I'm a big boy, Detective—"

He paused for deliberate effect, causing Mark's eyes to spring wide. Was Edward Newton flirting with *him*? Well, not exactly flirting. Goading was more like it. Even so, back the fucking truck up, because there was nothing, *nothing* flustered about Edward in that particular moment, and everything Mark thought he knew about him went tits up.

Sandy watched from not too far away, but Edward kept his voice low as he continued, "You'll find I'm a far harder nut to crack than you think, Knight. Don't mistake reserve for naivety. I eat lightweights like you for breakfast, but I doubt there's enough substance in there"—he poked Mark's chest with his finger—"to warrant the effort." He winked and stepped back. "Just saying." Then he walked off, leaving Mark scrambling for mental purchase in a universe that had just changed orbit.

Beside him, Liam chuckled. *Damn.* Mark hadn't heard his partner return, too busy being put in his place.

"Need some oxygen there, boss? A chair, maybe? I mean, I can see how getting crushed at your own game could be... disturbing."

"Shut up."

"It's just that he kind of—"

"*Shut. Up.*"

"Yes, sir." Liam sighed dramatically. "Jeez, try to help a guy out..."

From across the room, Edward locked eyes with Mark and grinned. *Oh, yeah. Game on, mister.* Mark gathered a decent eye-roll for the other man and left it at that... for now.

"So, you ready for my summary?" Edward wandered back across.

"I'm all ears." Mark sent him a wry smile, which was duly ignored.

"Cause of death was blunt force trauma to the back of the head with a large flat instrument like a shovel or block of wood. The victim was dead before he hit the water. The cigarette burns and a wealth of contusions and lacerations were all inflicted antemortem and indicate a sustained and deliberate pattern of assault over a period of time lasting maybe a few hours up to a day, but probably no longer.

"Time of death sits between twelve and twenty-four hours prior to being found. Harder to get much closer than that, sorry. Too many other factors involved including the unusually cool sea temperature for the time of year. I've taken blood and tissue samples, and I should have the preliminary tox screen results back this afternoon with the full report tomorrow, so don't pester me." He eyeballed them. "I'll let you know when I have them; I don't need a reminder. Anything else I can do for you, gentlemen?"

Mark answered, "It's enough for now. The wife is being brought here at noon for the official ID. She wanted to wait until her son could be with her. We told her the autopsy was happening this morning but she still wanted to wait. We'll interview her after that."

Edward nodded.

"Great. Then I'll look forward to hearing from you later. Just one more thing." He eyeballed Edward, who narrowed his gaze warily in return. "What does the R stand for?"

Edward frowned. "The R?"

"The R in Edward R Newton?" Mark kept a straight face, ignoring Liam's soft snort of amusement.

Edward's eyebrows lifted, and Mark's lips turned up in what he hoped was a Cheshire-cat-worthy grin—satisfied to have thrown the exquisitely buttoned-up doctor off his game. Oh, yeah, this was far from over.

Edward's sigh was big on annoyance, although Mark wasn't at all convinced, if only because of the twinkling blue-grey eyes that accompanied it.

"Good day, Detective."

Mark leaned in. "After this morning, *Edward*, it absolutely will be."

"Ed."

Mark grinned. "Talk to you tomorrow, *Edward*." He turned and left, knowing that there was no way in this universe or any other he was ever going to call the sexy pathologist anything but Edward, ever again. He glanced back through the window in the door, gratified to find Edward still staring after him. *Yeah. Bring it on, Edward.*

CHAPTER THREE

"So, Mrs Bridge"

"Evie, please." The woman's bloodshot eyes brimmed with unshed tears. Evelyn Bridge had been grief-stricken after formally identifying her husband, and in deference to her obvious distress, Mark had decided to interview her in her home rather than the station, and with her son in support. He wanted to make this as easy as possible, there being little evidence she had any involvement in her husband's death.

Finn Bridge, her son, was a tall, not unattractive, rake-thin young man with kind, restless grey eyes, a generous mouth, killer cheekbones, and a slight breakout on his chin. He wouldn't have looked out of place on a high school volleyball team, having yet to grow into his long bones and substantial hands. But when he did, with the benefit of a bit of muscle and a settled hormone profile, Finn would scrub up nicely, possessing all the elements of hot and handsome simmering just under the surface of awkward.

"Evie. Can you tell us again about the last time you saw your husband?"

Liam entered the lounge and placed three coffees on the table before taking his own to his seat. Finn reached for his, and Evie immediately wrapped both hands around hers in a white-knuckled grip. She took a sip, sat the cup back on the table, and drew in a shaky breath.

"Sunday night," she said with a sigh. "Rowan was teaching at Waikato Uni this week. He had an early class Monday, so he was staying over Sunday night. The hour-and-a-half drive is hell on a Monday morning."

"And when was he due back?"

"Wednesday, yesterday." Her lip quivered, and she reached for a Kleenex.

Liam asked, "Was there anything different about him? Did he appear anxious or worried?"

Evie shook her head. "No, nothing like that. Things were... normal. Except he always called when he got to Hamilton so I wouldn't worry, but this time he didn't. And he never answered any of my texts or calls either. It wasn't like him. I thought maybe his phone was dead, so I tried not to worry until I still hadn't heard anything by Monday morning. Then I knew something was wrong."

Mark flicked through his notes. "You said that you tried to call the motel, right? The Empress?"

Her frown deepened. "Yes. It's where he always stays when he's down there. It's walking distance to the university. But they said he hadn't stayed with them since last year. I never even checked—I just assumed that's where he'd be. He looks after all his travel bookings himself."

"Can you think of a reason he might have stayed somewhere else, maybe with a lecturer or someone he... knew?" Mark pressed.

There was no escaping the implication, and Evie Bridge bristled accordingly. "He wasn't having an affair, if that's what you're insinuating. Rowan and I have always had a good relationship. I can't imagine him having a... fling. If you knew him, you'd know how preposterous the idea was. Rowan was a huge introvert. It took him over a year to ask *me* out, and I practically threw myself at him from day one."

"I'm sorry, but it had to be asked," Mark apologised, watching the woman carefully. She was affronted but not obviously hiding anything. She believed what she said, though that meant very little in terms of whether her husband had actually been faithful or not. Mark had heard it all before. "So when the motel said he wasn't staying there, what did you do?"

"I called Finn, and we went through a list of motels close to the university. When none of them had his name on their books, I tried calling Carey Miller, the person Rowan was teaching with. All I got was a message to say Carey was away—until today, I think. Then I tried the university itself, but they didn't seem to know anything about Rowan, and they wouldn't give me an alternative contact for Carey because of some privacy policy."

She took a sip of coffee and a few deep breaths. "That's when I rang the police to report him missing, around noon on Monday. They took his vehicle registration and said they'd put it in the system, but that it had been less than twenty-four hours so there wasn't much more they could do. On Tuesday, when he still hadn't been in contact, he became officially missing, and... well, you found him Wednesday night." Evie's head slumped to her chest.

Finn threw a concerned look his way, and Mark nodded, giving the woman a moment to collect her thoughts. "You both said you can't think of any reason someone would want Rowan dead, but it looks like somebody did. And the evidence suggests it wasn't just a random act or opportunistic thing. Someone targeted your husband, and whoever it was spent some time with him before he died. Chances are they wanted something from him. Money? Information? Something. Do you have any idea what that could be?"

Both Finn and Evie shook their heads, and Mark was inclined to believe their wide-eyed ignorance. There was no hint of deception— they were simply bewildered and desperate for answers.

Evie said, "I don't know what to tell you. We don't have a lot of money. We still have a mortgage, for heaven's sake. And there's only about fifty thousand out on deposit. That's it. And neither of us come from money, Detective."

Mark already knew that. The Bridges were middle class, solid and relatively conservative—the first in both their families to even attend university. Rowan had a PhD in science—chemical engineering, to be specific, and Evie a degree in education. Their eighteen-year-old son Finn was in the first year of a science degree at Auckland University. They owned an unassuming house on the North Shore, a late-model Toyota, and an older Nissan. They screamed predictable suburbia with every coffee loyalty card pinned to their fridge, and a family photo hung in their conventional living room adorned with a nineties black leather lounge suite, large-screen television, and ubiquitous potted plants. If you were going to pick a prospective victim to torture for their PINs, it *wouldn't* be Rowan Bridge.

Mark had very little to work with. He needed something, anything. "What about his job? You said he worked from home. Consulting, right? Tell me more about that."

Evie sighed, slender fingers worrying the hem of her soft floral shirt. "Rowan is, *was*—" Another sob broke, and she took a few seconds to settle. "Rowan *was* quite brilliant as a scientist, but he never fitted well in a regular job in an office or lab environment. He was a very... private man, quiet. He could be... brusque. Never with us, of course. He was very gentle. But others often found him... abrupt. Detached."

Someone very similar sprang to Mark's mind. "Is that why he chose self-employment?"

Evie Bridge swallowed another sob. "I'm sorry. I just don't... I can't believe..."

Finn grabbed his mother's hand, and Liam pushed the box of Kleenex Evie's way. She took a handful, sending him a grateful half smile. Then she dabbed at her eyes and continued. "Yes, I guess. There's more opportunity than you'd think to be self-employed in Rowan's line of work, especially if you're as talented as he is, *was*.

Companies sometimes outsource aspects of their research and development to people who have more specialised knowledge. Or they contract them in-house for short-term assignments. Rowan did both. In the last twelve months he had two contracts for a pharmaceutical company in the US, a four-month contract in-house with Morgan and Associates here in Auckland, and then the teaching assignment at Waikato. He had no trouble finding work—there were always two or three companies lurking in the wings at any one time. He could pretty much cherry-pick his projects."

"Must have been nice. What was his specialty?"

She thought a moment. "He's been involved with a variety of things, but if you asked him he'd probably say, *have said...* dammit, I'm never gonna get used to that..." She sucked in a stuttered breath, her eyes welling again. "He'd *have said* alternative fuels. He's worked for the oil and gas industry for years, but his real interest was in renewables—they were the subject of his PhD. Having said that, chemical engineering is used across the board in a number of ways, and Rowan mostly worked with formula development for R & D—"

"Research and development?"

Evie nodded. "Rowan had experience in developing both catalytic processes and hydroprocessing in fuel production, but he'd done work in improving manufacturing processes for pharmaceuticals as well."

Mark's brows peaked. "Seems an odd combination."

She sighed. "He worked mostly on the formula side, which is bound by the rules of chemistry and physics, regardless of what the end product is. For the contract with Morgan's, he worked on their renewable energy programme, but for the US pharmaceutical company, he worked on streamlining the production of a new bowel cancer treatment."

"And he did all this from home?"

"Mostly. For the pharmaceutical job he teleconferenced, used some local private lab facilities here to do some testing when he needed it, and made a couple of trips to Dallas. But for Morgan's, he worked on-site with their team in their downtown offices. It really depends on the contract. Mostly companies used him for contained aspects of their research which he had more experience in, or to problem-solve a particular issue. He was rarely given all the information for any one project—too risky for the company to have all that out there with a contractor."

"You said he had access to a private lab?"

She frowned. "It used to be Pinlab downtown, but I know he recently changed. I'm just not sure where to."

"How recently?"

"Three months, maybe? After he left Morgan's. Why? Do you think it's important?"

Mark shared a look with Liam. It was the first hint of something out of the regular for a man who, up until then, had maintained a strict routine and whose life appeared woefully lacking in any spontaneity. His only indulgence? A penchant for restoring classic Ford Prefects, of all things, and that was about as exciting as it got. One sat partially completed in the family garage—all its accompanying parts meticulously arranged on the floor.

He bypassed Evie's question. "And this teaching job?"

She frowned, taking time to think. "Something about catalytic cracking of fuel, I think. Although I'm guessing it ended up being more work than he bargained for, because he was putting in some long hours. I'd hardly seen him the last few weeks, but I assumed that was because he had a lot of planning to do before the students arrived. Carey Miller's the one to ask about that."

Mark had his own suspicions about this teaching job of Rowan's, but he kept his thoughts to himself. "Did your husband seem out of sorts lately? Depressed, angry, secretive, drinking more than usual?"

She shook her head. "None of those. Or rather, it was hard to tell with Rowan. As I said, he kept himself to himself and always seemed... level, if you get what I mean? He didn't drink alcohol, couldn't stomach it, and I rarely knew about any work problems he had, because he didn't discuss his contracts with me—a lot of what he did was confidential. I might know the general idea, but no specifics. He just seemed... normal, I guess." Her attention flicked to her son, who was busy frowning into his coffee. "Finn?"

The young man looked up. "It's just... well, you remember, Mum, a couple of months ago... I don't think he was depressed, but he *was* kind of... off, I guess. Remember, we were supposed to go to the Drayton Players that night? They'd started their new three-act-play season. But then Dad begged off at the last minute, something about some mate of his—"

"Oh, that's right," Evie interrupted, eyes wide. "Gosh, I'd forgotten all about that. Some work colleague had his home robbed. It really rattled Rowan. He got our security system upgraded and a new lock put on his study."

Mark and Liam shared another look.

Evie continued, "Some of the work Rowan does, *did,* for companies was commercially sensitive. He had to have a good security system in place. It was part of the contract requirements."

Liam asked, "Was there anything particularly sensitive he'd been working on recently?"

Evie closed her eyes for a second, and Mark was about to repeat his partner's question when she opened them again. "I wish I could tell you, but I just don't know. As I said, he wasn't allowed to tell me much at all. He was excited about whatever he was doing, though, I can tell you that."

"Excited?"

"Yes. Working with formula development and testing isn't always a thrill seeker's haven, Detective."

Mark smiled at the small attempt at humour.

"But every now and then, Rowan got to work on something he really loved, and the last couple of months were more like that, I guess—" Evie's voice hitched, and another wad of tissues made its way to her eyes. "I thought it was the teaching, but now I don't know what to think. I'm not painting a great picture, I know." There was a silent plea in her expression. "But he was a good man, a good father, and we loved each other. We had a good marriage—" She dissolved into tears, both hands dragging down her face in wretched misery.

Finn scooted over and wrapped his arms around her, physically placing himself between her and them. "Don't you have enough?" he snapped.

Mark sympathised. "Almost. We'll need the name of the friend who was robbed and the security company."

Evie wiped her face with her palms and pushed her son a little to the side. "I'm okay, Finn. They're just doing their job." Then to Mark, "I afraid I can't remember the friend's name. It was while he was working at Morgan's, though."

Finn got to his feet. "I'll get you the security company's card."

Evie collapsed in on herself with a shaky sigh and grabbed another handful of Kleenex. "I just can't understand why anybody would want to hurt him. He was a good man, an honest man."

Mark reached over and squeezed her hand. "You've been very helpful. We'll need to have a good look around the house and particularly his study. And someone will be taking his computer and laptop, so we'll need his passwords as well, if you know them."

"Of course. Take anything you want. You won't find any of his consulting work on them, though, if that's what you're looking for."

Mark's confusion must have been obvious.

"Most of Rowan's contracts required him to do all his work online in-house, using the client's servers. He signed locked-down nondisclosures and every other sort of hush-hush imaginable. Some of the R & D he worked on was worth a lot of money to rival companies."

Mark's ears perked up. "How much money?"

She shrugged. "Hundreds of thousands of dollars, even more."

Finally a possible motive. Excitement tugged at Mark's belly.

Evie continued, "Anything he worked on, offline or on his own computer, or with pen and paper, he wiped at the end of each contract, if not each day. If it was ever discovered he hadn't, his career would be over. And I don't know all his passwords, but I can give you the main ones."

"That would be a big help."

———————

Sounding more like a law firm than a research facility, Morgan and Associates was not at all what Mark expected. In place of a run of sterile labs in some nondescript building, it was instead housed in a beautifully renovated Ponsonby villa, hidden behind a discreet façade of subtropical plantings with not a test tube in sight.

Morgan's might not have been Rowan Bridge's most recent contract, but Waikato University was a two-hour drive south and Morgan and Associates was an easy fifteen-minute detour on the way back to the station. Mark secretly hoped a phone call might suffice for the university—he wasn't keen on leaving town in the middle of a murder investigation.

"The labs, both computer and testing, are all located underneath us," CEO Doug Morgan explained as he led them through to his office at the back of the building.

Soft lighting, a palette of cream and soft green, leather furnishings, and luscious prints added to an overall sense of calm and opulence. For all of that, it had none of the warmth of Edward's office, and Mark grinned, picturing Edward working quietly at his desk surrounded by his photographs. The image felt oddly reassuring.

"We had the villa lifted and a concrete basement purpose built before the refit on the rest of it started." He directed them to take seats around the highly polished coffee table set in one corner. "Morgan and Associates is a fully accredited lab and advisory service. Coffee, gentlemen?"

"No, thanks." Mark refused for both of them and joined Liam on the couch.

Doug Morgan chose a contemporary curved chair that screamed designer price tag, sat, and steepled his fingers. In his early fifties, he was an average-looking, tight-eyed, middle-aged, Pakeha man, who was struggling with male pattern baldness and the beginnings of a double chin. He appeared relaxed and welcoming, if not warm. Impeccably groomed, he wore a suit that likely cost more than Mark's monthly salary and an attitude that said he knew it.

"I can't believe Rowan is dead." His pained expression didn't quite meet his eyes. "It just... defies belief. I'm not sure how I can help, but I'll try, of course."

Mark made a point of studying the lavishly decorated office. "I have to say, Mr Morgan, this is a striking work environment. Not at all what I envisaged for a lab."

Morgan beamed with obvious pride. "I'll take that as a compliment, Detective. We try to attract the best people to work for us, the crème de la crème, and I've always believed in the importance of an agreeable ambience to getting the best out of people."

Mark suppressed the urge to roll his eyes.

"The testing labs are, of course, more... functional, but they still possess wonderful light, good art, the best in computer technology, state-of-the-art equipment, and a comfortable break room with a well-stocked snack and refreshment fridge. In addition, all our employees get full health insurance and flexible hours."

Morgan sounded like a damn brochure. A two-day-old sandwich and a barely drinkable coffee would be considered a win back at the station. And who the hell used phrases like "agreeable ambience"?

"Sounds... expensive," he commented dryly.

Morgan chuckled, completely missing the sarcasm. "It is. But in return we get loyalty, reduced staff turnover, better productivity than most labs in the country, and more than our fair share of the top-end clientele who bring in the money. We have people queueing to work here, Detective. I'd say that was a win-win."

The CEO bordered on the irritating side of smarmy, and Mark wanted to slap him, maybe twice. Then again, he couldn't help having an oily personality, and the feedback from Mark's investigation team had shown the company to be as prosperous as its CEO touted, so there was that.

He gave a cool smile. "So it would seem. Can you tell us what exactly your company does, Mr Morgan?"

Morgan leaned back in his chair. "We offer a range of services from food and agricultural testing to pharma development and environmental and product testing—pretty much anything in that arena that might be needed by the business sector. That's our bread and butter, but it isn't our raison d'être."

Lord help me.

"Those *mundane* services support our own R & D, which is rooted in working on renewable energy."

Bingo. "Is that the area Rowan Bridge was contracted in to work on? His wife mentioned it was his passion."

Morgan's face pinched, his expression almost apologetic. "It was..." He hesitated.

"But?"

Morgan blew out a sigh. "Look, I hate to speak ill of the dead, but I was recommended Rowan by a colleague who said he was brilliant in the area of renewables, a genius at coming up with solutions to tricky problems."

"I take it you had a tricky problem?"

Morgan sank into his chair. "We did. I can't give you the details, as they're commercially sensitive, but we had a processing issue that defied every solution we threw at it. So, at considerable cost, we contracted Rowan to solve it for us."

"And did he?" Mark asked, then waited as the CEO hesitated in his reply.

"No," Morgan finally answered. "He didn't. In fact, he made no progress at all in the four months we had him. In the end I had to terminate his contract and let him go."

Mark frowned, surprised. "And yet he'd been recommended?"

"I know." Morgan shrugged and gave a weary sigh. "All I can say is that we expected great things, but in the end, Rowan Bridge turned out to be somewhat... ordinary."

Huh. Very much at odds with what they'd been told. "What

exactly was he was working on?" Mark suspected he wouldn't get the answer, and Morgan's patronising apologetic wince confirmed it.

"I'm sorry, Detective, but it would be entirely inappropriate for me to comment on that. The market for our work is highly aggressive, and in our competitors' hands the data would be worth a great deal of money. Besides, Rowan hasn't worked here for a number of months. I would've thought his more recent employment would be more likely to give you the information you need. Come back with a warrant and our doors will, of course, be open."

Mark didn't need to see Liam to hear the rattle of his eye-roll. He bit back a smile. "We may just do that," he warned the smug CEO.

Morgan shifted uneasily in his seat. "I don't mean to put road-blocks in your way, but it would ruin us if it got out that we simply handed over material to the police willy-nilly without the proper warrants. And I can't imagine that anything Rowan worked on *for us* might have led to his death. His role simply wasn't important enough here. I've no doubt he was a talented pharmaceutical engineer, but for what we needed from him, he just didn't deliver."

"And yet his latest job was lecturing at Waikato University in precisely the same renewables area, not to mention it was the subject of his PhD."

Morgan opened his hands wide, his frustration evident. "I don't know what to tell you. Just because someone can teach doesn't mean they are capable of groundbreaking application. All I can say is that *we* were underwhelmed by the man."

Mark got to his feet. "One last thing." He pinned Morgan with a stare. "Rowan's wife mentioned she thought a colleague of his had their house robbed during the time Rowan worked here."

Morgan shrugged. "Not that I know of. Sorry, Detectives."

CHAPTER FOUR

"Your opinion?" Mark threw the question at Liam as he drove them back to the station. The rain might've stopped, but it left a sodden city baking in 90% humidity and counting. He'd tossed his coat along with his tie into the back seat the minute they returned to the car.

"I don't get it." Liam cranked up the air con and took a slug from his ever-present water bottle. It bore the logo of the school where his wife taught—a fundraiser having resulted in half the detective squad lugging around identical bottles, Mark included. It made for some confusion.

Liam continued, "According to the wife, Rowan was brilliant—God's gift to chemical engineering—good enough to peddle his skills from home and work for big-name offshore companies, at least. And yet Morgan painted him as little more than an average employee. Now, even allowing for a bit of fangirling about her husband, that's a pretty big discrepancy."

Mark took the on-ramp to the motorway and jockeyed for position with the school pickup crowd. "Maybe the contract with Morgan wasn't his forte?"

"Then why accept it? Evie said her husband was always in demand, that he had multiple offers on the table at any one time. Why take on something he wasn't good at? I don't see the reasoning."

Mark agreed. "And the big question is, why *wouldn't* he be good at it? Renewables was his baby, or so Evie said. Plus the guy was *recommended* to Morgan by presumably someone else in the industry."

"Which meant he should've been good at his job."

"Precisely." Mark took the turn into the underground car park at the station, pulled into his spot, and cut the engine before turning to Liam. "So, why wasn't he? I think we need a lot more information on this project he was working on for Morgan. Maybe Bridge's laptop will give us a clue. Did Connor say when he'd have something for us?" The station's tech expert had been sent to pick up all Bridge's computers and drives.

Liam pulled a face. "Only inasmuch as he'd be able to say fairly quickly what he *could* access and what was gonna take some time, depending on the passwords."

Mark locked the car, and they headed for the elevator to the detectives' bullpen. "Okay, so you get on with a warrant for Morgan, and I'll follow up the Waikato University lead—see if I can track down this Carey Miller. He should at least be able to clear up whether Bridge had the intellectual manpower upstairs or not. And let's hope Connor or Edward can give us something more this afternoon."

"Edward, huh?" Liam smirked.

Mark flashed him a warning glare. "Not. A. Word."

Liam hit the button for the fifth floor and put his back to the elevator wall, eyes dancing in amusement. "My lips are sealed. Wouldn't want your reputation dented by anything getting out about your inconvenient crush on the man."

"I don't have a crush."

Liam bit back a smile. "Of course you don't."

"What do you mean he had no contract?" Liam threw down his pen and cocked his head in disbelief.

Mark's desk butted up against Liam's, but Liam's was considerably more organised—unnecessarily so, in Mark's opinion. He preferred a more organic approach to filing, one that involved piles of papers with sticky notes atop. The system appeared to give Liam hives, another thing Mark liked about it.

He opened his hands. "What I *mean* is that Waikato University has no record of Rowan Bridge being on *any* sort of contract with them since way back last June. He's not on any of their teaching schedules either, and Carey Miller says he hasn't even talked to Rowan since before Christmas and certainly never asked him to teach. Rowan's specialty doesn't even come up on the curriculum till next semester. And his credit card statements back it up. Nothing booked from Waikato on any of the dates Evie gave us."

Liam arched his brows. "So he lied about where he was?"

Mark shrugged. "Apparently. But why? And exactly what *has* he been doing for the last couple of months if he wasn't tripping down to Waikato a couple of days each week? We need Connor to get us something useful from Bridge's computers, like yesterday."

The tech had accessed a lot of the man's files and search histories but had uncovered little of interest. Of the few obvious work files, virtually none covered the previous year, and the few that did appeared to be innocuous. Hardly the stuff of murder. The US pharmaceutical company he'd worked for had agreed to send some information about his contract, but just like Morgan, they couldn't see it providing any explanation for what had happened to the man.

"He's working on it," Liam answered. "Don't lean on him."

Mark's phone shuddered with a call, making it halfway across his blotter before he picked it up. After a quick look at the name, he grinned and flashed the screen at Liam, who rolled his eyes and leaned back in his chair with a shake of his head.

"Edward." Mark drew out the man's name and winked at Liam. "So nice to hear from you."

Silence greeted the comment, and Mark bit his lip. Riling Edward was just too easy and way too much fun.

"Detective." So much irritation conveyed in a single word. "I have the preliminary tox screen results for you."

Mark glanced at his watch. Four p.m. "Awesome. Let's hear them."

"Check your email and I'll walk you through it. Just remember, these aren't final till the full report comes tomorrow." His voice carried an exhausted note Mark related to. He sat upright in his chair and opened the email. "Fire away. I'm putting you on speaker."

Edward cleared his throat, and Mark pictured him sitting at his desk in his comfortable office, the top button of his pristine shirt rakishly undone, his hair slightly askew from tunnelling his tired fingers through it, a coffee in hand. The idea of a dishevelled Edward Newton only added to his appeal.

"To keep it simple, there were only two things of note," Edward began. "And I've highlighted both in red."

Mark found them straight away. "Well, fuck me." He smiled at the sharp intake of breath on the other end. "Sorry"—*not sorry*— "Edward, but ketamine in the guy's urine? Who'd have bet on that?"

"It's Ed—"

Mark grinned delightedly, and Liam wagged a scolding finger his way.

"—and yes, it was a surprise. Not most people's first choice to incapacitate somebody. You have to know what you're doing with that stuff. As a depressant anaesthetic, too much ketamine and you kill your victim—not overly helpful if you're trying to get information from them. And if you keep going down that list, you'll see MDMA was also present, and a drug called piperazine."

"Ecstasy and ketamine—a pretty common club combo," Mark mused. "Ketamine's a downer and Molly's a stimulant, right?"

"True, but again, tricky. If you were looking to use the combo to subdue someone, you'd have to get the ratios just right. End result: a compliant, unafraid, and euphoric hostage who loses motor control. A perfect storm to abduct someone with minimal fuss. *And* it can be hidden in a liquid—you'd hardly notice it in most alcoholic drinks, and I found no injection sites."

"Okay, so that works then." Mark threw a pen at Liam, who scribbled the information down on his blotter. "How long would it take?"

"Ketamine, about twenty minutes, a bit longer when it's ingested. MDMA, much the same. Or you could give the MDMA first to get a person to go with you, and then administer the ketamine to stop them leaving. Both stay detectable in urine for two to three days, but I also sent blood and hair for analysis. The blood results corroborate the urine screen, but the hair will take longer."

Mark thought for a minute. "Bridge wasn't a drinker though."

"Coffee, a soft drink, anything would do."

"You mentioned piperazine?" Liam asked.

Papers rustled on the other end of the phone. "Ah, yeah, it's a cutting agent. I checked with pharmacy, and it's currently banned in New Zealand as a Class C drug, like cannabis. But there was a spike in its use a couple of years back. It's actually an antiparasitic, but most forms of it act as a tranquilliser."

Mark ran a frustrated hand down his face. "Is there anything to help us track the source?"

"Drug combos have signature profiles based on the ratios used, and piperazine adds a less common element, which makes it easier, but I won't know until tomorrow."

It was something, at least. "Anything else."

Edward sighed. "Not at this stage."

Mark twirled his pen in his fingers, then switched the phone off speaker and put it to his ear. "You sound tired, Edward."

Liam's eyes flickered in amusement. Mark dismissed him with a wave of his hand, which only encouraged Liam to lean forward instead. He rested his chin in his hands and batted his eyelashes at Mark.

"I'm... fine," Edward answered, and Mark could almost hear the man's walls slam into place.

"So..." Mark's voice slipped into a lower tone. "I think it's Robert." The remark was met by silence, and Mark could only imagine the crunch of Edward's puzzled frown lines.

"I'm afraid you've lost me."

Mark's mouth twitched at the corners. God, if only he could see Edward's face. "Your middle name. It's Robert, right?" He spun his chair so he didn't have to watch Liam's reaction, though he couldn't block the man's delighted laugh.

There was a beat of silence from Edward's end, then...

"No, Detective, it's not Robert."

Mark would have sworn there was an edge of mirth tucked in there somewhere. "Huh." He slid down in his chair. "You know, you may as well tell me, Edward. I *will* find out."

A grunt of definite amusement. "I'm sure you will. But far be it from me to deprive you of any modicum of pleasure you might gain in the pursuit."

Jesus, the man spoke like he had a dictionary rammed up his arse, and was it wrong that Mark wanted nothing more than to fuck him from A to Z and straight on through the addendum? And wow, that particular rabbit hole had appeared out of nowhere.

"Speaking of pleasure—" He turned back to Liam. "—could I maybe interest you in a quiet drink... after work? We could... pursue the research."

Liam snorted, and Mark flipped him the bird while at the same time wondering what the hell he was doing. Crossing his own line in the sand, it appeared.

"No."

Not a lot to work with there. "Not even an innocent, welcome-to-the-city-and-get-to-know-a-colleague drink?"

"I've been here three months, Detective. And somehow, you and the word *innocent*, don't sit well together in my head. What do you really want, honestly?"

Damn. Honestly? Mark had no idea whatsoever about what he wanted. Then again, when had that ever stopped him? "Okay. Well, I think I've made it pretty obvious that I'm attracted to you, Edward, and I think maybe you find me, well, at least not *terrible* to look at." He grinned as a choked-back laugh came through the phone. "So I just thought maybe we could... talk?"

The responding silence said it all. But just in case Mark didn't get the message, Edward filled in the gaps.

"Detective—"

"Mark."

Two beats of silence. "Mark. I appreciate the offer, but I sincerely doubt we have anything much in common. Yes, you're not... terrible to look at—" Edward paused, and Mark could almost see the quirk of the man's lips. "And I'm not sure I want to know how you even knew to ask me—"

Didn't, actually, but good to know my gaydar is still working. "That you're gay?"

"Bi, actually. But as we both know, being under the same rainbow umbrella doesn't necessarily a friend *or* attraction make."

Under the what? "How do you know? We might have more in common than you think."

"Really?"

Mark winced at the tone which sounded more like, *Have you lost your fucking mind?*

"Do you read, Detective? As in, for pleasure?"

"Not a lot."

"Do you enjoy galleries and museums? Country music?"

"Hey, I can get into country. I liked that stuff you had playing this morning. As for the others, well, no, but—"

"How many long-term relationships with men... *or* women... have you had? As in longer than three months?"

Mark barked out a laugh. "You don't mess around, do you?"

"You're late thirties, right?"

Mark grunted assent and wondered how this conversation had suddenly veered into a summary of his dismal dating track record.

"So, how many, then?"

Shit. "One, two maybe."

"One or two." Edward paused for effect. "That tells me you prefer relief to relationship."

Mark's head spun, and he could see the man's smirk. *Oh, he's good.* But Mark was a master. "Okay, Edward, I'll play your little game. But it's men," he answered firmly. "No women... ever. Just so we're clear. And yes, so what if I prefer my sex uncomplicated and... efficient?"

Edward snorted. "Well, I don't, Detective."

"You don't have sex?" The question came out a little louder than Mark had intended and caught a couple of raised brows from a colleague seated across the way. Mark also caught Edward's sharp intake of breath. He lowered his voice. "Are you saying you're ace, Doc?"

Silence followed, and Mark wondered what line he'd crossed this time. After all, he wasn't the one who started the conversation.

"No, I'm not ace, but if I were, would that be a problem?"

The question threw Mark. It wasn't something he'd ever considered, because... well, Edward was right. Mark pretty much avoided anything beyond sex with *any* man he was attracted to. He had friends, and then he had hookups—nothing in between. And he wasn't too sure what that said about him, or if he even wanted to know. *And what the hell kind of question was that, anyway?*

Could he partner long term romantically without sex? He'd never thought about it. But now that he had, he knew he'd keep thinking about it. *Goddamn the man.* Mark had spent a long time cultivating superficial and shallow. He had it perfected and polished, his life tidy and... uncomplicated. He didn't do deep conversations at four p.m. on a Thursday, and he certainly didn't do them with a guy he was cruising in the faint hope of a little dancing between the sheets. *What. The. Fuck?* Because now, well, now he had... questions.

Mark had screwed up the few relationships he'd ever tried, the last being Jeff, and at that he'd drawn a line in the sand. Pump and dump? Friends with benefits? No problem. It had always been enough for Mark, until *this* man. If Mark just had the hots for Edward, he'd slap himself and walk away. But something was stopping him. Did he want more? Surely not. Dear God, how did people do this shit?

"It's okay not to know," Edward said softly.

"Gee, thanks."

"It's also okay to do what you've been doing."

"I'm so glad you approve."

"Each to their own, right? All I'm saying, Mark—"

"Hah! You called me Mark twice now. Admit it, Edward, you like me."

"All I'm saying, *Detective*, is that I don't do one-night stands, I don't do friends with benefits, and I sure as hell don't do the club scene. Nothing wrong with any of those, but they're not me. If I were interested in *anyone*, it would only be on a dating basis—a very *slow* dating basis, I might add. Still interested, Detective?"

Mark could barely swallow, let alone answer, far too many scary words banging around inside his skull.

Edward snorted. "I thought not. I can almost see those running shoes laced up tight. So, now that we have that out of the way, perhaps we can get along professionally without all the sexual innuendo. Good talk, Detective. We must do it again, or not. Have a good evening."

Mark held the phone out from his ear and stared at it, unable to stop the spread of a huge grin. *Holy shit.* He'd never been grilled like that. What a fucking rush. He glanced down at the burgeoning semi in his chinos and shook his head. *Well, looky there.* And all from a damn phone call.

"You okay there, boss?"

He spun back to face his partner, still grinning. "Absolutely." Whatever judgemental stick Edward had up his arse, and whatever rules and regulations he liked to live by, it hadn't made a single dent in Mark's fascination for him. He'd actually enjoyed the ballsy interrogation. Few men caught him on the back foot like that. Another layer, another glimpse of all the fire and intensity that pulsed just beneath all that studied calm. If anything, the dressing-down only ramped up his interest—although the whole dating scare tactics thing had been an admirable play by the other man and had almost worked.

What's more, Edward hadn't denied being attracted to Mark—hadn't admitted it exactly, but hadn't denied it either. It did, however, spell trouble with a capital *T* for Mark. Then again, Mark was never one to shy away from a challenge.

Liam chuckled. "So, um, it sounded suspiciously like you tanked there, boss. I can understand if you might need a moment to recover from the... embarrassment."

Mark waggled his eyebrows. "Now that's where you'd be dead wrong, my son. What you heard was merely the opening salvo of the first game. Don't count me out yet. Edward Newton is clearly crazy about me."

"Hah! You know, I wouldn't have pegged you for the pursuing type."

And you'd be right. But Mark wasn't about to go there with his partner.

"The rumour mill will be smoking when word gets out that the infamous Mark Knight was actually doing a bit of chasing."

Mark shrugged. "Different men, different strategies. Plus, the rumour mill isn't going to know a damn thing about it, because you're not going to open your mouth, understand?" He narrowed his gaze pointedly.

Liam blinked twice, then broke eye contact. "Whatever. It's not like I give a shit anyway. Just don't come crying to me when you get your arse handed to you."

Now there's a thought. "I don't think that's the dire warning you think it is." He smiled. "Still, we'll see. Now pull up a chair, negative Nancy, and let's talk about what the nice man had to say."

CHAPTER FIVE

Ed hit the refresh button to make sure he hadn't made a mistake. Then he sat back and waited for the machine to do its thing once more—troll through all the relevant files looking for possible drug matches. Speedy, it was not.

With only one autopsy that morning, he'd retired to his office after lunch, put the Dixie Chicks on replay, and tried to put a dent in the mountain of paperwork in his inbox. And he'd been doing pretty well up until the data-mining report he'd requested based on the previous day's toxicology results arrived in his email.

With the intriguing ketamine-MDMA result from the day before, he'd set up a full comparative search on the specifics of the drug combo, including the national database. It had run while he was busy with the autopsy. Street drugs were often cut with other substances in a way unique to their cook. Something in favour last year might not be available currently. So comparing the drug result profile to others on record could be useful in tracking the source.

He mulled over his coffee as he waited for the repeat search to finish. He was more awake than yesterday, having caught up on some sleep, despite the intrusion of a certain irksome detective into his dreams. Mark Knight was a menace to Ed's peace of mind, and he still couldn't believe how close he'd come to accepting the guy's invite for a drink. The "No", had been reflexive, and thank Christ for that.

Mark played with Ed's emotions in a way that short-circuited his brain, and circumvented all those iron-clad walls he'd spent so much time reinforcing. Every time they met, Mark was all up inside Ed's mental space like a damn virus, cloning pieces of himself that later showed up randomly when Ed was cooking, or showering, or dreaming, or... well, whatever. What's more, he seemed powerless to stop the infection or even slow its spread.

Worst of all, both Mark and Grace had been right. Ed *did*, in fact, like Mark. *Dammit.* For all the effort Mark put into that carefully cultivated man-whore image he had going, Ed had caught the odd glimpse of a far more complicated character beneath the bluster. Whether that person could live in the light of day, Ed had his doubts. It was just... interesting. Okay, maybe intriguing was a better word. Intriguing and... charming. *Son of a bitch.*

Still, regardless of what his sister had said, there was no way the two of them were compatible. Ed had been willing to open his mind, as Grace suggested, but those few quick questions on the phone to Mark had highlighted the futility of that. And yet Ed had hung up feeling disappointed, something so out of character that he'd stumbled at the realisation and spent far too long ruminating on the why of it.

After that bizarre phone conversation, Ed had given up pretending he could focus on what he'd been doing, and instead downloaded the files he'd needed, and gone home to continue over a glass of wine—a definite break in his routine. He preferred to keep work at work—something he'd learned from his therapist after the Christchurch debacle. But Mark had unnerved him, and not in a good way. Staying at his desk had only made Ed more... itchy.

Still, a smile tugged at his lips. That Mark had tolerated the personal interrogation had been surprising. And not just tolerated, but given back as good as he'd received, seeming to enjoy the banter as much as Ed. It wasn't that Ed was rude, just... blunt. Forthright, he liked to call it. Regardless, it kept people at a distance—and that's where Ed preferred them.

As for the whole middle name thing? Okay, it was amusing, even flattering in its absurdity. But he really should've just told Mark what it was and buried the whole ridiculous flirtation there and then, because that's exactly what it was, and they both knew it. By not putting a stop to it, he'd silently given a green light for Mark to keep trying. And why? Because he liked the man's attention on him— hated and liked it. Yep, there it was again.

He even secretly liked the sound of his full name on Mark's lips, a name he'd always loathed. He shouldn't, because it would only cause a problem when Ed shut the whole thing down—which he would, because there was no way his heart would survive the inevitable pain that someone like Mark would hand it. But yes, Ed liked Mark. And that was a big fucking problem.

The search finally finished loading, and Ed scrolled through the results for the second time. Bingo. There was the identical match alert he'd gotten from the first search. *Damn.* There'd been no mistake, and he'd really, really hoped there had been.

"What the hell?" He sank into his chair and tried to make sense of what he was reading.

The exact same ketamine-MDMA-piperazine profile found in Bridge's blood had also been found in a lab report archived just a few months before in Forensic Pathology's own system files at Auckland Med. Other than that, no other matches for over three years, which meant that combo wasn't current on the streets. So either it had been home brewed or it was part of an old supply.

In one sense it was good news, because it narrowed the potential sources and would carry some weight in court. But it also eliminated the more straightforward option of simply tracking the drug from street to supplier to cook, and that meant nowhere to start. Needle-in-a-haystack stuff.

But there was more bad news, the worst. The archive match was a floater, unattached to the case file it should have been a part of—the stuff of pathologists' nightmares. *Holy fucking shit.*

And it only got worse. As Ed kept looking, he located the file the result *should* have been attached to—an autopsy done by his predecessor, Tom Spencer, just before he retired.

Thank Christ it wasn't his own case, was Ed's first thought.

The autopsy had been on one Adam Greene, a guy the coroner later ruled as having committed suicide by hanging—a case where tox screens should have been standard evidence, so Greene's file couldn't have been missing that particular report. Ed's heart slowed. That was good news. Maybe it was just a duplicate? But no, it couldn't have been, because with those drugs in Greene's system, there was no way the coroner would have been happy to rule the case an uncomplicated suicide.

Ed searched again, and sure enough there *was* a report in Greene's file, it just wasn't the same as the archived one. The one in the file made no mention of the ketamine-MDMA-piperazine mix; neither did the urine screen or the hair sample. All were clear other than a slightly elevated blood alcohol.

Son of a bitch. In a pathologist's line of work, it didn't get any more grim. Why two different results? Had someone sanitised the original report? If so, why? To get a suicide verdict? It was the only reason that made sense. A compliant person, happy and high on that particular drug cocktail, was certainly less likely to follow through on suicide.

No matter how many scenarios he ran through his head, Ed couldn't come up with a better explanation. One body, one autopsy, one case file, two different drug screen reports. And the last person to have worked with the file, the same man who presented it in court: Tom Spencer. *Holy shit.* There was no way Spencer couldn't have known.

Just in case he'd missed anything, Ed placed a call to the lab and asked them to check their file. It took a few minutes to find they had the exact same result as was in the official case file, no trace of the ketamine mix result that had been in the archived file.

But how could that be? Everything was stored on the cloud these days. Someone had to know what they were doing to wipe the original results from the system. Ed rang the head of the lab, who said he'd get back to him with an answer. A few minutes later they called back.

As it turned out, no one had tampered with the system. Tom Spencer had called the lab the day after Greene's autopsy and logged an incident report over potentially incorrectly labelled samples of blood and urine. He'd then sent the lab new samples for testing, and it was those results that had gone into the official notes. The lab worker remembered the case because he'd been responsible for the testing on the new samples. The incident report would be on file somewhere.

It raised all sorts of alarm bells in Ed's mind and did nothing to satisfy his concerns. It suddenly became very important that he print out a hard copy of that original report, right fucking now. He downloaded a copy to his laptop, got a printout, and saved one on a flash drive as well.

He didn't want to jump to conclusions, hoping he was wrong, but there weren't many, if any, likely alternatives. Done with the copies, he sat back and pondered his options. The police needed to be told about the possible match, but Ed felt some collegial obligation to check with Tom Spencer first before unleashing the hounds of administrative and judicial hell on him. At the very least, the coroner's office was going to have fucking kittens.

Spencer's cell rang for a good thirty seconds before he picked up. Ed had met Spencer a couple of times during the handover process but really didn't know him beyond that. First impressions? Nice enough, good at his job, respected by his colleagues, if not exactly warm and inviting. But who was Ed to talk? Cool and detached were familiar words on his own performance appraisals. Ed preferred to call it careful and professional, but what would he know?

The man's sharp intake of breath and tell-tale hesitation when hearing of the conflicting reports told Ed all he needed to know, and his heart plummeted. *Dammit.* Spencer absolutely knew something, but what? Ed couched his questions with as much professional respect as he could muster, all the while cursing the arsehole for landing a shitstorm of trouble in his lap. He had no doubt Spencer had cocked up big time, possibly even criminally—it was written in every carefully articulated syllable of the man's answers. But why?

"Yes, I remember the case." Spencer was far too calm for a man whose professional reputation was on the line. "It was fairly routine. The guy had divorced about a year before. He had no children, was living alone, and had a recent history of depression. His ex-wife said he'd increasingly isolated himself since they'd split, burying himself in his work and not responding to her calls or texts. He was found hanging in his garage by the woman who walked his dog. The animal had been shut in the backyard. It was a shock to his ex, but he apparently hadn't wanted the divorce and had fought it all the way."

The words were slick and practised and simply reeked of a lie. "What did he do for a living?"

Spencer paused just a fraction too long. "Some kind of scientist, I think? I can't quite remember, to tell you the truth."

Another scientist. A coincidence? Ed didn't believe in those. But then again, he also knew better than to jump to conclusions. Scientists were as prone to depression as anyone else. In the wake of the terror attack on two of Christchurch's mosques, he'd worked non-stop alongside every other available forensic pathologist in NZ. They'd done their best to get the victims autopsied and back to their families for burial as quickly as possible.

It had taken an emotional toll on them all, and for the first time in his career Ed had signed up for a few therapy sessions to cope with the fallout. The tragedy had changed Christchurch and New Zealand forever. And Ed couldn't deny it had played a role in his decision to take the position in Auckland. Life was too damn short.

"Why all the questions?" Tom Spencer was finally sounding a bit flustered.

With all his alarm bells ringing, Ed decided to rattle Spencer a bit further—see if anything interesting fell out. "Because the Greene case was flagged in a database search I ran on a probable homicide."

"Homicide?"

Oh, yeah. Spencer was clearly nervous now.

"Flagged why?"

Ed told him the details and could almost see the colour drain from Spencer's face. A set of sirens was added to those damn bells. *Son of a bitch.* What the hell had Spencer done?

"It'll be a mistake. Some kind of computer error," Spencer insisted.

"I've checked and rerun the whole thing. There's no mistake, Tom. So what I need from you now is *any* reasonable explanation for why there are two sets of the same tox screen results for this man and why you ordered a second set of blood and urine work. You and I both know how bloody careful we are with those specimens. It's damn near impossible to mislabel them."

"What the hell are you suggesting—"

"Tom, listen. You need to understand that, regardless of what you say now, I'm going to have to push this up the ladder to the powers that be, both here and in the coroner's office. You need to prepare yourself. At the very least there'll be a second coroner's enquiry on the man's stated cause of death, especially with this new drug match showing up. And there'll also likely be an exhumation, since there are no leftover samples. They'll want to rerun the tests.

"The fact you're retired is a good thing, but shit is gonna rain down one way or another, on you *and* this department. And I'm gonna cop a load of it as well. Not only that, but if this drug match proves a link between the two cases, then we're talking possible homicide in the Greene case as well. So I'm waiting, Tom. If you know *anything* about this, you need to tell me, now."

Silence.

"Tom? Come on, man, give me something here. If it was a simple error, I could work with that, present it the best way I can for you. But you were the last to handle that file, the one to upload the report, the one to lodge the incident report. Are you in some kind of trouble?"

Still nothing.

Frustration gnawed at Ed's gut. Spencer was making it impossibly hard on himself. "Tom, I—"

"Look, I'm sorry. I can't do this now, Ed. It's not what you think. I'll, ah, I'll have to come in and talk to you... tomorrow. I promise. But right now... I have to go."

"Tomorrow's Saturday, Tom. We're not—"

"I'll be in around ten thirty."

"Tom—"

"Tomorrow." And Spencer hung up.

Ed dialled back immediately, only to be sent straight to voicemail. He threw his phone on the desk and roared, "Son of a bitch."

Sandy poked his head in the door. "You all right, Dr Newton?"

The very definition of irreverent but astounding efficiency, Sandy Williams had an angular face, sharp nose, and pointed jaw that somehow worked together to form a pleasing whole, all wrapped up in six feet, three inches of lanky anatomical Lego. He sometimes wore trousers, sometimes a dress... or skirt... and once, a lava-lava. The last hadn't gone down well with the powers that be, even though Sandy swore black and blue he had Samoan ancestry on his mother's side.

Ed idly thought Sandy was more likely to have ancestry in common with a praying mantis than with any hominid, but what would he know? Not that Sandy wasn't handsome, he was just... startling. And after checking with the intriguing man which pronouns he preferred, Ed simply sat back to enjoy the show that was Sandy Williams. And what a delightful show it had proven to be.

"I'm fine, Sandy, and it's Ed, dammit," he answered much louder than he'd intended. "Why is it so difficult for people to grasp my damn name?"

Sandy's languid brown eyes popped open, and he regarded Ed warily. "Okaaaay... Ed." He cheekily underscored the *d* for effect, and Ed almost smiled. Almost.

Instead he said, "See, what's so hard about that?"

Sandy rolled his eyes with his usual drama. "Well, if you wanted me to call you Ed, you only had to ask... which you didn't"—he wagged a finger Ed's way—"until now. So, for the sake of clarity, I'll repeat. Are you sure you're okay... Ed? Would a hug help?" He grinned cheekily.

Like a hug was anything Ed would *ever* ask for, and Sandy damn well knew it. Cheeky as all hell, and Ed loved it. He snorted in amusement. Few people messed with him this way, and it made him feel oddly... safe. Like he didn't need to be on his best behaviour— didn't have to walk on eggshells so as not to offend people by his introversion, which was so often misread as standoffishness.

Sandy had already been employed in the forensic pathology department when Ed had arrived, and Ed had been slightly dismayed at the idea of working with the seriously out-there and touchy-feely young man. Boundaries were a fluid concept to Sandy, as was pretty much everything in his life, from what Ed could tell. But there was just something about Sandy that Ed couldn't ignore. Sandy was... alive, in every sense of the word, and something deep inside Ed thrummed to attention when he was around. Not dissimilar to his experience with Mark Knight, he mused, except Ed wasn't attracted to Sandy. It was more that he admired him. An unlikely admission.

"When I need a hug, you'll be the first to know," he deadpanned. "Not that you've ever needed an invitation."

It had been a standing joke between them since the day Sandy had first barged through Ed's defences after a depressing autopsy on a baby. No sooner had Ed thrown his gown in the linen bag than an arm slid around his shoulders in a one-armed hug, and he'd been subject to all those Sandy-shaped gaunt angles and edges.

He'd been startled speechless, frozen on the spot. Then Sandy had released Ed with a pat to his cheek and an order to go eat his lunch and not show his face in the autopsy room for at least an hour. A coffee made to perfection had arrived on his desk minutes later, the music had changed to a band Ed hadn't recognised but which fitted his playlist perfectly, and his pressure cooker brain had safely defused. And that had been that.

Sandy grinned widely. "Pshaw. My hugs are the best, everyone knows that. The day you arrived, your human-touch meter was red-lining so bad, I had no choice but to make it my mission to correct it. I'm nothing if not a humanitarian." He threw Ed a wink, and Ed's eyes pricked alarmingly at the simple truth in the words.

"How did you—" He cleared his throat under his assistant's watchful gaze and changed tack. "Why on earth would you think that about me?"

Sandy chewed on his cheek before answering. "You're a good man, Dr Newton—Ed. That's all I have." And with that he closed the door between them, leaving Ed a bit bewildered and wondering, not for the first time, if their working partnership was really such a good idea. Sandy was altogether too perceptive.

Sandy wasn't just impeccably efficient at his job, he seemed to *get* Ed, dismissing Ed's often cool, introverted manner as one would a two-year-old's tantrum—ignoring it and positively reinforcing only the stuff he approved of. Sandy managed Ed, *handled* him—he knew it, and Ed knew it. And, for some reason, Ed let him.

He'd eventually need to talk to Sandy about the old case and the lab reports, check if he knew anything, but first Ed wanted to speak to Tom Spencer. In the meantime he shook off Sandy's parting words, took a couple of deep breaths, and focused his thinking. Then he called Mark.

Mark picked up on the second ring. "Edward, how nice to hear from you."

Ed rolled his eyes and tried to ignore the annoying way his lips quirked up in a smile at hearing his name on Mark's lips. "It's Ed, and I hope you feel the same after you hear what I have to say."

The change in mood was palpable. "Hang on while I go somewhere I can hear better."

Ed waited.

"Okay, what have you got for me?"

"First, tell me how the interview with Bridge's wife went. Anything I should be on the lookout for?"

Mark gave a brief summary of what they'd found, their visit to Morgan and Associates, and the surprise discovery about the non-existent university lectureship contract.

"Hmm. Can't see that type of research facility giving him access to ketamine, but I can check. It would be more likely if it was into animal research."

"I'd appreciate anything you can find out."

"No problem. So, the man's not as straight up as you thought?" Ed commented.

"Apparently not. Now, I'm sure you rang for a reason, unless it was simply an overwhelming urge to hear my voice?"

Ed found he could picture in surprising detail the smile on the man's face, the sparkle in his gold-flecked eyes. He relayed what he'd learned about the drug, the flagged match, and the conflicting reports. "I had a quick look at Greene's autopsy notes, and there were no drugs found at his house, which means that if he wasn't a regular user and he died quickly after the ingestion of the cocktail, any hair follicle test would've come up clean anyway. The drugs wouldn't have had long enough in the man's system to cross into the follicle."

Ed paused, considering his next words. "I also think that archiving that report in the pathologist files was a mistake. I think whoever was responsible, meant for it to be either deleted, or buried with similar reports that aren't available for comparison searches because of their unreliability. Without it, we'd be none the wiser about any possible connection." There, he'd said it. He waited.

Mark whistled long and low. "Holy shit. You're positive about this?"

If only. Ed sighed. "No. I can't say anything for sure other than a second report exists, and blood and urine tests were repeated with dubious reasoning. I'm finding it difficult to swallow the mistaken labelling—we're just too damn careful about that sort of thing. But it could happen and does, sure, and if it weren't for the drug screen match, maybe I'd be fine with it. But it just seems there's way too many ducks conveniently in a row for comfort. Not to mention Spencer was all kinds of strange about it when I put him on the spot."

"I agree. Explain about Spencer."

It was a gut feeling more than anything, but Ed wanted to be as accurate as possible for Mark. "He was just... off. At first, he played it as a mistake—that I'd got it wrong. Then, when I pushed, he got all defensive and refused point-blank to talk about it—said he would come in to the morgue tomorrow and talk, even though it's Saturday. To be honest, he sounded guilty as shit. If it were me and someone confronted me about something like this, and I was innocent? I'd have beaten the land speed record to clear things up—or at least find out what the hell was going on. This is his reputation on the line, after all, retired or not."

Mark took a moment. "I trust your instincts."

Oh. Ed didn't want to dwell too long on why that sent a glow to his cheeks, but damn.

"When do you have to push this higher?" Mark asked.

Good question. "I'll need to talk to Spencer tomorrow, then Sandy, triple-check my facts and write a report, so... Sunday, Monday at the latest for an official report. But I'll need to call my boss before then and give him a heads-up."

"But can we begin to work with this information? At least start looking into the other guy?"

"I don't see why not, but I'll hold off emailing you any official report until I've talked to Spencer and the powers that be. But yeah, as long as you keep it casual and quiet. We need to keep it out of the media until I get some answers. The Coroner's office isn't going to like it if this gets leaked, especially as I may be barking up the wrong tree—"

"But you don't think you are, do you?"

Ed thought about that nagging itch in his belly. "No, I don't think so. But that whole Greene autopsy will be compromised. All results, including the discarded screens, will be inadmissible in court until they're checked and likely redone. There'll be an exhumation, I guarantee."

"Jesus, what a mess." Mark's frustration bled through the phone. "Okay. It is what it is. But at least we have something to go forward on. The Greene guy was a scientist too, you said."

"Physicist, I think."

"Okay, I'll pull anything we have on him at this end and get back to you."

"Thanks. I'm heading home."

There was a two-second pause. "Long drive?"

Ed snorted in amusement. "Nice try, Detective. Talk to you tomorrow."

"Randy."

Ed blinked. "I'm sorry?"

"Edward Randy Newton."

He barked out a laugh, surprising the hell out of himself. "No, not Randy... on so, so many levels. Goodnight, Mark."

"Hah! That's the third time you've called me Mark. Face it, Edward. You and me? It's destiny."

"Goodnight, Detective." Ed hung up. And if he stared at the phone with a stupid smile on his face for longer than was strictly necessary, it was no one's business but his own.

So he was warming to the man. So, what? Mark was... amusing. And yes, Ed felt a little... flattered. There, he could say it. Nothing wrong with that. Didn't mean shit in the scheme of things. Mark Knight was to relationships what the dodo was to flight. Never. Gonna. Happen. He shut down his sister's nagging voice in his ear, grabbed his laptop and all the copies of the archived report, and headed home.

CHAPTER SIX

MARK MADE HIS WAY BACK TO HIS DESK MULLING OVER THE NEW information. He wasn't sure what it meant, only that he trusted Edward's suspicions. Someone's butchered birthday cake sat on a nearby filing cabinet, and he swerved to grab another slice of sticky chocolate heaven.

Auckland Central Police Station housed one of the largest investigative teams in the country, and it's detective enclave was a notoriously busy, noisy place to work. For all that, the atmosphere was welcoming, even for an out gay cop like Mark. There'd been a few struggles at the beginning—bigotry loved company, and homophobia was rife in his early days on the force—but times had changed. Things weren't perfect now by any means, but they were a fuck-ton better. Hell, they even had diversity liaison officers now. Mark's first boss would've tossed his cookies at the mere suggestion.

An incident room had been set up to work the Bridge's case. Two other detectives plus a few extra uniforms had been pulled in, and they'd spent the afternoon cataloguing information, chasing up crime scene results, getting boards set up, and dividing the workload. Edward's call had come at the end of all that.

Liam leaned back, his gaze calculating. "So, what does our esteemed pathologist have to say for himself?"

Mark replied through a mouth full of cake, "He thinks he's found a case match with the exact same drug profile." A lump of chocolate icing fell down the front of Mark's white T-shirt. "Goddammit."

Liam pushed a box of Kleenex his way. "Jesus, you're as bad as my kids. Here."

He dabbed at his shirt, managing to spread the stain further. "Shit. I'm never gonna get this out."

Liam waved a hand dismissively. "Soak it in Spot's Gone, then put it in a cold wash."

Mark frowned. "The fact that you even know that is frightening on so many levels."

Liam spread his hands wide. "Hey. Man with two kids under three, here. I could write a book on what I know about various stain removal solutions. But find me one for explosive diarrhoea on my carpet and I'll love you forever."

A quick check confirmed he wasn't joking. "Jesus, Liam. Just no. There is to be no mention of the ejection of substances from toddlers' orifices ever again at these desks. Do. You. Understand?"

Liam saluted. "Hey, it's not like I need a reminder of the sad state of my daily existence, anyway. You said Ed found a match?"

Mark gave up on his shirt and threw the Kleenex in the bin. "Maybe. Some physicist"—he glanced at his notes—"but it's a bit of a long shot because, according to the coroner's report, he hung himself after a divorce he allegedly didn't want."

Liam chewed on his pen and said nothing.

"Earth to Crowley?"

"I'm thinking. I have no idea how that fits—"

"It doesn't. That's why we'll just keep it in mind for the moment, unless we find something more. There's some question around the reliability of the tox screen report, so Edward's going to check with Tom Spencer tomorrow—see if there's a reason for that, and then get back to us."

Liam pursed his lips. "Okay, so what do you need from me, then?"

"Nothing."

He arched a brow.

"Not tonight, leastways. Go home. I'll take a quick look at the file, see if anything jumps out, though I expect there's not much to go on since it was quickly ruled as suicide. And keep this between us, for now. The coroner won't be happy if word spreads about a potential mix-up, and then we find it was all above board."

"I hear you." Liam grabbed his red parka and bag but hovered by Mark's desk. "I don't mind staying, you know. Joe's putting money on the bar at the Phoenix tonight for their new baby. Gina's not expecting me till late."

Mark waved him off. "No point both of us wasting a Friday night."

Liam nodded. "Okay, well, thanks." He clapped Mark on the shoulder and headed for the elevators, giving a shout-out to the remaining detectives as he passed.

Mark spent an hour tidying up his notes and catching handovers from the other members of his team before picking up the police file on Adam Greene. He quickly focused on the autopsy results which pointed to the cause of death as brain ischaemia, likely caused by self-inflicted hanging, and with no indication of foul play. All of which meant there was little follow-up investigation needed by the police. At that point Mark stopped reading and put a call through to Edward.

"Detective, so soon." The doctor's voice had the flinty edges smoothed off, like he was a glass of wine down, and Mark idly wondered what a relaxed Edward Newton looked like—what he wore in his own home when no one was watching. Not sweats and an old T-shirt, that much he was willing to bet. Edward likely just kicked off his work shoes, untucked his shirt, rolled up his sleeves— and oh, yeah, that worked nicely.

He cleared his throat. "Edward. Any chance we can catch up and talk about Greene some more? I was reading the autopsy report... but then it occurred to me that having you alongside to answer questions would be far more... fruitful."

Edward hesitated. "Riiight. And of course you mean tonight?"

Come on Edward, throw me a bone. "Well, I'd really like to get ahead of the game before tomorrow if that was at all possible?" And if it meant spending a little more time in the doctor's company, Mark wasn't about to complain.

"I'm at home."

"Well I can, um... come to you?"

Edward groaned. "Is this some sorry excuse to get invited to my house?"

So suspicious. Mark grinned to himself. "Do you want it to be?"

"Goodnight, Detective—"

Oops. "Sorry, sorry. Don't hang up. I was being an arsehole."

Two beats of silence. "I'm listening."

"Look, I just want as much info on this other case and your thoughts as I can get before I hit up the ex-wife tomorrow."

"You're going to interview her?" His concern was evident.

"Is that a problem?"

"I guess not. As long as you don't mention the fuck-up in the reports at this stage."

"I won't say a word. Only that I'm looking to close the case and want to be sure we have all the info we need."

Edward sighed. "When the shit hits the fan, she'll know that was an excuse."

"So we'll deal with it then. If there's a genuine connection and we *don't* follow up, we'll all have egg on our collective faces. At the moment it's just *your* department... Edward."

Edward snorted. "Gee, thanks."

"You're welcome. Now, can we talk?"

"Are you sure we can't do this over the phone?"

"Jesus, Edward. Am I that scary?" It was hard not to take offence at the man's obvious lack of enthusiasm.

"Ugh. Fine. Come here, then."

"I'll be on my best behaviour."

"That gives me no reassurance whatsoever. I wonder why?"

"I don't know," Mark shot back. "Maybe it's that devastatingly low opinion you seem to hold of me." And, yeah, that might have come out a little more offended than he'd intended.

There was a hesitation at the other end of the phone before Edward answered more softly, "Touché, Detective. You clearly don't have the monopoly on arsehole behaviour. I'll text you my address."

Mark chuckled. "You know, I don't think that was the apology you thought it was."

"See you soon, Detective."

Mark hung up just as his phone dinged with Edward's address. He printed a copy of the file, stuffed it in his bag, and was just finishing clearing his desk when his boss ambled over.

"Got anything new for me, Knight? I've got the media breathing down my damn neck on this thing already." DCI Rick Kirwan was a short, earnest man in his early fifties, with a developing paunch and a mop of red curls, the latter due in no small part to his strong Irish ancestry. Mark got on okay with the man. Kirwan let them do their jobs without too much interference, took the political heat without passing it down, had their backs most of the time, and pulled rank when he needed to keep the troops in line. Warm and friendly he wasn't, but then Mark didn't need that in a boss.

"Maybe... I'm not sure yet."

Kirwan glanced at Mark's computer screen. "Who's this guy?"

"A three-month-old suicide, flagged in the pathologist's files as having a similar drug profile as our guy. But it's screwy. There are apparently *two* reports: one in the man's official file that makes no mention of the drug combo, and a second report Edward found randomly archived in the system. That one has an exact drug profile match to our guy, and Edward's spidey senses are tingling. It was supposedly a mislabelled blood sample, so the test was redone and the original results discarded, but Edward's not buying it."

Kirwan perched on the edge of Liam's desk. "The man seems to have good instincts."

Mark shrugged. "Yeah, but he's not sure. It happened under Tom Spencer's watch, so Edward's gonna talk with him first before he reports it."

Kirwan paled. "Hard to see Spencer involved in something like this."

"I agree. But we'll know more tomorrow. He's meeting Edward at the morgue in the morning. I'm gonna start working on the possibility anyway, just in case. Edward asked us to keep it on the quiet until he's talked with Spencer and the coroner's office."

Kirwan pursed his lips. "That'll put the cat amongst the pigeons and send a crapload of hell their way. Maloney's gonna blow a gasket. He's only just introduced another round of protocol fail-safes intended to stop this exact thing happening. But even if it's true, it's a long shot to tie it in to this new guy."

Mark tended to agree, but he trusted Edward's instincts more. "You're probably right, but I'm gonna head over to Edward's place now and go over the files to get a head start. Then I'll do a quick follow-up on Greene's ex-wife tomorrow—just say I'm reviewing the case notes before it's closed."

Kirwan looked doubtful, and Mark didn't blame him, but in the end his boss nodded. "Do what you need to, but don't tie up anyone else until you know if it's a wash or not."

Mark agreed. "At this stage it's just Edward and myself. I'll bring Liam on board tomorrow."

Kirwan nodded. "So, you're not coming to wet the head of Joe's new baby?"

Mark gave Kirwan a wry smile, knowing how much the other man hated socialising. "Sorry."

The DCI sighed. "Lucky you. Wish I had an excuse. I'm too old for all this."

"The perils of seniority, sir."

"Tell me about it." He rested a hand on Mark's shoulder as he got to his feet. "Keep me in the loop if you find anything."

Mark threw his satchel under his arm and followed Kirwan out. At his car he changed out of his chocolate-stained T-shirt into a fresh one bearing the logo of their station softball team, the Switch Hitters, a name that paid homage to the increasing diversity on the team and which was a supporter favourite. Then he texted Liam.

Hey.

Liam: Find anything?

Mark began a reply, deleted it, then simply called the man. "How's the party?" He grinned at the raucous noise in the background and the sound of Joe's voice loud above the crowd.

"Joe's tanked already, in case you missed that." Liam sounded more than a few drinks down already himself. "You should come over."

"Nah. I'm heading to Edward's. Gonna compare notes on this new guy. You and I can visit the ex-wife tomorrow."

"Really? Five bucks says the whole thing's a blow. He's working late at the hospital, then?"

Mark said nothing.

There was a pause on the line. "You're going to his place?"

"Maybe."

"Ohhh. Right. *I* know what's going on. You're gonna hit on that poor man again, aren't you?"

"No comment. We simply need to check this out, and Kirwan doesn't want any numbers on it if we're not sure."

"Okay, I get that. But be careful with the doc. I'm thinking all that secret-squirrel shit probably comes with a black belt or something. You might get more than you bargained for."

One could only hope. Mark could absolutely see the so very precise, clean and measured Edward Newton packing some lethal moves, and, yeah, his dick might have also perked up with the idea. And Jesus George, since when had that ever been a thing for him? *Since fucking never, that's when.*

CHAPTER SEVEN

THIRTY MINUTES LATER, MARK WAS SCANNING THE SWANKY neighbouring houses as he made his way to Edward's front door. He was definitely in the wrong profession. Herne Bay was one of the posher Auckland suburbs, and the properties that backed directly on to the water, like Edward's, bore all the hallmarks of exclusive living: security cameras, privacy, lush gardens, pools, and driveways that looked like luxury car dealerships.

It was more than just a step or two up from Mark's tiny one-bedroom downtown apartment, with its rowdy upstairs neighbours and a view over his local Italian restaurant dumpster. The apartment's one saving grace? The smell of Angelo's amazing marinara sauce wafting through his lounge windows three times a week. Plus it was close to the police station, close to Downtown G—his preferred gay club—close to transport, and cheapish. All distinct selling points for a man whose life revolved around work, clubbing, and one-night stands. No excuse for a hookup to overnight when a taxi stand sat literally at his front door, the train station a one-minute walk. Problem solved.

Edward, on the other hand, seemed to have no trouble making

ends meet. Mark wasn't usually intimidated by those kinds of comparisons, but then again, he wasn't in the habit of visiting the home of a guy he was interested in either—didn't do interest, full stop, at least not like that. His interest bar was set fairly low, mostly to do with getting a man out of whatever club they were at and into a bed, and he wasn't too fussy whose bed it was. To that end, jobs and income meant nothing. His needs were simple. Or they had been.

He checked his watch. Eight thirty. *Shit.* Should he have brought something? No. Not. A. Date. He rapped on the door and jumped at the booming bark that greeted him from the other side. *What the...?* A dog? And not just any dog, judging by the muscle behind that bark—a *big* 'Keep your hands to yourself or lose your whole arm' kind of dog. And that was a surprise. In a million years, Mark would *never* have picked Edward for a dog guy, ever. Too much hair and dry cleaning for all those pristine suits, for a start.

There were a few muffled words before the locks snapped and the door opened to reveal Edward... and wow. He sported a light scowl, hand-tousled hair, pursed lips that accentuated his cute-as-fuck dimples, those damn black-rimmed glasses, and a million points of contact for Mark's lips. Mark's tongue landed on the roof of his mouth and stuck there. It was marginally better than having it on the floor in full living colour, but not by much, because... *holy shit...* Mark had been in no way prepared for *this.*

The image of Edward R Newton in soft sweats, bare feet, a hint of scruff on his jaw, and a slim-fitting Rascal Flatts T-shirt that did nothing to hide a considerably tighter, fitter body than Mark had ever fantasised damn near sucked the breath from his lungs. It was all he could do not to back Edward against that very expensive wall and sink into those succulent, disapproving lips.

Oh, yeah, as if he didn't already know how much trouble he was in. Yet he seemed completely unable to stop himself from walking straight into it, like a damn prisoner to the executioner's block. Now why in the hell was that? *Oh, right. Still no fucking answer.*

"Detective Knight." Edward motioned Mark inside with a sweep of his arm. "Straight down and to the left." Business as usual.

For Mark it was anything but. He hitched a brow and did his damnedest not to drool... or pant... then turned and made a dramatic point of scanning the neighbourhood, giving himself some much-needed time to get his shit together.

Finally he turned back to Edward and pulled up his most confused expression. "Excuse me, sir. Do I know you? This is 16 Holsworthy Drive, right?"

Edward bit back a smile. "Why? Is there something the matter, Detective?"

"You know damn well there is." He eyed Edward sideways. "You did this deliberately, didn't you?"

"Did what?" Edward's brow creased.

"This." Mark gestured with a sweep of his hand. "This mellow, breezy, 'I'm not buttoned up tighter than a drag queen's tuck' look you've got going on here. Just a regular Joe, relaxed, take-me-as-I-am kind of guy, in my obscenely revealing sweats and painted-on fucking T-shirt—just your everyday sexy piece of intelligent gorgeousness, right?"

Edward's eyes popped. "I have absolutely no idea what you're talking about. These are my at-home clothes. And... obscene?"

Mark's gaze narrowed. "All of that, and you focus on obscene? You know very well what I mean. You're a tease, Edward Newton. I can not only see you're circumcised in those, at the right angle I could quite possibly read the date stamp of the procedure. Come close enough and I can probably scan the bloody QR code with my phone."

Edward chuckled. "You have a serious problem."

"No, I damn well don't. You don't play fair. Who are you, and what have you done with Edward? Where's the suit? The exec shirt with its labyrinth of teeny-tiny Alcatraz-style buttons, and chastity-level belted-up trousers with their ubiquitous No Trespassing sign plastered across the fly in neon lights. And, for the love of God,

where the hell are your shoes? Look at those toes—those feet are seriously sexy." He threw up his hands. "You can't fuck with me like this,
Edward. I may need therapy."

Edward gaped, his expression part amusement, part serious
concern over whether Mark might have lost his freaking mind—
which Mark suspected wasn't far from the truth. And if a little bit of
flirting had troubled the good pathologist, spewing sex talk was never
gonna be a winner. Mark figured he'd cooked his goose. But then
Edward laughed, loudly, and everything in Mark's world got a little
brighter with it.

"Just the outcome I was looking for," Mark said. "Total derision."

"No, um, it's not..." Edward took a few breaths in a seeming effort
to calm down and waved Mark inside for the second time. "Just so
you know, I'm not going to furnish any reply to that nonsense, mostly
because I have no idea what you're talking about. I'm at home, in at-
home clothes. It happens."

"Nuh-uh." Mark waggled his finger in Edward's face as he
stepped inside. "At-home-Edward clothes have always, in my imagination—and believe me when I say I've spent some considerable time
imagining it—have *always* been a pair of conservative, relatively ugly
(sorry) beige corduroys or chinos, belted, of course, quite possibly
padlocked even... with added chain. And maybe, just maybe, a loose
button-down shirt, untucked if you were feeling particularly risqué.
But nowhere, and it bears repeating, *nowhere* did you *ever* appear
barefoot and tousle-haired. Never. Slippers, at the very least. Deal-
breaker, Edward, deal-breaker. You cannot expect me not to flirt with
all this on display. You have no one to blame but yourself."

Edward shook his head in disbelief. "Your imagination is a
dangerous place, Detective. Remind me never to visit. But it's nice to
know you fantasise about me. Now, head down the hall and to the
right before you say something you'll regret."

Mark eyed him up and down. "Like that horse hadn't already
bolted from the stable a paragraph or six back."

Edward grinned. "I promise not to hold it against you."

"Such is my luck. Shoes off?"

"No need."

Mark paused. "By the way, the scruff looks good on you."

Edward's hand lifted to his jaw, and Mark smiled to himself.

"You should keep it," he said, and Edward's cheeks tinged pink. At least Mark wasn't the only one off balance.

They stared at each other for a few more seconds before Edward cleared his throat. "After you, Detective."

Mark wandered down the wide hallway, noting the pricey furniture and eclectic selection of colourful modern prints—nothing at all like the photographic landscapes Edward seemed to favour. It was almost jarring. Trying to scope any further clue to the other man's personality, he failed to notice the lumbering obstacle in his path until a throaty rumble alerted him to a huge drooling mouth parked within snapping distance of his groin and he slammed to an abrupt halt.

Holy shit. The steely, focused attention of fifty to sixty smoke-grey, quivering kilos of wary hound sent Mark's pulse, not to mention his balls, rocketing north at such a speed he wasn't sure he'd lay eyes on them again.

Goddamn, it was big. He didn't dislike animals—hell, his best friend was a damn dog handler, and Paris, Josh's German shepherd, lounged all over him with complete disregard for personal space every time he visited. But this monster was in a whole other league, and Mark's breath lodged painfully in his throat as the animal stared him down.

"Ah, Edward?" It resembled a squeak more than a question, but hey, Hound of the freaking Baskervilles, or pretty damn close.

Edward sidled up and fondly scruffed the dog's head. "Leave the poor man alone, Tinkerbell. She's a Neapolitan mastiff."

Tinkerbell? "Are you sure about that? I heard the zoo's missing one of its baby elephants."

Edward clapped him on the shoulder. "Not frightened of a wee pup, are you, Detective?"

Mark narrowed his gaze. "You're joking."

"Not at all. Tink's only eighteen months. Neos can get to seventy-odd kilos."

Mark eyed the dog in horror. "Holy crap, that's two-thirds of my weight! And, fair warning—I've seen what you drive. Trust me, you're gonna need a bigger car."

Edward's eyes glittered a steely silver in the half light of the hall as he laughed, and damn, Mark loved that sound. Gone was the stern, unapproachable schoolteacher, and in his place was this relaxed, sexy, almost fun man that Mark had not the slightest idea what to do with. Edward Newton was messing with Mark's head big time.

"Never fear, I've got a Ford Ranger in the shed. The BMW isn't actually mine, and I wouldn't let Tink anywhere near it for more reasons than size alone." Edward dropped to his knees and grabbed the dog by her ample jowls. A huge pink tongue flashed out and caught his nose. He chuckled and let her wash his face before rubbing noses with her, and Mark found himself a sudden believer in parallel universe theory—one where Edward Newton allowed a gigantic dog to lick his face and even seemed to like it.

"These guys were bred from the Molossus, a huge Greek war dog," Edward explained, still face to face with his dog. "The Romans brought them back when they conquered Greece and further developed the breed. They're supposed to look frightening—"

"Oh, good," Mark scoffed. "They succeeded."

"They were guard dogs. They even went into battle. Some were fought in the gladiator arenas—"

Mark's heart stuttered. "What the hell? What is up with people? War is one thing, but making animals fight for spectator pleasure... it was wrong then, and it's wrong now. It makes my blood—" He broke off mid-rant because...

Edward was staring at him with soft eyes.

His cheeks warmed alarmingly. "What?"

Edward shook his head. "Nothing."

"Don't do that. Don't brush me off."

Edward breathed a small sigh. "I just, um... I don't know. It's silly, but I guess I didn't expect..."

And, yeah, the subtext hurt a little. "What? That I would care about shit like that? 'Cause I'm such a douchebag and all, right?"

Edward winced. "Sorry." And, to his credit, he looked it. "Yeah, it was a pretty shitty thing to think."

Mark grunted, "Forget about it. And can you please get up off your knees? It's... distracting."

Edward's mouth twitched. "Oh, right. Sorry." He got to his feet. "And it shouldn't have surprised me. It's just that sometimes you—"

"Piss you off? Get under your skin? Flirt relentlessly with you?" Mark chuckled, then sobered. "And make it hard for you to take me seriously." The last wasn't a question.

Edward gave a half grin. "A little, maybe. You come on a bit strong for my tastes. But that's no excuse for dismissing you as a lightweight."

Mark's hand landed over his heart with a dramatic thud. "Ouch. A lightweight? Wow. All because I flirt with you? Well, I'll let you in on a little secret, Edward. I flirt because you're hands down the sexiest man I've seen in a long time."

"Don't be ridiculous." Edward seemed genuinely affronted, his gaze sliding from Mark to Tinkerbell at his feet. He reached out a hand and scratched the dog's head. "You flirt with everyone, Mark. I'm nothing special. You flirt because that's how it's done in the one-and-done crowd. Flirt-hook-fuck-leave, right? And I've got zero interest in being a notch on your belt."

Mark's mouth dropped open. Well, he had said he wanted to get to know what Edward thought. But yeah, not so much, maybe.

"Wow, I guess that tells me, then, right?" he said in a flat voice. "Got me all figured out there, Edward, don't you? Didn't realise you could tell so much about a man from a little innocent flirting, but I'll be sure to remember." He eyed the room at the end of the hall. "I'll just go through, then, shall I?"

He took a step, changed his mind, and tipped Edward's chin up with a finger till their eyes met instead. "Just one more thing. I've said many, many ridiculous things in my life, Edward Newton, but you being drop-dead sexy was not one of them. That said, I take your point about the notch thing—"

Edward arched a brow.

"—but you've made your position very clear, and I respect that. Anything more than one night, two at a push, makes me itchy in ways you don't understand, and yet against all odds, here I am, still trying, not running for the hills... so call the damn marines. I have no clue why I'm still here, and I'm not sure what that says about me—out of my ever-loving brain springs to mind—but I'd suggest it at least moves me out of the purely one-and-done crowd, as you so eloquently put it. It might be a mere step to the left in your world, but it's a fucking country mile in mine."

Edward drew a sharp breath, looking slightly stunned. *Whatever.* Mark was tired of the one-way traffic. Edward didn't get a free pass on judging him. No one did. His gaze slid to Tink, who looked even more unconvinced by his presence, if that were possible. *Well, that makes two of us.*

A touch on his arm drew his gaze back to Edward, who now looked stricken.

"I screwed up. I'm sorry. That was inexcusably rude of me. Look, can we take this into the family room, please?"

Mark nodded.

"Thanks. Come on, Tink. Leave the nice detective alone." Edward headed down the hall, and the massive dog immediately thundered after.

Mark followed at a safe distance, coming to a stop by the break-fast bar while Edward continued into the kitchen. Tink plopped her large frame down on a sheepskin rug the size of a double bed, and Edward threw her a chew bone that wouldn't have looked out of place in a woolly mammoth exhibit. She growled and attacked it with concentrated gusto, her gaze lifting every now and then to check that Mark was behaving himself. It was so comically deliberate that he wondered if Edward had briefed her about him in advance.

"Look, I worded all that poorly. I don't even know why I said it." Edward kept the breakfast bar between them.

"Yes, you do," Mark argued. He locked eyes and saw the uncertainty there. It likely mirrored his own.

"Maybe. You, um... rattle me, Mark, and I'm not easily rattled."

At least they had that in common. "But you also like me, right? And I think that's the real problem."

Edward's gaze softened. "I do... and yes, that's a problem, a big one."

Finally they were getting somewhere. "You say that like you're the only one affected by... whatever this is. The only one with anything on the line. You do realise that it's a problem for me, too, right?"

Those two little creases between Edward's brows notched a little deeper, and Mark barely suppressed the urge to reach out and smooth them.

"I um... I don't understand."

Mark blew out a sigh. "You know, for a smart guy, you can be really dense sometimes."

Edward snorted. "Humour me."

"Okay. I get that you don't want to like me, because I have an apparently shitty reputation, dating wise that is—not that you should believe everything you hear, or even half." He eyed him pointedly. "And it doesn't make me a bad person."

"Fair comment."

Mark nodded. "Good. But just so you know, me liking you is *equally* a big, big problem for me, Edward. Don't get me wrong, I tend to like the people I fuck. All gossip aside, I'm not a total arsehole—"

"I said I was sorry—"

He held up a hand. "But wanting to get to know someone, concocting excuses to spend time with them..." He paused for that to sink in. "Questioning my rules..."

Edward drew a sharp breath. "You've been doing that?"

Mark blew out a long sigh. "You know, as irresistible as you are, Edward, I'm not overly fond of getting the stuffing knocked out of me on a regular basis, just for the sheer hell of it. And so we're clear, if I wasn't as confused as you are about this"—he waved his hand between them—"whatever the hell this is that we *both* feel and *both* want to run the hell away from, I'd have stopped blowing smoke up your arse weeks back and left you to it. I hardly need the aggravation. It's not *that* much fun riling you." Not quite true, but Edward didn't need to know that.

A flicker of doubt crossed Edward's face. "I, um, I don't know what to say. If anything, that makes me even more nervous, and I'm not sure it—what did you mean before, about you still being here trying?"

"I meant exactly what you think I did. That for some terrifying and completely baffling reason I can't just seem to walk away from you. And I should. For a number of very sound reasons, not least of all your obvious aversion to me, not that you even know me."

Edward opened his mouth, no doubt to argue, so Mark covered it with his hand and tried to ignore the warm press of Edward's lips on his palm. "Don't even go there," he warned. "I don't want to get mad at you again."

Edward rolled his eyes, and Mark slowly removed his hand. "Look," he said. "I'm not asking you to abandon your concerns. Lord knows those things seem locked down in triplicate with a few hundred penalty clauses attached. Not to mention my own issues come with sets of bells I'm surprised you didn't hear ringing a mile away, and I can't promise that I can silence them. I'm just... putting it out there that I'm... thinking about... things. And maybe, just maybe you could give me a little bit of rope here and be patient, not dismiss the whole idea out of hand. But only if you're interested as well. Of course."

Edward blinked slowly. "I, um. Wow. Um... okay. Lord help me, but okay." He blew out a breath. "I guess I can do that. But no promises, mind."

"Does that mean you might also be... interested?"

"Interest was never the problem, Mark."

The tightness Mark had carried in his chest all day unfurled a little. "Right. Good. That's... good, then. I think. So let's just mosey along and see what happens. You promise not to jump to conclusions and sully me with unwarranted disapproval"

"Sully, huh?" Edward's eyes danced.

"Yes, sully, and I promise not to jump your bones without contract-level consent, *and* to keep working on my issues around... longevity. In fact, to avoid all possible risk of miscalculation on my part, I think it best to leave all overtures in your court. I'll simply follow your lead. Agreed?"

Edward's eyebrows almost climbed into his hairline. "Jump my bones?"

Mark winced. "Too much?"

"A little." Edward sent him a wry smile, then narrowed his gaze. "You were baiting me, right?"

Mark grinned. "Quite possibly. So, are we agreed?"

Edward studied him. "If I agree—and that's a big if, Detective— then you're saying any first move would be mine? And if I decide not to, then it will end there?"

"Absolutely." God help him.

"You won't push?"

"Never." *Goddammit.*

"And you'll be respectful in my workplace and yours?"

"Goes without saying."

Edward dipped his head in thought. Then, raising only his eyes, he studied Mark through those long, gorgeous lashes for a few seconds before adding, "And no flirting."

Mark cocked his head cheekily. "Ah, and we were doing so well there. You have to leave a boy a little fun."

Edward's eyes flashed warm with amusement. "All right. You know you're way too charming and slippery for your own good."

"Aw, you think I'm charming?"

Edward steeled his gaze. "Don't push it. But yes. I agree to keep an open mind, that's it—though I think you should shoot me now, as it'll probably be less painful." He turned his back and began rooting in a cupboard beside the fridge. "I can't believe I'm doing this."

"I'll be the model of chivalrous, you'll see."

Edward snorted. "I won't hold my breath." He spun back with a bottle of whisky in one hand and a red wine in the other. "Merlot, or scotch—a Laphroaig triple wood, to be precise?"

Right. Of course Edward drank *scotch*. Mark leaned over the breakfast bar to take a closer look, and Tink gave a soft warning growl. He turned to where she still lay on her mat and spread his hands. "What? I'm nowhere near him." Which only earned him another growl.

"She's a teeny bit protective, wouldn't you say? And whisky, please."

Edward shrugged and reached for some glasses. "She has good instincts, what can I say?"

"Oh, really." Mark poked his tongue out at the mastiff, who shook her head in reply, sending a ribbon of drool flying from behind the curtain rolls of skin that fell from her jaw. It landed on the rust-painted wall behind, looking like a gluey Rorschach inkblot test. He shook his head in horror. "Oh, and by the way, Edward: Tinkerbell? Are you fucking kidding me?"

Edward laughed, and the warmth of the sound settled low in Mark's groin.

"My niece named her. Do you want ice?"

Mark feigned horror. "Ice in scotch, Edward? You shock me. I'm going to have to re-evaluate my opinion of you. No, not for me. And you let your niece name your dog?"

Edward laughed and added a cube to just one glass before

pouring the whisky. "That's what you get for letting a four-year-old fleece you at cards."

"Your niece beat you at poker?"

"No, Go Fish. And *Peter Pan* was her favourite story at the time. I should've known better. I still think she cheated."

Fucking adorable. He couldn't hide his grin. The hard-arse pathologist was actually a big softie. Yet another piece in the why-the-hell-am-I-so-stuck-on-this-man puzzle.

Edward handed Mark his whisky and led them to a pair of matching cream leather couches that framed the family room, each sporting a dark-coloured, slightly tatty woollen throw. Decked out in neutral beach tones, with high-vaulted whitewashed ceilings, the space was light and airy, and the seating had been carefully arranged to make the most of the stunning view through the twelve-foot glass wall at the end of the room which boasted a silky calm Herne Bay lit in early sunset blues and rose pinks.

He took a sip of his whisky and hummed in appreciation. It was satin smooth, with just the slightest edge on the swallow and a smoky finish on the palate. He sank into one of the couches while Edward claimed the one opposite, and from there they studied each other, circling their wagons.

"I know that look." Edward notched a curious brow, his eyes a blue-grey match with the deepening sky behind. "Something's tickled your fancy."

"Just that you're not as gruff as you'd have everyone believe. Dogs? Kids? Who'd have guessed?"

Edward's mouth quirked up. "You just keep thinking that, Detective. Here, help yourself." He pushed a readymade tray of cheese, olives, and grapes across the coffee table towards Mark, while the clack of teeth on rawhide broadcast Tinkerbell's ongoing obsession with her bone.

"I was hungry," he said in answer to Mark's raised brows. "And I didn't imagine you'd eaten."

Mark was oddly touched, and his stomach rumbled on cue.

"Thanks." They ate in silence for a few minutes, and Mark's gaze landed on a stack of old-style comics sitting off to one side of the coffee table, a few still in their plastic sleeves.

He nodded to them. "Yours?"

"Guilty as charged." Edward sipped at his whisky and sank back into the cushions.

Huh. Mark would've bet a month of Sundays that Edward's reading matter didn't veer far from medical journals or whatever professional shit pathologists read that Mark was likely better off knowing nothing about.

"Can I?" His hand hovered over the top comic.

After the briefest hesitation, Edward shrugged. "Sure. Just, um, be gentle. They're collector editions."

He picked the comic up, slid it out of its sleeve, and leafed through it. "Wow. This is amazing. How long ago was it published?"

Edward's expression lit up. "Yeah, it's cool, right? 1950s. It was the first *Adventure Comic* featuring the Legion of Super-Heroes—" He hesitated. "I, um, collect them... and others."

The retro artwork was amazing, and Mark could totally see the attraction. "You know, as a kid I loved Deadpool and Hellblazer."

Edward's eyes flashed cobalt. He licked his lips and leaned forward. "Really? I've got the entire *Hellblazer* series. A complete unit came up at auction about ten years ago in Australia, just after I'd got my first pathology residency. I drained my savings to win the bid. Put me back buying an apartment a couple of years, but man, I love those comics."

His voice grew more animated as he talked, clearly passionate about the subject, and Mark found himself unable to do anything but stare.

"DC Comics really went out on a limb with that one," Edward kept up the commentary. "So political for the times. And Constantine was such a great character, right? I don't have them with me. I only brought a few favourites here. The remainder are in climate-controlled storage with the rest of my collection until I get a permanent place, but I, um, I could show you them... one day." His face flushed and his voice dropped. "If you wanted, that is."

Hell, yeah, Mark wanted. It was the most Edward had said about something other than work since they'd met, and he was spellbound. This Edward was light years from the uptight pathologist he thought he knew. This Edward was animated and passionate and so damn intoxicating, Mark wanted to crawl across the coffee table, straddle him where he sat, and kiss him senseless into tomorrow. He didn't, having given away his rights to first moves and all that, but it was a close call.

"I'd, um..." He cleared the roughness from his throat. "I think I'd really like that. You said this one's valuable?" He held up the comic. He wanted nothing more than to keep Edward talking, and if that meant comics—well, if he hadn't already had an interest, he'd have conjured one up on the spot.

Edward gave a pleased smile. "It depends on the market, but yes, the one in your hand is probably worth between $4,000 and $20,000 US, depending on how badly someone wants it."

Mark's eyes flew open. "You're kidding me."

"No, I'm really not." Edward leaned forward, encouraged by Mark's obvious interest. "They're pretty popular, especially with all the modern superhero movies. People are now looking for lesser-known characters. It's on-trend, as they say—not that I collect for that reason. And their value depends on their condition and rarity. Unopened is always more valuable, of course, but where's the fun in that? I only keep a few of those, as investments, and I make sure to have well-thumbed copies around to slake my appetite for actually reading the things."

Mark slid the comic back into its plastic cover and returned it to the pile... carefully. "Is it difficult to let go and sell them?"

Edward shrugged. "I don't, as a rule. Only if I end up purchasing a bundle that has repeats of what I already own. I'm not a dealer, as such. I just like having them, reading them. They relax me. It takes me back to being a kid, I guess. My uncle got me started. He loved them, especially the French ones. Graphic novels have always been big in Europe, even when they weren't fashionable elsewhere. I used to hide in my bedroom with a couple whenever I needed some space. My uncle died quite young and left me his collection, and it went from there. Anyway, I've battered you enough with my hobby."

"No, it's interesting. I'm enjoying getting to know this side of you. Tell me more about Edward Newton, the kid."

Edward popped a slice of cheese in his mouth, and Mark suspected he was buying time as he decided how much more he wanted to reveal. He waited for Edward to reach whatever conclusion he was going to. He wouldn't push, much as it killed him. Mark had no strategy in his playbook for a man like Edward, a man so unlike all the men whose company he typically sought. This stupid crush he was building was fucking relentless, and he really, really needed to get a handle on it, because as Edward had said himself, he was in no way a sure thing as far as Mark was concerned. And Mark was beginning to think that might become a big problem for him down the track.

Edward made a show of clearing his throat and reached for his scotch.

Mark dragged his gaze up from that tempting mouth to meet the other man's smirk and fell back against the cushions with a disgruntled sigh. "Hey, it's not my fault," he grumbled. "You want me to stop looking? Then stop sitting there doing that whole broody sexy nerd thing you've got going on. It's damned irresistible."

Edward snorted his whisky, sending a spray of the expensive stuff over the coffee table, narrowly missing his comics.

Mark smirked. "You wanna be careful. I hear those things are valuable." He snagged a cracker and cheese and watched Edward mop the droplets off the varnished wood.

When he was done, Edward threw the cloth into the sink and returned to his seat. "That was your fault."

"Why? It's true." It so fucking was.

"So you keep saying."

Mark leaned forward, elbows on his knees. "It's true whether you want to believe it or not. So deal with it. God knows, I have to."

Edward stared at him a minute, then shook his head. "You're impossible. I think we should talk about the case so you can head home. It's been a long day."

And just like that, warm Edward left the room and cool, distant Edward was back in spades.

Mark put his glass on the coaster. "Okay. But there's one thing I absolutely have to know."

Edward watched him warily.

"About Tink—"

The mastiff pricked its ears and looked at Mark.

"Did you just suddenly decide one day that your life needed the addition of a dog the size of a small continent? And how did that even happen? 'Cause I gotta tell you, that behemoth was a huge surprise."

Edward's smile lit his face almost enough to rival the whole comic thing. "Really? Why? I'm too much of an ice queen to share my home with animals? Now who's jumping to conclusions?" He leaned sideways to snag a few olives, the movement lifting his T-shirt to reveal a sprinkling of silky flaxen hair on a lean stomach.

The effect on Mark's libido was immediate and somewhat of a puzzle. *Jesus Christ.* He'd be heading to a fucking bear convention next.

He cleared his throat, drawing a curious glance from Edward. "Not at all. It's just that I had you pegged for a bit of a neat freak. Dogs in general, but I'm guessing this horse-dog in particular"—he indicated Tink, who was currently lying on her back, all four paws paddling ridiculously in the air and a bone hanging out of that ample, slobbery mouth—"doesn't strike me as being the most easy-care option."

Edward stared at the mastiff with undisguised affection. "You're not wrong about the neat thing, and no, she's far from easy care. But she's big on getting me out of my head and a whole lot cheaper than a therapist."

Oh.

"You don't mind the, ah... mess? I mean, this is a nice house. Amazing view."

Edward's gaze swept the room. "It is, and that's what mats and rugs are for. It's not mine, by the way, the house I mean. I'm house-sitting for friends who are in Somalia for six months with the Red Cross. The BMW is theirs as well. I just run it every now and then to keep it going. Damien's a plastic surgeon and Linda's an ENT specialist. It's not my thing, but I admire the shit out of them for doing it. And the timing meant I could stay here and avoid any rush finding a place of my own."

"Not a bad place to crash." Mark held up his glass in a toast.

Edward grinned and raised his. "My thoughts exactly."

As they both took a drink, Tinkerbell lumbered across to sit at Mark's feet, a single strand of drool bobbing like a bungee cord just above his knee.

He started to reach out, then snapped his hand back. "She won't mistake me for dessert, will she?"

Edward regarded him patiently. "No. In fact, you should feel honoured. She clearly likes you, which isn't her fallback position, just so you know. She's usually more standoffish."

Mark's brows shot to his hairline. "And you know this because...?"

Edward flashed those gorgeous eyes. "Because she isn't growling and eyeing you up as if planning how to get the most out of her first bite."

Mark's alarm must have shown, because Edward suddenly erupted into laughter.

"Glad I amuse you," he grumbled.

"Oh, you have no idea." Edward wiped at his eyes.

"Fucker." Mark wound the ribbon of drool around his finger and then fed it back to Tinkerbell. She licked it up greedily, then frowned as if realising he'd tricked her.

Edward chuckled. "A sweet idea but inevitably futile. My life is an endless cycle of drool, wipe, wash, rinse, repeat. After the first month I simply learned to dress for it, protect stuff from it, clean it, and then forget about it. If not, that shit will drive you nuts."

"Ah. Explains the dark throws, the huge sheepskin rug—"

"And the attire." Edward swept a hand over his sweats and the telltale lines of dry saliva painted across his... groin. "All accusations of flouting my *alleged* circumcision aside."

And shit. Just like that, Mark's gaze was laser focused.

Edward cleared his throat.

"Not. My. Fault," Mark answered the raised brows. "You're the one who went there."

There was an attempt at a scowl, but the distinctly amused edge to it counted as a win in Mark's books. Then again, the bar on that had been set at an all-time low for Edward Newton. Pretty much anything not directly hostile got a tick of success.

Tinkerbell chose that moment to slide her head on to the throw alongside his thigh, her tongue lashing his hand, fingertip to wrist, in a single swipe. He barely held back a shudder and fired a look of disapproval at those big limpid eyes. But the battle was lost the minute she nudged his thigh, and his hand found her ears in a solid scratch instead.

She keened in appreciation, and Mark snorted. "I think that's the first time I've coaxed a filthy groan from any female."

Edward choked on his mouthful of whisky. "Is that right? You were never tempted as a horny teenager, while you were working things out in that brain of yours, just to see?"

"Nope. Gay all the way. Can't remember not knowing it, if I'm honest." His fingers worked Tinkerbell's ears. "Whereas you, on the other hand, are bi—a subject already covered in a previous excruciatingly awkward exchange." He met Edward's eyes. "For two men who aren't fucking, or dating, or doing anything other than dancing around each other, we seem to have incredibly personal conversations, wouldn't you agree, Edward?"

Edward's cheeks flushed. "I'd hardly call it dancing," he said, dryly. "Or at least if it is, I doubt we've been listening to the same tune. You've been tangoing, *hard*, I might add. Whereas I'm more your awkward line dancing nerd—if you can get me on the dance floor at all, that is."

Yeah, Mark could see that.

"Maybe that explains you and me. Attracted to our differences. Yin to yang? If we leave it alone, it'll all blow over."

Doubtful. "Maybe. I do know I'd introduce my yin to your yang any day, or vice versa. I'm, ah, flexible in that regard... in case you were wondering. Were you? Wondering?"

Edward closed his eyes for a moment, and when they opened, they held that familiar unwelcome wariness that Mark had hoped he'd seen the last of. *Damn.* A bristly tongue swept across his hand once again, damn near stripping his skin in the process.

"You realise you could earn a fortune hiring your dog out as a floor sander."

The comment elicited a laugh and broke the awkward silence. "She's way too lazy for that. Thinks she's a fairy princess."

Mark choked on a mouthful of pistachio cracker. "Has she taken a look in the mirror lately? She's about twenty kilos and a couple of facelifts shy of that, I'd have said."

"Don't you listen to him, sweetheart," Edward addressed the mastiff. "Haters will hate." He eyeballed Mark. "You better hope she didn't hear that."

Mark patted the animal's head. "Nice doggy."

Edward rolled his eyes. "Question. Why do you insist on calling me Edward? Other than the obvious piss-off factor." He looked truly at a loss.

Mark chuckled. "Well," he said. "Ignoring the fact that there is *indeed* a great deal of personal satisfaction to be had watching you bristle with indignation every time I use it, the truth is, I *like* your name, Edward. You suit it. It's kind of old-fashioned—decent and principled. It's you, alongside prickly and suspicious, of course." He grinned at the scowl that came his way. "Plus, it keeps me in your orbit."

Edward blinked. "My orbit? What the—"

"How about *you* tell me why you hate it so much?"

Edward's mouth slammed shut, and his teeth set about worrying the inside of his cheek. Mark got it. He did. This was need-to-know stuff, and Mark wasn't sure he'd earned a high enough security clearance yet. And so he waited.

He had more patience than people gave him credit for. As an only child who was very definitely *not* the centre of his parents' world, he'd mastered quiet and patient pretty damn well. It would've been a lonely-as-hell childhood if he hadn't, not that it didn't have its moments.

He saw the minute Edward conceded. A little crease formed at the corner of the man's mouth, a slight softening around his eyes, and a shiver of delight ran up Mark's spine.

"I don't *hate* it," Edward answered. "But let's just say it wasn't the best name to have as a nerdy science and debate team kid, let alone being bi. And my sisters gave me endless shit about it as well. Ed was just more... regular. And heaven knows all I wanted was to be fucking normal. Didn't you?"

"Hell, yeah. Adolescence was bad enough, right? Were you out in high school?"

Edward snorted. "Nah. I wasn't exactly popular as it was, so there was no way I was gonna add in the fact that I hankered after both sides of the coin—something that had been evident pretty early —so, no. My family knew, but no one else. It wasn't a problem, because I didn't really date... anyone."

Mark's mouth dropped open. "No one? How is that even possible? How did this"—he swept a hand over Edward—"not bring all the boys *and* girls to your yard?"

Edward regarded Mark as if he'd sprouted two heads, and then he blushed. Hand to God, a full-on blush.

"I think you're overstating things again." Edward pushed on

quickly. "I was awkward as hell, to say the least, gangly and thin as a reed, and I didn't..." He paused. "What I mean is that I was what you'd call a... late bloomer. Sexually, I mean. I never really had that huge hormonal drive that everyone else seemed to have. It took me... a while."

There was such earnestness in the man's expression, like he was worried Mark would mock him. *Hah.* If only he knew. It was all Mark could do not to tuck Edward into his arms and bury his lips in his hair.

"Well, all I can say is you're lucky you weren't at my school," he said. "'Cause one look at you and I'd have risked that beating."

Edward shook his head, making it clear he thought Mark was full of shit.

Mark let it go. "So, when *did* you come out, publicly?"

Edward's gaze slid across to the blazing lights of the Chelsea Sugar building on the other side of the bay. "I had a huge crush on my best friend all through school and well into university. Anton Carmichael."

Mark winced. "And this Anton was straight, I take it?"

"As an arrow," Edward answered without looking back. "Not that he ever knew anything about my feelings for him. I just dealt. Went out with a girl in my anatomy class instead. Much safer bet. I eventually came out to him and everyone else later that year. The girl didn't last, of course. Being bi was a definite deal-breaker for her, but Anton and I stayed friends."

Tinkerbell gave up leaning against the couch and collapsed on top of Mark's feet, a fifty-kilo slobbering furnace.

"You said you had sisters?" Mark pulled his toes free before they became pancakes.

"Yeah, four."

Mark's eyes popped. "Four! Holy shit." Then understanding hit. "Ah, that explains the need to escape to your bedroom. Now I get it."

Edward pulled a lopsided grin. "Don't get me wrong, they're great as far as sisters go, but yeah, they were... a lot." He reached across to a side table, grabbed a framed photo, and handed it to him. "That's a fair few years ago now."

Mark studied the image. It had been taken somewhere around Otago way, judging by the scenery. It showed Edward in the middle of a quartet of laughing, attractive girls, all making a mockery of him in some form, from rabbit ears to held noses, with the parents off to one side looking delighted with the shenanigans and proud as Punch. The siblings were in their teens and twenties by the look of it. The perfect family. Mark's chest clenched for a second.

"Wow," he said. "As an only child, I always imagined having siblings would be cool. But four sisters? Yeah, I feel your pain. Must have been..." He scrambled for the polite word as he set the photo back on the table.

"Loud is the word I think you're looking for." Edward laughed and took the photograph back, taking a minute to study it with undisguised affection.

Goddamn, Edward had to know how much he was letting Mark in and how intoxicating that was for Mark. After all, Edward did *nothing* without careful thought, and the very idea that on some level he trusted Mark enough to share like this, well, the thought nestled deep in Mark's chest and bloomed a little. Dear God, he was in so much trouble. Not least because a fearful part of him just knew that he would continue to like *and* thirst after Edward, even when Edward turned Mark down flat, as he inevitably would if he had any sense. Mark was a bad bet in anyone's books.

Was *this* what Josh had been yapping on about since he'd first met Michael? The classic love-hate attraction? *Son of a bitch. They should really vaccinate for this shit.*

"But hellish, frustrating, and terminally chaotic at times, would also work," Edward continued. "And yes, it drove me up the wall. But as the solitary boy in the family, I did have my own room, and that was my salvation. Plus the comics. I'm a huge introvert, and my parents understood that well enough to ban my sisters from crossing the threshold of my bedroom without permission. To this day I credit that single rule as having saved me from the desire to perpetrate homicide on a daily basis."

Mark snorted. The more Edward talked about his family, the more his shoulders dropped their defensive tension, and Mark relished the slide of a slow easy smile across the man's face—a smile that transformed Edward Newton from untouchable to... irresistible. He was like an intriguing book that Mark couldn't put down, and it was too damn late to tape the cover shut with a warning sticker: "Known to cause quivering resolve."

He side-eyed the other man. "Robin."

Edward arched a brow.

"Edward Robin Newton?"

Edward bit back a smile. "No, not Robin."

"Damn. I was sure I had it that time."

"Name me one guy you know called Robin." Edward leaned back and folded his hands across his stomach.

"Reece?"

"Give it up."

Mark threw up his hands. "Okay. I'll behave."

"I'm not sure that's remotely possible."

Mark sent him a slow smile. "There, see how well you know me? Anyway, these four sisters. Are they the reason you keep your distance from people? Still guarding that need for space?"

Edward narrowed his gaze, and the temperature in the room slid ten degrees south. "Don't imagine you know me well enough to analyse me, Detective."

Shit.

CHAPTER EIGHT

Mark was going to drive Ed to drink. Actually, that was a damn good idea. Ed got to his feet, feeling so tightly strung he was surprised he didn't vibrate.

"How about another whisky and then we hit the files?"

Mark held out his empty glass. "Sure."

Ed headed for the cool of the kitchen, opened the freezer to grab some ice, and bathed in the cool air for a few seconds. So Mark was "flexible," huh? Was Ed surprised? Maybe. A parade of images appeared unbidden in his mind. And Mark had had the gall to ask if Ed had wondered? Of course he damn well had. *Jesus Christ.* Wondered, imagined, obsessed over, all of the above. And that was when he was busy walking the "Absolutely not, I'm never ever going there," line. Now?

An untethered Ed had free rein to take that obsession to the next level: daydreams. And daydreams were even more dangerous. Because the very nature of daydreams meant they had perilous feelings attached. Fantasies and imaginings were physical, at least in Ed's world. They led to a quick jerk-off and some kind of satisfaction.

Daydreams were a whole other matter, ethereal wishes with little substance.

"How about I order some Uber eats," Mark called from the couch. "We could be a while."

Ed turned and stared. It was starting to feel like a damn date.

"Just a suggestion." Mark picked up on the vibe. "But I'll tell them to hold the candles." He dimpled up nicely.

"Very funny. How about this suggestion? We work at our respective homes and meet up in the morning."

Mark threw a less than convincing pout. "Aw, Edward, don't be like that. Two heads are almost always better than one, right?" He let the double entendre stand in all its glory.

Ed made sure his eye-roll was particularly scathing. "I'll take your word on that, but okay, order whatever you like. And no, no candles," he added with a smile.

Mark shoved Tinkerbell from where she'd encroached on his feet yet again and stood. She groaned in protest, pinned him with a forlorn stare that Ed knew well, and then headed to her mat.

"Do you have a favourite go-to takeout, then?" he asked.

Ed poured two fingers of whisky into each glass and added ice to his. "There's a couple of local places on the fridge. The Orient Express—no, Orient Foodbar, I think it's called; that one's pretty good."

"Right, I'm on it." Mark took a few steps, then stopped and glared at his feet, and it was all Ed could do not to crack up on the spot. He didn't even need to look.

"Holy shit." Mark lifted his trouser legs and stared. The tops of both socks were sodden with drool.

"Yeah, um... sorry about that... I think." The apology was somewhat undermined by the punctuation of snorting laughs.

Mark eyeballed the mastiff. "You're a menace."

Tinkerbell buried her nose in her paws and regarded him sorrowfully, adding a soft whine for good measure.

Mark crossed his arms. "Nope. And don't think I don't know what you're up to, missy," he added. "Dog saliva is full of enzymes. Give it an hour, and I guarantee you'll be back to see if I'm tender enough for you."

The mastiff's gaze swept the ceiling before she collapsed on her side. Ed wasn't sure it counted as an eye-roll, but it was a close call.

"Wow, tough crowd." Mark dropped to his knees and roughed the animal's ears, then pulled the mat till it was under her jaw to catch any fresh seepage. Tink never batted an eye, and Ed's heart squeezed just a little. *Or not. Definitely not.* "You're a soft touch." He tried and failed to hide the roughness in his voice.

Mark eyed him playfully. "Have to say it's not my usual feedback."

He squeezed past Ed on his way to get the menu from the fridge, his chest grazing Ed's back—something Ed was sure Mark could've avoided, but damn, he smelled good—a little whisky, a little citrus, a little musk, and a fuck-ton of temptation.

The heat of the contact lingered, sizzling against Ed's skin like it had stripped him raw. And, curious fact? Ed had seen it coming and hadn't moved a muscle to avoid it, giving Mark the opportunity to repeat the manoeuvre on the way back. Which he did... slowly—Ed cataloguing every millisecond of it—before he made a beeline to the couch, dug his phone from his pocket, and left Ed to collect his composure and the glasses and follow. *Goodbye rattled, and hello, turned the fuck on. Ugh.*

"It'll be forty-five minutes." Mark pocketed his phone.

"Perfect." Ed slid plates and utensils on to the breakfast bar, then returned to his seat opposite Mark. "We should easily be done by then."

Mark eyed Edward salaciously. "I'd hope we could do better than that."

Ed offered him a cracker. "Here, consider it foreplay."

Mark's jaw dropped. "Edward Newton, did you just flirt with me? 'Cause if you did, you really need to warn a guy next time. My heart can't take too many more surprises."

Ed threw the cracker at Mark and grabbed his pen. "Come on, Casanova. We've got work to do."

Mark rubbed his hands together. "Ooooh. Casanova, I like that. The gay version, of course."

Ed sent him a long-suffering look. "Of course."

They swapped files and began to read, Mark scribbling in his notebook as he went. Ed did the same with the police file, although as Mark had warned, there wasn't a lot there.

Ten minutes later, Mark looked up. "Did you bring that printout of the toxicology report?"

"Yeah, sorry." Ed fumbled in his bag and drew it out. "Here."

Mark scanned it quickly, his expression unreadable.

"I, um, dropped it on to a flash drive as well," Ed added. "It seemed—"

"Prudent?"

Ed sighed. "Yeah."

"You got it somewhere safe?"

"Well..." Ed's gaze slipped sideways to the small hand-thrown pottery bowl on the coffee table.

Mark took a peek and cocked a brow. "How about you think of somewhere better?"

Edward felt his cheeks heat. "Right." He pocketed the drive in his sweats. "I'll stow it in the office safe before I go to bed. Satisfied?"

"Extremely." Mark pushed his laptop over so Edward could scroll through the police file on Greene, and Edward did the same with his. They perused each other's respective notes in silence for ten minutes or so before Edward suddenly stiffened and leaned forward.

"You said you'd read this, right?"

Mark frowned. "A cursory once-over is more accurate. My boss interrupted, so I shoved it in my bag and figured we'd go through it together. Why?"

"I take it you hadn't reached the part where Greene and Bridge had both worked for Morgan and Associates at one point?"

Mark sprang forward and swung the laptop around. "Holy shit. No, I obviously hadn't got that far."

Ed watched as Mark read, noting the way he worried his right thumbnail as he did, an endearing habit Ed had been quick to log early on, one that meant Mark's interest had been piqued. It was pretty cute... dammit.

"So their contracts overlapped by just over a month. Greene was at Morgan's for eight months before Bridge arrived, and left about five weeks later while Bridge was still on contract." Mark slouched in his seat and stuck his pen behind his ear. "What the hell does that mean?"

Edward shrugged. "That's your job, but it seems a pretty damn big coincidence to me."

"You're telling me." Mark rubbed his hands down his face. "We're gonna have to go back to Morgan and ask him about this guy. Funny he never mentioned him in our discussion."

"Should he have?" Edward unfurled and stretched his legs in front of himself. "It was determined a suicide, after all. Why should he make *any* connection?"

"Maybe. But *two* ex-employee deaths in three months?" Mark's brows peaked. "That's pushing coincidence just a little far. He couldn't have forgotten, surely."

Ed thought about it. "Yeah, if it were me, I definitely would've mentioned it. But not everyone thinks like that, right?"

"True. What about that incident report you talked about?"

Ed sighed. To be honest, he wasn't sure what to think about it. "Well, I did find it, eventually. The lab had it in their system, it just wasn't in ours—which could simply be a cock-up and nothing deliberate. Not that it helps much, because all it does is cite the incorrect labelling and steps taken to remedy it and the persons involved, blah blah. There's nothing there to raise any flags. If it hadn't been for the tox screen match, I wouldn't have even known about it. And if I'd just stumbled over it in a file, I would've thought it unusual but not suspicious. Interesting that there was no trace of the original urine screen report, so that got wiped as well. We have really good systems in place to avoid mislabelling, as you can imagine, so I'm going to have to talk to Sandy about what he remembers."

"Do you ever work alone?"

"Not usually."

"So whose name is there?"

"Just Spencer's. And I think that's why I'm reluctant to let this go. That, in addition to the tox match. The specimen labelling side of things is usually left to our assistants, or mortuary technicians. In the event of a stuff-up, the assistant's name and the pathologist's and anyone else involved would all be on the incident report. So why it's just Spencer's in this case, I'm not sure."

"Unless he *did* do the autopsy alone, maybe? Is there any way of finding out if the second samples were still from Greene?"

Ed thought about it. "I'm not sure. The blood group was the same in both, but that's not definitive. Unless they stored any of Greene's blood, which would be unusual seeing as the death wasn't ruled suspicious, it would be hard to find out. Of course, then you'd need to have more blood from the source of the second sample to compare." He threw his hands up. "It's a nightmare. I can't see how an exhumation is going to be avoided."

"And it gives us bugger all to go on. Without that, we can't conclusively say whether the cases are related or not, just that there's some suspicion around them. Kirwan isn't going to be pleased."

The doorbell heralded the arrival of their dinner, and Edward left to answer it.

––––––––––––

Twenty minutes, a scrumptious egg foo young, half a dozen wontons, and a fiery Cantonese beef later, Ed's head was swimming. And not just from trying to work out how the two cases might fit together. Oh no. The principal causative factor behind all that confusion could be laid squarely at the feet of the boyishly charming detective sitting opposite him. Mark was so far under Ed's skin, Ed was gonna need vacuum extraction to get the sucker out. *Crap.*

So much for taking it slow and keeping an open mind. If Ed's mind was any more open, it would collapse into its own black hole. He sighed and glanced down the hall to where Mark had disappeared into the bathroom, giving thanks for the few scraps of headspace to get himself together. He hadn't wanted Mark in his house for this very reason. Mark simply fucked with Edward's head, and not in a good way—well, mostly not.

To be honest, the evening had been a huge surprise, Mark's refreshing frankness included. And it wasn't like Ed could deny the physical attraction—something just sizzled between them. It might be faster than Ed was used to, but the arousal Mark sparked in his body was addictive as hell. Still, for all that, there was nothing Mark had said or done yet, beyond stating good intentions, to justify a total rethink. A part of Ed still feared Mark was a man with a slick line and a tight body to catch you when you slipped on it.

That said, something *had* changed between them. An element of respect had unexpectedly wormed its way in and was burrowing deep, undermining Ed's caution. Until that evening he'd been happy to keep Mark in a mental box labelled 'Dynamite': something to be appreciated only at a distance, like a good fireworks display. Nothing to get up close and personal with, nothing to risk being burnt for. Pretty but dangerous. And to some extent Ed still thought that—all that sharing of childhood and family dynamic snapshots aside. What the hell had he been thinking?

He'd been thinking Mark was... nice, of course. And that right there was the problem. Ridiculously sexy and *nice*. Ed hadn't been prepared for that. Nice was his kryptonite. You could say all you liked about hot bodies, sexual chemistry, guys strong enough to hold and fuck you against a wall. But nice? Nice was a highly undervalued personality trait in Ed's mind. Nice came with respect, manners, caring, and loyalty, if you were lucky. And nice had *not* been the first word that sprang to mind when Ed had been introduced to Mark.

He'd been primed for sexy, self-assured, and arrogant, like a bad club hookup. He'd been in no way equipped to handle the version of Mark he'd seen tonight: funny, friendly, self-deprecating and... kind. He let Ed's gigantic shaggy excuse for a pet drool all over his Vans with nothing more than a smile, for Christ's sake. And only hardcore dog lovers ever got *that* girl's approval—those willing to do battle with a fifty-kilo slobber machine and come out the other end smiling. It had been a low blow if ever there was one.

All of which begged the question of what the hell was he going to do now? He was tempted. God, was he tempted... but he couldn't get past the feeling that it would be a bad, bad idea. Or would it? Hell if he knew.

"Penny for your thoughts." Mark retook his seat, startling Ed out of his musings.

He snorted. "Never gonna happen."

"That bad, huh?"

Was it? Did Ed risk asking what he really wanted to know? Could he risk *not* asking? "Maybe you should tell me," he finally said, burrowing back into the couch and twisting his legs sideways.

Mark's expression turned serious. "Okaaaay, I'm listening."

Ed didn't need to think. "I guess I'd like to understand why you avoid relationships... if I'm gonna try to keep an open mind, that is."

Mark blew out a heavy sigh. "And how exactly do you plan to do that?"

"Maybe you could start by telling me a bit about your family."

Mark opened his hands. "So you can analyse me?"

Yes. "No, so I can understand you."

Mark snorted. "Yeah, well, good luck. How about I *don't* start with that?"

Huh. Ed held his tongue and waited.

The stand-off dragged on for an awkward moment until finally Mark hauled a pillow on to his lap like he needed the comfort. Ed wasn't sure the other man even realised he'd done it, and the whole thing tickled his radar something fierce. "Okay. Give me a place to start, at least."

Ed nodded. "Your parents."

Mark sucked in a deep breath. "Tom and Lucy Knight." He paused while he got himself comfortable, but the pillow remained on his lap. "I was lucky in lots of ways. No divorce, no fighting—they loved each other without question. But it was kind of an intense, unhealthy love, you know? All-consuming, almost selfish. A love that left little room for anyone else... not even me. I'm not complaining, mind you. It could've been a lot worse. They raised me with care and consideration, supported everything I did, made sure I never missed out on stuff, and never blinked an eye when I came out as gay..." He dropped his head and rubbed his eyes.

"I sense a 'but,'" Ed remarked softly.

Mark looked up, lips pursed. "*But*... let's just say I wasn't exactly planned. They never wanted children, something they were very clear about with friends, family... even with me."

Damn. Ed sighed heavily.

Mark shrugged. "Yeah, I think they missed that memo. I was pretty much a third wheel in their lives, if you get what I mean. I was never mistreated or yelled at or anything like that. Just more like an interloper, a fond curiosity they were responsible for until I left home.

"And when Mum died of a heart attack at fifty, Dad was devastated. He disappeared into the vegetable garden and his memories, and I hardly saw him. It was like he'd died as well. I was old enough to look after myself, and so he left me to it—" He hesitated. "God, I hate talking about this shit. Which is why I *don't* talk about it."

He unfolded himself and practically ran to the kitchen. "I need another drink."

Ed followed him to the breakfast bar and held out his glass. "Good idea."

Mark grabbed the whisky and nearly dropped it, juggling to keep it from hitting the floor. Splashes of amber flew across the granite, and Ed reached over and seized the bottle from his hands.

"Shit." Mark backed off, dragging a hand across his face. "Sorry. I'm sorry."

Ed rounded the breakfast bar and rested a hand on Mark's arm. "Hey, it's okay." He locked eyes with the other man and caught a flicker of deep-seated anguish. It was so unexpected he almost hauled Mark into his arms on the spot. But then the moment was gone just as quickly, leaving them standing staring at each other, not six inches between them.

Mark's body heat sizzled under Ed's hand, and he knew he should let go—but damn, he didn't want to. And it didn't stop there. He tightened his grip, leaned in, and slowly, softly, brushed Mark's warm, dry lips with his own, pressing at the corner just a little, their cheeks aligned, the citrus musk of Mark's skin and the graze of stubble filling his senses along with the slight intake of breath between them.

Mark froze at the kiss, stiff and uncertain under Ed's lips, and hell, who could blame him? If there was a prize for sending mixed messages, Edward figured he'd just taken the jackpot. But he didn't pull away, and slowly Mark's lips turned up in a smile against his own and pushed softly back, a gentle reply but no more than that, leaving Ed to lead, as promised.

That reassurance bubbled warmly in Ed's chest, and his eyes drifted shut, giving in to the tenderness of the moment. He drew his lips along Mark's once again, every nerve ending zeroing in on that two inches of molten shared skin. The tip of his tongue teased at the seam of Mark's lips: no pressure, no question, just... hello.

Then he pulled back and caught his breath, shocked at the surge of desire and storm of emotions that rallied in his head. A reminder of every reason he'd fought this whole idea all along. Without a doubt he'd just fucked up, but he didn't regret it.

With his eyes still shut so he didn't have to face Mark, and close enough to feel the puff of the man's breath on his chin, Ed tried to pull himself together, convince himself Mark had been upset, that Ed just wanted to comfort him. But it was a bald-faced lie, and he knew it. He'd kissed Mark because he wanted to, because that one glimpse of vulnerability had changed everything. *Shit, shit, shit.*

"So," Mark whispered at his ear. "That happened."

Ed lifted his gaze to find a pair of smiling hazel eyes locked on his. "Yeah, it did." His tone was flat, wary, even to his own ears.

Mark's smile faltered, and Ed could see the cogs of disappointment spinning. He popped a kiss on Ed's cheek and stepped back. "Don't worry. I can see that mind of yours scurrying for the hills. I didn't read anything into it. You felt sorry for me. I get it. So, whisky or wine?" He reached to grab a clean glass, but Ed held on to his arm.

Mark froze. "What?"

"Don't do that. Don't joke everything away." Ed dropped his hand and put his back to the cupboard. "And I'm not scurrying for the hills, as you put it." He so fucking was. "I'm a grown man. If I kissed you, I meant to kiss you. I just... surprised myself, is all."

Mark turned so they were shoulder to shoulder, his brows creased in concentration. "Is that a good thing?"

Ed shrugged. "It's not a *bad* thing per se."

Mark banged the back of his head against the wood and groaned. "Jesus Christ, do you ever give a straight answer? You're a dark horse, Edward, you know that, right?"

Ed grinned. "It may have been said, once or twice." He added, more seriously, "I like you, Mark Knight."

Mark cautiously met his gaze. "So you've said."

"I still think you're a danger to my common sense, and on that basis of that kiss, a whole lot more than that, but I *do* like you."

Mark grunted. "I don't know whether to be flattered or offended."

Ed slid his hand down to squeeze Mark's. "Definitely flattered." He let go. "And I'm sorry about your parents. A kid deserves to be the centre of their parents' world, not an also-ran."

"Thanks." Mark's gaze tracked away. "And as you already know, I like you too, Edward. Also more than I should. Maybe we should save ourselves the heartache and just have a little fun—if you're worried about my... unreliability, that is. I'm hardly boyfriend material, or so I'm told." He slid Ed a wry grin.

And that was precisely why the two of them weren't a good idea. Ed heaved a long sigh.

Mark elbowed him gently. "Relax. I'm joking. It's not your style, I know. The funny thing is, Edward, the idea doesn't exactly appeal to me any more either."

Fuck. Ed had no response to that, he was too damn busy scrambling to gather all those neurons that had just been blown to hell. Goddamn the man.

Mark chuckled, put a finger under his chin, and lifted Edward's gaze to meet his own. "Ah, there you are. Now focus, Edward. I might end up being that disappointment you're so convinced I will be, and we'll just pass like ships in the night—but it's gonna be a hell of a ride finding out, right?"

Maybe. But Ed wasn't at all sure he'd survive the journey. As if to underline that fear, something warm and hopeful skittered in his stomach. He grabbed its tail and threw it back into the dark where it belonged. He had enough to think about without his reckless heart getting involved. It had taken less than twenty-four hours for Mark to completely fuck with Ed's orderly world, and he was hanging on by his fingernails.

Tinkerbell lumbered over to where they stood in the kitchen and collapsed once again on top of Mark's feet. It thankfully provided a distraction and eliminated the necessity for Ed to reply to what had been said.

Mark didn't kick her off, just wiggled his toes under the dog's chin and grinned as she grumbled in delight.

A smile tugged at the corners of Edward's mouth. "You don't have to indulge her, you know."

Mark eyed the contented animal. "She's fine. It's not her fault she's the size of a tank with enough body heat to rival a sauna."

Ed elbowed him out of the way. "Go on. I'll sort us a drink if you open the door and let Tink outside for a pee."

Mark backed away with his hands raised. "Done. Safer for all concerned. I get it." He eyed Ed pointedly, then bent down and scruffed the dog's head. "Come on, Tink. You and Uncle Mark are gonna bond in some fresh air. Piss on my foot and you'll be in trouble, understand?"

Tink dragged an eyelid open and studied Mark with weighty disinterest for a good second or so. Then she hauled herself to her feet and trudged after him, the cool night air rushing in to fill the void as they headed outside through the patio door.

Ed poured their drinks, heard Tink huff a raspy bark from the garden, and imagined her bounding after a wayward moth—one of her favourite pastimes. What the hell had he been thinking, kissing Mark? That he wanted the nice detective in his bed and under his body as soon as humanly possible, *that's* what he'd been thinking. And because of that, one more drink and Mark needed to leave, like *really* needed to leave. Finally, a plan Ed could get on board with.

"She's not too bright, is she?" The amused comment filtered through the open door.

Ed called back, "Bright enough to get you doing her bidding, I notice." He stowed the scotch back in the cupboard, out of reach in case he had the ridiculous idea to offer Mark any more. Then he reached for the glasses thinking he'd take their drinks out to the deck.

He never got there. The smashing blow came from nowhere, catching him on the side of the head and hurling him sideways into the pantry door with a sickening crack. A single panicked thought —*Mark*—punched through the ringing pain in Ed's skull before his eyes shuttered closed and his entire world went black.

CHAPTER NINE

MARK WAS PRETTY SURE IT WAS THE BIGGEST POOL OF DOG PEE he'd ever seen in his life. Paddling pool capacity at the very least, and he counted his lucky stars he'd kept some distance. Not to mention another ice age could've come and gone in the sheer amount of time it was taking the animal to get the job done—so much so, he was beginning to wonder if she'd actually gone to sleep in her squat.

"Hey, girl, you nearly finished?"

She started, and an eye shot open. *Definitely asleep.*

He chuckled. "Well, can you hurry it up? I'd like to get back in sometime before Christmas, if you think you can manage it."

She fired him a withering look, scratched a few clods of urine-soaked grass into the air, and shook herself hard enough to flatten nearby shrubs. Then she plodded towards him, jowls all a-wobble, and he grinned from ear to ear watching her. It was pretty damned hard not to fall under the big dog's spell. She was just so fucking... there.

He was still smiling when a muffled thump came from inside the house and Tink's gaze shot from Mark to the patio door. She froze, mid-stride, hackles up. An unearthly howl tore from her throat and every hair on Mark's body stood at attention. *What the...?*

He spun and saw nothing, but he wasn't about to second-guess the animal's keen intuition or his own spidey senses. Tink wasn't happy about something... or more likely, someone. *Edward. Shit.* Mark sprinted for the open door, taking a second to register the darkness inside. When had the lights gone off? *Fuck.* His mind raced. Only the living area lights were out—the hall was still blazing. Something was off.

He slowed and tried to get a quick take on the shadowy interior before he charged in, but Tink was coming up too fast. He didn't want her bursting full tilt into whatever or whoever it was before he checked it out. But as soon as he pushed through into the lounge, the patio door slammed shut behind him, locking the mastiff out. *Fuck.* Someone else was in the house.

Mark spun, his vision slowly adjusting to the dim interior, but he still couldn't see anyone—not until his gaze swept the kitchen where a body lay in a crumpled heap on the floor. *Oh God, Edward.* No. Mark lunged toward him. The squeal of Tink's claws gouging the glass door jerked his attention back—but it was too late. A flash of white-hot pain shot through his neck and dropped him like a stone, and then a boot slammed into his ribs. Bile surged up the back of his throat. He clawed to stay conscious, but it was a struggle. *Son of a bitch.* All he knew was that whoever this was, they meant business, and if Mark didn't keep his head, he and Edward were in deep trouble.

He rolled to the side and struggled to get his knees under him as the metal tang of blood filled his mouth. He spat it clear, somehow got himself upright, and staggered backwards to the breakfast bar, desperate to dodge the next blow that might send him packing to la-la land. But the hit to his head had messed with his balance and his knees gave way, crashing him back to the floor with an excruciating crack to his elbow that sent nerves vibrating the length of his arm, rendering it momentarily useless.

He cried out, and Tink launched into full-blown frenzy on the other side of the door, its frame shuddering under the onslaught. A boot connected with Mark's loin, and then another to his stomach shoved him onto his back from where he had just enough time to capture the blurred outline of a man above him holding what looked like a damn gun before an almighty crack split the air. A snarling mass of spit and snapping teeth flew into view amid a rain of shattered glass and barrelled straight into the guy.

Catching the intruder side-on, Tink sent him careening into the dining table, shoving it up against the wall and leaving the guy scrambling on the floor, his gun skittering sideways across the tile. There was a grunted curse as the man's hip hit the table leg, momentum carrying Tink past her quarry and into the far wall with a whimpering thud. It gave the intruder just enough time to scuttle to his feet and take off through the wreckage of the patio door.

Gone for good, or just to get reinforcements? All Mark knew was they needed to get the fuck out of there, fast. He was in no position to fight anyone. But about that. Pain scored a savage line along the right side of his neck and shoulder from the blow that had felled him. And as for his ribs? *Holy shit.*

"Edward?" He wrestled his body to his side—doing his best to ignore the fiery crunch in his chest—and got up on one elbow, the nerves of his injured arm sparking like damn fireworks under his skin as they rebooted. Bile with the sour edge of malted whisky flooded his mouth, and he gagged, turning sideways to heave the wretched mess on to the floor. Then he remembered the gun.

Fuck. "Edward!"

The only answer was a soft howl from Tink, who'd crawled from her landing place at the foot of the wall to where her master lay on the kitchen floor with God-knew-what injuries. Mark couldn't see, and it was killing him. He wrestled his reluctant body on to one knee and tried to suck a decent amount of air into his lungs, not that much was moving past whatever the fucker had done to his ribs.

"Goddammit, Edward," he rasped. "If you're awake, you damn well better answer me, you hear?"

Still nothing. *Shit, shit, shit.*

"Tinkerbell, come here, girl." Mark finally got himself semi-upright, a cause for celebration in itself, just as the lumbering animal turned the corner of the breakfast bar and shoved her nose straight into his face. He pushed her away, protecting his injured arm, and only then saw the blood smeared across her muzzle. Hers or Edward's? He had no way of knowing, and his throat tightened with fear.

"Edward?" Silence. "Goddamn you, Edward." Mark grabbed the edge of the table and tried to uncurl his back to a standing position. He got halfway before his stomach unloaded itself again, this time on the shiny oak table. He paused and breathed through the wrenching in his gut before finishing the job, and then finally he was upright.

"It's Reginald, isn't it," he croaked, pushing off the table. "I know it's fucking Reginald. Just the sort of prissy pissant middle name for a guy who'd string along a mate who was worried sick about him. I'm gonna call you Reginald for the rest of your goddamn days if you don't answer me, now."

Mark lurched into the kitchen, switched on the light, and grabbed the fridge for support as his eyes swam over Edward's too-still body laid out on the floor. His gut clenched, and the spasm in his chest reached up into his neck and pulled even tighter. *No. Not on my watch.*

With his arm twisted awkwardly behind his back and his legs all akimbo, Edward lay prone on the tiled floor, his face turned sideways, one cheek lying in a pool of blood, the other at the mercy of his biological floor sander. Tink looked up from her attempts to wake her owner and growled softly.

"It's okay, girl." Mark stretched out his good hand. "I'm gonna help him, okay? Here I come. There's a good girl." He inched his way across, and Tink stretched to sniff his hand. She gave it a lick and he took that as a win, and an invite, and sank to his knees alongside Edward and the dog, who didn't back off.

"Not fucking Reginald," came a raspy voice, and Mark thought he might just pass out from relief.

He sucked in a shaky breath and pushed the blood-matted hair off Edward's face. "I knew you were playing possum, you bastard." He stroked Edward's cheek just as Tink's tongue found its way into her owner's open mouth.

Edward spat and lifted his head. "Get off me, both of you."

Mark slid back so Edward could roll over, but the admonition only encouraged Tink, who set about cleaning every inch of Edward's face as it was revealed. It was only then that Mark noticed the blood dripping from her mouth.

"Edward..."

Edward shoved at the animal. "Tink, move."

"Tink, come here." Mark grabbed the mastiff's collar with his good hand and pulled her away before tugging Edward upright. Tink growled at the moan that came out of her owner's mouth and Mark's gaze quickly swept Edward's body. "What's wrong? Are you shot? I didn't hear—"

"Shot?" Edward's eyes flew wide. "The guy had a gun?" He stretched his body gingerly. "No, no, I'm... fine, I think... other than a headache the size of a fucking planet."

Thank God. Mark released the breath he'd been holding and squeezed Edward's shoulder in relief, trying to push away the panic that had threatened to crush him when he'd thought, even just for a second, that Edward might've been dead.

"Um... ow?" Edward tensed, and Mark let him go.

"Shit, sorry. Look, we don't have time, I want to get us out of here, but I think Tink's injured her mouth."

"What?" Edward spun and nearly keeled over, but Mark held tight to his sleeve and steadied him as Edward opened the huge dog's mouth and peered in. "Fuck. I can't fucking see straight. You look."

Mark eyed the still-growling dog. "You're kidding me—"

"Look, goddammit."

And so he did, grabbing a tea towel from the floor to mop up the blood—all the while wondering how he'd managed to get a solid beating, have a gun waved in his face, and then find his head down the throat of a dog the size of a horse, all in under a quarter hour. "I think she's lost a tooth. That's where the blood's coming from, at least," he said, breathing in a lungful of blood-laced doggy breath. "Can't see much else."

Edward relaxed his grip on Mark's arm, but the nod he gave was shaky to say the least. Mark tugged at his sleeve. "Come on, we need to get out of here. Tink scared him off, but we can't be sure he won't come back."

"Who?" Edward rolled to his side and pushed himself on to one hip. Then both hands flew to his head. "Jesus Christ. Someone broke my damn brain."

"Shit." Mark gingerly bent over and probed at the large cut that ran just above Edward's right eyebrow, seeping blood down the side of his face. He grabbed a hand towel from the counter and pressed it against the laceration. "Put some pressure on that."

Edward jerked back. "Ouch! Get off. Let me."

"Baby." Mark let Edward take over and quickly ran his good hand over the rest of the man's head but found nothing other than a nasty lump by the right ear. "Think you can move?"

Edward snorted. "Of course I can bloody move." But Mark saw him wriggle a bit just to be sure, testing out his neck and stretching his legs. "I think I hit my head on the damn pantry door," he said. "Don't remember anything after that. You?"

"Nothing major. Now, come on, we need to go."

Edward blinked rapidly as though clearing his vision. "My car's in the basement, back through the hallway"

Mark thought about it for a second. "No. We don't know how he got in, or where he is now. It's too risky. Mine's out front. We'll take that."

"Okay." Edward latched on to Mark's good hand and allowed himself to be helped to his feet, where he wobbled but stayed upright.

One to the good guys. Mark's gaze briefly swept the room for the gun but saw nothing.

Edward froze. "Wait. The case notes, the laptops."

Mark checked. "Shit. They're gone. But we can worry about them later. You still got the drive?"

Edward patted his pocket and nodded. Then he suddenly pitched sideways.

"Oh no you don't." Mark grabbed his shirt just in time to steady him. "Now, hold on to me. We're getting out of here."

Edward blinked, long and slow, and took a deep breath. "Okay, ready." He reached an arm around Mark's waist. "After you." He tightened his grip, and Mark flinched.

Edward froze and let go. "Fuck, you're hurt."

"I'm fine."

"Let me see—"

He grabbed Edward's hand and eyeballed him. "No. We don't have time. Please, Edward. We have to go."

Edward searched Mark's expression. "Fine." He stepped back a little. "But I'm only grabbing your shirt."

"You need—"

Edward pushed him forward. "Quit talking. I thought you were in a hurry."

Mark sighed and skirted the broken door and its mess of shattered glass, in favour of the second set of sliders in the lounge. "You're a bossy little fucker, aren't you?"

Edward snorted at his back. "You have no fucking idea."

Tinkerbell pushed past them both, and Mark was quietly grateful for the small umbrella of warning and protection the animal offered. If their guy was still out there, he might think twice with a huge dog leading their way. Once bitten and all that. If only he'd been able to find the damn gun, he'd feel safer. He reached down with his good hand and roughed the mastiff's head. "Atta girl."

Mark's first instinct was to avoid the back garden—too many places someone could be hiding—so he angled them into the shadows of a wide garden that bordered a path down the side of the house. In the driveway at the end sat his car, waiting. If he could just get them there.

They'd almost made it, when a shift in shadows in the driveway entrance pulled Mark up short. *Fuck.* Someone was out there. He tugged Edward deep into the garden, out of sight against the neighbour's fence, Tink in tow. They needed another plan.

"What happened?" Edward leaned against the fence, keeping the towel pressed against his forehead.

"Someone's out front," Mark said in a hushed voice. "Could be the same guy. Could be a partner. Either way we can't risk it. Here, let me look." He peeked under the towel, but the laceration on Edward's head was deep and still bleeding. *Shit.* He let the cloth go and cupped his hand over Edward's on top. "You'll need to keep up that pressure for a bit."

Mark's gaze flicked up to the house, but this time there was nothing out of place. It was quiet. Too quiet. Like whoever it was, was waiting for them to make the first move. *Dammit.*

He drew his phone from his pocket and stared at it. This whole thing had felt off from the start, and he couldn't shake the idea that the attack wasn't random. Home invasion in New Zealand was rare— a gun even rarer. And Mark was willing to lay bets that nothing bar the case files and laptops had been taken. Which kind of narrowed the pool of suspects, and meant they were in bigger trouble than he'd initially thought. But why?

And why take them both on? If the man was after something Edward had, all he had to do was wait till Mark left. Someone had wanted them both, or at the very least what was laid out on that coffee table, and there was only one thing that tied the two of them together.

He led them to the rear of the property again—giving thanks for the privilege bestowed upon the wealthy of ridiculously large properties. He didn't stop until he had them well hidden in the far corner with a good view back to the house, and the soft lap of an incoming tide to their rear. Then he slipped behind a tree, pulled his T-shirt over his phone to dim the light and made two quick calls. When he finished and turned to Edward, the man raised a questioning brow.

"Liam and Josh," he explained.

"The dog handler?" Edward whispered.

Mark nodded. "And a good friend. I told him there might be a gun in play and that we needed to get somewhere safe."

Edward frowned. "We're not heading to the station, then?"

Mark peered through the foliage, then shook his head. "Not right now."

Edward's frown deepened.

"I'll explain later."

Edward's expression tightened. "You think this is connected to Greene, don't you?"

"Whoever it was, took the laptops *and* the printout."

Edward closed his eyes for a second. "Fuck."

"Exactly. Now, enough questions. We need to move. I told Josh to meet us at Point Erin Pools. That's only three blocks away. Can we get out this way?"

Edward screwed up his eyes. "I'm not sure... I don't... Jesus, my head's a mess."

"Edward!" Mark gripped his shoulders. "Think. Can we get out this way?"

Edward's gaze steadied. "Yes, I think so. There's, um, a public access to the beach on the left with a small car park."

Mark frowned. "Not my first choice. There's a good chance he has eyes on that."

Edward sucked in another breath. "Okay. Well, the beach is only a hundred meters long with cliffs at either end, but we could go through the neighbours'? They don't have a fence at the beachline, and their driveway comes out about fifty metres down the road and around the corner. You can't see it from this place."

"Perfect." Mark grabbed Edward's hand and headed for the sound of the waves. Tink followed close behind, a low growl rumbling in her throat, and Mark caught Edward's eye. "Look we can't have her—"

"Don't." Ed threw him a fiery look.

Mark huffed out a sigh. "Okay, just keep her close. We can't go looking for her."

"We damn well will," Ed snapped. "Tink, tight." The mastiff moved alongside Ed's thigh. "What about the house? It's wide open."

"Least of our worries. Liam will sort it."

They were nearly at the sand when the snap of a branch and a growl from Tink had Mark pushing Edward to his knees. He then dropped side-on in front of him. With their faces barely a breath apart, he put a finger to Edward's lips, drawing breath at the unexpected surge of affection that ran through him. Edward's expression gave nothing away, but he held Mark's gaze, and made no attempt to move.

When no one appeared and things remained quiet, Mark dropped his finger and stood to check before helping Edward to his feet. Then they ran as best they could for about fifteen metres along the sand before heading into the neighbours' property.

The modernist house was ablaze with lights, though Mark could see no one moving behind the glass, and the two of them slunk along the shadows at the driveway's edge. Tink moved at Ed's side like she was glued there, and not for the first time Mark was grateful for her solid presence. Another plus: his arm was back in play, the nerves no longer firing like shotgun pellets.

At the driveway's end, Mark pulled Edward to a stop and peered into the street. Clear. They headed out, made it around the corner seemingly without being spotted, and then picked up to a slow jog. It was the most either of them could manage. Every step crunched excruciatingly in Mark's ribs, but he gritted his teeth and kept going. A glance Edward's way revealed he wasn't doing much better.

At the pools, Mark headed them down the access road, and across the open car park into the dense bush on the far side. From there they had cover and a decent view of the road. The traffic on the motorway rumbled to their right, heading over the harbour bridge, but only brief flashes of head- and taillights sliced through the shadows that hid the two of them.

Tinkerbell fell at Edward's feet and finally relaxed, something Mark hoped was a good sign they'd made it without unwanted company, but he couldn't be sure. He kneeled and tugged Edward gently to the ground alongside him.

"How long?" Edward dragged a hand down his face, his lips tight with pain.

Mark sympathised. He was barely keeping his own shit together, his ribs raging their protest. "Ten minutes, or thereabouts." *Hopefully.* His gaze scanned the street and parking lot. In the condition they were in, if they'd been followed, it was only a matter of time. They were sitting ducks.

Edward faced him with one brow arched. "Why am I not surprised that the first time in my life I'm ever knocked unconscious, it happens to be when I'm with *you*, Detective Knight?"

Mark gave a lopsided grin. "What can I say? I'm special like that."

"You're a menace, is what you are. So, tell me what you're thinking. I need something to keep my mind off the fact someone's out there looking for us."

Mark scanned the road as he answered. "Nothing good, that's for sure. If Tink hadn't sensed something was off, you'd likely be in much worse shape."

Edward winced.

"I think whoever it was waited until one of us left the room, and me taking Tink outside gave him that opportunity. But when she sniffed him out, he had to leave you and deal with me sooner than he wanted."

"But it makes no sense. We've already found the report—shit!" His eyes went wide. "You think it could've been removed from the system files as well, don't you?"

Mark shrugged. "Maybe. Is it possible?"

Edward blinked slowly. "I have no idea. Everything's backed up, so I would think there'd have to be some trace of it still. Besides, I've still got the flash drive." He tapped the pocket of his sweats, and only then did Mark realise Edward was still barefoot.

"But *they* don't know that, right?" he said. "And getting the police files must've been a bonus. They'll know what we've got. Maybe that was what they were after. Or maybe they were just buying time."

"But why? And how did they know—Spencer, right? That's why he put me off till tomorrow." Edward pulled the towel from his head and studied it. "Damn head lacerations. Bleed like motherfuckers." He folded the fabric to get a clean square and then pressed that back against the wound.

"Spencer's a good guess but we can't be sure." Mark gingerly eased himself to his knees. "As to the why? Honestly, I have no idea. But if it's to do with Rowan Bridge, they're clearly not above murder. This whole thing is too slick and too complicated. Falsified reports, possible involvement of a forensic pathologist. It doesn't feel like a bunch of amateurs. There's something we're not seeing."

Concern registered in Edward's expression. "So why didn't he just shoot you? He had a gun, right?"

It was an uncomfortable thought. "Maybe because the noise would draw too much interest, but mostly I think because your tank of a dog took him down—smashed straight through the glass door, baying like fucking Cujo. Tink saved our damn lives." At the mention of her name, she looked up and Mark couldn't help smiling at her. Then a rough cough broke from his throat, and specks of blood flew to the dirt.

In a second Edward was all up in his business trying to take another look.

Mark elbowed him aside. "I'm fine."

"Shut up." Edward pulled at his shirt, and when Mark made to stop him, he slapped his hand. "Don't even think about it," he warned, lifting Mark's bloodstained clothing out of the way. "Holy shit." His cool fingers probed at the burgeoning bruises over Mark's ribs. "There're a couple of dodgy ones there—bruised, maybe broken. They'll need an X-ray and strapping, pronto. Not to mention the damn boot prints on your loin and stomach. God knows what damage that did. You need a hospital."

Mark pulled at his shirt, covering up. "Not happening. Not yet. I told you, I'm fine. And I'm getting you somewhere safe. For all we know, they're aware of the flash drive and are gonna try to come after it." He flipped open his buckle and pulled his belt free.

Edward quirked a brow, and Mark couldn't help but give a soft laugh. "I couldn't make a move on you if my life depended on it." He fed the belt through Tink's collar to fashion a make-do lead.

Edward nudged his shoulder. "And here I was about to drag you to the ground and have my wicked way with you," he deadpanned.

Mark chuckled. "Another joke, Edward? Be still my heart."

The hint of a smile played around Edward's lips for the first time since they'd fled the house, and it was reassuring. But neither had a jacket, and Edward was shoeless to boot. Not to mention Mark was feeling the backwash from a fading adrenaline rush. It only took a glance to confirm Edward looked to be crashing too. "You're cold."

Edward waved his concern aside. "I'm fine."

Mark shuffled close and tucked Edward under his good arm.

He shrugged it off. "I said, I'm fine."

Mark scowled. "Shut up and be sensible. You're in shock, Edward. Hell, *I'm* in shock, and I'm a bloody cop. Don't be stubborn. Let's just keep each other warm." He returned his arm around Edward's shoulders and this time Edward let him.

His fingers trailed the edges of Ed's slightly-worse-for-wear feet. "How are they?"

Ed shrugged. "Fine."

Mark fired him a dubious look. "You're a damn broken record..." He paused as a set of headlights flooded the road beyond the car park. They travelled slowly along Sarsfield Street towards the pool turn-off, and Edward held his breath and sank a little deeper into the crook of

Mark's good arm. Mark tightened his hold, but the vehicle kept going past the entrance to the pools and Edward finally relaxed. They both did.

A few minutes later, Tink's rumbling growl had Mark spinning to check behind them. "What is it, girl?" His eyes searched the ragged bush and saw nothing. But Tink kept staring... and growling. *Shit.*

Mark's phone buzzed in his hand, and his gaze flicked down just as another car came into view. "Okay. That's our lift." He squeezed Edward's shoulder and shuffled awkwardly to his feet before helping the other man. "We're meeting on the road to avoid getting trapped in here." He scanned the parking lot and surroundings again. Still nothing. He eyeballed Edward. "It's about a hundred-meters straight. Fast as we can. Got it?"

Edward nodded, his jaw set determinedly.

Mark blew out a sigh. "Right then, let's go." They shambled as quickly as they could across the parking lot, injured ribs and concussion notwithstanding. But they hadn't even got halfway when a second set of headlights lit up the ground almost directly in front of them. A motor gunned. *Shit.* Another car, heading straight for them down the access lane. Mark hadn't even seen it sitting there in the shadows.

"Move." Mark gave Edward a shove.

"Not your friend, I take it?" Edward picked up speed.

"No."

"But—"

"We can debate this later. Let's just get the hell out of here. Now, run."

Edward took off, and Mark followed as best he could, his legs pumping with a speed he didn't know he had left in him while his ribs screamed in protest. He couldn't say the words, but he'd needed to know Edward was all right—that's why he'd insisted Edward lead. If anything happened, it needed to happen to Mark, not Edward. Mark could live with that.

The mastiff bounded alongside, clearly spooked but also hyped in defence mode, gaze fixed on the following car, yanking all hell out of her lead to face it. It was all Mark could do to keep hold. But Tink was Edward's, and Mark wasn't letting go.

The chasing car was nearly on them as they leapt the elevated kerb of the car park and ran on to the grass, still twenty metres or so from the main road. The car's engine screamed as its front tyres hit the same prominent kerb, and the front of the vehicle lifted into the air, then slammed down on the grass and slid sideways.

Edward and Mark got to the main road just as their rescuer pulled in. The passenger door flew open. "Jump in," a familiar voice shouted.

Relief hit Mark like a freight train. He tugged the Mercedes SUV's rear door open and got Edward into the back seat with Tink in behind, and somehow got it slammed shut again before the dog tumbled back out.

Then he levered himself into the front seat yelling, "Go, go, go." The entire inside of the SUV lit up like a Christmas tree as the chasing car finally got a grip on the grass and made headway toward them.

"Holy shit...."

The SUV lurched forward and smoked it out of there in seconds as the other car barrelled towards them. Thank Christ for German engineering.

Mark turned to find arms, legs—human and canine—and a gigantic lethal tail all scrambling for position. "You okay back there?"

"Just dandy," Edward fired back, shoving Tink to the far side of the seat. "You worry about yourself and get that damned seat belt on."

Mark did just that, as the SUV wove into a line of cars bound for the northern motorway on-ramp less than a kilometre away. No one said another word until they were on it and away. Fast enough to get lost in the burgeoning Friday night traffic before the other car could catch them, or so Mark hoped. Finally, they'd caught a break, but he hunkered down and kept an eye on the side mirror all the same.

"I thought Josh was sending Michael," Mark said without taking his eyes off the mirror.

"He's working a shift." Cam glanced his way from the driver's seat. "He tagged me instead. And what the hell, Mark? Who *was* that back there?" Mark was still trying to wrap his head around that himself. When got no answer, Cam addressed Edward in the rearview mirror. "And what the fuck are you doing with this idiot, Ed?"

Mark sank deeper in his seat. *Goddammit. Of course they had to fucking know each other.* He glanced down at his shaking hand, fisted it, then dropped it to his lap, but not before Cam noticed.

A frown creased the nurse's brow. "Mark, what's going on?" Softer this time.

Mark shook his head. "When we get there, okay? Just... when we get there." He clamped down on the tears of pain pricking his eyes and tried to focus on the side mirror instead as the lights of the harbour bridge flooded their car and they were carried north of the city—to what he hoped would be a place of safety.

CHAPTER TEN

THIRTY MINUTES LATER, CAM PULLED OFF THE NARROW country road on to an unpaved driveway, the Merc's headlights painting the dense bush on either side a dazzling white. The adrenaline had finally abandoned Mark's system a few kilometres back, leaving him cold and jittery and turning an excruciating set of ribs into an almost unbearable burden. So much so that when the SUV finally pulled up alongside a modern concrete-and-steel home, he could barely move a muscle to get himself out of the SUV. He was so done with this night. Not that it was over, not by a long shot.

He turned to check on Edward in the back seat and smiled to see the man's arms wrapped around his dog, the two of them out like a light. At some point the cloth had fallen from Edward's head, but the wound had finally stopped bleeding, so Mark left it where it lay. Jesus Christ, he was turning into a sap. Even worse—he was turning into Josh. He'd never live it down.

Cam elbowed him gently and flicked his gaze to the back seat. "Something I should know about you two?"

Mark scoffed. "When I know, I'll tell you."

Cam's shocked expression almost made him laugh. *Yeah, weren't expecting that, were you?*

Mark had done little to counter his friends' belief in his player reputation. It kept them off his back. They gave him shit about his diehard clubbing-and-hookup lifestyle, and all of them worried about him. He knew that. But then again, they didn't understand his bone-deep fear of what they so desperately wanted for him—mostly because he'd never told them.

Even Josh only knew surface details about Mark's relationship with his parents. When Josh had met his match in Dr Michael Oliver just a few years before, he'd done his best to paint a wonderful picture of committed family life to try to sway Mark from his man-whoring path. And to be fair, those two pretty much walked the talk: bringing up a teenager, taking on two other foster kids, family holidays abroad—perish the thought—complaining about how busy they were... and still fucking like bunnies, apparently. It would've been inspiring if it weren't so damn terrifying.

But then Mark had always written Josh off as the hopeless romantic type, a concept so foreign to Mark that if he possessed even a scrap of it he'd need a goddamn map to find it. As long as Mark had known Josh, that man had been looking for a white picket fence. Who would've guessed he'd find it in a temporary medical import from the States, who'd been busy fucking his way through most of the available gay population in Auckland, until he ran into Josh.

And, against his better judgement, Mark had come to love Michael as a close friend. Michael was good for Josh—they sparked and soothed each other in equal measure, and Mark got it, he really did. The two of them fit, and if Mark missed knocking around with Josh, just the two of them together, he'd never say a thing.

He reached between the seats with his good arm and shook Edward's knee. "Hey, sleeping beauty, we're here."

Edward opened his eyes and blinked rapidly. Tinkerbell groaned and sat up to press her face to the window. A slurry of drool slid down the glass.

Cam grunted. "You failed to mention I'd be ferrying the dog from *Turner & Hooch*. I take it that... leakage, is a constant issue?"

"I'm sorry." Edward grimaced apologetically.

Mark chuckled. "Great, isn't it?"

Cam sighed. "Wonderful. You know how much Reuben loves this bloody car. He's gonna have fucking kittens when he sees that." His gaze swept the back seat, and with it came another groan. "Jesus, the thing sheds hair like a damn lawnmower has been through it. Ugh. I can't deal with this. Keep it as long as you need, just get it valeted before Reuben lays eyes on it again. Deal?"

Mark grinned and returned the high five. "Deal."

"Right, let's get you inside and checked out." Cam headed into the house while Mark hovered over Edward and Tink as they climbed out of the car, and then they both waited as Tink flooded a carefully maintained flower bed with pee. Cam came back, no doubt to check on what the holdup was, just in time to watch a pretty pink geranium cave under the canine waterfall.

He stared in horror and threw up his hands. "You know what, I'm just gonna pretend I never saw that, and we'll all go inside and have a nice cup of tea... or a shot of something stronger. Fuck, definitely something stronger." He turned and left them standing.

"Make that two shots." Mark trailed after his friend, who fired back that, in their state, neither of them would be getting a damn thing other than water, and did they think he was fucking crazy?

"I take it three shots is out, then?" Edward muttered to Mark's back as he followed him up the stairs.

Mark felt the heat of Edward's hand at the small of his back for just a moment before it was quickly jerked away. He stopped and turned slowly.

"What?" Edward frowned, but he couldn't hold Mark's gaze.

Mark leaned in and pressed a chaste kiss to the corner of Edward's mouth. On and off in a second. "I like it when you touch me."

Edward flushed crimson. "I'm sorry. I didn't mean—"

Mark put a finger briefly to Edward's lips. "Then that's a shame."

Edward scowled unconvincingly. "Just to clarify, I thought I had the rights on making the first move."

Mark eyeballed him. "I think that horse has bolted, don't you?" He left Edward pink cheeked and turned to find Cam watching from the door, wearing a furtive smile. *Bugger.*

"One word to the others and I'll let the paparazzi know where you two are headed for your honeymoon," he said as he jockeyed past Cam into the house before turning back.

Cam's eyes had narrowed to slits. Press interest in the first out gay All Black rugby player and his partner hadn't diminished as quickly as everyone had hoped, but they managed.

"You wouldn't dare," he fired back.

Mark cocked his head. "Try me."

They eyeballed each other for a moment before Cam finally grumbled, "Fine. As if I'd even consider telling that pack of gossip hounds anything. You know that Reuben's the matchmaker from hell. Drop a word of this his way and he'll have everything down to the poor doc's jockstrap size on a spreadsheet by sundown tomorrow. John Lively, that All Black prop Reuben set up on a blind date last month... well, let's just say it didn't go as planned and he's no longer talking to Reuben. So now I have to get the man over for dinner to try and mend some damn fences. And you know how much those guys eat! I'll blow a month's budget on the meat alone."

"Um, hello, still here." Edward edged around Mark and stalked into the room, looking decidedly pissed off.

Tink followed her master and then peeled off to take a position on the mat in front of the cold fire, where she went straight to sleep.

Edward sent Cam a pointed look. "For what it's worth, before you go way off track here, there's nothing to tell. Mark and I are a million miles apart on most things. We'd likely be an epic disaster together."

Well, shit. Mark tried to keep the sting of Edward's words from his eyes. "Yeah, what he said," he threw over his shoulder as he headed for the bathroom.

It sounded a lot less convincing than he'd hoped.

Ed watched Mark leave, wishing he could pull back the words, but it was too late. He'd been caught on the back foot by that kiss and by Mark's comment at the front door. And then again when Mark didn't deny the two of them to Cam.

It made Ed feel tight in his own skin, too exposed. He didn't know how things were going to progress between them, if at all, and it was way too early to have anyone else knowing. Not that it was all Mark's fault. *Fuck.* Ed really hadn't meant to touch the man. His hand had simply gravitated there of its own accord.

But it had been a mistake, like that damn kiss in the kitchen. It sent a message, leaked too much about how deep Ed's attraction ran. They liked each other and had said as much, sure. But Mark had no idea how strong that allure was for Ed, and Ed had no intention of telling him.

Still, he'd looked almost disappointed, and Ed struggled with that. Mark was nothing if not a loveable rogue, a charming tease, and all this was likely just part of his determination to get Ed into his bed. Not that Ed wasn't becoming increasingly consumed by that idea himself. But anything more than just a tumble between the sheets? He doubted Mark would go that route when it came down to it, and that had hurt written all over it for Ed.

Cam interrupted his thoughts. "There's food on the counter, soup and bread, crackers and cheese, and something for breakfast, plus dog food, as requested." He smiled. "Yeah, Mark mentioned that you came with... baggage... of the four-legged variety."

And Ed was struck, not for the first time, by Mark's thoughtfulness. He hadn't even gotten round to thinking of needing food for Tink. "Oh right, thanks."

"No problem. Better some kibble than Mark's left leg, right?"

Ed laughed. "Can I take a rain check on answering that?"

A wide grin split Cam's face. "Hah! I know, right? The man could drive anyone to drink. Speak of the devil..."

Mark returned and cast a suspicious glance between them. "What?"

"Nothing." Cam winked Ed's way. "Just extolling your considerable virtues."

Mark flipped him off. "Fuck off."

Cam waggled his eyebrows. "Right let's get you lot cleaned up. Pass me that emergency kit, will you, Mark. Who's first?"

Ed held up his hand. "Can we just... take a moment... before we start on all that. I just need to clear my head a bit... if that's okay?"

"Yeah. Me too," Mark chipped in.

Cam's gaze flicked between them and softened. "Of course."

Cam waved Ed to the couch, throwing a blanket over one end for Ed to park his filthy clothes on. Meanwhile, Mark spread another on the chair farthest away and avoided Ed's eyes. *Crap.*

Ed took a minute to scan the room—a mishmash of elegant casual taste and quirky memorabilia. Decorated in a palette of soft blues, greys, and creams, with bed-width linen couches strewn with lightly patterned pillows and throws and deep cushioned chairs, the room invited you to pull up a seat, sink in, and stay a while. In one corner, a huge quilted box spilled over with toys, videos, and kids' books. Behind it stood a chalkboard, a small music system, and a child-sized armchair. Cory's space. Ed knew only a little about Reuben's nephew —mostly from hospital gossip—that Cory sat on the spectrum somewhere and that the adoption had only recently been finalised. But if this set-up was any indication of how loved the kid was, he was one lucky boy.

The family and open-plan dining area led into the clean lines of a cream-and-stainless-steel kitchen clearly set up to cater for some serious cooking, and Ed wondered which one was the lucky cook. And lastly, on the walls, a plethora of photos, awards, and even a couple of signed and framed jerseys paid testament to one of the owners' profession and passion.

He drew his gaze back to find Cam watching him, a clear flush of pride on his face.

"He doesn't like to hang his stuff up at our other place, so I make him put it up here," he said softly. "I won't have him hide it away. He's so fucking talented. And no one comes here except close friends. He's safe here. We all are. It's our... hidey-hole."

Cam gathered himself, sat straighter in his seat, and turned to face Mark. "So, how about we use the time for you to fill me in? Josh gave me a brief rundown on the phone, which means I know practically nothing," he began. "Something about you two being attacked is about all. I don't suppose you'd like to add a few details, considering I nearly got T-boned by that car at the pools?"

Mark rubbed at his eyes, and a flash of guilt ran through Ed. Mark looked nothing short of exhausted.

"I'll try," Mark answered. "But to be honest, I'm still trying to work it out myself." He went on to explain what they did know and some of what they presumed.

Cam whistled long and low.

Mark added, "I asked Josh and Liam to take care of things at the house and get the crime scene guys there, but I wanted to get Edward safe and have some time to think before heading in and writing it up. Something about the whole thing just felt... off."

Cam's sharp eyes trained on Ed. "And you agree?"

He blew out a long sigh. "I do. I just don't know exactly how. There's a lot of loose ends. Nothing makes sense."

Cam said nothing for a minute, then reached for his emergency kit. "Okay, enough. I need to see what's going on with you two. No more arguments. Ed, scoot over."

It took a second for Ed to realise he'd been spoken to. *Goddammit.* He was so used to being called Edward when Mark was around.

"Ed." Cam waved his hand in Ed's face.

He moved closer and Cam took the towel from his head.

"Ow."

Cam peered closely. "Mmm. Nasty cut you've got there. Let's get it cleaned up." He pulled some dressing equipment from his bag and organised everything on the coffee table.

The man came well prepared. Ed was impressed.

Cam continued, "Well, whatever is going on, Michael warned me that if Mark was involved, you'd both likely need a bit of patching up, and I can see he was right."

Ed had run into Michael Oliver a few times in medical meetings, and they'd shared a coffee or two in the cafeteria. Michael had a stellar rep as a trauma surgeon but was better known for his part in a kidnapping incident when the daughter of his boyfriend—now husband—had been abducted. Ed didn't know the details, but it must have been terrifying. Michael's husband also happened to be Mark's best friend, Josh. Welcome to New Zealand, where six degrees of separation plummeted to around three or four—if you were lucky.

"I think I should take offence at that comment. I have an excellent track record for safety."

Cam simply stared at him.

Mark fidgeted under the scrutiny. "Okay, well, maybe not excellent. But good, right? Or at least fair?" He scowled. "Aw, fuck off. I don't need the opinion of a man who has more silk lingerie in his top drawer than they stock in the Playboy Mansion."

Cam snorted and returned to cleaning Edward's forehead. "Michael thought I could cover whatever you needed, what with Ed being a doctor and all." Cam rolled his eyes as if that meant close to zip in reality.

Ed, who was still stuck back on the silk-lingerie comment and whether it was a joke, thought Cam was probably bang on in that assessment because, hey, pathologist. A nurse was far more up on this shit than he was.

"I'd better let Josh know about the second scene, at the pool."

Mark pulled out his phone, got carefully to his feet, and moved into the kitchen to make the call.

When he was gone, Cam drew back and studied Ed with gentler eyes. "So, how are *you* doing? Been a hell of a night by the sound of it."

To Ed's horror, his throat closed and his eyes brimmed. *Fuck.* He bit his lip and tried to force some air into his lungs as a flicker of panic took hold in his chest. His hands shook. And his gaze slid off Cam's as he tried to breathe.

A hand landed over his, and his gaze jerked back to find nothing but soft understanding.

"It's okay to feel it." Cam squeezed his hand. "Your adrenaline's crashed, and you've taken a blow to the head. But even without any of that, someone assaulted you. It sucks, big time, and it's okay to feel it, Ed. It's important to feel it. Understand?"

Ed's eyes flicked to where Mark stood in the kitchen, his back to them, still talking on his phone.

Cam's gaze followed. "I won't say anything. But just for the record, he'd understand. He's got his own crash coming. He was attacked too, but more importantly, someone he clearly cares about was attacked on his watch. And that... does things to a person."

Edward snorted. "We aren't... things aren't..."

Cam smiled gently. "He's good people, Ed."

Goddammit. Edward glanced back into the kitchen. "Yeah, he is. I'm just not sure *we* would be good."

Cam studied him. "Maybe, maybe not. Kind of hard to know when you're busy convincing yourself you aren't. But that's just me."

Edward nodded, too muddled in his own head to reply with anything more rational.

Cam let go of his hand and grabbed a damp swab, his expression all business. "This is gonna hurt."

Edward nodded.

Cam set about cleaning the cut and Edward hissed as the first cold sting settled in the wound. It was about the same time he realised he'd just begun thinking of himself as Edward not Ed... again. *Son of a bitch.*

He rattled the notion around in his head as Cam worked, wondering what it meant. Nothing he wanted to think about too closely was the answer. Ed? Edward? Did it really fucking matter? He sat on the harping voice that answered yes, wincing as Cam drew the swab firmly through the middle of the throbbing wound. *Whatever.* Edward was just as much his name, so what if he suddenly liked it? It didn't have to be a *thing*, right?

Cam shrugged an apology but continued to dab away, so Edward took the opportunity to study him close up. He had stunning eyes, wickedly sharp and immaculately lined in emerald green. Dressed in a pair of tight-fitted black jeans and a T-shirt that read 'Fabulous since Forever,' he moved through a room like silk but with an indisputable authority Edward wouldn't want to mess with.

He'd seen Cam before, of course. He might not have much to do with Auckland Med's ER, but everyone knew the name Cameron Wano, and not just because he was the very public boyfriend of an All Black. He took no crap from anyone, was a machine in the ER, a talented charge nurse, and a fierce advocate for his staff and patients —not to mention unapologetically fabulous in every sense of the word. Over a year from their very public outing, paparazzi still hung around the ER hoping to catch a photo. Edward would never have survived the horrific intrusion on his privacy, but Cam was clearly made of sterner stuff.

"So how'd you get the clanger?" Cam asked as he cut down a dressing to pack the laceration.

Edward snorted. "I got hit behind the right ear and then bounced off the pantry door, knocking me out. I've got a bitch of a headache, some ringing in my ears, and a need to sleep until the next century, but that's about it."

"Let me be the judge of that." Cam taped the dressing in place and fingered behind Edward's ear. "Ah, yeah. There it is. Nice little golf ball." He pushed Edward's head to the side and took a look.

"Skin's intact. Looks okay from the outside, but you know the drill. Sound it off, Ed. Let's see how much that brain of yours got a reboot."

"I want Tink's mouth looked at first."

Cam bit back a smile and got to his knees. "Okay. Here. Clean the rest of your face while I'm at it." He handed Edward a clean, damp facecloth and then waved Tink over. "Come on, sweetheart. Open your mouth for the nice nurse." Without batting an eyelid, the dog sauntered over, sat, and put her head in Cam's hands.

Edward paused in his cleaning and gaped. "That's some freaking bedside manner you have there."

"Not the first time I've heard that." Cam winked his way and Edward swallowed hard, not doubting for a minute, because *holy smokes*, Cameron Wano oozed enough sizzling sensuality and toppy airs to blow the lid off a pressure cooker.

Tink tolerated the affront to her person with little more than a mortified glance Edward's way as if to say, "And you're allowing this?" But Cam was done in a minute, and when he bent to rub heads with the dog, Edward swore Tink's mouth turned up in a smile—an attention slut of the highest order. The move also highlighted a flash of lace and silk beneath the hem of Cam's T-shirt. *So, not a joke.* It brought a smile to his face.

"The canine tooth's gone, but that's it, as far as I can tell." Cam smooched his cheek against Tink's. "It looks like it was knocked out whole, not broken, so she shouldn't need anything more. But I'd keep an eye on it regardless, just in case." He returned to the couch. "And now, back to you."

Edward grumbled and handed the blood-soiled facecloth back to Cam. "I thought I was the damn doctor."

That earned him a sly grin. "It's almost sweet how naïve you are. But at least you smell better. Dried blood is the pits, but then I guess you'd know as much about that as me." He tipped Edward's head up with a finger under his chin and flicked a penlight in and out of his eyes. "But in my ER, I rule. And my ER extends to this particular house, in case you were wondering. But if pretty boy over there dies, he's all yours—dead bodies are your skill set, not mine—"

Mark snorted. "Gee, thanks, Florence."

"—but until then," Cam continued, "you *both* answer to me. And the fact that you're a doctor only makes that *more* imperative." He flashed Edward a wicked grin. "Keeps you lot from getting ideas above your station. Having said that, I've seen you around the hospital, Doc, *and* I've heard about you, so don't worry, you're not on my shitlist... yet."

"How—"

"Sandy is a friend."

Edward groaned, and Cam beamed. Of course they bloody knew each other.

"I'll bear that in mind," he muttered. "For future reference."

The nurse eyed Edward pointedly. "Give that lovely man any grief and you'll be on that list of mine faster than a drag queen at a wig sale. Sandy's a good man."

Edward nodded soberly. "He is. The best."

Cam studied him as if checking for any sarcasm and then nodded. "Good. I knew I'd like you. Right, then." He threw the penlight back in his bag. "That eye's a little sluggish, so I'm gonna need those level-of-consciousness cues."

Before Edward could protest, Mark said, "Just do as he says, Edward. It'll go a lot easier. And don't forget to get your feet checked. We ran a fair way."

"I don't need—"

"Just do it."

Edward sighed and rattled off his name, age, time, date, country, prime minister, and so on till Cam held up a hand. "Good enough. Now show me your feet."

Edward grumbled but did as he was told.

Cam nodded. "They'll pass. Now stand and do a circuit of the room."

"I'm not—"

"Just do it." Mark.

They locked eyes for a second, and Edward managed a passable glare under his dressing. "I'll remember this, Detective." He stood and proceeded to wobble his way around the perimeter of the lounge. *Dammit.* Sure enough, when he sat back down, two pairs of eyes drilled into his skull.

"Okay, so I'm a little bit unsteady," he said sheepishly.

Cam cocked a brow. "Yeah, like I'm a little bit fabulous."

Mark snorted.

"You need rest, sleep, quiet, light food, and more rest. Then rinse and repeat, got it?" Cam locked eyes with him. "And nothing more than a couple of Panadol—you know the drill. You should have a damn X-ray, but I won't waste my breath. Tomorrow, understand? And no excuses. Michael's on duty."

Edward rolled his eyes and nodded. "Yes, Mum."

Cam pinched his cheek. "Good boy. You're growing on me."

"Yes, well, I'm reserving judgement on you," Edward shot back, and Cam's face lit up with mirth.

"Oh, yeah, we're gonna get along famously," he said with a chuckle.

And funnily enough, Edward believed it. "Well, I don't live in a dungeon, you know. Come down and visit us sometime."

Cam cocked a brow his way. "You know, I might just do that. Brighten the place up a bit." He spun to Mark. "Your turn."

"Fuck."

Cam snorted. "No, thanks. Now get over here and lie down. I can see you holding those ribs a mile off."

Edward moved aside to let Mark have the couch so Cam could poke about his ribs for a bit.

"There's some graunching movement there," Cam commented as Mark winced under the manipulation. "But nothing major. You might've escaped with just bruising or a nondisplaced crack, but only an X-ray will tell. I'll strap them anyway."

He did and then tended to the small lacerations on Mark's face—

mostly the result of the spewing glass when the patio door exploded, Mark explained. After that, Cam prodded at the bruising on Mark's shoulder from the initial blow that felled him, but didn't seem to think any bones had been broken there either, and the tingling in his arm from the jolt to the nerves in his elbow had vanished completely. Cam still added it to the list of things that needed follow up. But the bruising around Mark's abdomen got a much more thorough examination and accompanying murmurs of disapproval. That injury Cam wanted checked out at a hospital. But Mark wasn't having a bar of it, and that was that.

Edward wanted to slap him. Mark was a pig-headed fool. A ridiculously attractive pig-headed fool—but yeah, best not to go there. He at least agreed to get them done the next day, so Edward would count that as a win.

Headlights grazed the front of the house as Cam was finishing, and Mark's gaze shot to the window. Cam put a hand on his shoulder. "Relax. It's Ruby. He texted to say he was on his way. He had to bring Cory with him, so he won't come in."

But a few seconds later the door swung open, and Reuben was halfway inside before Cam even made it past the couch. One look at Reuben Taylor in the flesh and Edward nearly swallowed his tongue. Reuben was stunning. Unruly hair framed surfer good looks, giving Reuben a boyish, cheeky appeal. But all that youthful energy sat atop a thick and tightly muscled athlete's body that had absolutely nothing boyish about it.

Reuben's gaze swept the room until it landed on Cam, and the reaction was instant. He stalked over, cupped Cam's arse in those famously skilled hands, and hoisted him into his arms. Cam wrapped his legs around his boyfriend's waist and took Reuben's mouth in a blistering kiss that almost singed the hair on Edward's arms from the reflected heat alone. When Cam finally demanded his boyfriend put him down, Reuben obliged with a playful slap to that pert arse, and Edward decided the two of them together were the hottest damn thing he'd seen in ages.

Edward chanced a sideways glance at Mark and caught him watching the couple with a curious expression—even wistful? *Huh.* Maybe he *should* give Mark the benefit of the doubt.

Cam peeked around his boyfriend's shoulder. "Where's Cory?"

"Asleep in the car." Reuben's gaze ran over Edward and Mark, quietly assessing. "You two okay? Josh filled me in, not that there was much to tell. We can stay if you need us."

Mark shook his head. "We're fine. Cam will vouch for that. And no one knows we're here. I don't mean to keep you in the dark, but I'm honestly not sure yet what the fuck's going on. But you saved our arses tonight, so thanks. Take your family home, Rube. Your fiancé will be crawling up our arses tomorrow as it is."

Reuben grinned widely. "Fiancé. Huh. Not sure I've gotten used to the word." He pressed a kiss to Cam's lips. "And you should be so lucky as to have him crawling anywhere near your arse, just saying."

Mark groaned and threw his head back. "Ugh. Don't even with the sex talk, man. Please. Dear God, he's insufferable enough as it is."

Cam smacked a kiss on Reuben's cheek. "You just got yourself lucky tonight, mister."

Reuben cradled his face. "I'm always lucky with you."

"Oh, for fuck's sake. Go. I can't stand it any longer." Mark walked over and shooed them both towards the door. Edward got to his feet and joined him.

Cam grinned. "Fine. I'll see you two tomorrow for those X-rays, and stay safe."

Reuben added, "Call if you need us. And don't forget to turn the water heater on, or you'll be having cold showers. Josh said to tell you he'd meet you at the station at eight and that the glass door will be boarded and the house locked before they leave tonight."

Relief swept through Edward. *Thank God.* He still didn't know what the hell to tell his friends. The truth, he supposed. "I need to thank them."

"You'll get the opportunity," Mark answered.

They were nearly at the door when Reuben caught sight of Tink on the mat and pulled up short. "What in the ever-loving name of God is that?"

Edward had to laugh. "A Neapolitan mastiff. Reuben, meet Tinkerbell."

Reuben stared at Edward as if he'd lost his damn mind. "You're shitting me. Tinkerbell?"

Mark laughed. "That's what I said."

Edward shrugged. "She's a sweetheart. You can pat her. She's quite friendly."

Reuben looked less than convinced but walked over and gave Tink's head a scratch anyhow. When he pulled his hand away, a ribbon of drool stretched from his fingertips to the dog's jowl, and Edward stifled a snigger at the horror evident in his expression. Adding insult to injury, Reuben shook his hand and sent the whole slobbery mess hurtling through the air. Mark and Edward parted like the Red Sea as it sailed past to land on the breakfast bar, and the room fell deathly silent.

Reuben turned slowly to Cam, who had suddenly found the latch on his bag mighty interesting. "And did Tinkerbell travel in *my* car, *sweetheart?*"

Cam snagged his man's hand and brought it to his lips. "She might have, *petal*. She's very well behaved. Now, we need to leave before Cory wakes up. See you guys later." He tugged at Reuben's hand, and the two of them left, Reuben still demanding why Cam hadn't given them Cam's beat-up car instead, and Cam explaining that Ed and Mark needed one that actually ran and that Reuben needed to get his head out of his arse and deal. It was just a car, after all.

Mark closed the door on their bickering, set the external alarm, and then cracked up. Edward joined in until Mark was holding his ribs like they were about to snap and Edward was cradling his head against the blades of pain slicing through it. It hurt like hell, but damn if it didn't feel good to just let go for a few seconds.

He stumbled his way back to the couch and collapsed, still chuckling.

Mark followed. "You're still not good on your feet."

Edward flicked a hand. "I'm fine. Just need some sleep. So this is their house, then?"

Mark nodded. "It's their 'get-away-from-the-media-and-paparazzi-safe-house' cabin."

"*Pfft*. Some cabin."

Mark's gaze swept the room. "Tell me about it. But there's no one for a kilometre or so in any direction, no direct line of sight for photographers, no hint it even exists from the road, and a gorgeous view to the Tasman Sea through that wall of glass when the sun comes up. It's also down in the name of some relative or other of Cam's, so there's no official record of them even owning it. Peace and quiet on a big budget."

Edward considered all of that. "Not sure I could do it, even so. Put up with all that shit? Not for me. But they seem really good together."

Mark rolled his eyes and shuddered. "Sickeningly so. They're planning a wedding next year, if Cam can ever give up enough control to let someone help him with the details. You didn't hear it from me, but I have a pretty good idea who runs that particular bedroom."

Edward thought of the peek of lace and the sassy mouth. "I don't doubt it for a minute." He hooked one leg under him and turned to face Mark, seated at the other end of the couch. "Okay, it's just us. Tell me what you're thinking."

A crease formed between Mark's brows. "Will you be angry if I don't?"

"Depends on the reason."

Mark grabbed a cushion, punched it into submission, and cradled it against his ribs before answering. "It's just that we won't really know anything until I can talk with Liam tomorrow. Until then it's all guesswork. I value your clear and methodical head... and I don't want to prejudice your opinion with my own."

Well, damn, if that wasn't nice to hear. "Okay, I can live with that." Edward pressed his fingers lightly to the dressing on his head, and Mark followed the move.

"Still sore?"

"Not the wound so much. The headache's a bastard, though." He dropped his hand and caught Mark's eye. "Okay, no second-guessing, but just tell me one thing. Why are we here? Why didn't you want to go to the station?"

Mark's gaze slid away, and he looked uncomfortable. "If it's to do with this case, then someone knew we were meeting tonight, and where."

"Not Spencer. He knew I found the report, but nothing about our meeting. Maybe it was only me they wanted."

"Then why not wait to get you alone?"

"Because when you arrived they decided to see what you had? It was an opportunity."

Mark nodded. "See, there's that cool head. And yes, maybe. But we can't know that for sure. So I have to consider the possibility it was both of us they wanted."

Edward's heart ticked up. "But that would mean—"

"Yes. So who knew about our little evening meeting on your end?"

Edward didn't have to think. "No one."

"So that leaves whoever I told, which was my boss and... Liam. Though Liam didn't know the name or specifics of the other case, he did know about it in general terms, and he knew about the tox match."

"Shit. You can't think..."

"I don't. But until I know if those two shared it with anyone else... well, I just think we should be careful."

Edward's head spun. None of it made sense. "But even if they were targeting us or what we knew, they failed in their bid to shut things down the minute we got away."

"We don't really know what exactly they were after. We're only guessing. And until we know for sure, I'm not risking you, Edward, and that's all there is to it."

They locked eyes, and Edward saw the earnestness, and just for a second basked in what it would be like to have this man watching his back as more than a friend. He liked it. More than liked it.

"Which reminds me," Mark said. "Do you still have that drive?"

Edward fished it from his pocket. "Here. Keep it."

Mark walked into the kitchen and took a look around. Then he dragged a stepladder from the pantry with his good arm and carefully climbed to a bookshelf above the fridge. A bit of shuffling and he managed to get the drive behind a stack of cookbooks. "That'll have to do till the morning." He returned to the couch and sank back down in his seat, clutching his chest and still keeping his distance.

Edward blew out a sigh. "For God's sake, scoot down on the couch and pull up your shirt."

Mark blinked slowly. "Now, don't tease me, Edward."

Edward snorted. "Behave. You're holding that chest like it's a goddamn newborn. This place has to have some ice or cool pads in its freezer, right? Professional rugby player and all that. Plus we need to get a little light food on board, maybe some of that soup and crackers Cam brought."

"Good idea." Mark shuffled down and on to his back as directed, while Edward weaved his way in search of ice and something to eat.

CHAPTER ELEVEN

AN HOUR LATER AND THEY'D BARELY MOVED, EXHAUSTION AND
the adrenaline crash finally taking their toll. Mark was still laid out on
the couch, partially on his side, with Tink curled in a large ball at the
far end pretending to be invisible—epic fail. Edward sat on the floor
alongside, holding a large wrapped cooling pad in place over Mark's
lower ribcage while trying to keep his eyes averted. Also an epic fail.
Not to mention he could've easily left Mark to hold it... but he
didn't... and Mark didn't move to change things either. So there was
that.

They'd nibbled on some crackers and cheese and a little soup as
they sat and talked. About anything, about everything, about nothing,
just... talked. Nothing too personal at first—some unspoken rule it
appeared they'd both signed up for, but one Edward was about to
break after throwing every shred of common sense he possessed out
the window. But after the day he'd had, it barely rated.

Edward shuffled around slightly so he could face Mark better
without removing his hand from the cool pack. Mark's gaze dipped
and his lips quirked up, but that was as far as either of them went in
acknowledging the fact that this close contact between them had

moved beyond practical or casual, oh, about thirty fucking minutes ago... which was a relief to Edward, who might otherwise have felt obliged to put an end to it.

Edward's behaviour was confusing, even to him. God knew what Mark had to be thinking, especially after all the energy Edward had expended brushing his advances aside. Edward would've put it down to Stockholm syndrome if he weren't so patently aware he'd been attracted to the other man since he'd first laid eyes on him. So, yeah, busted—internally and externally. God help him.

"Can I ask you a question?" he said.

Mark's eyes flicked to his. "Why do I feel I'm not going to like this?"

"You don't have to answer."

"I'm well aware of that, thank you. Go on."

"Just don't hit me, okay?"

Mark waited in amused silence.

"Okay, so I was wondering why you avoid relationships... or anything, it seems, beyond a hookup. I mean, you mentioned your relationship with your parents... so I guess that had something to do with it, right? I know I'm prying, but I'm just... interested. When you let someone see beyond that cool act you wear like a suit of armour—" He winced. "Sorry. But well, when you do, you're a... nice guy. Surprisingly."

Mark snorted. "Surprisingly, huh? High praise indeed."

Edward flushed. "You know what I mean."

"No, I don't, actually."

God, why did Mark have to make everything so difficult? "Just that you walk around giving everyone the impression that you're this joking-around, notch-on-your-bedpost player type, but I don't buy it, not completely. You say you don't want a relationship—"

"Didn't want," he corrected.

Edward fought an eye-roll. *"Didn't* want, but I saw the way you looked at Cam and Reuben, like you... envied what they had."

Mark bristled. "I don't *envy* them. I'm glad for them. There's a difference. They fit together and make each other happy. They're my friends. Why wouldn't I want that for my friends?"

"And Josh and Michael? You can't tell me that with two happy couples crowding you, that it never crossed your mind about getting the same for yourself—something more than a nameless guy to just get off with?" *Shit. Open mouth, insert mammoth-sized foot.*

Mark's expression hardened. "Well, in that case I could ask *you* why you're so... unapproachable... as if it's beneath you to have casual sex, and why you feel it's fine to judge me for being okay with it?" He shifted away, and Edward's hand fell from the cool pack. Not an accident.

Edward dropped his head to his chest and took a breath. *Way to go, dipshit.* An injection of subtlety—hell, plain old good manners—wouldn't have gone amiss. Story of his life.

He lifted his gaze back to lock with Mark's manifestly pissy one. "I'm sorry. And I'm not judging you—"

Mark arched an eyebrow, and Edward put up his hands. "Well, maybe. Okay, yes, I admit I've been a dick about things on occasion. I can be a little... blunt, or so I've been told." The corner of Mark's mouth twitched just a smidgen, and Edward took that as a promising sign. "But I had my reasons."

Mark shifted back. "So, name them."

"Now who's being blunt?"

Silence.

Oh, for fuck's sake. "Okay. Well, I, um... Let's just say I don't handle casual sex well."

"Why? You got hang-ups?" Mark asked flatly, looking for a tender spot.

He found it. *Count to ten.* "No. I don't have *hang-ups*... though there'd be some who'd argue that, I'm sure." He sent a self-depre-cating smile Mark's way. "But I guess I deserved that."

Mark sighed. "No, you didn't. I was being a prick."

"Maybe, but maybe it's not as far from the truth as you think."

He could tell he'd caught Mark's interest when Mark shoved a pillow under his arm and leaned in. "Do tell."

Edward rolled his eyes. "I'm not saying I haven't had hookups, because I have. More than you probably think. I just almost always feel worse after them than before, to the point I stopped. Good sex for me is linked far more to how much I like the person. The more I like and know them, the better the sex. So a hookup leaves me flat, and sometimes... well, I could, um... lose interest... during." His gaze slid sideways as the heat rose in his face.

"Oh... *ohhh*." Mark's gaze softened.

Edward wished he'd never said anything. Like maybe for once the universe would be on his side and the floor would just open and swallow him up. "Yeah. It can get... awkward."

Mark frowned. "Someone give you a hard time about it? Pardon the pun."

Does "What the fuck's wrong with you?" count? Edward's face must have given him away, because Mark reached over and ran a finger gently down his cheek.

"Then they were arseholes," he said. "Not worth a second of your time." He leaned back. "So, are you, like, demi... or something?"

"No. God, I hate labels. Well, maybe... Hell if I know, actually. It's not that black and white. I love sex, when it's good. It's not that I don't want it, per se. I can get turned on as easily as the next guy, especially if I know someone well and like them. But then other times, especially if it's casual, it's like the sleep of the undead trying to get any reaction... down there. I'm just... me, I guess. And that's where you come in."

"Me?"

"Yes, because for some reason, you... *affect* me."

Mark leaned even closer, close enough that Edward could smell the remnants of his cologne, still there after the night they'd had. How did he do that?

"Are you saying I make you hot, Edward?"

Edward looked to see if he was being mocked, but there was

nothing bar curious affection in the other man's eyes. And heat. Oh, yeah, lots and lots of heat.

"You know you do," he answered flatly, then narrowed his gaze. "And stop that." He tapped between Mark's eyes, and Mark withdrew a little. "But what's more important is, you make me want to break my own rules."

"I do?" A wicked smirk rolled into place under that sizzling gaze.

Edward found it hard not to lean over and kiss it right off. *So, yeah, see above regarding the whole breaking-rules thing.* "Don't get cocky," he warned. "I should be running from you as fast as I can, and yet here I was, holding that bloody cold pad in place over your damn ribs and praying my hand would sink right through so it could roam all over your skin."

Mark froze, and a flood of heat washed through his body. He cleared his throat and rested a hand over Edward's. "Okaaay. I um, hadn't expected that, but—and I might be missing something here—that's a problem because...?"

Edward stared at where their hands touched. "Because I don't do this. I *never* do this. I don't moon after some guy *or* woman I barely know"

"But you *could* know me"

"—and I need a lot of... space, something a lot of people I've dated don't understand. I like spending time on my own. I need it. I don't like people all up in my business all the time. Which makes for an awkward set of criteria, right? I don't want hookups, but I don't want my life cramped with someone else's agenda either.

"I think that's part of why it takes me so long to warm up to someone. And it's what makes this"—he waved a hand, implying the closeness between them—"so damn unnerving. No, scrap that. It makes it fucking terrifying. Hell, the last relationship I had, I knew the woman a year before it even occurred to me to take things further. And then I get here, and you walk into my autopsy suite and five minutes later I'm wanting to..."

"What Edward? What are you wanting to do?" Mark leaned closer again.

Edward turned and eyeballed him. "I'm wanting to drag you into my office, spread you over my damn desk, and make you come so hard you walked funny for a week." *Holy shit, where did that come from?* But Jesus, he wished he had a camera to capture the look on Mark's face as his jaw damn near hit the floor.

Mark cleared his throat as a rush of red claimed his cheeks, and Edward had to smile.

"That's, um... that's... good to know," Mark managed to choke out. "I think. Though I feel we really need to discuss the details of exactly how that might have happened... just so we're on the right page here... compatibility-wise." He stared at Edward as if he wasn't sure whether to devour him or run screaming. No: devour, definitely devour.

"Don't press your luck."

"Oh, Edward, I intend to do exactly that and a whole lot more down the track." Mark eyed him with amusement. "But in the meantime, yeah, probably not *strictly* demi, I'd say."

Edward arched a brow. "Ya think? Imagine how I felt."

"Oh, I do, regularly." He shot Edward a wink and put his hand back on the cool pad.

"You're just enjoying the fact that you know what I'm wishing would happen with that hand," Edward accused.

"That you wish you could touch me? Hell, yeah, I like knowing that. Fucking payback."

"You're impossible."

"No, I'm really not, Edward. For you, I'd be dead easy."

Edward's jaw tightened. "And therein lies the problem."

A thoughtful look passed through Mark's eyes. "Okay, I get that. And I'm sorry that I made things... hard for you." He bit back a smile.

Edward just shook his head. The man was incorrigible. But God, he liked the way Mark made him feel: sexy, desirable, wanted. "So, does this mean I get an answer to *my* question?"

"You'll have to repeat it," Mark said cheekily. "I got sidetracked into the whole 'losing interest during sex' bit. Which, by the way, I cannot imagine being a problem between us, but if it were, we'd just ride with it, understand?" He held Edward's eye till he nodded. "Good. And, just so you know... even dyed-in-the-wool man-whores like me can have the odd... performance issue."

Yeah, right. "Fuck off."

"Or not, as the case may be," he said in a serious tone.

Edward fired him a dubious look. "You're kidding me."

Mark scoped the room with a furtive gaze and then leaned in. "Strictly between us, of course, but it might surprise you to learn that not every hookup follows through quite as expected. Some over-promise and under-deliver, and others are just... disappointing.

"And at thirty-eight years old, let's just say I wouldn't wager everything I had on a guaranteed meet-and-greet any more. Not if the stars weren't aligned right. Just saying. So yeah, it's not a regular thing, but I have experienced the odd... hiccup. So I get it at some level. But breathe one word of this and I'll deny everything and haunt you for the rest of your miserable life, understand?"

Edward pulled a serious face. "Scout's honour. Now it's your turn, I believe. Why the relationship moratorium?"

Mark's eyes glazed over. "Jesus Christ, who uses those words? Since meeting you, I've discovered a hitherto unknown dictionary fetish. One good multisyllabic word and I'm halfway to naked and sucking your dick." He waggled his eyebrows. "Just citing an example, of course."

"Riiiight." He barked out a laugh. *Goddamn.* Being with Mark was like playing bloody ping-pong. In twenty-four hours Edward had travelled the full gamut of human emotion, including terror, shock, arousal, anger, and hilarity. His quiet life had been turned on its head, and he still wasn't running... yet.

He reached for his glass of water and handed Mark his. "You need to keep hydrated." Mark cocked a brow, letting Edward know he saw right through the play for time, but obliged anyway, and then Edward returned both glasses to the coffee table.

Mark waited.

"So," Edward began. "Back to you and your non-relationship status. Seeing as you've hardly been shy about wanting to get in my pants"—he pinned Mark with a pointed glare—"I figure I have somewhat of a vested interest in your reasons."

Mark gave a sharp nod. "Fair enough. Well, the short answer is, I've never met anyone who made me want to rethink it."

"Oh. Perfect answer... I suppose." But only if he meant he had now. Did he?

Mark cottoned on quick. "You gonna hear me out, Edward?"

Did he have a choice? "Go ahead." He gave Mark his full attention.

Mark covered Edward's hand with his own and threaded their fingers together. "Well, first of all, and don't fall off your chair, I *have* had an actual relationship."

Edward nearly fell off his cushion.

"I lived with a guy for almost a year. Jeff. I really liked him, and we got on well together. It was an open relationship, until he wanted to change it. I didn't, so we went our separate ways."

Edward grappled for what to say. There was so much to unpack in those few words. He settled on, "Did you, um, love him?"

Mark said nothing for a minute. Then, "No. Although if you'd asked at the time, I would have thought I was pretty damn close. But when I look at Josh and Michael, or Cam and Reuben, I know I didn't feel anything like what I see they have—that drunk-on-the-other-person thing. And it wasn't about the open relationship, either, because I can see your mind working. I know couples who are stupidly in love and seem to make an open relationship work. It can be done if it's what both parties want."

Edward swallowed. *May as well get things out in the open.* "I agree," he said. "Although, fair warning, that would never be me. Not a judgement, just an acknowledgement of personality. Shocker, I'm sure."

Mark eyed him warily. "Hardly. Pretty sure I'd have guessed that about you."

"And yet you're not running?"

Mark leaned over and pressed a gentle kiss to Edward's forehead. "No, I'm not running."

Edward shivered, thinking about the implications of that statement. *Okay, then. Main engines on.* "You said earlier that you hadn't met someone to make you change your mind about trying another relationship, and that was the short answer. I guess I'm interested in the long answer."

Mark huffed. "Trust you to remember. I guess the long answer involves why I think I have that relationship allergy thing to start with."

"So you *have* thought about it?"

To his surprise, Mark glared at him. "Of course I bloody have. Jeff was always on at me about how wrapped up I kept myself. How I wouldn't let down my walls long enough to let anyone in, let alone have them make a home there. How, apart from sex, I treated him more like a flatmate than a partner."

Mark blew out a long sigh. "Believe me, I could write a six-volume treatise on all the ways I'm a relationship screw-up. Not to mention Josh lets me get away with bugger all when it comes to my propensity to avoid dating other men. And believe me, none of what he says is very flattering. And it's all true, to some degree. I just haven't seen any reason to change it."

His gaze slid off Edward to where Tink was having an ear-twitching dream that had to involve at least a rabbit or two, or a bag of kibble. A smile played on his lips as he watched the dog's paws race on some imaginary track. Whether he knew it or not, his grip on Edward's hand had tightened, and Edward drew small circles on the back with his thumb to let Mark know he wasn't going anywhere. It was obvious he'd been hurt by what his ex had said, far more than he'd been willing to admit. And Edward got it. He did. It sucked not being in control of why you behaved as you did sometimes.

"You said your parents were kind of uninvolved in your life. That they were focused on each other. Do you think—"

"That they screwed me up?" Mark released Edward's hand and threw the cool pad on the floor. "Yes, Edward, even I can have some insight. After all, it seems the likeliest scenario, right? Poor little unseen boy."

He stabbed Mark's thigh with a finger. "Don't be petulant. I didn't mean that, and you know it."

Those hazel eyes popped a little. "Not sure I've ever been called petulant."

"Stop distracting," Edward said, not backing down. "You asked me to be patient. Well, I'm asking you to help me understand." They locked eyes.

Mark blinked first. "Okay. Fire away."

"Good. Well, all I meant was, we learn a lot about love from our parents' relationship and how they make us feel loved. You said you never felt that kind of unconditional love, that you felt sidelined, a third wheel. And that the love they shared was almost cloying, selfish even. Hardly a shining endorsement of the state, right? But I wonder if you realise that's not what genuine love actually looks like."

Mark seemed to roll that idea around in his head for a minute before answering. "Maybe. I mean, of course I've thought about it. Even watching Josh and Michael—I catch snapshots of my parents, that intensely private thing they shared, finishing each other's sentences, all that shit, and it freaks me out. I know they're nothing like my parents, but it doesn't change my reaction. Every time someone gets close or has any expectation of me in that couple way, all I want to do is run a fucking mile. So I don't go there." He winced. "Sorry if that's not what you want to hear."

Edward held up his hands. "Hey, cards on the table, right?" Mark gave a quick nod, and Edward was about to ask another question, but something in Mark's edgy demeanour made him sense Mark wasn't done with what he wanted to say.

"So here's the thing," Mark finally said, eyes dancing on and off Edward like a yo-yo. "In the spirit of honesty, which is what we appear to be doing here, who the hell knows why"

Edward had to smile.

"—what you said before, about me having you want to break your rules..." He dragged a flustered hand across his mouth, and Edward's heart ticked up a beat. "I know how you feel... about the breaking-rules thing."

Edward froze, worried any sudden movement might send the other man skittering back into the shadows. He didn't need anyone to tell him how much of a limb Mark had just stepped out on. A troop of angels singing and riding fucking elephants couldn't have made it clearer.

"I can't say more than that, right now." Mark's gaze landed solidly back on Edward's and rested there, searching for... something.

Son of a bitch. Edward chose his words carefully. "I don't need more, Mark. We're still moseying along here, right?"

A nod.

"Getting to know each other?"

Another nod.

"Then how about we keep doing that?" He found Mark's hand again, squeezed and received a squeeze in return.

"With one slight amendment," Mark said with a sparkle in his eye. "I think we might have changed gears up to a solid walk. Definitely not moseying any more. But no pressure. No promises."

Edward broke into a laugh. "Fine. No pressure. No promises. Jesus Christ, we're a couple of fucked-up losers, yeah?"

Mark's expression became one of mock outrage. "Speak for yourself. I'm not the one with a penchant for comics, zero social life, and a monstrosity of a dog as my best friend. Just being seen with you lowers my pull factor exponentially."

"In your dreams, arsehole. Now pass me some of those damn

crackers. All this emotional vomiting has left me hungry." Edward took a handful from the proffered bowl and nestled back against the edge of the couch to eat as they talked... and talked. This time nothing was off the table: comics, rugby, doctoring, policing, favourite holiday spots, Tink, murders, all took a turn.

It shouldn't have felt as intimate as it did, but there was no denying it ticked the conversational components of an actual first date without even trying. And throughout, Mark kept hold of his hand, and Edward pretended not to notice because it felt so damn nice. He suspected Mark pretended not to notice that Edward pretended not to notice, and bingo, everyone was happy.

CHAPTER TWELVE

THE SOUND OF LIGHT SNORING IN HIS EAR STARTLED EDWARD'S eyes wide open. But they shut again almost immediately as he scrambled to make sense of a jumble of competing sensations, not least the suffocating heat radiating against his front and back—like being grilled in a sandwich press. On top of that, the stench of old blood, stale sweat, and a mix of other unsavoury aromas clung to his nose, and every bone in his exhausted body protested the very idea of lifting even a single eyelid again. It was all so much more than he was ready to deal with at the arse crack of dawn.

He slowly cranked his eyes open again, and, okay, this bit he got. An exceptionally unattractive set of wet canine nostrils sat level with his gaze, without doubt the source of at least part of the dubious odour. Grey, fleshy folds hung loose around a set of serious teeth, minus one canine, and a pink tongue the size of Manhattan lolled out to the side. Edward freed his hand from where it was pinned to his chest, while deciding he wasn't quite ready to face exactly what had pinned it there. The presence of a large, lightly haired arm across his. waist, however, really ought to have given him some clue.

"Move over, Tink," he hissed, pushing at the animal's head. "Goddammit, dog."

A low rumble shuddered up his back, and he froze as the owner of the arm shifted and pushed up against Edward with a groan... and something else. Definitely something else. *Shit*. And nope, still not looking. Meanwhile, glued to his front, Tinkerbell grumbled and finally rolled to her back, all four paws in the air... and went straight back to sleep.

Thank God. Delicious cool air licked at Edward's bare chest, and he could breathe again. Wallowing in the moment, he took a few seconds to do just that before the nagging question returned. Exactly why the fuck was he bare-chested?

Last Edward remembered, he was definitely wearing a shirt. He peeked down at his exposed and hairy leg—oh, and trousers. Yep, trousers got a mention last night as well. *What the hell?* He tucked his hand under his pillow and into a big wet patch from Tink's drool. He wiped it absently on the top sheet and thought about all the possible scenarios that might have got him into this predicament, and his options from this point on.

That the body pushed hard up against his back—and, it was worth repeating *hard*—was his friendly neighbourhood detective, was a no-brainer. Just how Mark had gotten there, and how Edward had managed to end up sandwiched between Mr Sex on a Stick and New Zealand's answer to the threatening global water crisis, remained hazy. And exactly why Edward was still lying there in said detective's arms debating how to extricate himself instead of actually doing it, while at the same time trying to ignore just how long it had been since he'd been held by another man and how damn good it felt, was a point Edward was even less willing to dwell on.

"Morning." The soft, raspy voice came over Edward's shoulder accompanied by an adorable squeaky yawn and a further graze of the man's morning wood against the back of Edward's hip. He closed his eyes, thought of Tink's morning breath, and wished his sudden plumped-up semi a quick demise. *For fuck's sake.*

"Good morning." Not bad. It came out relatively cool and calm, completely at odds with the raging impropriety in Edward's head. Not *that* head. Well, okay, maybe that one too. *Ugh.*

Mark sighed and rolled to his back, the weight of his arm lifting from Edward's waist until he was free of all contact. He should have felt good about that, right? Wrong. He just felt... cold. He rolled to mirror the other man, the two of them lying on their backs like sardines in a can or a pair of awkward virgins, take your pick.

Meanwhile Tink, sensing an opportunity, rolled towards Edward to fill the void, pushing her damp nose into his neck, her clumsy legs and huge paws dangling over his chest.

"She always sleep with you?" Mark croaked in his morning voice, blinking hard at the mastiff but looking oddly amused. "'Cause I have to say, that may be a problem."

Gravity had done its job, and Tink was now mostly lying on top of Edward. "Are you on drugs?" he fired back. "What about this scenario makes you think I would willingly endure this on a nightly basis? She stays in her own damn bed. Which raises the question about last night and... this." He waved a hand between them.

The blush that stole over Mark's cheeks was not the slightest bit adorable. Nope. Not one bit. And it had better not mean what Edward thought it might.

Instead of answering, Mark rolled off the bed and got to his feet, dragging half the duvet with him before realising and throwing it back over Edward, but not quickly enough to avoid a gander at Edward's boxers. His eyes popped wide.

Shit. Edward didn't need a mirror to know his face flushed bright crimson. He supposed he should be grateful he was wearing any underwear at all, considering what else was missing.

Mark's surprise turned into a wide grin. "Wolverine, huh? Now, who would have guessed the studious Dr Newton wears superhero boxers? Not me. It was kind of dark when I wrestled you out of your trousers last night, so I, um, missed the show."

Edward tucked the duvet in under his thighs. "Yeah, well, yours don't leave anything for the imagination, and somehow that's *not* a surprise."

Mark glanced down at the skimpiest pair of black briefs Edward had ever laid eyes on—and the perky morning wood bobbing inside them.

God in heaven.

"What, these old things? Pfft." Mark sauntered over to the chair, sat and wrestled his jeans on singlehandedly, and oh so slowly.

It was all Edward could do not to race over and help him. That is if he weren't already glued to the mouthwatering exhibition. His tongue found the roof of his mouth and took up residence. The man was killing him. But when Mark turned to grab his T-shirt, the full effect of the mottled bruising around his waist slid into view above the ridiculous scrap of black material, and Edward's thinking was instantly redirected. Could he be more of an arsehole? Unlikely.

"How are the ribs?"

Mark shrugged the question off. "Fine."

Edward raised a dubious brow, and Mark blew out a sigh. "Breathing's a little tight, and my kidneys feel like a tractor rolled over them, but I'm okay," he amended. "How about your head?"

Edward rolled his neck and winced. "Still got the headache, but I think it's getting better. As for the vertigo? Get back to me after I've gotten out of bed."

Mark nodded, then made a show of shrugging into his T-shirt and rolling it at glacial pace down his fit, firm body while Edward pursed his lips and bit back an offer of help. Coming within arm's distance was not an option right then. Mark was incorrigible.

"You can just stop all that," he muttered. "It isn't going to work." If his voice hadn't sounded so hoarse, it might even have been believable. He cleared his throat and eyed the bed, a safer option than the temptation of the man standing in front of him.

"So, I take it we slept like this, then?" It came out a little pissier than he'd intended.

"Ah, yeah."

Another blush. "Is there not another bed, or some equally satis-factory explanation?" For a moment Mark looked taken aback, but for the life of him Edward couldn't seem to dial back the sarcasm. One of them could've slept on the couch, goddammit.

Mark's expression was hard to read, other than some frustration, but then his gaze narrowed and raked over Edward with obvious appreciation, and oh, yeah, *this* Mark, Edward knew.

"Sure there are," he murmured in a voice like silk. "The main suite is upstairs, but I'm not in a rush to jump into their bed, if you take my drift. God knows what those bedside cabinets contain. And after what happened on the couch"—he flashed Edward a wicked smile—"I just thought we could... you know."

Edward choked on his tongue. "What happened? What the hell did you do?" He scanned the room furiously. "And where the fuck are my clothes?" Even as he said it, he knew it didn't feel right. This was Mark. They'd talked. He wouldn't—

"What did I do?" The grin slid from Mark's face, and he studied Edward with a mix of disappointment and frustration. "Holy shit, Edward. It was a joke. You don't really think... Relax. Your clothes are in the bathroom. You were unsteady on your feet taking a piss last night before bed. It just seemed... safer for me to stay close, in case you got up in the night. You didn't appear to mind at the time."

"The bathroom? I don't remember..." But then suddenly he did, as parts floated back into his head like a badly edited movie. Flashes of him teetering over the toilet and Mark on the phone to someone—some doctor—then asking Edward questions, shining a light in his eyes. *Crap.* "Sorry. I must have taken a harder bang to the head than I thought."

Mark ambled across to the end of the bed and took a seat, his jeans zipped but not buttoned, and *oh, dear God*, Edward didn't trust himself not to touch. He clambered away to sit at the top end of the bed, leaving a good metre between them, duvet tucked modestly around his hips, looking... ridiculous, no doubt. Mark fucked with his equilibrium without even trying, and Edward found it harder and harder to control his responses around the man.

Mark seemed to have no contextual filter when it came to letting Edward know he wanted him, really wanted him. It was in every look and every flirtatious comment. And Edward could feel himself reacting in kind, craving Mark in return. It was messy... and untidy... and completely addictive. He'd been so busy pulling Mark's issues apart, so focused on Mark needing to sort his shit out, that he'd ignored his own neurotic edge.

He'd built a comfortable life, one that offered him the space and peace he craved. He loved his job, loved his comics, loved his dog. And he hadn't been short on romantic interest. He'd had a couple of great girlfriends and a guy he'd really liked for a while. Shared interests were good. Building a life with someone you respected and liked was good. Being independent was... good.

Sexual attraction was an added bonus, but it never started with that, not for him. Friendship was far more important. He'd always believed he'd find someone long-term, one day, but if not, he'd convinced himself it didn't matter. Peace and stability were no small achievements.

And then Mark Knight danced into Edward's world with his flattery and innuendo, his whole-fucking-other-world-sexy bedroom ridiculousness, not to mention his blatant appreciation of Edward, and threatened everything he'd built.

It wasn't rocket science. Mark was dangerous to Edward's fragile heart, and his reaction had always been to shut down and pull away, to put plenty of space between them. And yet Edward had been the one to initiate the first kiss between them, not the other way around. But Mark's footprints were all over his boundaries, alarm cans jangling with every intrusion. It should have sent Edward running, but he was still there, equally appalled and intrigued by the strength of his own attraction to a man who had "broken heart" written in capital letters all over his goddamn face.

"Look, Edward." Mark regarded him as one might a small child who'd yet to learn his manners. "Nothing happened last night, so you can stop giving me the evil eye. I might be an arsehole, but I'm really not *that* big of one—"

It finally hit Edward what he'd done. "Of course you're not. I'm sorry. I didn't mean to suggest—"

Mark snorted. "Yeah, you kind of did, but I get it. And I kind of encouraged the idea, but only because it pissed me off that you thought I had any ulterior motive. What was it you called me the other day? An unrepentant flirt, right? Well, I don't deny it. Though how that equates to having enough dodgy morals to—"

"Look, I didn't mean—"

Mark held up a hand. "Forget about it. So here's the deal. Last night you fell asleep, like completely out. After the whole bathroom toppling-over incident, and seeing as how there's only one bedroom downstairs—and there was no way I was going up those stairs, with or without you—I compromised on a solution. Plus we both needed a good sleep. Neither of us were in any fit state to cope with a couch. I have to admit, Tinkerbell wasn't part of the plan, but I figured a stranger telling her fifty-kilogram arse to sleep on the floor wasn't gonna cut it.

"And so here we are. Yes, I took your trousers and shirt off, but other than admiring your eminently delicious body, I took a totally hands-off approach. I can't help that I may have slung an arm over you sometime during the night; I'm a cuddler, or so I've been told. Now, you can believe me or not, that's up to you, but just so you know, I don't make a habit of sexually assaulting my colleagues or friends. Or my enemies, for that matter." He stood and headed for the door. "Breakfast in fifteen. We need to be at the station by eight. You take the shower first." And he left.

Fuck. Shit. Damn. What the hell was wrong with him? He'd been a total prick. And what's more, he knew exactly why he'd done it, none of which had anything to do with anything except his own insecurities. Mark had done nothing but look after him.

Tinkerbell opened an eyelid and groaned her own disapproval.

"That's enough from you," he grumbled. "And get off the damn bed, you're drenching the pillow." He shooed the mastiff out the door, then gingerly made his way to the shower room to find a fresh towel and disposable razor set out for him on the vanity, with a glass of water and two paracetamol alongside. *Double fuck.* Mark Knight had guilt down to an art form.

CHAPTER THIRTEEN

Mark wasn't sure what this unfamiliar mood was toe-kicking his gut with a sulky pout, but he suspected it might be what his mother would call a strop... and he didn't like it one little bit. He snatched the toast from the toaster and attacked it with some butter, ploughing a bloody great gouge in it in the process. *Shit.* He dropped the knife and took a couple of deep breaths. What the hell was wrong with him? He didn't normally do self-indulgent navel-gazing, and he wasn't overly precious about his feelings, but dammit, he was pissed. Edward R-for-ridiculous Newton could just go suck an egg. The man was a dick.

Tinkerbell nudged at his thigh, and Mark offered her an edge of the burnt toast. She sniffed at it warily, then looked up as if Mark had lost his mind and walked off.

He watched the sway of her hips with a snort of amusement as she left the room heading for the blanket Cam had generously provided in lieu of a mat. "Everyone's a critic. I'll make sure to bring some bacon the next time I get a beating and a gun waved in my face, all right?"

Tink stared back as if the answer were obvious.

"You and your owner are a fucking matched pair," he grumbled, and returned his attention to breakfast.

As if Mark would take advantage of Edward. Jesus, what the hell was in that man's head?

Yeah, and who started that whole train of thought going, huh? Okay, well, maybe the whole what-happened-between-us-last-night tease hadn't been one of his better ideas, but really, who'd have thought Edward would swallow it? He might not approve of Mark, but Mark didn't think the man's opinion of him had sunk that low.

It stung, more than it probably should. And, *shit*, he hoped no one else thought that about him. A shiver of unease rolled through his stomach. *Ugh.* No, of course they didn't. Edward was just messing with his head. Mark had great friends, and everyone knew he was a stand-up guy, right? A flirt? Sure. But most took it with a laugh and a grain of salt. Okay, so maybe he'd pissed off a few along the way, mostly those who had their heads too far up their arses to take a joke —his gaze flicked to the closed bathroom door, and his lips twitched— but he'd have anyone's back who needed and deserved it, and that was the goddamn truth.

So, yeah, it stung. And in truth, Mark had spent some considerable time studying Edward when he'd fallen asleep on the floor next to the couch the previous night. One minute Edward had been talking about his favourite comic con event he'd like to attend, and the next he'd face-planted on the couch alongside Mark's hips and was out for the count. It would have been funny if it weren't so damn cute, and yes, sue him, Mark had taken an extra second to thread his fingers through the man's silken hair as he'd shifted his head aside so Mark could get up and get them both to bed. And maybe he'd more than appreciated the way Edward had leaned on him as Mark helped undress him and get him into the bed, but that's as far as it had gone.

Mark had been concerned at the time that Edward was actually okay and not suffering some downturn in his state of consciousness. So after he roused Edward and sat him in the bathroom, he had put in a quick call to Michael Oliver. The doc had already received a report from Cam, and he got Mark to ask Edward a few orientation questions, which Edward had answered correctly. Michael then had Mark run a couple of quick tests, like checking Edward's pupils and having Edward follow his fingers and squeeze his hands. After all that, Michael was satisfied that Edward was no worse, but he still wanted to see him in the ER by ten in the morning to check again. Mark agreed.

He threw another couple of slices in the toaster and took the scrambled eggs off the heat. *Whatever.* He had enough to worry about without walking on eggshells around everyone's favourite pathologist. Edward needed to get over himself. It was going to be a shit of a day as it was, and damn if his ribs didn't hurt like a motherfucker. He reached for the bottle of ibuprofen Cam had left for him and chugged two down with a slurp of coffee. He wished Edward could take something stronger than Panadol for his head, but... no, not a good idea.

He was tucking into his own breakfast, with Edward's in the warmer, when Edward appeared in the doorway and hovered for a second as if unsure if he was welcome.

"Yours is in there." Mark pointed with his knife at the oven's warmer drawer, then kept on eating.

Edward got his plate and sat opposite, hair still damp from the shower, smelling of citrus, toothpaste, and something earthy. He pushed his eggs around for a bit, then downed his utensils, broke a corner off his toast, and set about chewing it distractedly.

"You need to eat more than that." Mark nodded to the eggs. "It's gonna be a long day."

Edward said nothing for a minute, then forked a few mounds of eggs into his mouth, looking for all the world as if Mark were forcing him to eat dirt. Then he dropped his fork to the plate and looked up. "I'm sorry."

Mark kept his gaze steady on the other man but said nothing. A crooked crease formed between Edward's eyes, something Mark had picked up on as one of his tells. Edward was nervous, maybe more than that, and all of Mark's pissiness drained away.

"I knew you would never have done anything," Edward said. "I don't know what made me say that, because it's not you. It could never be you."

"You didn't seem so sure earlier."

"I'd like to say it was because I'd been hit on the head"—he slid Mark a half smile, and it was all Mark could do not to respond in kind, but yeah, call him petty—"but I think I was just being a jerk. You... unnerve me, Mark, and I have enough trouble keeping this distance between us when I'm awake, without the thought of what I might have done when I wasn't fully with it."

Mark dropped his head and chuckled. "What *you* might have done? You were worried about what *you* might have done? Not me? I'm clearly losing my touch."

Edward shrugged. "Maybe both. What I might have done to encourage you, is perhaps more the point."

Mark stared. What was Edward really saying here? And did it even matter? "Well, you didn't do or say anything in that regard, so you have nothing to worry about. Now, eat your breakfast." He reached for his coffee and watched as Edward picked up his fork, then put it down again and reached for Mark's free hand instead. Then he held his breath as Edward threaded their fingers together and squeezed.

"Thank you for taking care of me last night." Edward's eyes grew soft at the corners, his cheeks pink. "You could have left me on the couch and taken the bed for yourself, but you didn't, so... thank you. And I'm sorry for being such an arsehole about it."

Holy shit. If taciturn, solemn Edward was a turn-on, open, vulnerable, and heartfelt Edward was damn near irresistible, and Mark wanted nothing more than to haul him off his chair and into Mark's lap and kiss him till the frown fell off that beautiful face.

Instead he simply said, "You're welcome." And then, because he was such an unrepentant flirt, he added, "But just so we're clear, there was never *any* chance I'd be leaving you on that couch last night. It was the most time I've had to watch you uninterrupted without you getting all up in my face about it since we met." He grinned. "Just saying."

Edward stared at him for a second as a crimson flush crept up his throat, then burst out laughing. "Duly noted." He dropped Mark's hand, took back his fork, and shovelled the remaining eggs into his mouth with a little more vigour.

Mark watched Edward eat for a moment. "How's the head now?"

Edward remained focused on his food. "These are good, thanks. And, yeah, not too bad actually. The headache's still there, but I'm much better on my feet. I managed to bend over and wash my toes... and everything." He paused and glanced up as Mark dropped his fork to the table with a clang.

"You did *not* just say that." Mark grinned again. "That was almost a flirt, Edward Newton. You want to be careful, that'll get you a reputation." He eyed him pointedly.

Edward's gaze slid away, and he shovelled another load of eggs into his mouth. "Noted."

When he was done, Mark gathered both their plates and walked them to the dishwasher. "We should get going," he said as he stacked them. "There's a pair of Cam's shoes in that bag that might fit until we can collect some of your clothes."

He spun back from the sink, straight into Edward standing right behind, and froze. *Shit.* He needed to move before he did something else to offend Edward, like drag him to the floor and kiss him top to toe. And that was another thing. Since when did just kissing a guy become so damn enticing? Forget losing his touch, Mark's mojo was falling off in great whacking chunks.

"Sorry." He tried to shuffle sideways out of Edward's way, but a hand landed at his waist and another slid tentatively around his neck to hold him in place. He sucked in a breath and let his eyes track to Edward's silver-blue ones.

"Is this okay?" Edward whispered, leaning in, floating the unexpected words between them like a gentle wish, one Mark was far too shocked at to respond. The silence stretched between them like a rubber band, and Edward's head dropped. "I'm sorry." He went to pull away—

Oh, hell no. Mark's hand clamped over Edward's at his hip. "Yes. More than okay."

Edward's head lifted, a coy smile in place, and that probing, heated gaze returned to land on Mark like a net. The terms hook, line, and sinker flicked through his foggy brain.

"That's... good." Edward's gaze dipped to Mark's mouth. "Really... good. I, ah... I don't normally do this."

Mark brushed a lock of hair from Edward's lashes, and Edward looked up. "No kidding. Well, if you're a bit rusty, feel free to practice."

Edward smiled, but with enough of a hesitation that Mark felt he had to ask, "Edward, are you sure about this?"

Edward nodded absently. Then his eyes flashed, and that intense gaze dipped to Mark's lips like he wanted to—*fuck*, who knew? Eat Mark alive was what it damn well felt like. A flash of nerves swam through Mark's belly, and for just a second, he had the wildest notion that he'd maybe bitten off more than he could chew. That he'd mistaken a fucking crocodile for a pussycat.

Then Edward crossed that tiny distance between them, rested his warm, dry lips against Mark's, and all doubt evaporated in a blaze of sizzling heat. Edward's hand firmed at the back of Mark's neck while the other gripped his hip. Then he stepped in, and Mark was effectively pinioned between the granite bench and Edward's whole body pressed up against him. And, *holy shit*, Mark was going nowhere. Then—

A wet tongue grazed his foot and something warm and... slimy slipped between his toes. *Ugh.* "Ah, Edward?"

"Mmm?" Edward's nose brushed Mark's, and a pair of blue eyes came into focus just a heartbeat away from his own.

"We have company."

Edward glanced down. "Tink, mat."

The mastiff grumbled and lumbered off somewhere, who the hell knew where?

"Now, where were we?" Edward licked at Mark's lips, teasing and tracing a line from corner to corner, and God, Mark wanted a taste of the man, wanted inside that mouth like yesterday, but this was Edward's show, and damn if he wasn't running it with an iron fist. He had Mark pressed up against the bench, their groins on point, pressed solidly together, cock beside cock, getting to know each other, exchanging numbers, being polite—no movement, just pressure, enough to raise the temperature of the kitchen to just under molten... and still no fucking tongue.

Finally Mark risked a slide of his along the seam of Edward's lips, and Edward pulled back instantly, eyeing him with a wry smile. He cradled Mark's face and blew puffs of breath on Mark's lips, keeping his own just out of reach. Desperation curled in Mark's gut as he tried to capture those lips and gain entry but was thwarted every time as Edward pulled back and licked a path up his throat or nibbled on his jaw, before returning to Mark's mouth only to keep just out of reach again.

And that wasn't the only problem. A little left of centre, a smidge below Mark's belt, a whole other source of frustration was gently brushing across his straining cock, laughing at him. Edward's lips might have been firmly invested in all things skin above Mark's shoulders, but his cock was definitely aiming for the big guns in the game down south, and Mark couldn't grab anywhere near enough of its attention to suit his needs. He zigged to Edward's zag, thrust to Edward's parry, snagging not much more than the odd tantalising brush of something thick and hard as steel pressed up against him. It was all he could do not to simply fall to his knees and beg. *Always a good look, right?*

The dance continued, amping up Mark's arousal till he damn near saw stars and was a sparrow's breath away from slamming Edward on to the nearest flat surface and just getting on with things. And then, just like that, Edward committed, teasing thrown to the wind, and was all over Mark's mouth like he fucking owned it. And he did. *Hell,* Mark would've sold him the complete body package to use and discard as he pleased if Edward had asked, though he wasn't entirely sure he'd survive the experience based on current findings, because, whoa, that went nuclear fast.

So much for fantasies of throwing Edward anywhere. Mark was barely hanging by an orgasmic thread as it was, their tongues locked together as Edward's fresh taste exploded in Mark's mouth like manna from heaven. His mind was still spinning somewhere left of centre, grappling with the overwhelming sensation, because sure, he liked kissing as much as the next man, give or take, but nothing, nothing had prepared him for the experience of being kissed by Edward R-for-R-rated Newton. And when a hand disappeared from his cheek and popped up under his shirt to graze his nipple and squeeze lightly, Mark damn near came in his fucking jeans, saved only by a last-minute firm squeeze to his despairing dick.

They paused, the two of them panting, and Edward chuckled into Mark's open mouth. "Got a problem down there?"

Mark nipped the man's lower lip. "Nope. Just an itch."

Edward rubbed their noses together. "An itch, right." He ground up against Mark, eliciting an embarrassing groan. *Jesus, who the hell was this dude?*

Somewhere between finishing their eggs and packing the dishwasher, Edward R Newton had left the building and some seriously hot alpha had filled the void. That the two might exist in the same body and point in time was seriously screwing with Mark's head, but the dilemma could wait. Because regardless of the answer, Mark was freaking loving every goddamn minute of it.

The grinding continued, Edward laser focused on Mark's eyes, every tic, every reaction. "Still no problem?"

Mark sucked in a shuddering breath, trying and failing to hide how damn turned on he actually was, how close he was to blowing an epic load and likely causing the second great mass extinction—a piddly dust cloud or two had nothing on what was currently brewing in his briefs.

"*Pfft.* Don't know why you would even ask that," Mark whined, neck arched and corded as Edward's lips grazed his jaw, pressing tiny kisses along its length, while further south their cocks rode a wave of pressure. The butterfly assault continued down Mark's throat to the slope of his shoulders, where Edward bit down lightly, making Mark groan and arch up under him. Then... nothing.

Edward stepped back, resting just their foreheads together, his breathing ragged. Mark damn near keened in frustration. "What the hell was that?" he gasped, wrapping both hands around Edward's head, keeping the connection as he drilled his gaze into the other man's.

"A kiss?" Edward grinned wolfishly, his cheeks spotting pink.

"Nuh-uh. Nope. No." Mark pushed him back a step and leaned against the bench, shaking his head. "You do *not* get to do *that* to me... whatever *that* was... and just brush it off as a kiss. That was so much more than a kiss. I'm fucking destroyed here, Edward. Wait... where are you going?"

Edward had turned and was making his way out of the kitchen. "You said we needed to leave, right? So I'm getting ready to leave. Don't forget the flash drive."

Shit, he nearly had. "Yes, but... Stop. Come back here. You didn't answer my question."

"Didn't I?" Edward chuckled as he kept walking. "How remiss of me."

Mark had no choice but to follow. "Remiss? Edward!"

"Mark."

Oh, for fuck's sake. "Stop. Police. Put your hands up."

Edward's rumbling laugh barrelled down the hall as he turned with his hands in the air, wearing a grin from ear to ear. The air rushed out of Mark's chest at the sight.

"Yes, officer," he deadpanned as Mark strode up, pushed him back against the wall, and pinned his hands above his head.

"I repeat, what was that, Edward? I thought we agreed we were up to a solid walk—because, in case you misread the criteria, that was *not* a solid walk. *That* was at least a lope, a trot, possibly even a jog. So, I repeat, what just happened?" The question was deadly serious. For whatever reason, Mark needed the answer.

Edward's expression grew equally serious. "It was the sound of a door opening, Mark. Just a door. Nothing has changed about what I've said all along. This is not a game to me. *That* was deadly serious. You could hurt me, and you know it. I'm just letting you know where I stand. So, the question is, understanding all that, will you walk through that door or not?"

Mark stepped back, and Edward's hands dropped to his side.

"That's a pretty risky thing for you to do," he said. It so fucking was, and Mark wasn't at all sure how he felt about that. This was so far out of his comfort zone he needed a damn passport.

Edward's gaze slid sideways for a moment, then returned. "It is."

"So, are you saying you trust me?" Mark arched a brow. "An unrepentant flirt like me?"

Edward blinked slowly. "I trust that we might have something here—enough to break my own rules, as we discussed last night. Whether you see the same, and what you want to do about it, if anything, is now up to you. I just wanted to give you... information. So, think on it." He disappeared into the bedroom, leaving Mark standing in the hall wondering just how much further the universe would have to tilt on its axis to drop him straight off the side. About a whisker, he thought.

They drove to the police station mostly in silence, having left Tinker-bell with a bowl of food and a nest of blankets for a bed. Mark made a mental note to replace those for Reuben's sake once things were settled. Tink was asleep before they even closed the door.

Bitching ribs notwithstanding, Mark took the wheel of Reuben's

SUV, as Edward's concussion ruled him out, and steered them into town. The Auckland Harbour Bridge glistened under an early morning summer sun working hard to evaporate the remaining slick from an overnight shower. Westhaven Marina, nestled under the city end of the bridge, was chequered with an array of rich-boy toys, all bobbing gently on a rolling tide. On any other day, Mark would've soaked up the view. But just keeping his eyes on the road was proving a damn mission this morning, Edward drawing his gaze like metal to a magnet. His little crush on Edward Newton had blossomed into a full-on, sappy, cavity-forming infatuation, and Mark was pissed. And infatuated. But mostly pissed... at himself. Mostly.

He wasn't used to being on the back foot, wasn't used to feeling off-kilter about a man, any man. Wasn't used to not having control. And that's exactly what had happened. Somehow that sly, gorgeous, irritating man sitting next to him—the one calmly watching the world go by outside his passenger window—had managed to suck up all the damn power in the room without drawing a breath. And what's more, Mark hadn't even seen Edward do it. He'd sneaked up on Mark like a damn redback on the toilet seat and bitten him fair in the arse.

It was foul play in anyone's book. Up until then, Mark had Edward Newton firmly placed in the cute-and-nerdy-but-had-potential-in-the-bedroom-with-the-right-guidance (which of course was Mark) column. Yeah, right. That playbook hadn't just been thrown out the damn window, it had been incinerated on the floor of Reuben and Cam's kitchen.

That kiss... holy hell. Edward had kissed the living daylights out of Mark like he'd been born to the task, shoving him up against the bench and owning Mark like he fucking deserved it, like he'd take what he wanted, when and where he wanted it, end of story. Worst of all, Mark had let him—and not just let him, had caved without a single question and then followed him like a damn puppy up the hall, demanding an explanation. Had he mentioned he was pissed?

And somehow the tricky little bastard had managed to leave everything to Mark, as if Mark had all the power. *You just make a choice and let me know*, kind of thing. What the hell? Worst of all, Mark wanted Edward even more now, like *really, really* wanted the guy, and in a lot of fairly uncomfortable, better-left-unmentioned ways that had more to do with conversation and dates than burning up the sheets. Ways Mark sucked at, ways he'd left behind with Jeff and his parents and all that stupid romantic shit that did nothing but suck the life and independence right out of you.

Just the thought of that cloying, suffocating, insular *thing* he'd witnessed between his parents still raised every hair on Mark's body and sent his brain skittering for cover. It had been what kept him firmly in the lurk-and-flirt lane for years and was the reason he'd needed Edward Newton to dodge and dislike the Mark Knight he thought he knew. One look at Edward, and Mark had known he was in trouble. He didn't trust himself to walk away—he'd needed Edward to push him. But not anymore.

And by leaving the decision to Mark—oh, he was a clever bastard all right—Edward had slid a nasty tendril of conscience in alongside the offer. And make no mistake about it, it was an offer. Mark wasn't stupid. Edward was offering Mark a chance at something between them, *if* Mark wanted more than just a one-night thing. He'd put the whole thing up front and centre. *You can have me—but not just for one night, and decide now.* And Mark did... and didn't... and oh, he just wanted to drag Edward through brambles backwards and be fucking done with it. What the hell was he supposed to do with that? He couldn't even flirt his way through an answer. He really liked the guy, didn't just lust for him, and Edward knew. Somehow, he knew.

Ugh. Think on it, Edward had said. Well, good luck getting Mark to think on damn near anything else. *Goddammit.*

CHAPTER FOURTEEN

Mark's plan was to get their statements done, discover what Liam, Josh, and the scene techs had turned up, if anything, and then get to the hospital for their medical check and down to the morgue in time for Tom Spencer to arrive. Mark knew Kirwan wouldn't be pleased about him being at that meeting, but since Spencer expected to see Edward, there was no way Mark wasn't going to be there to keep an eye on him.

He hoped the fact it was a Saturday would play in their favour in that maybe DCI Kirwan wouldn't show his face this early. He could only hope. Kirwan would be pissed that Mark hadn't come in the previous night to formalise all the shit, and especially that he hadn't gotten them both seen to by a doctor straight away, but Mark's reasons were good and Kirwan would come around. He could just do without the aggro in the process. Not to mention he still wasn't sure how their attacker had found them. He didn't really suspect his boss, but his cop instincts were tingling something fierce that *someone* in the know was involved.

At that hour of the morning traffic was light, and they made it into the building's half-empty car park only a few minutes late, having picked up a bevy of coffees en route. A sober atmosphere greeted them as they exited the elevator into the brightly lit detective's enclave. A dozen or so detectives gathered over files and computers in the modern space, their solemn murmurings underscored by the shuffle of papers and furious tapping on keyboards. That was, until Liam's booming voice broke through the thick tension. Everyone turned and got to their feet, and Mark felt a prickle of guilt for leaving them in the dark as he'd done.

"Mark!" Liam strode across to them, looking exhausted, relieved, and thoroughly pissed off. Red eyed, unshaven, and tie askew, he looked to have been there most of the night. "Thank Christ you're here. Are you okay? Josh said the intruder broke your ribs." He switched to Edward without waiting for an answer. "And what about you?"

Mark held up both hands to ward Liam off from attempting a full-on body search just to confirm things for himself. "We're fine. We're heading to Auckland Med after this to make sure, but just bruised ribs... most likely. Edward's concussed and a bit unsteady, but nothing serious, all right?"

Liam's hands dropped to his sides, fists clenched. "No, it's not all fucking all right," he spat. "What the hell, man? You drop some serious shit on me last night and then disappear off the face of the fucking planet and don't tell me. Just as well Josh set me straight that you were okay—I was about to pull this damn city down looking for you."

Mark slid his load of coffees to the table and clapped his partner on the arm. "I'm sorry. I just needed to get Edward safe and time to think. I didn't mean to worry you."

Liam eyed him dubiously. "But for some reason you didn't want to tell me where you were."

Mark said nothing. He didn't need to, and Liam caught on quick.

"Okay. I'm gonna let that go for the moment and chalk it up to shock, and a trip down stupid street, because if you don't think you can trust me, we may as well call it quits right now." He cocked a brow at Mark, and the whole detective enclave fell quiet.

"Liam," Josh warned.

Liam shrugged the caution aside.

Mark winced. "Look, how about you lot have your coffees"—he pulled Liam aside—"while *we* talk."

Josh stared for a moment, then nodded, and he and Edward began to hand the drinks out.

"Keep your voice down," Mark snapped at his partner.

Liam was rigid with fury. "Why? So everyone can keep speculating about why I had absolutely no fucking idea where my partner stayed the night *after* he was attacked and refused to come in to do his statement, and why even his best friend wouldn't tell me... *partner?*"

"I said I was sorry. We were at Cam and Reuben's second house out west. But come on, Liam, that attack was deliberate, on both of us. It wasn't some light-fingered rando caught in a house he shouldn't be in. That guy waited for us, timed his attack for when Edward and I were separated for a moment and the dog was outside. If Tink hadn't caught on to him, we might not be here talking right now. So forgive me for being a little bit paranoid. Apart from Edward, only you and Kirwan knew about our meeting. Or at least that's what I thought at the time."

They stared at each other for a moment before Liam finally relaxed his shoulders and parked his butt on the edge of a desk facing Mark, arms crossed. "I took that call by the bar with at least six or seven guys around me, and to be honest I don't know how much any of them heard. It wasn't that noisy. The problem is, I was still there when you called about the attack, and most of those same guys were as well, which makes me their alibi and vice versa. One or two had left, and I'll follow up on those just to be sure, but we have no idea who Kirwan might have talked to, seeing as how the coroner's office is in play. Maybe he felt the need to give someone a heads-up."

It was true. There was no way to be sure exactly who knew about their meeting. Liam was right to be pissed at him. "Yeah, I'm sorry. I realised that when I thought about it. So, we play it by ear. You write a list of who was in that group at the bar and follow it up, and I'll check with Kirwan—see if he talked to anyone. We'll likely piss off half the station checking their alibis without being able to tell them exactly why, but hey, what could possibly go wrong?"

"Well, don't count on being popular at the softball game on Sunday, that's all I'm gonna say. Three of our team were at the bar with me. It'll be your round at the pub for the foreseeable future, I'm thinking."

"Shit."

"And just so we're clear on this, *partner*, there is no *we* in this investigation any more. Cracked ribs, assault, and a witness? You're gone for a week easy, desk duty at best. I'll send you flowers. But whatever. Besides, you're not done explaining yet. I want to know what other ideas are simmering in that butt-ugly head of yours. So go ahead. I'm listening."

Mark filled Liam in on the details of what went down the previous night and his suspicions about the linked cases. To his credit, Liam listened without saying a word until he was done. The remainder of the detectives present went about their work, casting the occasional curious glance their way, but no one interrupted. Partner spats were like domestics, rife with the potential for blowing up in the face of anyone who interfered unnecessarily. Only Josh and Edward stayed close, keeping an eagle eye and sipping their coffees as they watched and talked.

"So why not just OD on the stuff?" Mark finished. "Why go to all the effort of hanging yourself? Edward said the hair samples showed no evidence of long-term drug use, and the ketamine mix is kind of an odd choice for a scientist who you'd expect to know better. Plus there was no trace of drugs in his house. Meaning he did what—clean up, then go hang himself? That's pushing it, don't you think?"

"But we can't know that's not what happened. It *is* possible."

"Barely. But if you're a guy, home alone and depressed, what's your first port of call?"

Liam sighed. "Booze."

"Exactly. And the guy's blood alcohol only pointed to a couple of drinks at most."

"Okay, then." Liam cast an eye around the enclave and kept his voice low. "No one here knows about the Greene case, only about you and the good doc getting done over last night. Though I have to tell you, there were more than a few amused expressions wondering exactly *what* you were doing at his house on a Friday night." He held up a hand. "Don't worry. I told them Newton had some additional autopsy notes you were picking up."

Mark sent him a weak grin. "Thanks. Edward won't appreciate any gossip."

Liam nodded. "You're welcome. But I'm at a loss how to explain the attack if you want to keep the other connected case quiet, that is."

It was tricky. "Maybe just don't say anything for now. Leave it as a random and hope we get something more solid to give them tomorrow. We need Connor in those hospital computer systems now, to see if he can find us something, anything. Get the warrants sorted and get him up there. I have a sneaking suspicion that the report Edward found will be gone. At least he had the wherewithal to download a copy."

He dug in his pocket. "Here, give this to Connor. I want copies coming out our ears. Not that it's any good on its own. We need Spencer to come clean or we don't have any fucking idea what it actually means, what ties the two cases together. It has to be something big to warrant all this shit going down. Did Connor have any luck with Bridge's laptop?"

"Not yet. He got in, but it appears anything relevant has been deleted or he kept it somewhere else."

"Damn."

"And you think Tom Spencer is going to cough up to fiddling the report? Not much in it for him to do that, I'd have thought."

And that was the problem. Mark wasn't sure Spencer was headed that way either. "Won't know till we talk to him, I guess."

"What about Kirwan? He's gonna be all over my arse about this. And I repeat, he doesn't want you anywhere near this case—and he's right, you know he is."

Mark did know. He wasn't sure how to get around it, just that he would. No one was going to keep him out of the loop if he had anything to say about it.

"Which raises another point." Liam leaned in and lowered his voice. "You're a witness now, and so is Newton. You need to keep your hands off the guy."

Mark tensed. "What if that's too late?"

Liam's mouth dropped open. "Are you saying—"

"I'm saying it's none of your business either way, but if we were already *involved* in some form, that would kind of negate the need for the whole stay-away thing, right? Too late, horse already left the stable, as far as any jury is concerned."

Liam stared as if trying to fathom the relative truth of his carefully chosen words, and Mark was mindful to keep his expression neutral. He didn't fully understand what made him say it. It wasn't exactly the truth, but it wasn't exactly a lie either. Edward had left the decision to Mark, whose earlier confusion had abruptly cleared with Liam's warning to stay away from Edward. Something on a gut level railed against the very idea, and Mark wasn't having any of it. Which answered several questions in one troubling emotional jerk to attention. Not that there was any time to unpack that shit now.

"Look," Liam hissed, his gaze steeling. "I don't know what you think you're playing at, *partner*, but you better be damn sure you know what you're doing *and* what you're risking."

Mark held his gaze, unflinching. "Noted. Now, is Kirwan here?"

Liam shook his head.

"But he knows? *Everything*?"

"Of course he knows. He's our boss. And he's pissed as hell that you haven't already made your damn statements. Not to mention you weren't answering your phone last night, *and* I couldn't tell him where you were. Be prepared for an arse grilling of epic proportions when he gets here."

Hardly news. "Well, he was the one who wanted to keep it a side investigation with just you and me until we were sure. And I'm guessing if the coroner's office didn't know before, they will this morning." He glanced Edward's way. "Let's get Josh and Edward in on this conversation, and then we can do the damn statements before we head to the hospital and catch up with Tom Spencer." Mark took a step towards the others, but Liam grabbed him by the arm.

"You don't seriously think Kirwan's gonna let you anywhere near Spencer, do you? Did you hear nothing I said?"

"I heard *everything* you said. And yeah, I know I'm off the case. But there's no way I'm letting Edward anywhere near Spencer if I'm not close by, officially or unofficially, *partner*. And I'd like to think you'll keep me in the loop."

Liam worked his jaw but said nothing for a bit. Then finally he groaned and blew out a frustrated sigh. "Whatever. Let me know what you need, and I'll add it to the mountain of other stuff I'm juggling. And I'll try and keep Kirwan off your arse. Jesus Christ, you're a stubborn bastard."

Mark's face split in a huge grin. "Like you didn't already know that."

"Shut up." Liam released his hold on Mark's arm. "But ghost me again and you're on your own. And just so you know, if this all goes tits up, I won't go down with you. I have a family, arsehole."

Mark gave him a serious nod. "I wouldn't let you. And thanks." He pulled Liam into a loose one-armed hug that protected his ribs, and chuckled at the man's jerk of surprise. It took a second before Liam relaxed, and another before Mark realised he'd kept Liam at arm's length for the entire eight months they'd partnered, always unsure where Liam stood on the whole LGBT thing. Now, he couldn't understand why. They'd crossed a bridge, and it felt good, really good.

"Scared of the gay cooties, partner?" he teased.

Liam snorted and shoved Mark away. "As if, dipstick. Scared your dismal dress sense might rub off on me, more like."

That was more like it. This was a Liam that Mark was going to enjoy partnering. If he didn't get himself fired first.

"Yeah, you tell yourself that, straight boy. Come on, let's go appal the others with my lack of common sense." Which was possibly less of a joke than he thought, judging by the gaping mouth on his best friend, unused to seeing this side of Mark at work. And Edward? Edward was busy studying Liam with something pretty damn close to annoyance. *Hah!* Edward talked a big game, all that aloof, I-don't-care, leave-it-up-to-you shit. But there was no mistaking the posses-sive heat in the gaze that now fell his way. Edward Newton wanted Mark. End. Of. Story.

He winked at the other man, and a puff of pink blossomed on those cute-as-a-button cheeks a second before Edward scowled and turned away. Mark smiled to himself. *Oh, yeah. Game on.*

As it turned out, neither Josh nor Liam had much more to offer in the way of promising leads from the night before. The crime scene techs had finished with the house, taken prints and blood samples, but Mark pretty much knew they'd be a washout. Both he and Edward had their prints on file for comparison already, and Josh had grabbed a couple of personal items to lift the house owners' prints, but the intruder had worn gloves, Mark was sure.

On top of that, no gun had been found, and no sign of the laptops or paperwork—so either Mark was wrong about the gun or the intruder had gone back to retrieve it, a thought that had him squirm-ing. As for his laptop, it was well enough encrypted, and as soon as it was taken online the police techies would be able to lock it up and wipe it remotely. He'd need to check about Edward's.

Hoping for a scent trail, Josh had run Paris, but the only track the shepherd picked up stopped just short of the beach public car park next to the house. And there was nothing at the pools, although the techs had managed a cast of the vehicle tyres from the grass, and one neighbour had caught sight of a dark-coloured four-door sedan, navy or dark green, she thought, but couldn't be sure. Nothing else.

"There was nothing to track." Josh rounded the desk with Paris, his police dog, glued to his side. Conjoined twins had nothing on those two. The shepherd stretched his nose to Mark's hand and gave it a friendly smooch. Mark was at Josh's house almost as much as his own and had to be pushing uncle status at the very least—more, in those moments he was sneaking the dog illegal titbits from the table, but the less said about that, the better.

"Hey, darlin'." He roughed the dog's ears. "This bozo still treating you okay? I have a girl stashed away to introduce you to, if you play your cards right."

Paris cocked his head, ears pricked, totally focused on Mark's every word.

Beside him, Edward snorted. "All I'm gonna say is he'd better like them big and bossy. Tink is no shrinking violet."

Mark dropped his voice to a whisper. "Don't listen to him. *I've* heard she might have a thing for men in uniform." Paris whined and rubbed his nose along Mark's thigh. "It's true, I swear."

Edward elbowed him gently. "You're a dork, you know that, right?"

Mark turned and dropped his voice to a whisper. "I think you like that about me, Edward." Edward's neck went red. "Maybe like it a lot."

Edward's gaze fell away. "As I said. You're a dork."

"I hate to interrupt this tête-à-tête"—Josh flicked an interested gaze between the two of them, accompanied by a curious half smile, and Mark knew he'd need to be more careful around his astute friend. The last thing he needed was Josh all up in his business. Cam was bad enough—"but Paris and I have an invitation to a drug bust in about an hour, so can we wrap this up? What's the plan, other than keeping you two alive?"

Mark flicked Liam a look, passing the question along, and his partner gave a weary sigh. "Don't know why you're handing this to me. We all know you top from the bottom, arsehole."

Mark nearly fell off his chair, while Edward choked on the dregs of his coffee, delivering a spray over Paris, who promptly shook, coating anything Edward happened to have missed.

Liam stared around the small group and laughed. "What? Just because I'm not gay doesn't mean I'm not down with the lingo, you losers."

Mark was busy brushing Edward's coffee off his shirt. "Jesus, Liam. Your face lights up beetroot if I even stare at some guy too long."

"That's because you have crap taste and I'm embarrassed to be seen with you. I'd rather not hear the details about *anyone's* sex life, not just yours, so get over yourself."

Huh. So Liam wasn't quite the prude Mark had thought he was.

Liam continued, "You guys might have the inside line on Adam Greene and whatever Tom Spencer says about that doctored report, but you're off this case, Mark, so it'll be me in on that meeting, understand? We have no idea what Spencer intends to say or do. I want Edward set up with a listening device, and I'll be right outside his fucking door."

Mark steeled. "I'll be there too."

"As long as you keep it zipped and take a back seat, understand?"

Like hell. He nodded.

"Good. After that, I'll hit up Greene's wife with a few questions about her husband's suicide, and you meet me at Rowan Bridge's place to see if we can nail the connection with his wife. Mrs Greene doesn't know you, and I'm not having it bite me in the arse down the track when this whole report fiasco comes up. Evie Bridge at least knows you. She won't think too much of you being there. And, as I'm probably laying my career on the line here, you can damn well cough up for lunch."

It was a good plan. Mark nodded. "Done. You're pretty good at this for a junior partner, you know?" He winked.

Liam glared. "Fuck off, Knight."

Mark laughed. "What about Morgan and Associates?"

"Yeah, well, we're gonna need help regardless of what Kirwan said last night. Things have changed, and I think Kirwan will agree. The warrant for what Bridge worked on is bogged down in legalities because of the sensitive nature of the projects and the fact he hadn't worked at the firm for months. We might have to try a different angle. I'll get one of the other guys, maybe Stevens, to revisit and see if Morgan will at least give us access to his company's employment records and maybe let us talk to Bridge's work colleagues as long as we avoid the contract project information and keep it personal, around his friendships and character. It fits as a normal line of enquiry, with Bridge being a murder victim, so it shouldn't raise any flags to interested parties. Leastways there's no harm in trying, and if Morgan shuts us down again, we'll just file for a warrant."

"Let's get on it." Josh reached over and dragged a couple of gym bags from under the desk. "I'll try and catch you at Bridge's, but if not, I'll call when I'm done." He handed Edward a bag presumably holding some of the man's things from his house. "Nice collection of underwear you had there, doc."

Edward's cheeks instantly flamed, much to Mark's amusement.

Josh handed him the second bag. "Can't say the same about yours, sadly."

"Hah. You just wish you had my taste, loser."

"Nope. Michael wouldn't let me inside the house. We have standards, you know."

Mark flipped him off.

Josh simply grinned and handed each of them a prepaid cell. "Anyone who needs to get hold of you uses these numbers. Let them know. Liam will keep your personal cells on him, so give him your passcodes or whatever so he can check if he needs to."

Mark took it and frowned. "You sure they're necessary? As soon as the info on that flash drive hits our system this morning, whoever was after it is done. There's not much point in them pursuing us any longer to keep it quiet: it's too late."

It was Liam who answered. "We're not taking any chances. As you said, we have no idea what the reason is behind the doctored reports—which have yet to be substantiated, remember? And we've no idea what the connection between the two men is, if there even is one. So I'm taking no chances on your safety until we do. And that means you keep staying at your friend's place too, got it?"

"Understood. I'll also need a copy of the files again, and a spare laptop... please?"

Liam sent him a look, then sighed. "What the fuck ever. I'll have them ready before you go."

"Thanks, partner."

"Don't. Just don't. You owe me big time, Knight. Not to mention, now that you're injured, who the hell's going to play second base tomorrow? *Your* husband"—Liam stabbed a finger Josh's way—"is gonna have a flying fit. You know he's umpiring, right? Which means he can't play himself. Jesus Christ, we're mincemeat."

The grin Josh sent Liam gave new meaning to the term wicked. "Don't worry. It's date night tonight. I'll soften him up, then tell him."

Liam snorted. "Muzzle him would be more helpful."

Edward cocked a brow Mark's way. "Softball?"

Mark shrugged. "Fast pitch. The station has a team in the league."

"Really? Well, hell. You're gonna have to invite me to a game now."

Mark frowned, not sure that was a good idea at all, judging by the shit-eating grin Edward wore. "Maybe. We'll see."

They stared at each other for a minute longer—the sexual tension between them about as subtle as a fucking sledgehammer—before a throat cleared beside Mark, and Edward's gaze slid sideways.

"So, Edward..."

Mark could hear the knowing amusement in Josh's tone. Jesus

Christ, could the two of them have been more obvious? He was never gonna live this down.

"You can get that door fixed anytime you like now that the techs are done. And you better let the alarm guys know and change the code. Do the owners know yet?"

Edward winced. "Not yet. I'll call this morning or send an email. I haven't checked the time zones."

They spent the next few minutes transferring the numbers they needed to their new phones, then Josh headed out and Mark and Edward took their gear to the locker rooms to change into fresh clothes before getting their statements done.

An hour later Mark was thinking that maybe, just maybe, they'd get out of there without even laying eyes on their boss, until Kirwan walked out of the elevator and silence hit the detective's enclave like an executioner's axe.

The minute he spotted Mark, DCI Kirwan made a beeline for their little group, and Mark cursed under his breath. If only they'd left five minutes before. But the ragged concern on his boss's face had him immediately second-guessing any suspicions he'd harboured about the man.

Rick Kirwan looked like he'd been up all night. Tight lines framed a pair of irritated eyes that blinked repeatedly as if trying to clear a thick layer of grit, while his shock of red curls looked like they'd had little more than the man's five fingers for a comb since the night before, and yeah, Mark felt a bit guilty knowing he was likely responsible.

The DCI grabbed both Mark's biceps and squeezed. "Thank Christ." He frowned. "You okay?"

"A bit of bruising—"

"Is that what they call broken ribs these days?" Josh piped up.

Kirwan's gaze narrowed. "Broken ribs? Have you had them checked out?"

Mark threw Josh a pointed glare. "Most likely just bruised. And not yet, but it's next on the list."

Kirwan stared at him for another long couple of seconds then turned his attention to Edward. "And *you* took a solid hit to the head, I heard."

Edward nodded. "Slight concussion, nothing more."

"We're headed to Auckland Med after this," Mark told his boss. "Just wanted to get our statements done."

"*Hmmph.*" Kirwan's lips formed a tight line. "Those should have been done last night. Do you understand how worried I've been, or how embarrassing it was to call Commander Stables and tell him one of my detectives, *and* our pathologist"—he cast an eye over Edward, who returned a blank stare—"had been attacked? And that no, I didn't know the extent of their injuries, and no, I didn't know where the hell they were, and no, I hadn't received a personal update from either of them, and... forget it. Are your statements done now?"

"Just finished, sir."

"Good. My office, now, detectives. I want an update. You too, Dr Newton."

Fuck. Mark tucked his tail between his legs and followed, Edward and Liam at his back.

CHAPTER FIFTEEN

AUCKLAND MED WAS UNUSUALLY QUIET FOR A SATURDAY morning, so Edward and Mark were taken straight through to where Michael waited for them. Auckland Med was the largest hospital in the city, and its ER was the first port of call for most of the population south of the harbour bridge. The job of keeping the whole shebang on track fell to the ineffable Cam, who was currently staring daggers at Mark over a wide roll of strapping tape. Edward was doing his best not to laugh, but Mark wasn't exactly making life easy on himself—and Cam was in no mood to be fucked with.

"I don't need to take sick leave," Mark huffed. "I can work at my damn desk. I—ow, what the hell was that?" He whipped round to face Cam, who looked the picture of innocence as he tidied off the last piece of strapping on Mark's ribs.

"Sit still, and it won't hurt so much," he said, matter of fact. "And, just for the record, if Michael says you're on three days' sick leave to be followed by a week's desk duty, then you're damn well on sick leave. If it had been up to me, I'd have had you off for five. Now, hand me those bloody scissors."

Mark rolled his eyes but obeyed without question, and Edward bit back another smile.

"Don't think I didn't see that," he griped at Edward.

But Edward had lived through four sisters. He ignored the bait and watched calmly as Cam finished the strapping.

The chewing out they'd all received in Kirwan's office could have been worse. Mark's boss had listened to them recount the events of the night before and then focused his anger on Mark. Not that Mark didn't deserve it, and he'd prudently held his tongue while Kirwan raged on about not following standard procedure over witness statements and a wealth of other things, including the fact the assault should have been handed to the team on call, not simply given to Liam—although it was clear to Edward that Kirwan understood Mark's reasoning. He was just mad at his detective for taking things into his own hands, and Edward couldn't really blame him.

Kirwan approved Liam's idea to try for a fast-track warrant so Connor could delve into Auckland Med's computer systems, and he okayed Liam's plan to bring another detective in to help. He was also on board with allowing Edward's meeting with Spencer to go ahead provided Liam was close by and with the use of a listening device. The interviews planned for the wife and the ex-wife got the nod, although Edward noticed Liam made no mention of Mark's intention to be present for at least one of those.

When asked whether he'd mentioned Mark's meeting with Edward to anyone when he'd left the previous night, Kirwan said he'd only given a heads-up to the district commander. Edward's heart had sunk. Added to the guys at the bar, it meant it would be pretty much impossible to narrow the field about who might have tipped their attacker off.

Kirwan griped about Edward and Mark's temporary living arrangements, although Mark had fobbed him off by just saying they were staying at a mutual friend's, so as not to drag Cam and Reuben's name into it. But it sounded to Edward's ears as if Kirwan's grumblings were mostly for the sake of it, although he did drop a few words like "witness" and "compromised testimony" in for good measure, but in the end, he didn't push. That horse had bolted, Edward guessed, and he was quietly delighted to have a legitimate excuse to spend more time with Mark.

Kirwan even offered a squad car drive-by every couple of hours, but seeing as Cam and Reuben's getaway was out of the city, protected by an alarm system, and not visible from the road, Mark turned it down. Josh had offered his and Paris's services if needed, which was light years better than the odd drive-by anyway, and until they learned how the leak about their meeting had occurred, keeping the location of their current whereabouts as quiet as possible made sense.

In the end Kirwan agreed, though he was significantly less understanding of Mark's insistence he remain close for the Spencer meeting, casting a sceptical eye between them. But since Mark was already going to be on the premises and Liam was the official police presence, there wasn't much Kirwan could say about it.

But, as expected, the DCI did pull Mark officially from the case and put him on immediate sick leave pending a medical assessment. Edward suspected Mark was damn lucky that's where it ended. Not that Mark saw any of the positives, hence his pig-headed unwillingness to take time off.

Michael took that moment to stride into the room and across to where Mark sat on the edge of the bed grumbling to himself.

"What are you bitching about now, Knight?" The doctor was cocky and hot as hell, and he sucked up most of the oxygen in any room he entered, but hey, even Edward could appreciate the scenery. And knowing Michael was married to the equally sizzling Josh Rawlins, Edward's mind delved into images it really, really shouldn't.

Mark pouted and avoided Michael's gaze. "I don't need sick leave."

"Jesus, will you just listen to the experts?" Edward added his two cents, which earned him a scowl. "You can't work with broken ribs, Mark. Show some goddamn sense."

"Thank you, *Dr* Newton." Michael smirked. "Which brings me to the point that unless you've suddenly acquired some medical degree I have no knowledge about, *friend,* that makes me still in charge here."

Cam cleared his throat loudly.

"Well, *second-in-charge*, after Mr Wano here." Michael batted his eyelashes at the charge nurse.

Mark chuckled. "You are *so* not in charge, Oliver."

Michael ignored the dig and threw an X-ray up on the screen. "Be that as it may, pay attention, police boy. That there"—he indicated a dark grey line on the image—"is a non-displaced cracked rib—"

"So, not broken, then?" Mark's expression took on a smug edge that Edward wanted to slap away.

Michael scowled. "Zip it, friend. Fractured, cracked, broken—tom-ah-to, tom-ay-to—it's not in one solid piece. Plus, you're lucky it was only the one, considering the amount of bruising around the area. The boot to your loin and stomach doesn't seem to have damaged your kidneys or anything else, but you're gonna feel it for a while. And although your lungs look relatively clear, the fact you've coughed up some blood and also taken a thump to that admittedly mostly empty head of yours—"

Mark flashed him a paint-stripping glare, one Edward was pleased not to be on the receiving end of.

"—not to mention almost being run down by a car, means I'm gonna play things safe. I also have to answer to your best friend when I get home, and if you think for a moment I'm screwing up my chances of getting laid on my date night with my husband just to send you back to work, you're out of your goddamn mind."

"Ugh. Spare me any more jerk-off imagery of you two burning up the sheets. I'm chafed enough as it is."

Michael's eyes danced. "And my work here is done." He turned to Edward, who found himself standing straighter under the attention. "Same goes for you, Doctor. You might not have a skull fracture, but you were knocked unconscious and are still shaky on your feet and dealing with headaches. One week's sick leave, no argument. Can't have you making complex assessments that have legal ramifications with your thoughts all... wobbly, can we? You don't even get to desk jockey. Take it home, Doctor."

The air rushed out of Edward's lungs. "Wobbly? But I can't... I need to—"

"Listen to the experts," Mark deadpanned.

Bastard.

Michael pulled down the X-ray and patted Edward on the shoulder. "I don't tell you how to conclude probable cause of death, and you don't tell me how to run my ER. You have a problem with that, you can take it up with our esteemed charge nurse here."

Edward's gaze slid sideways to Cam's raised brow and I-dare-you expression, and he let out a sigh. Never. Gonna. Happen.

Mark threw him a shit-eating grin. "Not so fucking cocky now, are you?"

Tom Spencer was late. Ten thirty had come and gone without any sight of the man, leaving Edward and Mark on opposite sides of Edward's desk, going over the autopsy and police reports to pass the time. Well, Mark was. Edward had his hands full just keeping his eyes on the files and not ogling Mark. Or drooling. It was a close call. Pretty much any other train of thought had flown out the window after that mind-blowing kiss in the kitchen, and it was doing his damned head in to think only a little under twenty-four hours had passed since he'd left this very office the previous night. How much his world had changed since then.

Liam was already seated with Connor Fielding, the computer tech, at a terminal at Sandy's station when Mark and Edward arrived from the ER. The warrant had been expedited with minimal fuss—a murder, a potentially tampered legal and medical file, and an attack on a police officer and a pathologist couldn't have hurt. But Connor had only been in the system a half hour and hadn't yet cracked anything helpful other than to confirm the original file Edward had stumbled on to was, as suspected, no longer there, and that sure as hell pointed to them being on the right track.

The two cases had to be connected, and the discovery of the original report must have prompted the attack. Nothing else made sense, and none of it boded well for Spencer's role in it all. Not to mention the whole complicated business stank of higher stakes being involved, something worth all that effort and risk. What the hell was going on? Edward was no less confused than he'd been the night before.

But getting Mark's injuries properly assessed and treated had lifted a weight off Edward's shoulders, even though Mark was behaving like a big baby about it. Edward had been worried the bruising was hiding more than Mark was willing to admit, so a cracked rib and a bang on the head came as somewhat of a relief. And as for his own injuries? Other than a persistent ear-clanging headache and a terminally stiff neck, he was doing okay, and he was much steadier on his feet.

What was happening inside that traitorous organ in his chest, however, was a whole other bag of snakes. A Mark-sized hole was burrowing into his heart, and that fucker was growing by the hour—and nothing Edward tried appeared to have made a single dent in its progress. His stupid jealous response to Mark hugging his damn partner paid uncomfortable homage to that, because Edward didn't do jealousy, ever.

There was no escaping the fact Mark was already under his skin and setting up camp. He was irritating, arrogant, good-natured, sexy, and intoxicating—all wrapped up in an intoxicating bundle of lean-muscled deliciousness. And no matter how many times Edward reminded himself of all the reasons anything to do with Mark beyond the professional was a bad, bad idea, he found himself relentlessly reeled back into Mark's orbit.

He glanced up through his lowered lashes to find Mark chewing on the end of his pen, staring at the large photo of Monument Valley above Edward's bookcase. His brow was furrowed in thought, and good Lord, the man was sexy. Either that or Edward was a few light years past needing to get laid. *Well, that too.* But Edward's needs in that area rarely reached combustible. He could, and had, gone well over a year at times without getting up close and personal with another body. Slaking his needs with a quick-and-dirty fuck tended to kick-start a depressing downer for him.

Casual sex rubbed something raw and uncomfortable inside him, left him too tight in his own skin, too needy for something... real. Like drinking a glass of flat 7UP when what you really needed was full-bodied red. But where exactly Mark Knight fitted on that continuum, Edward had no idea. He could only hope his instincts were right—that the man's carefully crafted, devil-may-care manner was a foil for a much more complex character.

At least that's the reason he gave himself for why the hell he'd gone and kissed Mark that morning... the second time in twenty-four hours. And why he'd given Mark an opening. All Edward knew was, he was done walking on eggshells around their obvious chemistry. The way he'd inexcusably gone off on the poor man that morning after finding they'd shared a bed—for all the right reasons he'd later learned—just went to show how very much Edward had lost the plot. It couldn't continue, and he didn't want it to. And so he'd sucked up some courage and jumped. Holy crap, he'd jumped. No one ever said he was smart when it came to relationships. But at least now the ball was in Mark's court, and in the meantime, Edward could try to knit his nerves back together. So, yeah, about that.

But getting things out there had felt... freeing. At least it had when he'd said the words. Now, he wasn't so sure. Mark hadn't exactly leapt at the offer. Edward remembered the flash of hurt when he'd stupidly implied Mark had less than squeaky-clean motives that morning. He'd been rude and ungrateful, and he'd regretted it instantly. Mark wanted more than a tumble in the sheets, of that Edward was sure. He just wasn't quite so sure if Mark could admit it.

But none of that had a single thing to do with why he'd kissed Mark. At the time it simply felt as if he couldn't *not* kiss him. Like he was wired to react. And holy hell, what a reaction. The cascade of sensations that rolled through his flesh when their lips touched, the heat in Mark's eyes, the sharp intake of breath, the sensual roll of his neck as Edward's mouth trailed down to that sweet curve of his shoulder, the puff of his breath in Edward's ear, the rumble of need in his chest...

"You keep looking at me like that and I'm gonna need a shower." Mark pushed his file away and leaned back in his chair, watching Edward with an amused glint in his eye.

Edward felt his cheeks heat. *Shit.* "Sorry, I, um... huh." He grinned sheepishly. "Actually, I have no excuse. You're a beautiful man, what can I say?"

It was Mark's turn to pink up, which surprised the hell out of Edward.

"And you have this whole half-frown dip thing happening between your eyes when you work. To be honest, it's pretty damn cute."

Mark opened his mouth to reply, closed it, then opened it again but still said nothing, and Edward wondered if maybe Mark didn't get a lot of compliments that weren't linked to a packet of pre-lubed condoms. And that right there was a damn shame, one he made it his mission to right. "Does it make you uncomfortable, to be told you're beautiful?"

Mark's eye-roll was lucky it didn't take out half the files on Edward's desk. "No, of course not."

Edward arched a brow.

He pulled a face. "Well, maybe, but you didn't hear that from me. Just don't mention the cute thing too loud. I have a reputation to consider." He twirled his pen in his fingers. "You, ah... think I'm beautiful?"

He could have dismissed the question as fishing, except for the nervous dart of Mark's gaze and the way his whole body tensed as he waited for Edward's answer. He slid his hand over Mark's and squeezed. "I do. Almost impossibly so. And not just on the outside, though that's mostly all you let people see." He held Mark's gaze, making his point clear.

After a minute, Mark turned his hand, taking Edward's. "You scare me, Edward. *This* scares me. What if I'm not good enough for something like this, for you? What if I screw it up?"

Edward paused before answering. "What if you are, and what if you don't? And maybe *I'll* be the one to screw it up."

"Yeah, right," Mark scoffed. "The honourable Edward *Richard* Newton screwing up? Like that's ever gonna happen."

Edward grinned. "*Not* Richard, and don't do that."

"What?"

"Put yourself down. There's a reason I'm still on my own as well, you know. I'm not exactly a safe bet either. I'm stubborn and set in my ways and... cool, or so I've been told. My sisters say I'm awkwardly introverted and clumsily antisocial."

Mark snorted. "I think I'd like your sisters. I think we'd get on."

Oh, Lordy. Edward shuddered dramatically. "As horrifying as that is, I tend to agree." Mark's thumb brushed over the back of his hand, and since when had that ever had a short circuit to Edward's dick? Since now, apparently.

"So, um, can I ask you a question?"

Edward nodded cautiously. "Sure."

"I just wondered... well, okay... and don't take this the wrong way... again." Mark threw him a pointed look. "As I was helping you get into bed last night... *politely* helping you... I... noticed the tattoo on your chest."

Okay. Not the question Edward expected, but... "Go on."

"It's a dragonfly, right?"

He nodded again.

"And the name underneath. Sarah. Is that one of your sisters?"

"The youngest, yes." Edward felt the atmosphere in the room thicken. Sarah's death was a subject he *never* discussed other than with family, and he wasn't quite sure how he felt about breaking yet another rule.

But Mark didn't press. He simply waited. And that was all Edward needed.

He took a breath and steeled himself. "I don't talk about Sarah much, or at all, actually."

"And you don't have to now," Mark reassured him. "I'm not prying..." He grimaced. "Or, rather, I am, but you don't need to tell me your secrets. We're... still new at this, right? Still feeling our way. It's just that it's quite a beautiful design. I'm sorry if—"

"It's not a secret. It's just personal, I guess. But I want to tell you, I do." And he did. Which was surprising... and kind of wonderful. "So, Sarah. Sarah died when she was eighteen—"

"Oh, shit." Mark left his chair and circled to Edward, taking a seat on his desk and wrapping Edward's hand in his... again. "I'm so sorry."

Mark's genuine concern nearly undid Edward on the spot. He swallowed hard so he didn't simply climb into Mark's lap to be wrapped in his arms. "Thanks. It was an aggressive form of non-Hodgkin's lymphoma." As always, the words felt sucked from Edward's chest like poison from a wound. Usually he covered the pain with stoic platitudes and sensible rationalisations, but not this time. This time the words kept coming, and he was apparently helpless to do anything with the hole other than fill it with yet more words, words that streamed unfiltered from his lips, words that left him aghast even as they left his mouth. This was why he didn't talk about it. After all these years, thinking of Sarah's death still left him... gutted. Raw.

"It was spectacularly fast. Barely six months between the image I carry of her as fit and healthy, yammering on about her high school science project on the mating habits of a rare New Zealand dragonfly —and then all skin and bone, pallid, chest sounding like a rattlesnake, with a hospice nurse sleeping in our lounge. It felt like our family was hit by a hurricane that left nothing standing in its wake."

Once started, Edward couldn't seem to stop. "She was five years younger than me. We always ribbed her about getting away with so much more than we had as kids, and then... in the end... she didn't get away with the one thing she really needed to. God, it was like the sun left our house forever. It took my parents years to recover—all of us in fact.

"Even now it feels so strange, so wrong, to not have her there at Christmas"—he continued to ramble, mortified at his own voice—"shaking all the damn presents. She was such an impatient little minx. Of all my sisters, I was closest with her. We shared a love of animals, and biology, and... comics. She was the only one allowed within a country mile of my collection." He grinned at the memory.

Mark regarded him with soft eyes. "It sounds like you two had something special."

"We did. It broke my heart when she died, I can't lie. And it made it hard to leave Christchurch, leave those memories, my family."

"So why did you, if you don't mind me asking?"

"It was time. And after the mosque shootings... let's just say I was ready for a fresh start."

"You were involved in the autopsies?" He shook his head. "Stupid question. Of course you were."

Edward focused on their hands, still locked together. "Yeah. It was bloody heartbreaking. And I was pretty angry about everything. It raised a whole lot of unresolved stuff about Sarah. I, um, needed a bit of help after, to work it through. A lot of us who worked on it did." He lifted his eyes for any inkling Mark might judge him for needing help, but there was nothing other than deep concern written across his face.

Mark squeezed Edward's hand as if he knew he needed some reassurance. "I had mates fly down to help the Christchurch police immediately after the shootings," he said. "They said exactly the same—how affected they were by the grief and the outpouring of emotion, and people's gratitude and kindness towards them just for being there. One of our brand-new constables said it changed him forever."

"Yeah, I can understand that." Edward gently freed his hand from Mark's, needing a bit of space, and Mark let him, even moving back to his own seat. There were no hurt looks, no "What did I do wrong?", no pressure to keep regurgitating the pain. The unspoken understanding Mark offered poured balm on something that had been eating away at Edward's resolve to give the two of them a chance. Maybe they were more similar than he'd thought. "Thanks."

Mark shrugged. "Nothing to thank me for. And I'm sorry about your sister. For what it's worth, if she was here today, I think she'd be proud of you. I mean, what's there not to be proud of?" He reached across, took Edward's hand, and lifted it to his lips.

Edward watched in fascination and was about to answer that Mark hardly knew him well enough for such approval, when the door swung open and Sandy burst in, causing him to jerk his hand free— but not before Sandy caught them.

"Ed... oh—" Sandy stalled in the doorway, his gaze flitting between them. He seemed so shocked that for a second Edward almost burst out laughing. There wasn't much that surprised his assistant, and he could just imagine what Sandy was thinking behind that all too calculating and insightful gaze. Sandy made Dr Phil look like a rank amateur. And, sure enough, once he'd picked his jaw up off the floor, a sly smile crept over Sandy's face.

"I should say I'm sorry for interrupting" he narrowed his gaze, addressing them both—"but I am so very *not*. So let's quit with the polite pretence that I didn't just interrupt a... moment between the two of you, and instead let me direct this short comment to you, Detective Knight."

Mark jerked upright in his chair, eyes wide.

Oh, for fuck's sake. "Sandy, you don't—"

"Nope." Sandy held a hand up to silence Edward. "You've been here, what, three months, Ed? And I'm probably the closest thing to a friend you've made in that time, am I right?"

Edward sighed and deflated against the back of his chair, idly waving his hand for Sandy to do his thing, as if he could stop him.

Sandy nodded pertly and drew himself up to his full six feet three, making a good effort to loom over Mark. "You have a good game, Detective, or so I've heard. But Edward Newton is one of life's treasures, and I will personally nail your balls to the wall if you so much as hurt a hair on his head. Are we clear?"

Mark's mouth dropped open for a second before he gathered himself and said, "Crystal. And for your information, Edward and I are not a... thing—not yet, leastways. Right, Edward?"

Edward gave his best crocodile smile. "What he said. Not even remotely."

That adorable little crease appeared between Mark's eyes and disappeared just as quickly. He turned back to Sandy. "See?"

Sandy huffed. "Judging by what I saw, and the for-fuck's-sake-get-on-with-it energy in this room, you two are *not* a thing about as much as I'm *not* gay. So"—he stabbed a finger Mark's way—"just you remember what I said."

It was time to move things along. "Thank you, Sandy, for your touching concern regarding my virtue, but was there something else you needed from me?"

Sandy looked puzzled for a second. "Oh, shit, yes. I just had a call from the relieving pathologist. He's been called to a traffic accident—"

Liam poked his head around Sandy's shoulders. "Spencer's dead. A car accident, apparently. I've got to go."

Mark shot to his feet. "Dead? What the hell?"

Sandy's mouth hung open. "Holy shit. That'll be Neil's call out. I better warn him." He grabbed his phone and stepped outside.

"What happened?" Mark demanded.

Liam zipped up his jacket and pulled out his car keys. "It must have happened on his way here. He ran off, or was run off, the road just south of his farm. Hit the side of a concrete block wall... at speed."

Jesus Christ. Edward watched Mark's jaw work as he digested this new twist.

"Does Kirwan know?" Mark stared at his partner, something unspoken passing between them.

Liam nodded. "As of now, it's gloves off. *Everyone* is being briefed on the possible link, coroner included." He directed his gaze to Edward. "So, I'd expect a call from his office, Ed—"

Oh joy.

"—I'm heading out to the accident site, then I'll interview Greene's wife. I'm meeting her at her ex-husband's house, since she hasn't put it up for sale yet. We'll have to put off Bridge's wife until tomorrow."

Liam eyeballed Mark. "If I ask you to make a simple phone call to Stevens, can I trust you to do nothing with whatever he says before I get back? He was gonna try and get Morgan to play ball with those employment records and staff interviews. I warned him you might call. I'm gonna be too busy with all this for a couple of hours."

Mark looked affronted. "Of course you can trust me."

The eye roll Liam gave was spectacular. "Riiight. And as for the guys at the bar who might have heard us talking on the phone that night? I got hold of the two who left early, and their partners will vouch they were with them at the time the attack took place."

"Shit. Doesn't mean they didn't pass the information on."

"No, it doesn't, but it still gives us zip without a link. I'll catch up with you later. And one more thing."

Mark's shoulders tensed. "What?"

"When Ed's done with that conference call, you two are to head back to the house and keep your heads down, yeah? At least until we've got more of a handle on what's going down. Subtlety seems to have flown out the window for whoever's behind this."

Sandy stepped back into the room before Mark could answer. "Neil's on his way to the scene now. He was pretty shaken to hear it was Spencer. I'm expecting the body to arrive this afternoon. Your boss has apparently demanded an autopsy ASAP..." he trailed off and took a deep breath. "Jesus Christ, what the hell's going on?"

Edward's cool-as-a-cucumber assistant had been shocked enough when Edward had told him about the attack, but they'd needed his insight, both into the Greene case and the workings of the morgue prior to Edward's taking over, so Sandy had agreed to come in on his day off and help. They'd yet to mention the matching tox screen reports, but Edward had seen the cogs ticking over in Sandy's brain when Connor had settled himself at a computer terminal, even though he'd said nothing at the time.

Mark stared at Edward, determination set in every line on his face, and it didn't take much for Edward to guess what the detective wanted.

"Fuck." Edward's head fell back, and he dragged a hand across his mouth. "No. I can't get involved in the autopsy, Mark. Neil won't have a bar of it, and neither should he. He's a straight-up rules guy. Besides, it will screw any legal standing the autopsy has. I'm sorry."

Mark held Edward's gaze. "I know you can't, and I'm not asking you to. But we really need to know what they find." He tipped his head at Sandy, who rolled his eyes.

"It's up to you," Edward said to his assistant.

Sandy nodded. "Okay. I'll keep you in the loop, *if* you tell me the rest of the shit you're both keeping from me, because I know you are. I'm not laying my job on the line without good reason."

Edward looked at Mark and shrugged. "You heard the man. Your call."

Mark barely hesitated before bringing Sandy up to speed, and Edward watched his assistant's eyes blow wide.

"Holy shit, you think Tom screwed with that report? That those second samples weren't Greene's? But—"

Edward saw the moment the enormity of the fraud sunk in.

"Oh, fucking fuck, the coroner's going to have a heart attack over this." Sandy grabbed a chair and sank into it. "The body will have to be exhumed, the whole thing done again... Oh my God. But why would he do something like that?"

Edward shrugged. "We don't know. That's what we're trying to figure out. But it's all related somehow. And we have to know if they find anything in that autopsy that might help us. Plus, I need you to get me Bridge's other tissue results as soon as they come in. In fact, we should send another lot off from the stored sample material, just to be safe."

Liam's eyes widened. "Shit, that's right. You keep extras until the coroner rules."

Sandy nodded. "And if it's homicide, we try and get permission to hold them longer, in case future testing improves."

"Were any kept for Greene?"

Edward looked apologetic. "Doubtful. A suicide ruling would mean all samples were likely either returned to the family or destroyed. You need permission from the coroner to keep them—and a good reason. Plus if Spencer went to so much trouble to change the results, he's hardly going to have kept anything that would destroy his efforts. But I'll get someone to check."

Liam dragged a hand down his face. "Shit."

Edward addressed Sandy. "Did you assist with Greene's autopsy?"

Sandy nodded. "Suicide cases tend to stand out. It was pretty straightforward as I recall, and I can tell you right now there was no incorrect labelling and resampling that *I* knew about. I've only ever known one instance of that happening in this office and it was a long time ago. And I would've been responsible for organising at least some of Greene's specimens even if I didn't personally label them. Tom often helped, he was good like that. And admin never spoke to me about any reported incident."

"Tom didn't put your name on the incident report."

Sandy gaped. "What? Oh... shit. Yeah. I guess he didn't want me questioned, right?"

Connor pushed his way into the crowded office, garnering everyone's attention. "Okay, guys, I can't say who, but I can tell you the report was deleted in the system from one of the morgue computers about ten p.m. last night. I can't tell you which one yet, but I ran a check and the security cameras show someone coming through the loading bay door about nine forty-five. Whoever it was, kept their face well hidden."

Edward locked eyes with Mark, and they answered at the same time, "Spencer."

Liam frowned. "He still had access?"

Edward blew out a sigh. "I wouldn't have thought so. At least not to *my* office, or from the hallway—that's all key carded. I suppose he could've got hold of one of those somehow. But the morgue loading bay has a digital code to allow for the delivery and removal of bodies after hours, and I doubt that's changed since he was here. It wouldn't give him access to the actual lab, sample storage area, or autopsy suite —not without a card, but it's a much less travelled entry point, and he would be able to get into Sandy's office. There's a computer there, and no security camera, so I guess—"

Sandy blanched. "Shit. He used my computer? Bastard." He pushed away from the wall. "I'm going to get those second lot of samples sent away for testing, okay?"

"Thanks." Mark turned to Edward. "This just went from threatening to all the alarm bells fucking ringing."

Liam clapped Mark on the shoulder. "I gotta go. Just... don't do anything without me... please?"

Mark was clearly anything but happy about sitting on his hands, but to Edward's relief he nodded. "Only if you keep me in the loop."

Liam nodded. "We'll talk later."

They'd just about made it out the door when Sandy barrelled up behind. "Bridge's spare samples are gone." He was red-faced. "And it wasn't me, if that's what you're thinking"

"Of course it damn well wasn't you," Edward muttered. "That thought never crossed my mind." He looked to the others. "So if it *was* Spencer, he's definitely got an access card."

Mark eyeballed Sandy. "All the codes and swipe passes need to be changed."

Sandy sucked in a breath and gave a sharp nod. "I'll get right on it. I'm so sorry—"

Edward laid a hand on Sandy's arm. "It's not your fault." He turned to Mark. "Why bother taking those samples? We still have Bridge's body. We can just take more."

"How long will that take?"

Edward shrugged. "Neil will have to get Spencer's autopsy done first, then get Bridge's body back on the table. By the end of the day, at the earliest—tomorrow more likely."

Mark's brow creased. "Maybe they just wanted to slow us down. Call us when the autopsy's done, Sandy. We need to go."

"Of course." Sandy wrapped Edward in that sharp-elbowed octopus hug he'd perfected and then eyeballed Mark. "Keep him safe."

Mark glanced Edward's way. "I will."

And, okay, Edward could admit to a tiny shiver of pleasure at the resolve in Mark's voice.

CHAPTER SIXTEEN

FROM HIS POSITION STRETCHED OUT ON THE COUCH, MARK HAD a prime view of Edward working in the kitchen of the ritzy cabin as he whipped up some kind of pasta and spicy sausage concoction with the groceries they'd picked up on the way back. Whatever it was, it smelled amazing, and Mark was salivating for a lot of reasons—not least of all how Edward's tight shorts framed his arse in all kinds of tempting possibilities.

They'd both taken an energy hit after the stressful morning, Mark's ribs screaming abuse while the tight lines around Edward's eyes and the thin cut of his lips told Mark all he needed to know about how his head was holding up. They'd agreed to a moratorium—God, Mark loved that word—on all case talk until they heard from Liam.

The conference call with the coroner's office had gone as expected: shock, horror, back-pedalling, and panic about the media catching wind of the mess. Edward ran defence like a pro and managed to calm the administrative shitstorm. Still, a little less concern about the politics of it all and a little more about Edward and Mark's well-being wouldn't have gone amiss.

He'd spoken to Stevens, the detective Liam had tasked with contacting Morgan. Stevens had been unsuccessful in getting Morgan to give up his employee files, and a warrant had been filed. He had, however, run down a couple of Morgan's employees via an internet search and cold-called them at home to ask about Bridge. After warning the employees to steer clear of any project specifics that might breach client confidentiality, he'd managed to get some useful information.

Both employees remembered Bridge and Greene as being highly skilled at what they did and that Bridge had been critical in solving the problem he'd been contracted for—something completely at odds with Morgan's take on things. Both also knew that Greene had supposedly killed himself, and stated the news had come as a shock. He hadn't seemed the sort, they'd said. According to them, Greene and Bridge got on well during the short time they worked together, sharing lunches and long conversations as they worked. Not surprising, one commented, since both had a passion for alternative fuels.

And there it was. Finally, the connection they'd been looking for. Two men dead, both with a passion for renewable energy. They knew each other and even worked on the same project together. Plus they were friendly enough to lunch together. Which again raised the question why Morgan hadn't brought up the sudden deaths of two ex-employees in under a few months—it defied belief to think he hadn't known, especially when it was apparently common knowledge in his company. And why had he lied about Bridge's ability?

Still, there wasn't anything more they could do until Liam got in touch except try to get some rest. To that end, the minute they'd walked in the door, after letting Tink out for a sniff and a piss, Mark had bundled a grumbling Edward into the bedroom to nap. He took the couch for himself, falling senseless for a good hour before murmurings and banging of pots and pans startled him back to life. Edward, it seemed, had achieved less success in the sleep department.

Since waking, he'd been riveted on the man's fluid efficiency around a kitchen, displaying the same contained grace he bore in the autopsy suite... which was a mildly upsetting comparison. But Edward clearly knew what he was doing and had rejected all offers of help from Mark. To be honest, Mark was grateful. His ribs still protested the lack of rest, and the pain pills hadn't done much but take the edge off so far. But at least he'd caught up on a bit of sleep.

Yes, they could've shared the bed, but Mark so thoroughly didn't trust himself that he wasn't sure any close proximity to Edward wouldn't simply end up in a sea of tangled arms and legs, which neither of them was ready for. Or to be more accurate, after Edward's sizzling kiss in the kitchen, Mark was no longer sure *what* they were ready for, and he wasn't prepared to make a mistake.

Damn the man. This confusing tangle of half-voiced feelings and ambiguous behaviour was exactly what Mark hated about relationships—not that he and Edward were in one, of course. This sticky, suffocating sense of becoming entwined with someone else's feelings. His head, not to mention his heart, was currently running twenty cents short of a dollar's worth of any-fucking-thing. Edward Newton had infected his mind, and with no sign of a cure on the horizon, Mark was caught between ridiculous anticipation and abject fear. Not even remotely dramatic, right?

Whatever happened to his simple life? Edward R Newton, *that's* what happened to it. Which raised a very important question... His thinking paused as Edward bent to slide the pasta dish into the oven. And, *holy hell*. Men with casseroles. Who knew that was a *thing*?

Edward turned and flashed a wry smile as if he knew exactly what had gone through Mark's head, and Mark's face heated instantly. Which deserved mention as yet another mortifying development. Mark didn't blush. Mark caused blushes, responded to them, delighted in them, but never blushed himself... until recently.

He sat a little straighter and plumped his cushions. "Don't mind me." He rolled a hand for Edward to continue his work. "Just, um... supervising your technique. Hygiene is important."

Edward snorted. "Riiiight. Hygiene."

He returned to the sink, which gave Mark the opportunity to contemplate that delicious arse once again and mull over why he wasn't more panicked about this decision he was contemplating... or that he'd likely already made, if he could only find the balls to own up to it. *Jesus Christ.* Was he really going there? The answer in his head was a resounding yes, accompanied by a tentative grin. *Fuck a duck and buy it a house,* he was in.

"Did you know there's a second fridge in here?" Edward called from the depths of the walk-in pantry. "Jesus, this thing is huge. How many kinds of flavoured water does a person need?"

"I know right? But Cam's quite the cook and Reuben's dedication to hydration is legendary."

"Do you want a beer?"

Mark's mouth watered. "Hell yes, but we probably shouldn't."

Edward's head popped back around the pantry door and he smiled. "Do you have a medical degree?"

"No, but—"

"Then relax. Professional athlete in residence, remember. It's a stingy zero-point-two percent. Pretty much means the transport truck passed a brewery on its way to the liquor store and some alcohol fumes brushed the label. I think we're safe."

Mark grunted. "Maybe from the beer, but there's a sassy nurse-dragon-type fella I wouldn't mention it to."

Edward froze, a frown creasing his brow. "Point taken. Let's keep it just between us. Pinky swear?"

Mark took the beer, and they locked little fingers. "Now who's the dork?" But he still swore the sacred pinky oath.

"Dinner will be about an hour. We can kick back and go wild." Edward tapped Mark's leg, and Mark scooted back to make room for him.

He watched as Edward sank into the cushions and made circles with his head, stretching out his neck muscles. "How does it feel?" he asked. "You looked steadier this afternoon."

"You keeping an eye on me?" Edward arched a brow.

"Answer the question."

He sighed. "Yes. I'm much steadier, though this damn headache's a bitch. I suspect I'm stuck with it for a few more days, though. How about your ribs?"

Mark stretched gingerly. "Not great, but no worse either, so there's that."

They drank in silence for a minute, and man, did it ever taste good. Sensing Edward had moved from the kitchen for the foreseeable future, Tink found her way back into the lounge and settled on the floor at his feet with a sizeable groan. She'd been pleased to see his return, ambling from the bedroom when Mark opened the door with an excited wiggle of her well-rounded hips and wearing guilt like a blanket from nose to tail.

One peek at the downstairs bed confirmed Mark's suspicion. A Tink-sized crater had been carved out smack dab in the middle of the crisp white duvet—who the hell had a white duvet—with a few puddles of bloodstained drool for good measure. In contrast, not a wrinkle was to be seen on the jury-rigged bed they'd made for her in the lounge. Another thing was added to the rapidly growing list of things *not* to mention to Cam or Reuben until they could be fixed, or replaced, or whatever... *damn dog.*

Edward put his drink aside and rubbed at his neck. He looked shattered.

"Come here." Mark placed his beer on the floor, spread his legs, and signalled for Edward to back up between them.

Edward raised a brow and stayed where he was.

"It's just a neck rub, not a damn marriage proposal. Now do as you're told for once and get over here."

Edward rolled his eyes but moved as requested and settled between Mark's legs. "Bossy bastard."

But when his thighs cradled Edward's warm hips, Mark's cock twitched its approval and Mark began to rethink his offer. Edward's head sat only a few tantalising inches from Mark's lips, the scent of Cam's apple body wash filling his senses. Tempting didn't even begin to describe it. So no, it perhaps wasn't the smartest idea he'd ever had. He wriggled back to get a bit of respite from the maddening pressure on his groin.

"Is there a problem back there?"

"No," he answered. "Just... adjusting position. I think you need to lose some weight, Edward. It's a tight fit."

Edward chuckled. "Sure it is. I'll get right on that."

Using mostly the hand from his uninjured side, Mark began to work Edward's deeply knotted shoulder and neck muscles, which did two things. First, it helped focus his attention on something other than his traitorous dick—he really did want to ease the pain in Edward's head. Second, and eminently less helpful, it elicited a series of porn-worthy groans from the man on the receiving end. And Mark would take anyone's bet that Edward knew exactly the effect he was having.

"Whatever—" he croaked and cleared his throat. "Whatever you made, Edward, it smells amazing. Who taught you to cook?"

Edward's chest rumbled in delight as Mark's fingers ran over the knobs of his spine. "Um, my sisters. Mum worked full-time in an accounting firm, so we... ugh, that's good... we took turns getting dinner ready. My sister Paula is the eldest by a couple of years, then me, then Connie, then Grace. Sarah... well, you know about Sarah. We all did our bit, and Mum never stood for any easy pre-made pack-aged cheating. We were expected to dish up the real deal— Oh God... right there." He rolled his head forward so Mark could work his thumb deeper. "Yeah. Fuck, that feels soooo good."

Christ on a cracker. Beads of sweat popped on Mark's brow that he was damn sure had nothing to do with any exertion on his part, not unless it involved biting his tongue and trying to ignore the terminal arousal bubbling in his briefs.

"I wasn't a natural in the kitchen, but now I really enjoy it."

More groans.

"To the left and down a bi—there, yes! Holy shit, your hands are good." Edward bent further forward, which only served to push his arse more snugly into Mark's balls and... stuff. Rigid-to-the-point-of-detonation stuff.

"Are you guys close?" The words squeezed their way through Mark's clenched teeth as he tried to wiggle back even further, only to have Edward follow to fill the gap until Mark was wedged solidly between the arm of the couch and Edward's arse with nowhere to go... but up in flames, it seemed.

His fingers must have snagged a sore spot low on Edward's neck, because the next thing he knew Edward tipped his head sideways to expose a lengthy, full curve from ear to shoulder, and Mark almost drooled. He couldn't shift his gaze from that long slope of pale skin, and before he could stop himself, his lips were pressed against it.

Edward froze mid-groan but didn't move, and Mark considered his options. Retreat or advance? The answer came when Edward leaned back and tilted his head even further, providing him easier access.

Mark smiled against Edward's shoulder and pressed another kiss in place. Then he put his lips to the man's ear. "Just breathe, Edward. I'm going nowhere without you on board. But I was thinking"—he shifted more upright to ease the stinging stretch on his ribs—"that maybe you wouldn't be averse to shifting gears a little between us... on a trial basis—a dummy run, so to speak."

Edward let his head fall back so it rested on Mark's shoulder, putting those full lips almost within Mark's reach.

"Is that so, Detective? 'Cause I'm thinking I might be the dummy in that scenario."

"Shh." Mark nibbled on Edward's earlobe and a shiver ran through the other man. He couldn't help but smile to himself. So now he was someone who nuzzled... *WTF.* "I know the rules." Mark blew softly into Edward's ear, which earned him a strained purr and a wriggling butt.

"Um—oh God—so you're saying... what, exactly?"

"Yes." Mark nuzzled in again, drawing the tiny soft nub of ear fully into his mouth to suck on it. "I'm saying yes, Edward. I want to give this a try."

Edward lifted up and spun to face Mark. "You're kidding." He put his hand to Mark's brow. "No fever... that I can tell." He grabbed Mark's wrist and counted out loud. "Pulse is fine, but I'm not ruling out a blood clot with all that bruising—"

Mark laughed. "It's like you have no faith in me."

Edward stared without answering, and Mark felt that heat in his face... again.

"Okay, so maybe that's almost fair, but I'm trying to be serious here."

Edward gave a half grin. "I'm sorry. But you did say you wanted to give this a try, so forgive me for needing a little clarification on exactly what *this* means before we... you know."

"Mmm," Mark hummed. "I like the sound of a bit of... 'you know.'" He pressed a kiss to Edward's nose, which made him jerk back in shock. Mark knew it was shock by the sound of the man's jaw hitting the floor at roughly the same time. It was so adorable he wanted to try it again, but something in Edward's wary gaze held him back. Okay, admittedly he wasn't a sure bet in most people's eyes, and Edward deserved a little detail.

"You wound me, Edward," he said. "Suspicious much? But yes, I understand your reservations, so to answer your question, *this* refers to us, you and me... doing things together. All sorts of things."

Edward cocked a brow. "Sex, you mean?"

Mark huffed. "Not *just* sex. Other stuff too. Talking, maybe... walking the dog, that's always good... and I'm not averse to a little board game activity, or movie nights... so, um, in general..."

"Dating?" Edward failed to hide his amusement. "I think the term you're looking for is dating."

"Um..." Oh God, the word ran through Mark's chest like a porcupine with its quills flat—all nice and slippery going in, but he just fucking knew that shit was gonna dig in and have all sorts of painful expectations that he wasn't going to be able to meet, then hurt like hell on the way back out.

Back out? Okay, maybe Mark was a little short on the whole trust and longevity thing still. But for some reason, for the first time, he wasn't gonna run from it either. *So, hey, how about that?* All grown up and shit. Josh was gonna piss himself laughing... once he picked himself up off the floor.

"You didn't hide that look of panicked horror as well as you thought you did." Edward chuckled. "Can you even say the word out loud?"

Mark's chin jutted a little. "Of course I can. Dating... there you go, easy."

Edward rolled his eyes. "Once more without crossing your fingers behind your back, laying down a ring of salt, and invoking a mental prayer for protection."

He wasn't far off. "I didn't... Oh, shut up. Yes, I'm scared. But so are you, Edward, don't pretend you're not. And yes, I'll probably be so crap at this you'll send me packing in a week, but I still want to try. Please don't analyse this to death. I don't have all the answers. I just like you, Edward. I like spending time with you, as frustrating as this stupid hideaway situation is. And the fact that you're hot as fuck doesn't hurt things either—"

Edward arched a brow, and Mark held up a hand.

"—but it's not the sole reason, as I've said, or even... and I can't believe I'm actually saying this... the main reason."

Edward was struggling, and failing, to keep a straight face. "I don't expect you to use the *word*, Mark. I'm happy with the whole trial idea. But regardless of what we call it, you're saying we're exclusive, right? Trial or no trial. That's non-negotiable, because we're so far past the first meet-and-greet, get-to-know-you thing, it's dust in our rear view mirrors. This is next-level stuff, for me at least. And I know that's never been you, Mark, so feel free to turn it down on that alone. I won't hold it against you, and we'll stay friends. It's a hard limit to protect *my* heart, and I'll understand if you walk away."

And you should walk away, a tediously familiar voice rattled in Mark's brain, accompanied by all the usual anxiety and panic. Instead he kept his gaze steady on the other man. "I knew that was the deal, Edward. So, yes, exclusive, but because I want that as well."

Edward's eyes grew wide and glanced up at the ceiling. "Just checking for lightning bolts and maybe airborne porcine."

Mark snorted. "Everyone's a comedian. So, now that I've initialled all the relevant clauses, can we get back to the whole kissing thing? Because, correct me if I'm wrong, but I've heard that kind of goes along with the whole *dating* thing—there, I said it again—and it seems I'm a bit of a fan. Shocker, I know."

And it *was* a shocker, not least of all to Mark, who tried hard not to confuse his hookups with that kind of intimacy, and who, to be honest, had never entirely understood the appeal beyond paving the way to the more interesting stuff... until recently. But tracking his gaze down to Edward's lips right then, *hell, yeah*, he was all over that kissing gig like white on rice. Lips, sure, but he was equally keen to get up close and personal with the rest of Edward's skin, in every geographical location.

"One last thing."

Mark failed to stop the groan that slid from his lips. "Really, Edward? At this rate I'm gonna be grey and fucking wrinkled before I even get to taste you. If I'm honest, right now you're not exactly selling the whole concept of dating. I need to taste you, I need to have my tongue down your throat and your legs wrapped around me—well, maybe hold off on the legs thing, injured ribs and all. I just want *you*, Edward, any fucking way I can get you."

Edward's pupils grew black, leaving just a ring of blue-grey at the margins. He was just as keyed up as Mark, a reassurance Mark hadn't realised he needed until then. But he also still had his hand on Mark's chest.

"I want to know what *you* need from *me*. I don't want to be the one calling the shots. Newsflash: relationships are about partnership.

You're scared, I'm scared. You're giving me exclusive focus to help my... issues. What do you need?"

Shit. It was a damn good question. Not that Mark was into a transactional quid pro quo, but Edward had a point. Neither of them was... *easy.* And then it was right there on the tip of his tongue.

"Honesty. That's all. Call it what it is, Edward. Let me know when I screw up, cause I will. Jeff stockpiled resentment for a long time before he let me know what was wrong, and I'm shit at reading people's minds—whereas I think you're probably pretty good. Just keep your expectations low."

Edward's expression went soft, thoughtful. He shuffled on to his knees and moved to straddle Mark's hips, settling himself slowly on Mark's lap while sliding his fingers gingerly over his battered ribs.

"This okay?"

Mark nodded. "Just don't expect anything vigorous, horizontal or otherwise. And please don't judge me by these early efforts. I'm... not at my best." He brought Edward's hand to his mouth and pressed a kiss lightly on the back.

"I'm not judging you at all." Edward leaned forward, careful of Mark's chest, and slid a teasing tongue along his jaw. Mark was pretty sure he purred, and Edward sat back with a satisfied grin. "And don't sell yourself short. You constantly surprise me, and I wouldn't have opened up to this chance with you if I wasn't pretty damn sure you were worth the gamble. You're a sexy, kind, generous, admirable man, Mark Knight, and it will be a privilege to *date* you."

Oh. Mark tried to breathe around the sudden well of emotion lodged deep in his throat. And he couldn't be sure, but there was a good chance his eyes were about to leak. *Fuck.* He fisted the front of Edward's Neutral Milk Hotel T-shirt and pulled him back down, his other hand cradling the man's jaw to keep that mouth just where he wanted it. Then he covered those delicious lips with his own before Edward could notice anything was wrong.

It started gentle, as far as making out went, nothing hot and harried, nothing even as breathless as that kiss at the kitchen sink, but it didn't matter. Once their lips locked, Mark was lost in everything Edward Newton, the man's unique flavour rolling like sunshine over his tongue. Spicy notes from the pasta sauce, the tang of hops, the edge of sweetness from who the hell knew what, all aligned with the sensual roll of his body straddling Mark's hips, the feel of him in Mark's arms, the muted sounds of delight that passed between their lips. It was magic.

Every movement, every touch drew Mark deeper. It was erotic, and exhilarating, and honest-to-God bone-chilling terrifying, but he rolled with it, choosing to believe he was safe with this man. No one had ever pulled at Mark the way Edward tugged at his senses, the way he left Mark breathless to get his hands on all that pale, soft skin, desperate to run his fingers through the smattering of flaxen hair he'd glimpsed on Edward's limbs and chest, and hungry to wrap those same fingers around Edward's cock, to feel the pulse of it in his palm.

Edward sat back, breathing heavily, pupils fully blown, and fumbled at Mark's belt buckle. "Off. Now."

"Let me." Mark swatted his hands away and finally got the thing undone, Edward glued to every movement. He went to slide his jeans off and paused. "Um, Edward?"

Edward's gaze jerked up. "Hmm, what? Oh, sorry." He slid off to the side and stood so Mark could wriggle his hips free. But the jeans were barely halfway down Mark's thighs when his ribs jammed against his belly. "Ow, fuck." He froze and blew a few shallow breaths. "Could you...?"

"Shit, of course." Edward tugged them the rest of the way, and Mark's cock bobbed free, looking delighted with the direction things were moving. But Edward wasn't... moving, that is. He was frozen to the spot, staring down at Mark as if he were an all-you-can-eat buffet, and Mark prayed to God he was about to follow through on at least a few of those thoughts.

"You just gonna stand there?" he asked with a smile. "Not that I don't find it sexy as hell to be almost naked while you're still fully dressed, but I've kind of been holding out for this, Edward, and you're killing me here. I need to see you."

Edward glanced up. "Oh, shit, sorry." He blushed furiously. "You're just fucking gorgeous, you do know that, right?" He reached out a hand and trailed it up Mark's thigh, bypassing his cock to cradle his hip. "I never let myself imagine this. I just never thought you'd... I've never had... other than in my fantasies... I just... fuck, you're beautiful."

Mark shuddered with an emotion he couldn't name. "Ah, Edward?"

"Mmm?"

"Clothes, Edward. Now."

The blush deepened. "Oh, right." Edward struggled out of his clothes, leaving them in a pile on the floor, while Mark shifted down a little further till his ribs stopped protesting. "You sure you're not too sore?" Edward's brow dipped in concern. Mark's shirt had pushed up enough to give Edward a glimpse of some spectacular bruising painted over Mark's ribs.

"Don't even," Mark warned. "I'll be fine as long as we don't get carried away. But what about your head? You sure an orgasm is a safe destination for that brain of yours?"

Edward scowled, and it was so damn endearing Mark almost laughed out loud.

"I'm sure there are a million journal articles that would agree with you," he said. "But I'm willing to take the risk if you are. I'm pretty damn positive it's a million light years too late already to avoid the associated raised intracranial pressure, but as long as I avoid any head-down scenario, an orgasm will likely be therapeutic in lowering it."

Mark chuckled. "Oh God, I love it when you talk dirty."

Edward sent him a filthy smile and climbed on board. "And don't think I don't realise that it's me who's now naked while you still have your shirt on. So let me just help you roll that sucker right out of the way."

"Yes, sir." Mark saluted and did as asked, and then Edward set about getting their groins aligned. He leaned over to cage Mark in, careful to keep his weight on his elbows, and brought their cocks into direct nestling territory. And at the first brush of skin on skin, a groan escaped Edward's lips that sent Mark's arousal rocketing.

"Holy shit, you feel good."

"Likewise." Mark wrapped both hands around Edward's arse and directed the grind where he needed it, while Edward found Mark's lips and invited himself in, tongue-fucking him in time with the grind. If it hadn't been for the odd twinge in Mark's ribs keeping things real, he was pretty sure he'd have embarrassed himself and unloaded between them in a flat second. As it was, he didn't think it was gonna take much longer. And by the sounds Edward was making, he likely wouldn't be alone in that.

"I'm close." Edward sat upright and wrapped his hand around both their cocks. Mark added his for good measure, unable to drag his eyes from the sight of Edward jerking them off together, head thrown back, eyes closed, mouth open, grunting and swearing as he rode them to the finish with complete abandon. Every preconceived idea he'd ever had about how buttoned up and repressed Edward might be flew straight out the fucking window. Edward Newton unleashed was a sight to behold, and Mark didn't think he'd ever seen anything sexier.

Edward's eyes sprang open and zeroed in on Mark. "Now."

And *holy shit*. Two more strokes and Mark arched up and was gone, flying undone in waves of pleasure at the other man's hands. Seconds later, Edward joined him, his grunt of release the only warning before his come spilled between them, splashing up on to Mark's chin and chest and mingling with his own.

Edward stroked them slowly through the high until Mark squeezed his hand to stop, and Edward slumped forward on his hands, his face hovering just above Mark's, sweat slick on his forehead. Mark draped an arm over Edward's back and traced small circles there, trying to make sense of the moment: the intensity of a simple hand job that rivalled most of the sex he'd ever had, and the ridiculous connection they seemed to share.

Edward's head bobbed as he caught his breath, those floppy locks of blond hair dragging through their spill—an image which would remain seared in Mark's brain with enough attached spank-bank material to last a lifetime.

Another soft grunt, and Edward lifted his flushed face to catch Mark's gaze. With their eyes locked, he licked a swathe through their come before feeding it directly into Mark's mouth. A whimper may or may not have passed Mark's lips as he wrapped a hand around Edward's neck to hold him in place while he delved into the taste.

Then he shuffled sideways so Edward could curl up in the crook of his good arm, and they made out quietly. Soft touches, gentle kisses, sweet sounds, intimacy by the fucking barrel, leaving Mark almost more shattered than the explosive sex. All that, and they hadn't even made it to a bed, or past a hand job. He had no idea what to make of the jumble of emotions filling his head, only that he didn't want it to stop—and wasn't that a fucking miracle?

A pair of mournful eyes appeared over Edward's shoulder and stared at him accusingly. Tink. *Shit.* "Um, Edward? I think your girl might have an issue with us... you know. She's looking at me like she just caught you cheating on her."

Edward rolled back far enough to catch a wet tongue across his cheek. He elbowed Tink back and scruffed her neck. "Nah, she just picks up on the... ah, smell and the... energy. She'll get used to you. We both will." He flipped Mark an insolent smile.

Cheeky bugger. Mark loosened his grip for just a second, and Edward flailed, teetering on the edge of the couch, until he gripped him tight again. "You wanna rephrase that?" He tipped Edward's chin up for the briefest of kisses.

"Maybe." Edward nipped his top lip. "Though I have a feeling it's gonna be more about you getting used to us and this whole... thing."

He wasn't wrong.

"So..." Edward slid off the couch and stood cock to eye with Mark —a temptation Mark had no intention of ignoring.

"Now, that's a sight that I'm looking forward to getting used to," he said wrapping a hand around and giving it a couple of gentle tugs.

"Behave." Edward backed just out of reach and held out his hand. "Here, come on. The others won't be long, and I don't know about you, but I'd rather not greet them smelling of... us." He blushed prettily.

Oh. Right.

Showering with a guy wasn't something Mark had indulged in since... well, since Jeff, and the flash of anxiety made no sense considering he and Edward were... whatever they were. So showering could be a thing now, right? But still... "Nah, you go ahead."

Edward arched a brow. "Stop it."

Mark tugged at his T-shirt. "Stop what?"

"Stop whatever it is you're telling yourself in that pretty little head of yours and take my hand. I want you to shower with me."

Mark scowled. "Bossy fucker." But he did as he was told and pushed up off the couch with a grimace. Okay, maybe orgasms and a cracked rib weren't a match made in heaven, but he could live with it.

Edward leaned in for a soft kiss. "Right, now we're gonna shower together, and you're gonna let me wash you... thoroughly." He waggled his eyebrows. "And then you're gonna let me dry you and look at those ribs again—"

"I don't need help to—"

"Shh." He put a finger to Mark's lips. "This isn't up for debate. You're gonna let me take care of you, understand? You're gonna let me in, Mark. That's what this is about, yeah? That's what this means. It's important. And I'm gonna do the same. I'm gonna let you in, God help me. Okay?"

Oh. They stared at each other for a minute while Mark digested that. *Take care of each other.* Right. Like that wasn't a whole bag of snakes to get his head around. Tension pulled at the muscles of his neck, choking the balled-up breath in his lungs, memories crashing through his head.

I can't make it to your game—graduation, birthday, prize-giving—Mark. Your father needs me. Your mother needs me. We take care of each other—we love each other—you understand that, right? It's not all about you. You'll understand when you grow up. You'll be fine on your own. Don't make a fuss.

But he hadn't been, fine, not really. And nothing had *ever* been just about him, ever: that was the problem. He'd been—*fuck*, he'd been *so* damn lonely. But he'd survived, learned to be tough, become good at his job, and developed a wide circle of friends who laughed at his jokes and found him fun to be with. He was attractive, no use pretending he didn't know it, and he'd used that and his natural gift of the gab to ensure a parade of men slid in and out of his bed with barely a second glance.

But being cared for? Being a *priority* in someone's life? *Jesus.* He didn't even know what that meant. Mark knew Josh loved him, but that was different. Josh also had Michael now, and Mark understood the difference. He'd watched the two of them—and watched them with Sasha, and the other children. He'd felt that tug of envy, but also the lingering sting of fear that lay beneath it.

He didn't know that kind of love, the kind that set you free, that encompassed kids and didn't exclude them. Michael had merged into Josh and Sasha's inner circle like he was made for it, and the circle was still growing. Not that the two men hadn't had their problems, but a lack of love had never been one of them. And Mark realised he wanted to know what that felt like.

Jeff had done his very best to care for Mark, but Mark hadn't let the man anywhere near that hollow part deep inside, that box of nothing. Jeff would run him a bath, and Mark would empty the bath and take a shower. Jeff would cook him a special meal, and Mark would be late home. He'd want to plan a holiday and Mark wouldn't like any of the destinations. Date night and Mark needed to work —*shit, shit, shit.* As for discussing being in an open relationship? Yeah, about that. For Mark it had been a hard limit, and he'd presented it as make or break. But he could have discussed it more openly. Mark had, in fact, been a bastard.

The couch dipped alongside him, and Mark became aware of Edward's arm around his waist. Nothing more, just sitting there, holding him, caring for him as promised.

So, yeah, Edward. Serious, beautiful, honest, and super-smart Edward promising to look after Mark—wanting to wash him, for fuck's sake. No one had *ever* washed Mark since he'd been a baby. He'd fucked in a shower, but never been washed in one. And what did that say about him? What could he possibly have to offer this sweet man? Would he screw this up too? He was so screwed in the head, but God, he wanted this... thing with Edward, almost more than he wanted to breathe. So he would try—try to deserve this man.

Fingers played up his back and pulled his head down to Edward's shoulder, holding him in place. A kiss landed in his hair, and Mark's hand found Edward's thigh and rested there.

Edward felt safe in a way Jeff never had, something Mark had been aware of from their first meeting. Maybe it was because Mark had matured; maybe it was the quiet, self-contained manner Edward had. He didn't seem to want to change Mark, just said what he needed and then left it for Mark to decide if he was in. Mark could rip out his heart and pass it to Edward knowing it was in safe hands. It was a chance at a different life, and Mark hadn't had a chance like that in a long, long time. Men like Edward Newton didn't come along every day. Mark just prayed he didn't hurt the guy.

Tears pricked at his eyes as Edward's hand caressed his cheek. No words, just reminding Mark he was there. And when he finally met Edward's gaze, he almost came undone at the tender concern he saw there.

But Edward didn't speak that concern. He waited on Mark, brow furrowed: patient, quiet, still, giving Mark space to... feel. To choose. And suddenly the tightness in Mark's throat eased and he could breathe again. Edward wasn't going to force him. Edward was an open door, not a locked room. Edward knew about space. Edward wasn't his mother, or his father, or Jeff, and Mark had a chance to do things differently, if he wanted.

And he did. "I'm sorry."

Edward's mouth quirked up. "Having a moment?"

Mark snorted. "You might say that." He wanted to tell Edward, but his brain was running circles in his head. Later.

"So, how about that shower, then?" Edward tugged on Mark's hand, but he resisted.

"You don't want to know why I freaked out?"

Edward's gaze remained steady. "You ready to tell me?"

Yes. No. Fucking hell.

Edward shrugged. "Then tell me when you are. When I said we're gonna let each other in, I didn't mean it's show-and-tell. You get to share your secrets when you're ready, not on my timetable—and vice versa. I get the feeling that's something we both need. And right now I want to shower with you because... well, shit, you're sexy as hell for a start."

Mark bit back a smile.

"But also, I think it's a trust thing, right? Being together, intimate but not sexual—well, not entirely sexual, because hey, wet naked dicks"—he grinned widely—"but not having to share words, right? Just... together. It has power, like a hug or a kiss. It's funny how those things so often strip us bare, way more than fucking." He leaned in close. "Remember, I'm scared too, Mark. But in the meantime, I'm kind of anxious to get my soapy hands on you." He stood and held out his hand.

Mark's cock twitched.

Edward noticed and chuckled. "Not to mention I'm standing here as aforementioned, naked." He spread his arms allowing Mark to drink his fill from top to gorgeous toe. "Just saying."

"Oh, believe me, it hadn't gone unnoticed." Mark stood and drew Edward close to press a run of kisses down his neck. Edward melted against him with a soft hum. "And who the hell says aforementioned?" Mark burrowed his mouth into Edward's hair. "Have I told you how sexy I find all those big words of yours?" He pressed their groins together, and hello, naked dicks, just as promised.

Edward pushed him away. "You're an idiot."

"That may be, but not enough to forget you promised me a shower, and soap, and hands, and... stuff. That is if that dinner of yours can wait?"

Edward eyed him dubiously. "It can wait." He turned the oven off then took Mark's hand and pulled him towards the bathroom. "But it'll be less *stuff* and more soap, Detective. The rest depends on whether you're a good boy or not."

Mark ran his free hand down those miles of creamy skin on Edward's back, patting his firm arse and making him shiver. "Oh, trust me, Doctor, I can be a very, very good boy."

Edward groaned. "That's just what I was afraid of."

CHAPTER SEVENTEEN

As they dried themselves after, Edward mulled over the sudden change his personal life had seen in the space of a few hours. A bit of soap, a little warm water, and a second round of hand jobs had helped Mark find space enough to finally share what had got him so worked up. Sitting on the shower's large tiled bench—and Edward didn't even want to think about how much action that bench had seen—Mark had scooted back against Edward's chest and started talking, shocking the hell out of Edward, who'd stayed as still as possible so as not to risk shutting him down.

Mark had talked about growing up with parents who saw him more as a nice picture to hang on their wall and talk about with friends as opposed to a living, breathing son who craved their attention for more than just a plate of food, or school fees, or clothes on his back.

Edward didn't get it. If you so badly didn't want kids, then you did something about it, permanently. You didn't risk a slip-up and then make your child pay for your selfish disinterest for the rest of his life. No wonder Mark had run a mile from relationships. If that was the model of couple-love he grew up with—suffocating, selfish, and ring-fenced, even from your own child—Edward wouldn't have wanted a bar of it either. The question was, could he show Mark a better example before he ran screaming for the hills once again? He was going to have to, or this whole venture they'd started would die a premature death.

But family, and trust, and having each other's backs? Those were things Edward knew to his core. As for a parent's love, he'd had that in spades—they all had. And he had enough of all the above to share. He just needed to convince Mark to accept it.

He couldn't pretend he wasn't excited as all hell that Mark even wanted to try being together. Edward's open door had been more of a Hail Mary pass. Maybe even an attempt to get Mark off his back so Edward could breathe. Either way, it had done the trick. It was like lifting the lid off a pressure cooker, even if Edward had been pretty sure the notion would be a bust. In the end, it hadn't. Mark actually wanted to try, and now Edward wanted more than he'd ever allowed himself to think about. A lot more.

Yes, he could get hurt. But for the first time in a long while, Edward had a man he thought was worth it, and that meant something. It meant everything. Grace would be so fucking proud of him.

Shit. He owed her a call. He didn't want to worry her, but Edward had learned enough from losing Sarah to know you didn't second-guess the opportunity to touch base when the future was uncertain. She'd be circumspect with the rest of the family, but Edward wanted her, at least, to know. He wrapped the towel around his waist and ducked into the bedroom with his phone, leaving Mark to finish drying.

Grace answered almost immediately, and he didn't waste any time bringing her up to speed. She was shocked and frightened for him, but she held it together, that gritty lawyer side coming to the fore. After a million questions, most of which Edward couldn't answer, she gave up the third degree and an uneasy calm fell between them.

"I, um... might have taken your advice," Edward finally

confessed. Grace would read it for the change of topic it was, but she said nothing, and he loved her for it.

Instead she chuckled. "Oh, and which piece of sterling advice would that be? I've given you so many over the years."

It was true, but still he snorted. "About that man I was telling you about."

A soft gasp came from the other end of the phone. "Oh, the detective? Really? Do tell."

He laughed. "There's not much to tell yet, but we're, um... seeing each other."

Two beats of silence. "Holy crap, Edward. That's huge!"

"Jesus Christ, Grace, you make it sound like I was a frickin' lost cause—"

"You were."

"Shut up. Just... please don't go telling everyone. It's brand new. I just wanted you to know... in case..."

"No. There will be no 'in case' scenarios. You understand me, Edward? You will get through this. They will find and arrest whoever needs it, and you will bring that miracle man down here so your sisters can scare the living daylights out of him, got it?"

And they would. Holy crap, what had he done? "All right, but give us time, okay? We both have... issues."

"Shocker." She laughed, and Edward joined in.

"Look I gotta go," he finally said. "We're expecting some investigators any minute."

"Okay, but Edward?"

He waited.

"This man? This is good. This is grown up and so fucking deserved. You deserve to be happy. Whether or not he deserves you is yet to be seen. But goddamn, I'm happy for you. And... I love you, big brother." Her voice broke, and Edward's heart nearly went with it. "Be careful."

"I will. And I love you too."

They'd barely gotten dressed when Liam and Josh arrived at the front door with Paris at their heels. Tink hauled arse out of the bedroom lickety-split, dragging the decidedly grubby white duvet behind her. *Goddammit.* As the two dogs came nose-to-arse for a canine meet-and-greet, Edward whipped the duvet away and threw it back in the bedroom.

Josh cracked up laughing. "Holy shit. Cam's gonna blow a gasket, you do realise that."

"Twenty bucks if you keep it to yourselves till we can replace it," Mark pleaded.

"Hell, no. This is way too good. This is Cam we're talking about here. You know that man is more particular about his thread count than just about anything else other than those silk-and-lacy bits."

Huh. Edward *really* needed to keep his mind off those images, which had morphed from Cam into Mark wearing—nope, not going there.

Jesus, what was wrong with him? He'd never been much for anything beyond straightforward sex, but now... well, a detective had to have handcuffs, right? *Ugh.* Edward had never seen the inside of a sex store or even an online catalogue. He was boringly pedestrian in his preferences. He suspected his few previous lovers would have voted him least likely to rock the kink category, ever. And yet when he thought of Mark, the man's playful energy made it feel safe... to experiment... maybe. And wow, who would have seen that one coming?

"Edward?"

He jerked his gaze up to find Mark staring at him like he'd read every dirty place Edward's mind had run to. "Sorry, I was thinking about something else."

Mark regarded him with a curious smile, and Edward was sure the words "take me now" had to be stamped in capitals on his forehead.

"No problem. I just asked if Tink would be okay outside with Paris for a bit."

"Oh, sure. It's all fenced. Here, let me." He approached

cautiously, let Paris sniff him, and gave the shepherd a gentle pat. When he opened the door, the two dogs rushed out and immediately set upon a game of chase and tag and roughhousing.

Josh watched for a bit, then shrugged. "It's good she's big enough to handle his play. He doesn't hold back."

"Neither does she," Edward answered. "Though he'd outrun her easily. She's built for distance, not speed—that is, if she ever gets off Cam's bed."

As they moved into the lounge, it was clear to Edward that their wet hair was earning them a few sideways glances, not to mention— oh God—the tapestry of scattered couch cushions still strewn on the floor. *Shit.*

Heat bloomed on his cheeks. "Damn dog." He quickly gathered the cushions and threw them back on the couch while Mark watched him with an infuriating, indulgent half smile tugging at his lips. Edward returned a pointed glare. Mark could at least help out with a bit of distraction while Edward tidied away the evidence of their... shenanigans. At least they'd remembered to pick up their discarded clothes.

Josh ran a sceptical gaze between the two of them but said nothing, thank God, and Edward disappeared into the kitchen to pull the pasta dish out of the oven before he gave in to the urge to blurt out that yes, he and Mark had gotten down and naked, and now could they all just get over that and move on. Mark might be willing to give them a go, but Edward doubted Mark wanted that particular morsel of gossip spread to his best friend and partner just yet.

Mark appeared at his side and laid a hand on his arm. "Hey, what's up? You flew out of there like you had a rocket up your arse."

Edward slid him the side-eye. "Wishful thinking."

The comment drew a choked laugh from Mark. "Holy fuck. When you commit, you really commit, don't you? Gotta say, I'm really liking this dirty side of you, Edward."

Edward grunted. "You would. And I didn't just *fly* out of there. I wanted to get this bake out so we could eat." He turned to check if anyone in the lounge was watching, but Liam and Josh were engrossed in some discussion that had their full attention.

"Liar," Mark whispered in Edward's ear.

Edward slid free of Mark's hand. "Make yourself useful and grab some plates and utensils, will you? Put them on the coffee table."

"Yes, Mum." Mark winked and did as he was asked, while Edward cut the bake into large slices ready to serve. But when he returned, Mark took the knife from Edward's hand and pulled him off to one side, out of view. Then he tipped Edward's chin up and placed a lingering kiss on his lips. The idea that Mark would kiss him and risk being found out by his friends caught Edward completely off guard, and the look on his face must have betrayed his astonishment.

Mark lifted a hand and smoothed the deep frown that had carved itself into Edward's brow. "Jesus, am I that much of an arsehole that you'd think I was gonna ask you to keep us a secret?" he asked.

Yes. Well, not the arsehole part. Ugh. He didn't get it. "I just thought—you've been..."

Mark stopped Edward with another kiss, then rested their foreheads together. "No, don't answer that, because I don't think I really want to know. We might have known each other for three months, but I'm well aware I've spent ninety nine percent of that time being that aforementioned arsehole. And can I just point out the timely use of that word there. See, I have dictionary game, too, you know."

Edward couldn't help but laugh.

"That's better." Mark nuzzled his damp hair. "God, you smell good. I'm gonna have to get some of that frou-frou shampoo Cam uses. I want you smelling like this when you come out of *my* shower."

His shower? Edward thought he must be having an out-of-body experience, because—*holy shit*—who the hell was this man?

"And, just so we're clear," Mark continued to whisper in his ear. "I have no intention of hiding us. If I'm gonna do this, I'm going the whole enchilada—"

God, this man. "But... but what if it doesn't—if we don't..."

Mark cradled Edward's face. "Then it doesn't. But at least I won't wonder if I could have done more. I wouldn't put money on me not fucking this up six ways till Sunday, but I can't just dip a toe in, Edward. If I do, I'm gonna get too nervous when it starts to get deep, and I'm gonna want to run. Overall, I think it's best if I just jump right in and try to swim."

Edward's heart squeezed, and he realised that Mark had the power to hurt him far, far more than Edward had ever imagined. It was time to buckle up and pull his big-boy pants on. "Well, if that's what you think, Detective Knight..." He looked Mark in the eyes, and the vulnerability he saw there nearly took him to his knees. "Who am I to argue? I'll follow your lead."

"Ahem..."

They spun as one to find Josh and Liam watching with unguarded amusement. *Fuck.*

"We, ah... were wondering what the holdup was." Josh smirked, his gaze travelling between them. "And looky here, now we know."

Liam laughed. "We do indeed. I guess that whole compromised-witness thing is old news. Better shut that damn stable door before it gets draughty there, Mark."

Fuck. Edward winced. This had to be Mark's worst nightmare. "It's not what you—"

"We're dating," Mark stated flatly without even the hint of a choke.

Edward's eyes bugged and his gaze jerked sideways, but far from being freaked out, Mark appeared... cool and composed. *What the hell?*

"What?" Mark regarded Edward with obvious amusement.

Edward narrowed his gaze. Mark needed to laugh it up while he could, because Edward was gonna kill him.

But Mark wasn't done messing with him yet. "Well, we *are* dating, right?" He held Edward's gaze. "And I do believe I just finished telling you that I wasn't going to hide this, us."

"Yes but—"

"You're *dating*?" Josh interrupted Edward, his bug eyes no doubt a perfect match for Edward's earlier ones, and with the added bonus of appearing as if he was about to swallow his damn tongue. "Since when... you don't... what the hell, Mark? Why didn't I know about this? Did you know about this?" he fired the last to Liam, who held his hands up in defence.

"Not exactly. Only that he's had the hots for Ed since he arrived three months ago. But to be honest, hearing the word *dating* come out of my partner's mouth? Hell, I'm inclined to buy groceries, run for the hills, and hunker down under a tinfoil hat. 'Cause that there's apocalyptic shit."

"Ah... standing right here, arseholes." Mark strode forward till he was eyeball to eyeball with his best friend, and Edward didn't realise Mark still had hold of his hand until he found himself pulled along for the ride. "I didn't tell you"—Mark's voice softened—"because it's new, brand new. And I'm not looking for any commentary, understand?"

The two eyeballed each other, and then Josh laid a hand on Mark's shoulder. "Yeah, understood. I'm just... fuck... I'm just so pleased for you, man." He peered around Mark's shoulder to where Edward stood. "Both of you."

Edward shrugged. "Thanks. As Mark said, it's, ah, still pretty new." He shot a questioning glance Mark's way, but Mark just smiled fondly. Oh, yeah, they were gonna have words about all this cutesy stuff. Edward had lost his handle on the other man, and he didn't like it. Well, he did... but he didn't.

"As in...?" Liam quirked a brow.

Mark checked his watch. "Oh, about two hours, I'd say... give or take." He pressed a kiss to Edward's cheek.

Lots and lots of words.

"Two...?" Josh's rumbling laugh rolled through the kitchen. "That is typical Mark fucking Knight, right there. Thirty-eight years of running from the very *idea* of a real relationship, and then he has a man he actually wants for all of two seconds and he's shouting it to the fucking world. It's like I don't even know you."

"Not the world," Mark cautioned. "But, yeah. I figured keeping this from you guys would be pretty much impossible and would earn me a whole world of pain, so call it self-preservation. Besides, Edward deserves to witness my enduring humiliation. It's the least I can do for all the shit I've thrown his way."

And the hits kept coming. "Can we just eat now, do you think?" Edward eyed Mark pointedly. "Is that too much to ask before I implode in a burst of mortification here?"

"Of course." Josh threaded his arm through Edward's and escorted him into the lounge. "And feel free to come to me if—no, *when* this oaf does something stupid. I have all the dirt."

Edward glanced back to find Mark laughing. "Just you wait," he mouthed silently to him, which only drew another chuckle. Mark had no idea what was coming his way when Edward got him alone.

Conversation stayed light during dinner, Josh and Liam throwing lots of good-natured teasing Mark's way, though they were careful to be more circumspect towards Edward, for which Edward was grateful. Mark's friends were also full of praise for Edward's cooking, and it felt good to be appreciated and drawn into the group. Edward had a circle of friends in Christchurch that he would meet up with on occasion, but his fairly introverted and contained lifestyle meant he didn't socialise much and rarely entertained, although he was beginning to wonder if that had been a mistake.

He was surprised to find he was enjoying himself with Josh and Liam, and their easy acceptance of him was something he could get used to. Most people considered him blunt and prickly, and kept their distance—Sandy being the exception. Maybe these men too. It felt... good, the first true sense of belonging he'd experienced since he'd moved to Auckland.

A sideways glance at Mark sitting next to him on the couch confirmed Mark was still exhibiting all the signs of being shockingly at ease with this sudden change between them. It was doing Edward's head in. He felt like he was playing catch-up with Mark's unexpected personality shift, like he'd grabbed a rattlesnake by the tail. Mark appeared disgustingly nonplussed about what should have been a terrifying leap into coupledom for him, and was busy burning all of Edward's preconceptions to toast.

Mark caught his eye and smiled, and a million butterflies took flight in Edward's chest. *Goddammit.* He could do without the twelve-year-old hormonal theatrics. But he returned the smile and couldn't help but wonder if had the same effect on Mark, hoping the flash of light in the man's eyes meant it did.

When everyone had finished eating, Josh and Liam cleared the plates and rustled up a couple of beers for themselves, while Edward saw to glasses of water for him and Mark and received a screwed-up nose for his efforts. "Suck it up. Be a good boy and you can have this pill for the pain as well." He held out a fisted hand.

"I don't need—"

"Yes, you do. You've had nothing since the one I forced into you at lunch. I know, because the bottle hasn't moved from where I put it."

They faced off for a few seconds before Mark finally held out his hand to accept the pill. "I'm not sure I like this bossy side of you," he grizzled.

"Oh, yes, you do." Edward added a wink, and Mark returned a sly smile. He sat and only then realised the others had caught the exchange.

"Well, well, well," Josh teased his best friend. "I never thought I'd see the day—"

"Shut it, Rawlins." Mark was blushing furiously. *Holy cow.* So, not quite so nonplussed, after all. Would this weirdness never end?

"Just saying." Josh turned his focus to Edward. "I like you, Edward Newton. But holy shit, I gotta tell you, these next few months are gonna be the best show in town."

"Josh," Mark warned, none too subtly.

"Okay, okay. Catch-up time. I'll get Sandy on Skype."

Once that was done, Josh led off the meeting with what he'd learned. He'd followed up on Mark's conversation with Stevens and discovered that the warrant for Morgan's files was moving slowly. The CEO's lawyer was fighting it at every turn. But the good news was that they should have employee record access by the following day, which was a step in the right direction.

The other piece of news was that Doug Morgan hadn't been at work for two days. When Stevens got there, the man's PA said Morgan was unwell and was working from home. When asked if that was unusual, the PA looked decidedly uncomfortable and answered, "a little." Interesting.

As a side note, Josh let them know the glass door in the house had been fixed and Edward's friends had been in contact with the police to confirm Edward as their house-sitter. It had been hard letting Damien and Linda know what had happened, but they'd been concerned for his safety over anything else.

Sandy listened intently but had little to add, the autopsy having shown Spencer had died of head trauma, all injuries consistent with the crash. They'd have to wait till the next day to get the full tox screen, but the initial blood alcohol levels indicated he'd had more than a few before he'd gotten behind the wheel—somewhat odd for an early Saturday morning, but then nothing about the case had proven straightforward.

Liam said, "The wife was home, and according to her, Spencer had been holed up in his study all night and morning. He'd had no visitors that she knew of, but she had no idea whether anyone had come or if he'd gone out while she was asleep. And he'd been on and off their landline since the previous afternoon—"

Edward guessed, since his phone call.

"—and yes, we've got a request in for those records. He'd also been drinking consistently. She tried to stop him leaving this morning, but he took off while she was phoning their son.

"He may have died of trauma from the crash, but there *is*

evidence of the car having been potentially run off the road. No witnesses, but there are some scratches and paint transfer that the wife didn't think were there when she drove it yesterday, so we're working on that."

"Jesus, when will we catch a break here?" Mark grumbled. "I'm sick of fucking waiting for shit to come in."

Edward rested a calming hand on Mark's thigh, and Mark grabbed on to it like a lifeline.

"Well, I do have one morsel of positive news." Liam smiled slyly. "We now know *why* Spencer tampered with the results."

Air whooshed out of Mark's chest, and he leaned forward. "Thank Christ for something. It's about time."

"Don't get too excited," Liam cautioned. "There's still lots of questions, but Spencer's wife revealed he had a gambling problem. Nothing new—he'd struggled for years but managed to keep it in check. They kept separate bank accounts, to be safe, and he gambled from an allocated budget they both agreed to. But, unknown to his wife, he'd racked up quite a nasty debt, in addition to going through most of their retirement funds which she thought he'd reinvested. The shit hit the fan last September when the debt was called in. She was pretty angry about it all."

"I bet. And that would've been just before Greene's suicide," Edward mused. "And not long after that, Spencer informed everyone about his retirement. How much did he owe?"

"Nearly three hundred thousand."

Mark whistled. "I've never heard a thing on the rumour mill about a gambling problem, or anything else for that matter. That's a lot of money, and a decent motive as well."

"Yeah. Apparently, that's why he retired so unexpectedly—for the golden handshake and the superannuation payout from the hospital. His wife said it had been enough to pay back the debt and give them a small buffer, without needing to sell the house."

"Son of a bitch."

"Yeah. According to her, Spencer started seeing a counsellor, and things seemed to be getting back to normal."

"But...?"

"But," Liam repeated. "When we checked his bank accounts, there had been no superannuation payout. He'd scrapped the contribution years ago, presumably to pay for his gambling. He'd clearly been hiding from her just how bad it was for a long time. He got a bit of a bonus and payout from the hospital, but not near enough to cover that level of debt. His account did, however, receive a deposit of around $280,000 the week after Greene's autopsy. That money was transferred out again in just over a day."

"To the bookie, or whoever he owed," Mark concluded with a nod. "And then he retired almost immediately, citing health reasons."

Liam swept his hand Mark's way. "Give the man a balloon."

"What did Spencer's wife have to say about that? I assume you told her?"

Liam winced. "Yeah. Believe me, you really don't want to know."

"What about Greene's wife," Mark pressed. "You got to interview her, right? Did she have any idea what he might have been working on, or if he knew Bridge or Spencer?"

Liam shook his head. "She didn't recognise either name. We met at Greene's house. He'd left it to her in his will along with everything else, although it's still all tied up in probate. The place had been ransacked since she'd last visited three weeks ago. The back door was jimmied, but it didn't have the feel of a robbery. Made to look like one, maybe. And it looked recent, no settled dust anywhere. Crime scene techs are there at the moment."

"No alarm?"

"No. It *did* have one, but she'd stopped payments on it after the funeral, cleared anything of value into storage and just left papers and clothes and some old furniture. Stevens is going through it all as we speak. She couldn't tell me if anything was missing, but someone had clearly been looking for something. His office was largely intact, but no computer or laptop. They'd been missing from the start. She'd mentioned it to the police, but they never found any sign of either—

and when no one suggested it wasn't anything but suicide, she dismissed it."

"Right. Was she surprised he took his life?"

"Yes and no. She said he never wanted the divorce and had still been struggling with it. And he didn't do well alone. But she *was* surprised it happened when it did—he'd seemed a bit brighter, more upbeat in those last few months."

"Exactly what Evie Bridge said about *her* husband," Mark commented. "But getting back to Spencer, can we trace that deposit?"

Liam rolled his eyes. "What do you think?"

"Shit."

"Connor's working on it. It was done through some third-party sleight-of-hand thing."

Mark grimaced. "Okay, let me know if he has any luck nailing it. Someone clearly knew about Spencer's gambling debt and bribed him to repeat those blood tests."

The room went quiet as everyone pondered the question.

"So, are you done with me then?" Sandy broke the silence. "I'll let you know about those results as soon as they're in, Liam."

"Yes, and thanks, Sandy."

Edward added his own thanks, making a mental note to treat Sandy to a meal for helping above and beyond.

"Anything for you, boss." Sandy beamed at Edward before focusing a glare Mark's way. "And don't think I didn't notice those looks you two have been exchanging. Don't make me pay you a visit, Detective. Signing off."

The screen went blank, and Mark huffed out a laugh. "I don't know why, but that guy scares the shit out of me."

Edward understood how he felt. "Sandy's good people, but don't forget he's friends with Cam. I have a feeling they're cut from the same cloth."

Mark's eyes popped. "Fuck."

Edward blew out a sigh. "Pretty much."

"The timing of the whole thing seems strange to me," Josh said. "It's clear someone knew about Spencer's gambling problem well beforehand. Then, when things went tits up in whatever they were doing with Greene and they needed his death to look like a suicide, all they had to do was shoulder-tap Spencer to fix it and pay off his debt. But not even his wife knew how bad his gambling problem was. So how did anyone else find out?"

"Whoever held the debt, maybe?" Liam turned to the sound of scratching at the front door and got to his feet to let the dogs inside. "At least it gives us a piece of the puzzle." He stood back as a very happy and exhausted Paris and Tink loped into the room.

"Down," Josh ordered, and Paris dropped in place like a stone. Tink, on the other hand, simply froze in place and regarded the shepherd as if he had lost his damn mind.

"Tink, on your mat," Edward ordered, aware every eye in the room was focused on the battle of wills.

Tink turned that same expression of disbelief on him and then made a move to the bedroom as if that were, of course, the natural place for her to settle.

"No," Edward growled. Tink paused, one leg raised.

"On your mat." Edward indicated the green woven rug by the fire. He could see the cogs whirring in Tink's brain, weighing up the pros and cons of disobeying. Then her ears dropped and she slunk to the rug. But just to make a point, she spent an inordinate amount of time circling and scratching until she was satisfied enough to drop and stretch out.

"See." Edward grinned at Josh. "Response time is all that separates them."

A grin split Josh's face from ear to ear. "Just what I was about to say."

Mark snorted. "Getting back to this being a piece of the puzzle..." He eyed Liam. "It may well be. But it's not the piece that tells us what the hell was actually going on with Greene and Bridge that warranted murder—and was worth having a go at us when we looked like we were stumbling on to it. And how does Morgan fit into all this? There's no connection between him and Spencer, is there?"

Josh answered, "None that we know of."

Mark shot to his feet and paced in front of the large glass sliders with their panoramic view to the rolling Tasman Sea. "But there has to be, right? I mean, come on. Bridge and Greene meet at Morgan's while both are on contract there. They become friendly, at least according to their workmates—"

Liam interrupted, "But Greene's wife said she'd never heard his name."

"They don't have to be bosom buddies outside of work to be friends. Plus they only formally worked together for a little over a month. *And* the couple were separated. She said herself she hadn't seen much of Greene before he died. I bet you have friends at work who never make it into your home or discussions with your wife, right?"

Liam nodded and took a swallow of his beer. "Okay, keep going."

Mark was working up a head of steam, and as he gestured, paced, and ran his fingers through his hair, Edward couldn't take his eyes off him. It was a side of Mark he'd never seen. Most of their encounters had been over a body, on the phone, or in court. This focused, ener-gised, analytic, and determined Mark was a revelation, and one Edward found sexy as hell. And the fact he was wearing a loose, soft-as-butter tank that showed off his muscular arms and gave tantalising glimpses of the solid, tanned chest lying just underneath only inflamed Edward's already incendiary interest.

The urgency in Mark's tone damped those fires a little and drew Edward back into the discussion.

He'd stopped pacing to face them all. "The two men worked the same contract together, *and* they shared a passion for renewable fuels. Greene's contract finishes before Bridge's, so he leaves—and two weeks later he's dead from suicide, a suicide we now know to be suspect. *And* whose blood results were possibly switched out by Tom Spencer within twenty-four hours of the event. *And* whose original report showed the exact same drug combo in his system as Bridge had, three months later.

"As for Bridge, *his* contract finishes and he goes AWOL doing God knows what except lying to his family, which is apparently totally out of character. He then washes up dead, seemingly tortured, three months later. Then Edward discovers an unexpected connection between them, one the bad guys must have thought they'd covered, so the archived report becomes a problem and they try to shut the connection down by getting rid of all traces of it—which includes Edward and myself at this point—and getting their hands on our files to maybe see what we know. So connect the dots for me, folks."

Edward protested, "But that doesn't make sense, because the report and the connection were never going to be able to be eliminated completely. It's still somewhere in the system as a deleted file, or in the cloud. It's just a matter of time. Besides, Liam and Kirwan knew about it, it wasn't just you and me. And they failed. The report is out there now, and there's no covering it up. Spencer's death was pointless."

Mark seemed to think on that. "So maybe they were just buying time," he said. "Or maybe Spencer was going to talk, that's why they needed him out of the way. But why would they need more time?"

Liam stood up. "I think you're on to something, though. And don't forget Bridge's son said his father was 'off' around the time Greene's suicide happened, and that he'd had their security system upgraded. Bridge had told Evie it was because a colleague had been robbed, but what if it was Greene turning up dead that really rattled him? And Greene's place was turned over. Someone was looking for something. Maybe they still don't have what they need and are hoping we can lead them to it. That's why they stole your files and the laptops."

Mark eased back down on the couch next to Edward. He leaned forward, elbows on knees, and Edward could feel his excitement at the threads coming together.

"Yes. I like where this is going," Mark said. "So Greene and Bridge meet at Morgan's, start talking, find they have common interests—renewables being one of them. And maybe they discover something in their work, or develop an idea" He waved his hand around in the air. "Whatever. Anyway, they start working on it together out of hours, but Greene dies or is killed, maybe because of what they were working on.

"But Bridge *keeps* working on it, and that's what he was doing when he was supposed to be teaching, and that's why he was tortured. They wanted something he had, something that they didn't get from Greene. The question is, did he give it to them before he died? And what the hell is important enough to warrant killing both of them, and to go to such lengths as to bribe a pathologist to alter blood samples in a coroner's case? Not to mention how they even knew about Spencer. But yeah, I'm liking this a whole lot."

"In my mind, that makes someone at Morgan's the most likely culprit," Josh offered, leaning down to scratch Paris's head.

The shepherd rolled over to stare at his handler in what could only be described as abject adoration, and Edward was sure he heard Tink's eyes roll.

Josh continued, "What if Morgan discovered what they were working on and wanted a piece of the action?"

Mark agreed. "It makes sense, but proving his company's behind whatever is going on, is gonna be a bugger without access to all their systems, including his private files. All we have are suspicions, nowhere near enough evidence to get a warrant. We need something solid."

But to Edward, there was something missing in Mark's train of thinking. "Why the lag between Greene's suicide and Bridge's death?" he asked.

A penetrating gaze turned his way. "Excellent question, Dr Newton." Mark beamed with what looked like... *oh, hell...* pride.

Edward's heart surged.

"Any ideas about that one?" Mark spread his hands wide.

Josh suggested, "Because people bought the suicide angle, and maybe they thought they'd gotten what they needed from Greene? After all, Bridge never said anything at the time. All he seems to have done is change his security. Perhaps they didn't know each other that well at a personal level?"

Liam disappeared into the kitchen. "Okay, I buy that," he said as he returned with two more beers and handed one to Josh. "Or maybe they were worried about moving on him too soon, after Greene. Attracting too much attention."

Everyone fell quiet. There were so many unanswered questions, Edward wasn't sure how they'd decide where to start. Mark was too quiet. He wore a troubled expression, and Edward knew it was driving him crazy not to be in charge of the investigation. Then he caught Edward's eye and leaned over to press a chaste kiss to Edward's cheek and... well, shit... sappy didn't begin to cover it.

Edward looked up to find Josh grinning like the cat who'd got the cream.

Liam broke the silence. "I think, first up, we need to reinterview Evie Bridge tomorrow. We've missed something."

Mark nodded, and Edward sensed he'd been letting his partner come to the same conclusion in his own time. "Agreed. And I'm coming with you."

Liam glared at his partner. "Mark, you can't be anywhere—" He broke off and sighed angrily. "Goddammit. You keep your mouth shut and let me do the talking. And you don't touch *anything*."

Mark nodded a little too enthusiastically, and Liam's scowl deepened. "You're not going to do either of those things, are you?"

Mark shook his head, adding a bat of those ridiculously long eyelashes for good measure. Edward bit back a laugh and settled for an elbow to his... *holy shit*... boyfriend's uninjured side instead.

"You better not be fucking with me," Liam grumbled. "I'll see you there at ten. And if you screw this up for me in court, Knight, I'll put in for a damn partner change, I swear it."

Another frenzy of nodding, which earned Mark a well-deserved pillow to the head. "Arsehole."

"I'll be good, I promise."

"Yeah, right. Tell it to someone who gives a shit. If I still have a job after this, it'll be a fucking miracle. My wife's gonna kill me." Liam slouched in his chair and guzzled the last of his beer.

Mark threaded his fingers through Edward's, much to Edward's surprise, and he jumped before he could stop himself. Why was he so damn nervous? He needed to get a grip, but considering he was working hard not to simply lift up on his toes and slam-dunk a kiss on Mark's lips in return, he guessed he was failing at that whole "get a grip" thing. Mark's thumb began a new round of small circles on the back of his hand, and Edward was sure his heart beat loud enough for the whole room to hear.

It was all so... unexpected. Everything: Mark, the case, the two of them, this shockingly affectionate side of a man who'd just told Edward he was going in boots and all and was ridiculously busy proving it. All less than two days since Edward had written Mark off as nothing but an annoying sexy piece of trouble that had no future in his life.

And now? Now, Edward was falling for the man like someone had gone and pushed him off a cliff—no safety net, no taking it slow, and little protection for his heart. He desperately wanted to believe in this new, improved Mark; he wanted to hope; he wanted... far, far more than he should. But most of all, he wanted to believe he'd done the right thing. He squeezed Mark's hand, earning himself a wide smile and another kiss on the cheek in reply.

Oh, crap. It no longer mattered what he wanted; the fat lady had sung, got herself an agent, and headed to the recording studio. Edward needed to get his hands on the handlebars and stop spinning his damn wheels.

He leaned over, placed a kiss on Mark's bare shoulder, and relaxed.

CHAPTER EIGHTEEN

MARK WOKE WITH A SOFT WARM EDWARD AGAINST HIS CHEST, and his feet pinned under what felt like the combined weight of a few solar systems. The latter he dealt a hefty shove that resulted in a reverberating thump and a loud, rumbling growl of disapproval. This was followed by the tread of heavy paws and a grunt from somewhere near the floor on Edward's side of the bed. Mission accomplished.

That left Edward, still wrapped safe and sound in Mark's arms and going nowhere, if Mark had anything to do with it. And wasn't that a fucking miracle—the Edward-in-his-arms bit? He pulled Edward tighter against his chest and nuzzled his hair, breathing in the scent of a man who was rapidly coming to mean a great deal to him.

"Was that my dog you just pushed off the bed?" an adorable sleepy voice came from under the mound of an increasingly grubby duvet.

Oh, yeah. Mark grinned to himself. That delicious heavy-eyed vibe warranted much closer inspection. He nudged his rapidly filling dick into the welcome heat of Edward's crease. Edward hummed and pushed back, and... mmm.

Neither had bothered with underwear following a round of spec-tacular blow jobs after Josh and Liam had left. At least this time they'd made it to the bed, although manoeuvrings had to be made, amid much hilarity, in order to accommodate Mark's recalcitrant ribs, which refused to play pain-free ball. The problem was eventually solved by a sideways sixty-nine that allowed for a fair amount of arse play by both parties—something Edward had turned out to be exceedingly good at, much to Mark's delight. A win in anyone's books.

"I can neither confirm nor deny," he answered, licking a trail up Edward's neck to his sensitive earlobe, which resulted in a full-body shudder. Mark had found Edward to be incredibly responsive to everything he tried, and the noises Edward made when Mark touched him, the writhing, the groans of appreciation, all drove Mark's arousal sky-high. Plus Edward seemed more than happy to share the lead in the bedroom, just as he did outside of it. Although the word *share* might have put too fine a point on it.

Edward's dominance had come as a surprise to Mark, especially given he'd claimed he wasn't as sexually driven as other men. Mark didn't often give up the reins, but it had become apparent that Edward didn't need to have them offered. He slid into the control seat like he belonged there, checked in to ensure Mark was on board —which, God help him, he always was—and off they went. It was unexpected, and sexy, and intoxicating, and Mark freaking loved every second of it. He'd discovered, in fact, much to his horror, that he could whine with the best of the dedicated bottom twinks who had put up with his shit and shared his bed over the years. Not that he would be advertising the fact. Nope. Nothing to see here, folks.

And if you could have explained that alarming conundrum of submissive neediness to him, he'd have been indebted. Because who the hell knew why getting Edward Newton inside his arse in all possible permutations had rocketed to the top of his to-do list. Not him. Although he expected it was the same reason he found himself wrapped around Edward like he might disappear in a puff of introverted panic at having his space shrunk by a certain Mark-sized intrusion.

The last thing Mark wanted was to suffocate Edward with his own need, to become—God help him—his parents. Especially since Edward had been very clear about how much he needed his space. But hell if Mark could seem to keep his distance either. And did space mean physical, as well as psychological? Who the hell knew? Was a rule book too damn much to ask? For an alarming few seconds, Mark wondered if this was something he should discuss with his much-more-romantically-knowledgeable   best   friend.   Maybe not. *Ugh.*

Mark pressed a series of kisses down Edward's spine which resulted in another shiver of pleasure, and Mark decided that perhaps it should be Edward he talked to. Adulting 101. *God,* this was exactly why he avoided relationships.

"I can hear you thinking from here." Edward rolled over, and... *hello,* that felt nice. Edward's perky and substantial dick nestled alongside his own. "Good morning, beautiful." Edward pressed a kiss to Mark's nose.

"And good morning to you." Mark ground in a little, earning a hum of approval.

"You're... *up* early." Edward angled his hips for another pass at Mark's cock and ran a line of kisses along his jaw and... *oh, yeah...* Mark could totally get on board with this as a great way to start the day on a regular basis.

A pair of hands cradled his face. "So, you wanna share what you were thinking about?"

Damn. His dick deflated just a little. "I want to say 'nothing'"

"And you know I'd respect that."

Mark narrowed his gaze. "I *do* know, and that's some sneaky shit right there, Mr Newton. Just like last night, before our shower. You were all, 'I won't ever push you... we both need our space... in your own time.' It's all just part of that witchy magic you wield. Because you say that, and what happens? It makes me trust you, and then I'm damn well spilling my guts before I even realise it."

Edward laughed. "Oh my God, you are so adorable."

"I'm not. I'm nothing like adorable. I'm a badarse, mean, shoot-you-rather-than-talk-to-you, motherfucking detective. What I am *not* is cuddly and sharing and needy. Yeah. Did I mention needy... and cuddly? But I can't seem to stop that shit around you. So... there."

Edward's amused expression dropped, and in its place was such warm affection and concern, Mark almost couldn't hold the other man's eyes.

Edward simply waited.

Mark pursed his lips. "You're doing it again."

A single raised brow.

Son of a bitch. "Okay. I give up," he said, wriggling under the sheet and ducking his head to eye level with Edward. "I'm, ah... worried... that I'm cramping your style. I guess. I don't know what the fuck I'm doing here, in case you hadn't noticed, and I can't lay claim to a single shred of boyfriend nous. But I know you like your space, and I don't want to overstep any lines, like... maybe you don't want this—" He loosened his arms by way of explanation. "You said you didn't need a lot of... attention... or whatever. So I need you to, um... tell me if I'm getting it wrong. I just... Fuck. I want to get this right, Edward." Jesus, could he sound more of a dork if he tried?

But Edward didn't seem to mind. A huge smile flashed across his face a half second before he crashed his mouth over Mark's and that demanding tongue plunged inside as if planting a flag—and maybe it was. Every concern Mark had was swept aside in the overwhelming sensation of Edward kissing him as if his life depended on sucking the very air from Mark's lungs. Then Edward rolled him to his back and straddled Mark's thighs, carefully avoiding his ribs. He cradled Mark's face and leaned forward till they were only a breath apart.

"I love that you're worried," he murmured, his thumb moving in small circles on Mark's cheek.

Mark snorted. "Really? I'm glad someone is."

"Mmm-hmm." Edward's eyes roamed Mark's face. "It means you're taking this seriously."

Mark frowned. What the hell was Edward talking about? "Of course I'm bloody taking it seriously. You think I haven't run from something like this for... oh, let me see... my whole damn life just to suddenly say, 'Hey, you know what, I was wrong all along. I'm gonna go and get myself a boyfriend' and not be freaking out"

"Shh." Edward pressed a kiss to his lips. "I didn't mean it that way. I know this is a big thing for you. What I mean is, it tells me that I'm important to you." His gaze flickered for a second. "That I matter. And I kind of like that. A whole fucking lot, if I'm honest. Maybe too much."

Oh.

He ground down with a teasing smile, and stars sparked behind Mark's eyes.

"Does that make you nervous?" There was a cautious note to Edward's words that belied the casual tone.

Did it? Mark thought it probably should, but for some reason that familiar flight of panic wasn't happening in his chest, at least not about Edward's feelings. As to Mark's ability to screw the whole thing up? Well, that was another story.

"No, it doesn't make me nervous."

Edward arched a disbelieving brow.

"Well, not in the way you probably think." He left it at that. No need to dig that hole any deeper.

Edward studied him for a second as if deciding whether to press, but didn't. Thank Christ.

"I'll take that as a positive sign, then," he said, wriggling off Mark but keeping a leg casually slung over Mark's hips. "And to answer your question, no, I'm not feeling... cramped. I love this side of you. It's been totally unexpected, and I won't say I'm not still adjusting, but it's also been really kind of wonderful, and... cute—"

"Oh God," Mark groaned. "Don't even go there."

"Hey, I happen to like cute, and cuddly, and... adorable." He kissed Mark's shoulder. "So you better get used to it."

Mark was gonna have to hand his man card in at this rate. "Okay, but can we just, I don't know, keep that shit between us? I don't need to give Josh or Cam any more ammunition."

Edward saluted. "I promise."

"Besides," Mark teased with a wicked smile, "I suspect I was born with a limited supply of romantic drivel to call on. I'm already running on fumes—ow."

Edward licked over the fresh bite mark on Mark's shoulder. "You were saying?"

"Nothing," Mark muttered. "I was saying nothing."

"Good. Then you better get in that shower, or Liam will get to Bridge's place before us."

Mark narrowed his eyes. "Us? There is no us, not this morning."

"Don't be ridiculous." Edward rolled out of bed, nearly tripping over Tink in the process. The mastiff grumbled but didn't move. "If you think I'm staying here, you've got a screw loose in that pretty little head of yours."

"No." Mark intercepted Edward before he stalked out of the room, putting a restraining hand on his arm. "It's safer here." It damn well was. And Mark didn't care how stupid it sounded, he didn't want Edward stepping a foot closer to any danger. So fucking sue him.

Edward's expression closed like a goddamn vault, his gaze moving slowly from where Mark's hand held tight to his arm, all the way back up to Mark's face. "I thought you didn't want to let me out of your sight, *Detective,* or at least that's what you told your boss. And you know that little discussion we just had, about space? Cuddling gets a free pass. This"—he glanced back down at Mark's hand on his arm—"doesn't."

Shit. Mark dropped his hand instantly. "I don't want to... I just..." he said, flustered. "Aw, fuck."

Edward stepped in and his gaze softened. "You care. I know you do. You want to keep me safe—I know that too. I want the same for you. But I'm coming with you, Mark. This is how it's done."

Mark could refuse, he knew that. He could pull rank and exclude Edward from what was an official interview, not that Mark belonged there either. But he got that this was some kind of test between them. And okay, Mark could get on board with that, even if he didn't like it. Edward didn't need to be coddled.

"Okay, we go together," he choked out.

"Pleased to hear it." Edward flashed him a wicked smirk.

Mark huffed in defeat. "Fuck, you're gonna be trouble, aren't you?"

Edward beamed. "Like you didn't know that already."

"But you'll stay in the car at Bridge's, right?"

"No."

Mark shrugged. "Had to ask."

Edward patted his hand. "Of course you did. But I *can* be of help, Mark, and you know it."

There was no point arguing. Edward was as stubborn as Mark. "All right, but we are going to have words when this is over, Edward. Long, multisyllabic words."

Edward patted Mark's cheek. "Oh, I'm counting on it."

Mark didn't grin, not even a flicker. "But you *will* stay next to me like you're glued there, understand? Because whoever is behind this might also be keeping an eye on the Bridge's house—in fact, I'd count on it."

It would be fair to say Edward hadn't thought of that, judging by the spark of alarm that crossed his face. Call him petty, but the knowledge offered Mark a degree of satisfaction.

"Agreed," Edward replied, a little more conciliatory. "And I promise I won't take any chances. So, shall we?" He waved for Mark to go ahead to the bathroom.

Mark complied but then stuck his head back out. "Oh, and one more thing."

Edward sighed. "What?"

"I believe today calls for the Wolverine briefs." He caught the flame in Edward's cheeks and ducked into the bathroom before Edward could reach him.

Edward banged on the door nonetheless. "How did you know—open this—Goddammit, have you been looking in my bag?"

Mark grinned and set the shower running to block Edward's efforts to be heard, but before he slid under the steaming water he opened the bathroom door just a crack and poked his head out. Edward was halfway down the hall to the kitchen and spun at Mark's whistle.

"Ramon. Edward Ramon Newton."

Edward blinked slowly. "What the hell? No, it's not fucking Ramon. What is wrong—"

Mark lost the rest when he closed the door. *Oh, yeah.* He grinned. This was gonna be fun.

Evie Bridge invited them in with an expectant air, likely hoping for some news on her husband's killer. If she was confused about Edward's presence when Mark introduced him as the pathologist attached to her husband's case, she never said anything, and for that Mark was grateful. As it was, Edward was making it plain just how unhappy he was about the whole thing, firing Mark any number of filthy looks.

And okay, Mark probably deserved every one of them. Liam had texted he could be twenty to thirty minutes late, and Mark had refused to wait in the car twiddling his thumbs. Edward had fought tooth and nail against the decision, but Mark wanted to get in and get some answers. And now Edward's gaze kept darting around the lounge like he expected to be arrested at any moment.

Mark might even have felt a bit bad about that, but he had tried to stop Edward from coming in the first place. Now, as they waited for Evie and her son to bring the coffee, he glanced over and, yep, another glare of disapproval. Opting for silence as the safest option, Mark knew a reckoning would come later. Nothing was surer.

The home had a heavy, grey dullness about it that had nothing to do with its admittedly conservative, shades-of-tan-and-cream décor and everything to do with deep grief and mourning over the death of the man who featured in the swathe of photos strewn across the coffee table. Rowan's family had clearly been reminiscing when they'd arrived, the images drawing Mark's eye like an accusing finger.

Evie and Finn returned, laden with biscuits and coffee, and Mark let them eat and drink in silence for a moment. Then he took a big mental breath and bluntly broke the news that Rowan had not, in fact, been working for Waikato University when he was killed. The information dropped in the room like a bomb, levelling everything in its path. The gobsmacked look on both Evie's and Finn's faces and the anguished way she locked hands with her son made it crystal clear neither knew anything about Rowan's secret life.

With the revelation, Mark saw the wheels of doubt begin to turn in Evie's mind. What *had* her husband been up to? Where had he been? Was he having an affair? Was everything she thought she knew about him a lie? It cut at Mark's heart to see their trust in a husband and father blown apart—memories threatened—and he hated, hated to be a part of it. But there was no other way to get at the truth.

Now that he was sure they hadn't been hiding anything, he tried to reframe it in more palatable terms, away from the possibility of infidelity and more towards the idea of some project he might have been hiding from them. They grabbed on to that for all they were worth, and he didn't blame them one bit. But before he could take the questioning further, a knock at the front door sent his conscience running for cover.

Finn left to answer, and seconds later Mark heard his partner's voice in the hall. Footsteps headed their way and he took a deep breath. This wasn't going to be pretty.

"Started without me, I see." Liam's words sounded offhand, but there was nothing remotely accommodating in his expression as he rounded the corner into the lounge and pinned Mark with a glare acid enough to strip the meat from Mark's bones.

"Ah, Detective. More coffee?" Evie stood, seemingly oblivious to the tension in the room.

"Yes, thank you," Liam answered, his steely gaze still fixed on Mark.

Finn, who clearly *wasn't* oblivious to the icy vibes Liam was sending Mark's way, all but scooted after his mother as quick as he could.

The minute they'd gone, Liam crossed the carpet and lowered his voice. "What was there about you not going off on your own that you didn't understand, *partner*? Will you get it through your thick skull that you have *no* authority here and that it's *my* job you're fucking with? I have kids, you arsehole."

Shit. Guilt roiled in Mark's gut. He hadn't been thinking. Yeah, arsehole didn't even begin to cover it. He shot a sideways glance to Edward, to find his boyfriend shaking his head in a reproachful manner that didn't need any deciphering. "You're right. I'm sorry."

"Damn right. You fucking owe me for this, Mark, and believe it when I say I'm gonna collect. I'll let you know what it is when I decide, but it's gonna hurt your pocket big time."

Liam was letting him off easier than he deserved. "Fair enough." While they were still alone, he caught Liam up on what they'd discussed so far.

Once Evie and Finn returned, Mark sat back and let Liam ask the questions. His partner went over the statement from the previous interview and then moved on to possible scenarios about what Rowan might have been working on. But he couldn't prise anything free to help their case. That was, until he showed her the photo of Adam Greene, from his police file. She recognised him—was sure he'd visited the house once or twice to see her husband *after* he'd left Morgan's.

Mark struggled to keep the elation from his face. It put the two men together beyond their time at Morgan's. "Do you know the reason for his visit?"

A frown crossed Evie's brow. "Why? Is he important?"

"We don't know yet," Liam answered evenly.

"People did visit Rowan," she explained. "Not often, but sometimes, so I thought nothing of it. Max Harlowe, Rowan's old university professor, was always popping in... even Rowan's boss from Morgan's came around, and a guy from the lab Rowan used. He came regularly to drop off results—"

"Doug Morgan?" Mark had frozen at the name. His gaze jerked to Liam, whose whole body thrummed with tension.

Evie looked nervously between them. "I don't know his first name. Maybe?"

Edward's hopeful gaze briefly met Mark's, and Mark wished he were closer, wished he hadn't pissed Edward off so that he'd chosen the farthest chair. He scrolled through his phone till he found the Morgan and Associates website.

"This man?" He showed Evie the photo.

She frowned. "Yes. That's him, I think."

Liam leaned forward on his elbows. "So the man in this photo came *here*? *After* your husband had finished his contract with them?"

Mark knew exactly what Liam was thinking. Why would Morgan, a man who had rubbished Bridge's skills, visit him at his home *after* Rowan had finished with him? Not to mention, why *wouldn't* he have mentioned that to the police when they interviewed him after Bridge had been murdered?

Evie was clearly confused about the line of questioning. "Yes, I think, but—"

"Can you remember *when* he visited? Take your time and think carefully," Liam pressed.

She flushed and glanced at her son. "Oh, well, um, let me think. I don't know exactly—"

"Just take it slow," Finn said. He hesitated and glanced at Liam, who nodded his approval. He then shifted closer to his mother. "Mum?"

"Oh God." She put her hand to her head in concentration. "I'm sorry. I'm just not sure I can remem—"

"Evie." Edward spoke softly, and Mark's head whipped around. "Perhaps you can remember what you were doing the day he visited? For instance, were you at home when he arrived?"

It was something Mark had noticed very early on about Edward. There was a steady calm to his presence that people sank into like a pile of soft cushions. He wondered if it came from years of dealing with grieving families—but regardless of the source, Evie appeared no exception to its magic.

She visibly relaxed. She took a breath, and her eyes locked on to Edward's. "I was gardening out back. I remember, because I was nearly at the front door when Rowan raced ahead and told me not to worry, that it was his boss from Morgan's and he'd see to it. I was relieved because I was covered in dirt. I'd been moving that hydrangea that was blocking the path—" She turned. "Finn, you know the one."

Finn took his mother's hand and held it. "Yeah, I know. Can you remember *when* you moved it?"

"Of course I can."

Finn bit back a smile.

"It was in December. The second week. I know because I'd had coffee with the mah-jong girls beforehand. It was our last meeting before Christmas."

"That's good, Evie, real good." Edward thanked her and sat back.

Evie's gaze swept the room. "Do you think he was involved in Rowan's death? That would be just awful."

"At this point we're just collecting information," Liam reassured her. "Do you mind if we take another look at Rowan's study?"

Evie looked to Finn, who nodded. "Go ahead. Anything you need."

Liam got to his feet. "Finn, if your mum agrees, maybe you could come with us for a minute. You might have some ideas about where your dad might've put something he wanted to keep safe. There's nothing on his laptop to account for what happened, and you both said he was careful not to keep records of his contract work. But there's also nothing on anything he might have been working on for himself over the last three months. Plenty before that, but nothing since October."

Evie blinked slowly. "But that can't be right. He was in there every day he wasn't in Hamilton... or wherever he was—" She sent a devastated look her son's way, and he reached for her hand. "And he often worked till midnight on weekends, so if he wasn't teaching, he had to be working on something for himself. And he was meticulous about keeping data. He was a scientist to his core. It was his *life*."

Mark got to his feet, and Liam and Edward joined him, Edward's hand landing gently on the small of Mark's back as he moved alongside. It was a small gesture, but it meant everything. Edward might be pissed, but he had Mark's back. They were okay. A breath he didn't know he'd been holding gushed from Mark's chest.

"That's why we think he might have had another hiding place," Liam explained. "Maybe whatever he was working on had something to do with his death, maybe not. But it's the only lead we have. Did he have a security box, or someone he might have left it with, or *anything* outside the house?"

She shook her head. "Not that I know, but then... it seems I didn't know him as well as I thought."

Mark squeezed her arm in sympathy, and then they left and went through Bridge's office from top to toe. But even with Finn's help, they still found nothing. Mark was ready to throw something. They were about to call it a day when he saw Edward take Finn aside, and he wandered over to listen.

"Can you think of anywhere else we haven't looked?" Edward asked the young man. "Did your father help your mum in the garden, maybe? What about the shed I saw out there?"

Finn huffed out a laugh. "Dad in the garden? Never. He wasn't exactly your outdoorsy type. And the shed's Mum's domain. Nothing would be safe in there. No. The only time he spent anywhere was here in his study or tinkering with the Prefect in the garage."

Mark frowned. They'd already pulled the garage apart. Finn had told them his father used rebuilding the car as a kind of meditation, fiddling around as he worked through formulas in his head.

"No, he was kind of simple in his routines, really." Finn's eyes brimmed. "It was his work and his car, and that's pretty much it. I think he'd have liked me to show a bit more interest, but I'm not really a car guy, you know?" He looked wistful.

"I'm sure that didn't matter to him," Edward reassured him.

"But I should have tried, right? I did help him put the driver's door on the week he died—it had just come back from the panel beater. And all I could think of was that I didn't have the time, I wanted to meet up with my friends. Thank God I didn't. That was the day he told me I could have the car when it was done, which was kind of cool. He said it would be a reminder of something we'd done together. Don't know why he said that. I hardly ever helped with it. That was his thing."

Edward caught Mark's eye. "You need to take another look at that car."

It only took five minutes for Liam to locate and remove a small hard drive taped to the internal frame of the newly attached car door, and everyone blew out a collective sigh of relief.

Finn stared at it as if the thing were radioactive. "I can't believe he hid it there."

Edward rested a hand on the young man's shoulder. "We don't know what it is yet. But if it turns out to be important, then you know your father trusted you to remember, to realise something was odd about what he said. You did him proud. Now go tell your mum."

When they were alone, Liam said, "We need Connor's eyes on this like yesterday, but he's out west till this afternoon. I'll get it to him."

"No." Mark jumped in. "We can't wait hours for this. We need to take a look now."

Liam and Edward turned as one to stare at him, and Liam gave an eye-roll worthy of a Guinness record. "You better not be suggesting—"

"We still don't know how the attacker knew Edward and I were going to meet, and where," Mark said, trying to keep his impatience in check. "That means there's a chance someone in the department is involved—"

Liam huffed. "You still think—"

"Do you wanna take that risk?"

"What about chain of evidence?"

"Talk to Kirwan. He'll only get pissy if I call. Tell him our concerns. Connor can come to us and get a copy. It will still have chain of evidence if we get Kirwan on board and get the right authority. And you have to know that if what we find is a whole lot of scientific shit, Connor's not going to be any help. We'll need to get an expert to take a look, and—" He checked his watch. Just after noon. "That's not likely to happen until tomorrow, and I don't want this sitting around in the station evidence room until then."

Liam stared him down, but Mark wasn't giving up on this. He was right; he knew it and Liam knew it.

But Liam wasn't giving in that easily. "If we open it and it's primed to delete without the right password, we risk losing everything," he hissed.

"He breadcrumbed a trail so his son could find it. Why would he then booby-trap it?"

Liam worked his jaw as he fought some internal battle, and Mark hated himself a little more over what he was asking of his partner. But they didn't have time to mess around.

"Finn," Liam finally yelled, and the young man appeared at the doorway. "You got a laptop we can take a quick look at this on?"

"Sure." He headed back to the lounge, quickly followed by Liam.

Mark hesitated as his heart checked down a beat or two, and

Edward's hand appeared once more on the small of his back, grounding him. He turned and pressed a quick kiss to Edward's lips. "Thank you."

Edward cocked his head, his eyes full of affection. "You're welcome. But don't think you're out of trouble for that stunt you pulled earlier."

A smile tugged at Mark's lips. "It never crossed my mind."

Edward's gaze heated. "Just so you know. I've got plans for you."

Something twitched down south. *Oh boy.* "Does it involve punishment?"

Edward's fisted his shirt. "Do you want it to?"

"Knight, get in here." Liam shouted.

"Hold that thought." Mark glared up the empty hallway. "That man's in a for shitload of trouble when I'm back on duty."

Edward whacked him on the arm. "He better not be. He's saving your damned arse at the moment."

Mark grimaced. "Point taken."

Mark thanked all the gods and then some that the hard drive was not encrypted and there were plenty of dates and notes to make it clear it covered the time frame they were interested in. He had no doubt it held what Rowan Bridge had been working on all those months, the project important enough that he'd lied to his wife. It also appeared to be his own work, not a contract. There were a lot of notes about fuel transfer, decarbonising, hydrogen and gasification, and a ton of other stuff.

But having no encryption was their only piece of good luck, because most of the work may as well have been written in Swahili for all the good it did them. The entries were little more than a jumble of formulas and unintelligible scientific gobbledygook. Edward, with his medical background, could pick out a few scientific terms and chemical equations but not enough to give them much of a lead.

"It's definitely something to do with hydrogen fuel," Edward offered with a shrug. "But it's way, way over my head. There's comments about splitting off hydrogen, on-site processing, increasing vehicle range, and so on, but you need an expert to make sense of it."

Liam frowned. "But isn't hydrogen already a fuel? There are buses in the UK running on hydrogen. Nothing new about that."

Mark stared at his partner in surprise.

Liam shrugged. "What? I know stuff."

"But those buses use a mix of hydrogen and diesel. They don't rely on hydrogen alone, or they wouldn't have enough range." Everyone turned to look at Finn, who'd left the couch to appear behind them. He flushed bright red. "Sorry."

"No, go on." Edward smiled at the young man.

"It's just that Dad talked about it... a lot." He gave a dramatic eye-roll, and his mother chuckled. "I'm way better than you guys with the science side of it, but nothing like Dad."

"So tell us what's so special about hydrogen?" Mark prompted.

Finn took a deep breath and looked around at his mother, who nodded her head in encouragement. "Okay, well, everyone thought it was the answer, for one thing. It has twice the fuel economy of gas, with no vehicle emissions except water vapour. It's plentiful and can be made with renewable sources. But most importantly, we wouldn't have to change much about our current mechanisms to use it. It acts similarly to what we have now."

Liam crossed his arms and perched on the edge of the table. "Sounds like a miracle cure. I sense a *but* coming."

Finn nodded. "A couple of them. One, it's expensive. And two, it's highly flammable. To get an acceptable travel distance out of a tank, it has to be put under huge pressure, so there's that. There were a couple of fires in hydrogen fuel facilities in the US last year. Dad was on the phone with one of the companies trying to help at the time, right, Mum?"

"Yes, he was." Evie crossed to join them at the table. "I'd forgotten all about that."

"Anything else?" Mark pressed.

Finn thought before answering. "Well, we don't have the infrastructure yet, so there are hardly any refuelling facilities, and it's very expensive to transport because of the whole pressurised flammable thing. And last—Dad talked a lot about this one—although it can be made from renewables, it's currently not. They still use coal and gas in a process that emits CO_2, *and* it still needs batteries."

"Right." Mark understood. "Making it a no-go for the environmentalists still."

"Exactly."

"So how does it work?" Edward asked.

"It's a simple process. If you add hydrogen to oxygen, you get heat, electricity, and water. The electricity can power anything that needs it, from an electric car to a hairdryer. And theoretically you should be able to use water for the whole process, because H_2O, right? Hydrogen and oxygen. Split off the hydrogen, recombine it with the oxygen to produce electricity, and then split it again. Clean and renewable. That's what Dad said, isn't it, Mum?"

Beside him, Evie nodded.

Liam frowned. "But we can't do that because...?"

"Because of the problems getting the idea into large-scale practice. Dad said we needed to solve the storage problem, so that it could be made locally on-site and not need to be transported. And we had to stabilise the hydrogen to make it less... explosive. We also needed to find a way to produce it using wind, or solar or biomass, not as we are at the moment, and maybe even within the vehicle itself in a cyclical way to eliminate the battery issue—that would be the Holy Grail. So it's been a catch-22 for the scientific community for years. The perfect solution to our energy needs, if only we could make it work."

The room fell silent while everyone digested that for a moment.

Then Edward leaned forward in his seat. "And for the person who did solve one or all of these problems?"

Finn sighed. "If they held the patents, they'd have the international scientific and energy community beating down their door."

Liam cocked a brow. "We're talking a lot of money, then?"

Finn shrugged and sat by his mother who patted his hand in a proud-mother way.

"For the right solution to *any* of the problems, I'd say more than a lot," he said. "For whoever worked out how to make hydrogen on a local, ongoing cyclical basis from renewables and eliminated the need for both transport and storage, and so reduced the explosive risk? According to Dad, that would be worth tens of millions, and likely a lot more."

Goddamn. Go to the top of the class. Well, if they needed a big-time motivation for triple murder, autopsy tampering, and torture, it didn't get much better than tens of millions of dollars. The palpable silence that echoed in the room seemed to agree.

Mark turned to Finn. "Thanks. You've been a huge help."

"Do, um, do you think Dad might have actually been on to something to do with all this?"

Mark opened his hands. "We won't know till the experts take a look. But maybe someone at least thought he was."

"You'll let us know, though, right?" There was genuine longing in Finn's gaze, hope for a better memory and a more palatable solution to the question of his father's secrecy.

"I promise."

Standing alongside Liam's car, Mark hauled his still-pissy partner around to face him. "I said I'm sorry, all right, and I mean it. Can you just let it go?"

They stared at each other for a few seconds before Liam's shoulders relaxed from the 'I'm two seconds away from punching you' vibe they'd held since he arrived at the house.

"Did I mention you're an arsehole?" He stabbed a hard finger into Mark's chest.

Mark would've laughed in relief that they'd be okay, if it weren't for the biting pain in his chest. "Ow... ribs, remember?"

Liam's expression didn't even flicker. "Oh, I remember perfectly."

Message received. Mark cleared his throat and caught Edward's amused smile. "Something funny?"

Edward barked out a laugh. "Hell, yeah. Not sure I've ever seen you looking so sheepish."

Liam snorted and bumped fists with Edward while Mark squirmed.

"Yeah, well, don't get used to it." He eyeballed Edward. "And I thought boyfriends were supposed to have each other's back."

Edward flashed him an innocent smile. "Oh, they do, right up until they don't."

Liam slapped Edward on the back. "I knew I liked you. Now I'm gonna ring Kirwan. But if he says no to holding on to the drive, that's it, okay?"

Mark nodded and let out the breath he'd been holding. "Deal."

When Liam walked off to make the call, Mark joined Edward perched on the hood of the car. "You think you're so funny, huh?"

Edward eyed him up and down with a heated gaze that travelled all the way to Mark's balls. "Hilarious," he said, then pulled that plump lower lip of his between his teeth and bit down hard.

Mark's libido rocketed to a rolling boil. "You better have some damn good follow-through on all that teasing," he warned.

"You'll know soon enough." Edward pushed off the car and climbed into the passenger seat just as Liam returned.

Liam flicked a gaze between them. "What did I miss?"

Mark scowled at Edward, who smiled innocently. "Nothing. What did Kirwan say?"

"He was pissed as hell to start with, and it took some persuading.

He finally agreed, but he doesn't want us opening it again. We bag it and wait till tomorrow—let Connor get a copy. Meanwhile, Kirwan will clear it with evidence and the prosecutor. But they might demand to know where you're actually staying, you realise that?"

Mark blew a sigh of relief. "Yeah, I know. I just feel better if we can keep that to ourselves as long as possible." At least they had the breathing room they needed to try to put the pieces together.

"But we only get to hold it till the morning, and we're to keep it quiet," Liam continued. "Then the drive goes to an expert to make some sense of it. Kirwan's still not convinced about any leak, and he's climbing the wall about your name cropping up." Liam glared at Mark, who sensed another line of dollars added to his debt. "But if we're right about this fuel thing and the pay-off, then you guys are in big danger, and Kirwan's gonna put you both in protective custody if we don't have some answers by tomorrow night."

"Shit." That was all Mark needed. "But we're on to something, Liam, I know it. It makes sense for the first time. Are you heading back into the station?"

"Yeah. Unlike some others I know, I've got a shit-ton of work to do. The warrant for Morgan's employment records came through, plus a whole bunch of other crap. I'll swing by tonight, but it'll be late, like 'I might need to crash on your couch' late. Make yourself useful and try and have the name of an expert jacked up for me before I get there, but don't you dare touch that seal, understand? This really is your job *and* mine on the line, Mark. Kirwan was adamant about that."

Mark had already resigned himself to that. "I won't touch it. Kirwan's been good about this. Besides, there's no point until we have someone who knows what they're looking at. I just want it in safe hands."

Liam slapped the sealed bag containing the drive into Mark's hand. "You better damn well make sure of that."

Mark tucked it in his pocket. "Thanks, man. You're the best."

"Yeah, I am. And don't you fucking forget it. But there's one more thing."

Mark's heart sank. "What."

Liam threw him a shit-eating grin. "Kirwan wants you guys to check in at Auckland Med again this afternoon, or you won't get that clearance for work in two days. There was a message on my phone from Cam. He's expecting you both in an hour."

"Fuck."

Liam slapped him on the back and headed for his own car. "Yeah, I wouldn't be late for that if I were you."

CHAPTER NINETEEN

THE MOMENT EDWARD OPENED THE FRONT DOOR, TINK WAS gone—barrelling past without even a backward glance to greet Mark instead.

"Well, hello to you too, man's best friend," Edward chided, only half-joking. "I'll just be inside getting your bloody dinner, if that's all right with you?"

Still, poor Tink had been shut up for longer than they'd intended, the supposedly quick trip to the ER getting sidetracked by an unexpectedly full waiting room, which resulted in them not getting back to the house before four. Edward had intended to add another half cup of kibble as apology, but that was under reconsideration on the basis of the piss-poor welcome he'd received.

He was still muttering when the front door slammed behind him and he was squeezed between the wall and one very committed detective.

"Someone told me I've been a bad, bad boy," Mark murmured as he nipped and licked his way down Edward's neck to the collar of his T-shirt, and *oh, fuck*, it felt good. "I feel I need to be shown the error of my ways." He pulled Edward's collar aside and bit down... hard.

Edward gave a soft yelp and pushed his hips back, keen to feel that hard energy in exactly the right place. The feel of Mark pressed against him, demanding and needy, did fucking wonders for his ego. Mark cranked his shit no end, and Edward was happy to drown in the attention.

"I'm pretty sure this isn't how it's meant to go." He flipped their positions and caged Mark in, pressing their foreheads together. "If *you're* the one needing punishment, it seems only right that *I* should be the one leading, no?"

Mark arched to bring their groins into contact. "Details, details. But if you insist, I won't fight you on it." He covered Edward's mouth with his own and thrust his tongue inside, sweeping through to probe every nook and cranny.

The flood of sensation ramped up the action in Edward's briefs to just south of painful, and when Mark's hands fumbled at the zip of Edward's jeans, he grabbed them and pinned them above Mark's head.

The man's pupils blew black. "Yesss. Do it."

And fuck if he didn't want to. Edward struggled to catch his breath. But they were being ridiculous. They weren't kids. Was a bed too much to ask?

"No, no, no. I see what you did there." Mark dipped his head and peered up at Edward through those long fucking lashes that Edward was beyond desperate to feel against his inner thighs... again. It was one of his most vivid memories from their shared blow jobs the night before.

Mark went on, "You just went AWOL in that pretty little head of yours, didn't you?"

Edward scrunched up his face. "I'm just concerned about your ribs. Cam said we should—"

"Fuck Cam," Mark practically shouted. "Actually, no, that's an unsettling image. I'm fine, Edward. A bit sore, yes, but he shoved a couple of happy pills down my throat, so I'm kinda feeling pretty good at the moment. Unless *you're* not feeling—"

"I'm fine." He wasn't, not really. All day, Edward had watched Mark, caught between feeling excited at a chance with him and second-guessing... well, everything. He barely recognised himself— this self-assured, sexy, almost playful guy who showed up whenever Mark was around. It wasn't that he lacked confidence in bed. Edward liked control, and he was pretty sure he was a reasonable lay, even if he hadn't had as many partners as Mark.

It was more that Mark made Edward *feel* things—things he wasn't used to. And in Mark's presence, Edward felt... lighter, some-how. Desirable. Safe. Safe enough to risk letting someone past all those walls and into the well-protected space that Edward guarded so jealously. Well, it wasn't exactly a case of *letting* Mark in, more that Mark was already there, making coffee and sharing his bed, and Edward couldn't even remember unlocking the door.

Mark hadn't been wrong that morning, when he'd worried he might be pushing Edward's boundaries too fast. In every relationship he'd had, Edward had taken a long time to invite people into his bed, and even longer to let them into his life. Now? He was pretty sure he'd boarded a runaway train and it was too late to jump.

He didn't hate it. He just didn't know how to reconcile it with the serious, self-contained, controlled man he'd always known himself to be. Without even trying, Mark had laid bare Edward's normally cautious desire and fired it up until Edward was wanting... needing... demanding, just like that damn kiss in the kitchen.

And they were still only two days into this. What other changes would Mark rain down on Edward's life? And after turning Edward's world upside down, what if Mark then decided he didn't want him any more? *Fuck.* Edward wasn't sure he'd survive that.

Mark scowled. "You're doing it again."

Edward blinked slowly and released Mark's hands. "I'm sorry. You wanna...?" He indicated the bedroom door.

Mark shook his head and wrapped Edward up in those big, safe arms. "Look at me." Edward did, and Mark leaned in to capture his lips. "Fuck, you taste good, every damn part of you. How do you do that?" He cupped Edward's arse and pulled them together.

Heat rose in Edward's cheeks. "I think you're high." But he leaned into Mark's warmth and let it flood his body, leaving no room for questions.

"Just on you, Edward Newton." Mark licked at his lips. "Just on you." He ran a trail of kisses along Edward's jaw, then sucked on his earlobe while their hips moved together in a slow grind. It was all Edward could do to not buckle at the knees there and then, the urge to get Mark's cock in his mouth growing more desperate by the second. And from the increasingly laboured breaths at Edward's ear, Mark was feeling much the same.

Then he suddenly pulled off, and Edward was left chasing air. His eyes blew open in question.

"Focus, babe." Mark shoved his thigh between Edward's legs and ground down hard.

Dear God. "Kind of hard not to." Edward groaned as he stretched to try to lay his lips on Mark's once again, but Mark leaned away. "Get back here," he snapped in frustration.

"And there he is." Mark's eyes twinkled. "My stroppy pathologist. Look at you, so fucking sexy I can barely stand it. I love when you're bossy, when you take what you need. You're the first guy I've ever wanted to roll over for. Do you understand how scary that is, Edward?"

Oh, Edward understood exactly.

"And here I am, begging for you. You turn me on like no one else. So don't leave me hanging here, sweetheart. I don't need it pretty and clean and polite. I don't need a bed. In fact, with my ribs, I'll be better off if you just lean me over that damn couch and ruin me there."

Holy shit. Edward's hand slipped to palm his aching dick. *This man.*

Mark switched Edward's hand for his own. "Let me." He unzipped both their jeans, pushed their briefs aside, and had

Edward's cock naked and against his own in seconds, taking every last scrap of Edward's breath with him.

"Look at us," Mark huffed, staring down to where he slowly worked them together. "You're so beautiful." He swiped his thumb over Edward's leaking crown, sucked it clean and looked Edward in the eye before fusing their mouths together with a low groan.

The wanton sound made Edward's cock jump in Mark's hand. His mind switched off and he gave himself over to the surge of feeling that roared through his body. Wrapping his own hand around Mark's, the satin slide of soft, slick skin over their rigid flesh nearly did his head in.

"I want you." It was raw and gruff, and Edward couldn't have stopped the words if he'd tried.

"Then just take me already," Mark threw back as he peppered kisses down Edward's neck. "And get this damn shirt off." He broke away to deal with both their T-shirts, and the rest of their clothes, while Edward just stood there and let him, staring as Mark fumbled in his wallet and then slapped a packet of lube and a condom into Edward's palm. Then in no time at all Edward was back in those confident hands, being stroked towards something that threatened to bring far more into his life than a spectacular orgasm.

"Do what you want to me, Edward," Mark rasped against his ear, still working their cocks. "I don't care, I just want *you*. You in me, me in you—I'm not fussy here, babe."

Shit. "I um, don't bottom... much. It hasn't worked well for me... in... the past."

"Do you top?"

Edward grinned against Mark's cheek. "Oh, yeah, I top."

Mark's chuckle was a tight thread this side of explosive. He had to be close.

"Well, hallelujah. Must be my lucky day," Mark hissed. "You've been driving me wild all damn day—those looks and touches. Christ, I nearly came in my jeans from the scent of you alone. I'll never be able to eat apple crumble without sporting a semi, ever again."

Ugh. If Edward didn't get in this man soon, he was gonna shatter into a million pieces. He needed this. He'd sat in that house and bled that family's grief like it was his own, resonating with the ache of their loss like a damn tuning fork. He knew their pain inside out: every ragged breath, every crumbling thought, every choked-back tear, and the chasm of sorrow and pain where a loved one's heart used to be.

And in the middle of all that, he'd looked at Mark and felt the strength of his heart, soaked up his smile, and found the raw edge of the memories softening. Mark was life, he was promise, and he was hope. No guarantees—there never were—but if Edward was gonna do this, and there was no way in hell he wasn't, he needed to take a leaf out of Mark's book and just go all the hell in.

He spun them both around and backed Mark into the wall, being careful to stay off his ribs. "If you don't shut that sexy mouth of yours I'm not gonna make it past the next few seconds, let alone into your body."

Mark's face lit up with a sly grin. "Oh, yeah, now we're talking. If I'd known that was all it—"

Edward slammed his mouth over those cocky lips to shut him up, and Mark keened under the pressure. But he met every one of Edward's moves, demanding, passionate, rough, and so fucking sexy Edward couldn't see straight.

"Ow, ow, ow..." Mark froze, and Edward jumped back.

"Oh God, I'm sorry"

"Stop. I'm fine." Mark took a couple of deep breaths. "I just twisted too far to the right." He looked at Edward, and his eyes darkened. "Now, get the hell back here." He hauled Edward's lips on to his, and they were making out like desperate teenagers once again.

Then Mark pushed Edward back, gasping for air. "How do you want me?"

Edward ran his eyes over Mark's flushed skin, lingering on his bruised lips and swollen, bobbing cock, unable to digest the fact that every square inch of this man was his for the taking. *Holy cow.* He'd struck the mother lode. He ripped open the lube.

"Over the table, just... find a comfortable position. I don't want—"

"Got it." Mark stopped him midstream. "I'll be fine."

And just like that, Edward froze. *Shit.* Was he really going to do this? Not his house, not his table... *Aw, fuck it.* He was damn sure the piece of furniture had seen it all before. He jerked his head to hurry Mark along.

Mark smirked as if he'd read Edward's mind, and then sauntered across the room as if he had all the time in the world. He didn't. Edward reached out and slapped his arse, seeing a flash of heat pass through Mark's eyes. Mark picked up his pace, even throwing in a swish to jerk Edward's cock into overdrive. *Jesus.* Edward couldn't remember sex being this much plain fun.

At the table, Mark bent over, leaning on his elbows to support his weight and keep his ribs off the wood. Once in position, he gave his butt another sassy jiggle. "You gonna keep me waiting here? Or have you actually got something to back up those promises your eyes have been making all day?"

Edward lunged and pressed himself to Mark's arse, grinding his rigid cock into the space behind his balls and up into the tight heat of his crease, eliciting a deep, rumbling moan. He ran a hand slowly down Mark's back—down, down—while the slick fingers of his other dipped into Mark's crease, where Edward's cock already nestled, and grazed his hole, pausing, circling, slipping in and out.

He bent forward, and his lips found the run of Mark's spine, tracing the vertebrae downward until he was on his knees, spreading Mark's cheeks, tongue sliding between, over and around, pressing, licking, tasting... probing. Mark writhed and moaned under his touch, filthy nothings spewing from his lips. He pushed back, taking Edward's fingers deeper into that furnace.

It was almost too tempting to just keep going. Edward could come this way in a heartbeat. But he wanted to give Mark what he'd asked for. He wrenched his fingers free and stepped back while Mark swore his early death, or words to that effect. Then he suited and slicked up, and pressed against Mark's hole.

"Your ribs?" He checked one last time.

"Fine." The strangled word came with an edge of warning. "Please, babe."

Babe. Oh, yeah. Mark had used that word a couple of times now, and Edward liked it... a lot. He pressed past the ring of muscle and paused for a second, giving Mark time to adjust. But Mark wasn't having any of it and pushed back, taking him the whole way in, and... *oh God*, Edward thought he was gonna need to rewrite his bucket list —one to ten now taken by this man's arse.

He did his best to set a smooth rhythm, but he was so close to the edge he wasn't sure he'd last more than a dozen strokes before he went out in a blaze of mortified glory. He reached around and took Mark's dick in his hand and started stroking, not that it helped his own plight. Mark cursed and moaned in his arms, threatening to shatter Edward's shaky control. Jesus, he was so close.

He tried to ease up, grapple some control back, and he thought he'd even managed it until Mark's hand shot around, latched on to his arse, and pulled Edward in hard, holding him in place while he surged back and forth on Edward's dick, taking exactly what he needed—which wasn't slow, apparently. And goddamn if it wasn't the sexiest fucking thing Edward had ever seen.

But it put paid to any idea of lasting, and within seconds Edward felt the buzz at the base of his spine and his orgasm surged and he came undone with a single deep grunt, spilling himself into Mark and shuddering through the waves of pleasure that followed.

A few strokes later Mark joined him, back arched, head thrown back, neck corded as he rocked himself on Edward's cock, milking the last of the sensation. Then he rolled forward to hit the table, and Edward slid out, got rid of the condom, and wrapped his arms around Mark's waist—stretched like a contented cat over his back until they both calmed.

"How are the ribs?" Edward puffed out the question. "Sore?"

"Hell, yeah." Mark panted. "But so worth it. Holy shit, Edward, you fuck like a damn train." He shucked Edward gently off his back so he could stand.

When Mark was vertical, Edward took him back in his arms and sealed their lips in a languid kiss. He took his time, wanting to let Mark know just how much he'd enjoyed him. When he was done, he cradled Mark's face and stared him in the eye. "We're incendiary together—you know that, right? I didn't even recognise myself in all that. You do shit to me, Mark. I... I don't even have the words."

Mark beamed. "I'm a Big Mac to your French fries, huh?"

Edward rolled his eyes. "More like my sausage to your bun, *babe*. Now get in that shower."

"Ooohhh, you liked that? Me calling you babe?"

Edward narrowed his gaze. "Maybe."

"Nah, you love it." Mark stretched invitingly, his hands running down his torso and a wicked gleam lighting up his eyes. "My plump strawberries to your cream." He turned and ambled off, all six feet six of him, swishing that mouth-watering arse for all it was worth.

Edward grabbed a pillow and threw it at his back. "My stick to your balls. White one, corner pocket."

A middle finger shot up over Mark's head. "Ear of corn to sweet butter, baby."

Edward chuckled. "I've got a better idea. How about your handcuffs to my wrists?"

Mark froze and spun slowly in place, his dick bobbing again, and God, Edward was gonna need vitamins.

"Come here." Mark held out a hand, and Edward quickly crossed to take it. "I want you on your knees for me in that shower in two minutes flat—do we have an understanding, Edward?"

Hell, yeah, they did. Edward ran his tongue slowly over his lower lip, and Mark's nostrils flared. Then he turned and walked ahead, doing a fair impersonation of Mark's sashay and aware of two fiery holes burning deep into his back. Lordy, could this afternoon get any better?

Edward woke with a start, his eyes shooting open. The bedroom was quiet, evening shadows reaching deep into the room. He dropped his hand over the edge of the bed, expecting to find Tink, but found nothing. He reached for his watch. Nine p.m. *Son of a bitch.* He'd slept for three hours. Something moved at his back, and a soft smile broke over his face. *They. They'd* slept for three hours. An arm flopped over his waist and drew him close, the attached hand worming its way south of the waistband of his briefs to cradle his soft cock.

Between their six am start, their battered bodies, pain pills, awesome sex, and the stress of the case, they'd hit the bed straight from a few shenanigans in the shower, with the intent of catching a nap before making dinner. Liam was still not expected to show up until much later.

"What's going on in that head of yours?" Mark leaned over Edward's shoulder as he continued to fondle Edward's balls which had decided to wake up with all the attention.

Edward glanced down and then turned his face to Mark's, eyebrows raised.

Mark smirked. "Hey, I can multitask."

He rolled in Mark's arms and pressed their mouths together. "Oh, believe me, I know all about your multitasking skills." Mark had shown considerable focus and dexterity in his ability to receive what Edward had thought was a sterling blow job on his part while at the same time fingering Edward till they both got off.

"We've been out for three hours, sleeping beauty." Edward let his own hand wander down to wrap around Mark's semi. "Mmm, what have we here?"

"Well, if I need to tell you"—Mark licked his way into Edward's mouth, tripping all those needy nerve endings Edward tried so hard to hide—"then I think we might have a problem." He pulled Edward close so their cocks brushed, and damn, Edward didn't think he'd ever get used to that zing.

A growl filtered in from the lounge, and Mark froze. "Tink?"

Edward nodded and went up on one elbow, his gaze sweeping the darkening room.

Mark threw the duvet aside and tugged on his jeans just as Tink released another growl, louder and followed by an earnest bark.

"Fuck. She's warning us." Edward shot out of bed and pulled his own clothes on. "Someone's outside. Liam?"

"He'd have called first."

"Cam? Josh?"

"Same." Mark crept next to the window and peered around the drapes.

"See anything?" Edward slipped to the other side so they faced each other across the window and took a look. The thin spread of browning lawn out front quickly bled into the thick bush surrounding it—great for privacy, but for visual reassurance, not so much.

Mark frowned. "Nothing, but it—"

The rest was lost to a chest-rattling torrent of barks as Tink ploughed into the bedroom, mammoth-sized paws up at the window, eyes fixed on something only she could see. The window fogged in seconds, and Edward dragged her aside. "Shh, girl, what did you see, huh?" She struggled in his grip, a solid ridge of hair running the length of her spine.

Mark's expression showed his alarm. "Something sure set her off. Stay here. I'm going out to check." He grabbed his shirt and headed for the lounge.

Like hell. "Oh no you don't." Edward caught up, and Mark pushed him against the wall none too lightly.

"Not this time, Edward, please."

"But—"

"No."

Edward heard the desperation in Mark's voice and saw the resolution in his eyes. And suddenly Edward was afraid.

Mark cupped his jaw. "I need you to stay inside, Edward. If it's trouble, I don't want them getting their hands on that drive. You need to make sure it stays safe."

"But I can watch your back."

"I know you can, but if you're out there I won't be able to focus. I'll be too scared for you. Please just do this, for me."

"Then take Tink."

He shook his head adamantly. "No. She stays here too. I'll feel better knowing she'll protect you. And I can't afford to be keeping my eyes on her. She's no police dog. Please?"

Edward hated everything about the idea, just fucking hated it. But he also couldn't argue with Mark's logic. "Fine. I'll stay here. But you damn well better not get hurt, or I'll fucking kill you myself, do you understand? I... I care too much for you."

Mark's gaze softened. "I feel the same way. And I'll be careful." He pressed a quick kiss to Edward's lips. "If there is someone out there—and we don't know there is yet—I need that drive hidden until we can get help. Lock the place down, set the window and door alarm, and ring Liam. Hopefully the alarm siren will be enough to deter anyone trying to get in, but give the alarm company a head's up as well. Tell them we're not sure if it's anything yet and police are on the scene. I don't want them sending some poor security guard over just to get caught up in something he can't handle. So if the alarms go off, they're to call the police to send in the cavalry." And with that he opened the front door and disappeared into the gloom.

Edward slammed the door shut and pressed his back to it. *Fuck, fuck, fuck.* His heart kicked into overdrive. Damn the man.

He took a deep breath and did everything Mark had told him to, including moving the hard drive and his own small flash drive up into a crawl space above the kitchen that they'd scoped out earlier. But he couldn't reach Liam on the phone, both his and Josh's voicemail kicking in on every attempt. He left messages, then relayed Mark's instructions to the alarm company and sat back to wait. There was nothing he could do but keep trying

Meanwhile, Tink wouldn't settle, stalking from room to room, snarling and pushing at the drapes with her nose to get back at a window, any window. Edward tried to reassure her, but she was having none of it. And that, if nothing else, had his alarm bells pinging into overdrive. It wasn't usual behaviour for the mastiff, who could get easily excited but also tended to settle just as quickly with Edward at her side.

Edward's mind flew back to the attack when Tink had come to their rescue and hoped they weren't in for a repeat. Logic told him it was unlikely. The only reason for coming after them now was to get that drive, and only a handful of people even knew they had it.

He hunkered down on the couch and pulled Tink down alongside. "Nothing to do but wait, girl."

CHAPTER TWENTY

MARK HATED LEAVING EDWARD, BUT AT LEAST TINK WAS WITH him—and there hadn't been any choice, not really. He'd have been too worried about keeping Edward safe to focus properly, and that would put them both at risk. Edward was much safer where he was, and someone had to stay with the drive. Still, he wasn't jumping to conclusions. The whole thing was more likely to be a false alarm. But his spidey senses were tingling, and that never boded well.

He sprinted across the narrow patch of open lawn, not for the first time wishing New Zealand cops routinely carried guns. Then he made his way through the dense native bush that surrounded the house and lined the driveway on both sides to a depth of a hundred metres or so. It was one of the reasons Cam and Reuben had bought the property to start with: the protection it afforded them from cameras, drones, and prying eyes. But right then, Mark kind of wished they'd gone for a top-of-a-hill, all-approaches-exposed scenario instead.

So far, his search hadn't turned up a single thing out of place, though. The house surroundings were clear, as far as he could tell, and he'd moved on to making his way through the thick bush that framed the long drive. It was almost impossible to keep quiet, what with the dry bracken that crunched and crackled underfoot, but he did his best. The last of the orange sunset had dipped into grey, and it was getting harder and harder to find his way and keep his bearings. The unsealed driveway snaked five hundred metres from the road to the house. It was a lot of ground to cover. Oh, yeah, he and Reuben were gonna have words about trimming all this shit back, amongst other things.

It took him fifteen minutes to almost make it to the end, by which time he'd nearly convinced himself Tink had got her knickers in a twist about nothing more than a rabbit, when a flash of blue caught his eye and stopped him in his tracks. He slipped behind a thick rata, its red flowers still carrying a glow in the fading light, and studied the car.

It had been nosed deep into the bush on the other side of the drive—almost impossible to detect unless you were standing directly opposite, as Mark was. It was a blue late-model Honda. No way to see if there were any occupants without getting closer, but there were no voices.

Shit. He dropped his shoulders and maintained a low profile, moving a good distance past the car, before crossing the drive and circling back. He covered the last twenty meters at almost a crawl, his ribs burning every step of the way, but when he finally came to a stop, he was less than four metres from the vehicle and well hidden by a thick mass of gorse. From there he listened. Nothing broke the quiet of the dusk other than a morepork calling somewhere off to his right. He poked his head a little higher above the gorse until he could see in the passenger window. The car was empty. He stood and approached it cautiously.

A quick sweep of the inside revealed nothing about its occupants other than someone liked Diet Sprite—three empty cans lay in the passenger footwell. A phone charger poked out from the glove compartment, no phone attached, and a blue jersey lay discarded on the back seat. Other than that the car was empty. It was also minus its licence plates, which gave Mark pause and amped up his suspicion. He pulled out his cell and sent Edward a text to warn him they likely had company, and then tried calling Liam and Josh but was sent straight to voicemail. *Fuck.* He headed back as fast as his ribs would let him. He needed eyes on Edward as quickly as possible.

He'd made it about halfway when the first shot rang out from the direction of the house, and his heart rate skyrocketed with a burning need to get to Edward as soon as possible. It had been so bloody stupid to separate. If they'd stuck together, Mark could have protected him. If Edward was hurt because of Mark's decision... *fuck.* He couldn't afford to think about that. He just needed to get to Edward, now. He shoved through the underbrush and picked up his pace.

The house was nearly in view. A few more seconds and—

A second shot rang out, followed by a heart-shattering cry.

Goddamn this fucking driveway. His legs pumped faster, and his ribs screamed in protest. He pushed through a curtain of gorse, thorns jagging at his legs, on to the clear driveway and took off. It didn't offer any protection, but it would get him back to the house quicker than trying to navigate through any more of the choking bush.

A few more metres and the house came into view, its front door wide open.

Why the fuck hadn't the alarm siren sounded?

He heard shouting, along with the sound of furniture being dragged across the wooden floor. He reached the stairs and almost ploughed right on in without stopping to think what the hell he was gonna do without a firearm, but then his training kicked in and he swung back to the woodpile for a makeshift weapon. Club in hand, he slunk to one side of the open front door and listened.

His scramble up the driveway had hardly been silent, and even if it had, Mark was sure his heart had to be pumping loud enough to be heard clear into the room, but no one seemed to have noticed his arrival. Then it occurred to him that maybe, just maybe, they thought they'd caught Edward alone.

It was possible, especially if Edward had played along, which Mark was sure he would have. And it would explain the still open door and all the fucking noise—and it was the one thing Mark had in his favour.

He eased his head around the corner of the jamb for a quick look. The first thing he saw was Doug Morgan holding a gun in his outstretched, gloved hand. That answered that. Morgan looked like he hadn't slept for a week, and Mark remembered Liam saying he'd been AWOL from his business. But he wasn't alone—he was talking to someone out of sight in the kitchen. The not-so-good news.

He glanced at the log in his hand, but wishing wasn't going to change anything. Time was slipping away, and he'd yet to see any sign of Edward or Tink—and that filled his heart with terror. The back of the couch hid the floor between Morgan and the kitchen, and Mark could only hope Morgan had Edward flat in front of him, still alive. That would explain the need for the gun. Unless of course it was Tink laid out and Edward was... *No.* Mark couldn't let himself even begin to think about that or the two shots he'd heard, or he'd lose it.

He called the dog silently in his head. *Come on, girl. Don't disappoint me. You can sleep in our bed any time you want.*

Our bed. He sucked in a breath. *You damn well better be okay, Edward.*

Whoever was hidden from view was looking for the drive, Mark picked up that much from the conversation that leaked his way. Another quick look confirmed Morgan was distracted, talking to his colleague—but with a gun in play, Mark really needed to tackle them one-on-one to have a chance.

He left the front door, tiptoed along the tiled veranda, and peered around the far end. A second garage sat off to one side, separated from the rest of the house. Taking a wide swing, he threw the log in his hand high into the air and watched as it sailed towards the garage, landing with a crash against the siding. Then he whipped behind a magnolia in the garden and waited.

Two seconds later, the back door slammed open and a dark figure stepped out, flashlight in hand. From the person's height and build, it wasn't Morgan, but that's all Mark could be sure of. The flashlight ran over the garage as the individual made their way down the steps and along the path.

Mark didn't waste a second. With the assailants' attention drawn elsewhere, he darted out from his hiding place and back along to the front door. It was dead silent inside except for a gut-churning wheeze that Mark didn't want to think about.

Morgan, gun in hand—a hand that was visibly shaking—had his back half-turned to Mark, his gaze flitting nervously between the floor and the back door. Morgan was clearly out of his depth and shitting himself, and Mark had no doubt this whole scenario was way, way out of the man's comfort zone. This could be Mark's only chance. If only he knew where Tink and Edward were. Tink should have been raising merry hell. He shook his head free of the panic building there and focused on what he had to do.

It took a few seconds, but the next time Morgan's gaze turned to seek out his partner, Mark slipped through the door and across the room until he stood a couple of metres directly behind him, out of view behind a tall sideboard. Morgan was muttering under his breath, nervous tension rolling off him in waves.

From his hiding place, Mark had a clear view of the empty kitchen and the wide-open back door leading to the darkness beyond. How much longer he had till Morgan's partner reappeared, he had no idea—not long enough to second-guess himself. He had to get that gun and even the playing field.

Three, two, one, now...

He slipped out and around the couch, intending to rush the man, but before he'd gotten two metres he nearly dropped to his knees. The mastiff was slumped on the floor, deathly still. But that wasn't the worst of it. Lying over top of the dog, half-on, half-off, was Edward, face down, his back covered in blood. A bubbling wheeze filled the room, and Mark nearly keeled over at the sight and sound of the man he'd come to care so much about fighting for every life-giving breath he took.

No. No. No.

The determined thought broke through Mark's panic and stirred a driving rage inside him instead. The two-second hesitation could have made all the difference, and Mark didn't want anything more on his conscience. He roared and threw himself at Morgan just as he turned, and their heads connected with a crunch that sent fireworks spinning through Mark's brain.

The momentum carried them both into the breakfast bar, Morgan's arm catching the edge of the granite with a sickening crack. The gun went flying. Mark sank to the floor and prayed the blow had snapped the bone. The scream Morgan unleashed was promising, but there was no time to waste debating whether he could rely on that or not. He needed to get to his feet before arsehole number two was brought running by Morgan's scream.

But Mark had a problem. His ribcage had taken a further blow from one of the four bar stools they'd careered into, and for the moment he could barely breathe, let alone move. He was going nowhere until he got some air past the blazing pain in his chest.

"Mark?"

"Edward!" *Oh, thank Christ.* The man's voice was barely a whisper, but it was enough to galvanise Mark. He sucked in a breath, nearly passing out in the process, but the second was easier and then the third.

On the floor beside him, Morgan cradled his shattered arm and whimpered.

"Shut up." Mark crawled to his knees, his gaze sweeping the spinning room.

"Doug!"

Shit. The shout came from outside, but it was close, too close. Mark had seconds, if that. Where the fuck was the gun?

"Under the stool behind you," Edward hissed.

There was no time to even glance his way. Mark just spun and lunged in the right direction. But he landed short, and before he could crawl any closer, footsteps hit the kitchen tile and a shockingly familiar voice broke through the fog in his brain.

"Leave it, Detective. Stay right where you are."

Mark froze on the floor. *Holy fuck.* It wasn't possible. He couldn't even think it.

"Morgan, take your gun and get up," the voice ordered.

Again, the nauseating tickle of that familiar voice in Mark's head. A booted foot nudged the injured man's hip in front of Mark's gaze, and he raised his eyes to confront the truth. He *did* know that voice. He'd listened to it for fifteen years. And as his gaze slid from Rick Kirwan's face to the gun in the man's gloved hands, he knew something else: he and Edward were dead.

Morgan struggled to his feet as Mark and Kirwan locked eyes, the DCI's expression bordering on apologetic. Then Mark glanced Edward's way, desperate to know, but Edward was face down again, silent. And, *oh God*, Mark would never have thought he'd be praying for that horrifying rattle, but he was. Because at least it would mean Edward was alive. Now he didn't know what to think. A lance of fear skittered through his chest: fear... and raging, black fury.

"What the hell are you doing?" he shouted at his DCI and scrambled to his knees, gasping for breath as Kirwan backed away, gun held out. "Was it you that night at Edward's house, as well?"

Kirwan never even blinked. "No. That was... a third party." Not a trace of remorse.

"A third—but you told them where to find us, right? You signed off on it."

"Yes, but you didn't leave me much choice. Finding that report and the link between the two cases was... unfortunate."

Mark couldn't believe what he was hearing. "Unfortunate?" Then, louder, "Unfortunate? What the hell, Kirwan. How the fuck did you get involved in all this?"

But even as he said the words the pieces fell together in Mark's head. How Kirwan could've easily found out about Spencer's gambling. How it wouldn't have been hard for him to get the drugs he needed, or someone to do his dirty work. You work a city long enough as a cop and you just know where to go and whose shoulder to tap. Add to that Morgan's R&D contacts in the pharmaceutical industry, and it was a no-brainer.

Kirwan's gaze held firm. "That hardly matters. Now, get on that couch."

Mark shook his head in disgust and pulled himself to his feet before stumbling towards the couch. The lancing pain in his chest had eased enough for him to breathe a little easier, and he was feeling stronger in his legs, but he didn't want Kirwan to know any of that yet, so he played it up.

As he lurched past Edward, still on the floor, his heart squeezed, a pain so tight it almost choked him. His feelings for Edward had soared in such a short time—maybe not love, not yet, but hell, it had to be close. And God, it was terrifying. If they got through this, could he deal with the risk of losing Edward in the future? What if they didn't make it? What if Edward got sick? What if Mark screwed up?

But Mark knew he wanted the chance to at least find out for themselves, not to have this bastard take that opportunity from them. Tears stung his eyes, and it was all he could do to not just throw himself at Kirwan and hope for the best. Tink lay deathly still under Edward, her eyes rolled back in her head. Mark could see a gaping bullet wound in the dog's chest, her mouth frothing blood. *Frothing? Shit.* She was alive.

He blinked rapidly and kept his expression hidden from Kirwan as he tried to make sense of the bloody tableau on the floor. He could see it, the soft flare of the mastiff's nostrils, and there—a rumbling gurgle in her chest. Relief flooded through him. Tink's chest, not Edward's. It sucked to feel like that, but he'd take it over losing Edward.

His gaze darted to his lover's face, or what little he could see of it, and yes, there was still some colour, though the awkward angle made it impossible to tell if Edward's chest was moving or not. He couldn't afford to dwell on it, but Mark took the kernel of hope for what it was. Fuck if he was giving up on Edward, or himself for that matter. If they got through this, he would damn well take it for the gift it was and give everything to make this thing between them work. He'd never been a coward, and he wasn't about to start.

He lifted his gaze back to Kirwan's. The man's expression was unreadable.

Standing behind Kirwan, Morgan whimpered, his broken arm resting on the granite top of the breakfast bar as he tried to fashion a sling from the shirt he was wearing.

Kirwan ignored the man, his cool eyes focused on Mark. "I'm sorry about the dog. It ran at us when we entered."

And the shocking thing was, Mark thought the man genuinely *was* sorry. He huffed out a disbelieving grunt. There was no answer to the outrageous comment. "And Edward wouldn't think twice about turning off the alarm to let you in, would he? After all, you're the DCI in charge of the investigation, you arsehole. What about Newton? Did you shoot him too?"

"I had no choice. I didn't *want* any of this. You have to believe that, at least." He sounded almost indignant, and Mark just wanted to punch the guy.

"I don't have to believe anything, so you can save your excuses. If you regret either of those deaths, it's only because they made things messy for you, brought the shit right to your doorstep. And how about us? Are you gonna cry a few crocodile tears at our funerals? Talk about how brave we were, what a great service we provided to the police and the courts? You gonna do that, you worthless fucking bastard? No. There's no way this doesn't come down to plain old greed. What's on that drive is worth a fuck-ton of cash, we know that. You sold out, you piece of shit."

Kirwan's gaze narrowed, and he swung his weapon to Edward. "He's not dead, but I can easily remedy that."

Shit, shit, shit. Shut your damn mouth.

"You, have no idea what you're talking about, Knight. I tried to keep you out of it. I told you, that night at the station, that the report was probably a red herring and not to waste your time. If you'd listened, we wouldn't be here."

"But it wasn't a fucking red herring, was it?" Mark fumed. "And here we are."

"Yes. Here we are. So now you're gonna tell me where you've hidden the drive so we can get out of here. Newton was... less than helpful." Kirwan threw Morgan an accusatory look.

"Don't look at me," Morgan snapped. "No one told me anything about a fucking dog."

"And I'm not telling you anything either." Mark eyeballed his boss.

Kirwan smirked. "Yes, you will. Because if you don't, I'm gonna shoot your *friend* here."

Mark snorted. "You've already shot him. And there's no way you're gonna let either of us walk out of here anyway, so why would I give you what you want?"

Kirwan blinked slowly. "Because, as you well know, there are *ways* to die, Mark. And one bullet at a time in every joint is not the best of them."

Mark drew a sharp breath and glanced at Edward on the floor. *No.* He would never let that happen. "How can you live with yourself?" he spat at Kirwan, but the DCI simply smiled.

"The drive. Where is it?"

Mark had no choice. He told Kirwan where to find it, and Kirwan fetched a stepladder from inside the pantry to retrieve the drive from the crawl space while Morgan picked up his own gun again and trained it on Mark.

Mark studied the CEO, who was growing paler by the minute. Mark wasn't sure how Morgan was even still standing with his badly injured arm, but he held the gun on Mark without too much shaking, so Mark wasn't prepared to try a run at him. But he was fast running out of time for plan B.

But there was one thing in his favour.

With Mark's arrival, Kirwan knew Edward hadn't been alone, after all. So, he'd have to assume Mark had called it in, most likely to Liam. That meant help would be arriving at any time. Kirwan couldn't afford to muck around. He had to be itching to get out of there as fast as possible. Mark just couldn't work out how he was gonna turn things around before that happened.

Kirwan gave a satisfied grunt and started back down the stepladder, drive in hand, just as a slight movement on the floor caught Mark's eye. Edward's hand. The one hidden from Morgan. Five tiny but very definite finger taps, a pause, and then another five. Not a code, just a signal. *I'm awake. I'm ready.*

Mark's heart surged. *God fucking bless the man.* If they got out of this, Mark was gonna make it his mission to put a smile on Edward's face every damn day. After he'd killed him for getting himself shot, that was.

Kirwan brandished the drive with satisfaction and nodded at Morgan, who put his own weapon back on the granite, looking about two seconds away from keeling over.

"Thank you." Kirwan tucked the drive in his pocket. "And now, much as it pains me to have to do this—" He turned and put two bullets in Morgan's chest. The man's eyes hardly had time to register shock before he dropped to the floor.

Kirwan turned back to Mark. "You don't look surprised."

"How else were you gonna clean this up? This leaves Morgan to take the rap. Makes perfect sense. He comes to get the drive, shoots us but gets shot in return, all tied up with a big fucking bow. And best of all? You get to direct the investigation into the horrifying shootings of one of your detectives and a respected crown pathologist. I assume there'll be enough on Morgan's personal computers to tie him in but not enough to give away your part in all this or that money you're hoping to earn. You can't give away too much of that all-important hydrogen research, right? Just enough for motive but not enough to do you out of the millions it's worth on the market."

"True. And I'll need to find another partner, but I'm sure that won't be a problem. You think you're so smart, Knight, but it's not me sitting there with a gun pointed at his head."

Mark nodded sagely. "I have one question before you shoot us. What happened with Greene? Why did you need this drive?"

Kirwan grimaced. "Greene gave up the data he had, but the bastard didn't tell us they'd split some crucial stuff between him and Bridge. Neither man had the full workings. You needed both drives: one was the key for the other. We didn't know till we got it back and ran the figures. And then we needed to wait before moving again, so we wouldn't raise suspicion. But enough. You get a choice. You can go first or second, up to you."

Mark sucked in a ragged breath and pretended to think about it. There was no way of knowing if these were the last few seconds he and Edward had left. But on the floor, his lover didn't move a muscle. Mark had to hand it to Edward, he had nerves of steel.

"Second," he answered in a grim tone, holding his ribs as he coughed. "I can't let him die alone." His gaze slid sideways to the floor in the hope that Kirwan wouldn't read the lie hidden there. Second, in fact, merely meant there would be a fraction of time when the gun wasn't trained on Mark and he could maybe do something. What exactly that something was, he had no fucking idea, but he need to decide on it pretty damn soon. Morgan's gun still lay on the breakfast servery where he'd left it, but it was too far for Mark to reach.

"I'll make it quick." Kirwan took a step closer to where Edward and Tink lay sprawled on the floor—a step that angled the gun just that little bit away from Mark and gave him the only opportunity he was going to get.

When Kirwan straightened his arm to nuance his aim, Mark lunged, and Kirwan toppled. Mark was almost shocked how well it had worked, but he hadn't quite hit Kirwan where he wanted. It knocked Kirwan's gun hand, but not fast enough to stop him getting a shot off or hard enough to remove it from his grip. Mark had no time to worry where the bullet landed. He just had to believe he'd connected in time to send it off the mark—and maybe he had, but he'd also failed to seal the deal on Kirwan in any mean-ingful way.

The mistake proved costly, as Kirwan had only been temporarily knocked off balance. He was still on his feet, and when he rounded, furious, to take aim at Mark instead, Mark had nowhere to go. His last regret? Leaving Edward to die alone with that bastard.

Kirwan had the gun up in a split second, but it was a split second too long, as Edward's legs lashed out to sweep him off his feet. The move caught Kirwan by surprise, and though it failed to achieve its objective, it gave Mark the time he needed to wrap his hand around Kirwan's wrist and try to snap it back. Kirwan recovered fast enough to pull Mark towards him and release the tension on his wrist. They grappled chest to chest, Mark still desperately holding on to the man's wrist, the gun somewhere between them.

He was vaguely aware of Edward getting to his feet, but Mark was too focused on trying to stay alive to wonder what the hell his boyfriend was up to. A few seconds later, Edward reappeared behind Kirwan, Morgan's gun in his hand. *God bless him.* But his shirt was wet with blood, his face pale as a ghost, and the sight of him punched Mark square in the chest. Edward was struggling to stay on his feet, and Mark wasn't sure how long he'd be able to keep it together.

Edward placed the gun behind Kirwan's ear and gave it a push. "Drop it."

Kirwan froze but kept hold of his gun, Mark's fingers still wrapped around his wrist. "You try and shoot me, and I'll guarantee I can get a shot off before I die." He eased back to reveal his gun pushed up under Mark's diaphragm. It wouldn't be a clean shot, but it would be enough.

Mark sent an apologetic look Edward's way. "Just do it, babe."

Edward's eyes narrowed. "Like hell. In it together, right?" His eyes ticked down, and Mark didn't follow his meaning until he saw Tink laid out right alongside Kirwan's ankle. The dog was past actively helping, but maybe—

Mark jammed his fingernails into the arteries and nerves of

Kirwan's wrist and shoved his hand down as hard as he could while corkscrewing their bodies to try to overbalance the DCI, and fuck if it didn't work.

Kirwan slid his foot back to try to stabilise himself, connected with Tink's ample frame, and stumbled backwards over the mastiff, crashing to his back on the floor. His gun hand flew back with the impact, and a shot rang through the room. Kirwan's wrist exploded into a million pieces, and a half second later, a black-and-tan torpedo landed on his chest in a flash of snarling teeth.

Mark turned to the front door and came face to face with Liam, gun drawn on his boss, and behind him, Josh—both their faces set in deadly intent. Josh quickly scooped up Kirwan's gun and collected Edward's as well before shepherding him and Mark to the couch before they dropped.

Mark immediately turned and pulled at Edward's clothes. "Where did he get you?"

Edward gave a crooked smile and indicated his arm. "The bicep. Straight through. Could've been a lot worse. Nothing else."

Mark hauled him close and pressed a hungry kiss to his lips. "Don't you ever... *ever*... do that to me again." Edward tried to pull away, but Mark held on. "No. You're going nowhere. Where's the damn medics?" he yelled.

Josh squeezed his shoulder. "They're coming. We had to secure it first."

Mark grabbed his friend's arm. "How the hell did you know to come—"

Josh locked eyes with him, and Mark read all his worry and fear in a second. "Thanks," he said, squeezing Josh's arm. "You... I... fuck, man. Just thanks."

Josh nodded, his eyes full. He cleared his throat. "We found Morgan had gone to high school with Kirwan. They'd been good friends back then, apparently, or according to the online yearbook Connor found. There's been nothing to tie them together since, but adding that information to the question of a leak still hanging over the station, plus the fact Kirwan had asked Liam to give up where you were staying for some bullshit reason—we couldn't risk it.

"As soon as we suspected him, Liam asked me to put an unofficial tail on him, just to be on the safe side, while he did some fact-checking. Within the hour, Kirwan headed to a bar out west where he ditched his car in the parking lot and joined Morgan in one of his. That locked it up. I called it in to Liam, who called Stables, who approved an armed approach." His gaze swept the room. "Just as well. Anyway, the rest later."

"Josh?" The anguish in Edward's voice broke Mark's heart anew. "Tink, please. Don't leave her too long."

Josh nodded, and Mark knew that if anyone understood, his friend did. "They're gonna wanna take a look at you first, okay? But I'll tell them to work on Tink too, and we'll get her to a vet. I promise. She's in a bad way, though, Edward. Just... be prepared."

A wealth of emotions passed through Edward's eyes, every one of them heart-wrenching. Edward's hand grabbed for Mark's, but there was no way that was going to be anywhere near enough. He brushed it aside and drew Edward back into his arms, ribs be damned. It was a place Edward would be lucky to escape from in the foreseeable future.

He had a million questions for his partner and his friend, but all of them could wait. Nothing was more important right then than getting his hands on Edward in as many ways as possible, for as long as possible. He buried his face in Edward's hair, rocking them together until Edward stiffened.

"Ow?" he peeped from somewhere against Mark's bloodstained shirt.

"Shit, sorry." Mark eased off and ran his eyes over him.

Three paramedics arrived, and Mark reluctantly moved aside so they could work. One took Edward, another Kirwan, and the third dispensed equipment. Edward grabbed Mark's hand to keep him close, and the medic sighed.

"Just don't get in my way, Knight." He narrowed his gaze at Mark. "You okay to wait?"

Mark nodded. "Ribs hurt like a bitch, but that wasn't from tonight. Nothing new."

The medic cocked a brow. "I'll still need to check you." He went back to his work on Edward. "This is just a patch job, Doc. We'll be taking you to Auckland Med."

"Please, check on Tink?"

The medic glanced at the mastiff and sent the third medic to have a look.

A thought suddenly occurred to Edward. "Is Cam on tonight?"

The medic smirked. "On, and fit to spit tacks about you guys. Something about 'What the hell do they think they're up to,' and 'When I get my hands on those two,' and something else about balls and nails and walls, and—well, let's just say it was all very colourful."

Edward's eyes widened. "He knows already?"

The medic lifted his gaze. "What do you think?"

Edward shuddered. "You realise this is his house, right?"

The man's eyes popped as his gaze swept the disaster of a room, and then he cracked up. "Holy fuck. You're gonna need serious protection, my man."

Edward turned to Mark with an anguished expression. "We both are."

They sat in silence as the medic finished, Mark content to drink in every second of Edward by his side, amazed they'd survived. Edward's gaze was locked on Tink, who'd barely moved.

The bleeding seemed to have slowed, but her breathing was laboured and she wasn't responding. Liam helped Josh and the paramedic roll her on to a sheet, and they carried her out the front door—presumably to a car—with Paris following close behind, his ears down, nose all up in Tink's hair.

"The vet's on standby." Mark knew Josh was trying to sound reassuring for Edward, but Mark hadn't liked the look of her. Josh rested a hand on Edward's shoulder. "We'll let you know as soon as there's something to tell. One of the constables is taking her. She's in good hands."

Edward shivered and moved closer to Mark, the medic having finished with his patch-up dressings. "The wound in my arm was buried underneath me when I fell on top of Tink," Edward explained. "So they couldn't tell where I'd been shot without rolling me over. And Tink was gurgling and wheezing and bleeding something chronic. It got all over me, and I think they thought I'd been hit in the chest as well. I played it up, and then my fucking head checked out again—I wasn't knocked out, just... swimming. When I came to, I thought it best to stay still and pretend I was in worse condition than they thought."

Mark pressed a kiss to Edward's forehead. "Smart man."

"Yeah, well, then you arrived and all I could think of was how you were gonna get yourself shot as well. What were you thinking barrelling in here like that?"

"I was thinking I was gonna save your sexy arse."

The paramedic glanced up from his kit and smiled.

Edward snorted. "And instead I saved yours. How's that feel?"

Mark kissed Edward on the cheek. "How about we split the difference?"

Edward made a show of considering the suggestion. "I guess we could do that."

"Okay, your turn." The medic pulled at Mark's shirt to look at his ribs and grunted. "Strapping's still there. It'll do till we get you to hospital for another X-ray."

"I'll get myself there."

The medic rolled his eyes. "Of course you will."

Liam appeared behind the couch. "I'll take him."

The medic nodded. "In the meantime, we need to get going." He stood and waited for Edward to join him.

Mark rose at the same time and cradled Edward's face. He'd never take touching this man for granted ever again. "I'll meet you there, sweetheart."

Edward grimaced. "They're gonna want your statement—"

"I *said* I'll meet you there." Mark pressed a final kiss to Edward's lips and stepped back. "I'll bring us fresh clothes. Liam can interview me there. Besides, Cam needs a chance to yell at me. I'll take one for the team, okay?"

Edward's eyes were a turmoil of emotion. "I... We need to talk, you and me, when things... you know. I have words that need saying. Good words. Important words."

Mark's heart squeezed. "We both do."

They stared at each other for a long minute, until the medic interrupted with a grunt and an impatient roll of his eyes. "Anytime now would be good, gentlemen."

Edward nodded and let himself be escorted with a steadying hand at his elbow. Mark watched every step until Edward got to the front door, where he paused and turned back to face him.

"Just one more thing." He gave Mark a wry smile.

"I'm all ears." Mark grinned back.

"It's Remy," Edward said softly. "My middle name. R for Remy."

Mark gave a low whistle. "Goddamn, that's a sexy name."

Edward blushed brightly and turned to leave.

"So, which ones shall I bring?" Mark called out, before Edward disappeared from view.

"Fucking Avengers, of course," Edward threw back, and every head in the room turned.

Mark grinned widely. "Damn right, babe."

EPILOGUE

MARK FLICKED DOWN THE COLLAR OF HIS BLACK LEATHER
jacket which had been up against the bitter May wind howling
straight off the Hauraki Gulf. He got in the car making no effort
whatsoever to hide his frustration. He was about done with this day.
Three houses down the list and he was ready to haul Edward into the
nearest alley and take the man's cock down the back of this throat in
exchange for calling it a day. Then maybe they could go to the closest
bar for a drink and some hot food. And that might, in fact, have been
a viable option, if it weren't for Edward's sister Grace sitting in the
back seat. He glanced in the rear vision mirror and caught her
watching with a wicked smirk that said she knew exactly what he'd
been thinking.

"So, where to next?" he asked, not even trying to hide the grump
in his voice.

Edward patted his thigh indulgently. "Don't pout, it's not attractive. Twenty-five Maplewood Crescent. It's not far."

Mark put the car in gear and headed out, still grumbling.
"Haven't we already been to that one?"

Edward nodded. "Two weeks ago. I want another look."

Lord help him. "How many more are there after that?"

Edward turned with a smile. "This is the last one. Feel better?"

Mark knew he was being a prick. With the shooting two months behind them, Kirwan rotting in isolation in jail as he awaited yet another bail hearing, and the trial a full year away, Edward was only trying to get on with his life. And Mark was behaving like a spoiled baby.

There'd been more than enough evidence on Morgan and Kirwan's computers to fill in the gaps of their case and nail Kirwan's involvement. As it turned out, Bridge and Greene hadn't actually completed their groundbreaking research simplifying the process of using biomass to produce renewable hydrogen, but they'd been close. Evie and Finn were in discussions with Waikato University to co-fund the remaining work and share the patents that would see them financially secure. They'd generously invited Greene's ex-wife to be a part of that as well.

Mark and Edward had returned to work after a few weeks, and the time had flown since. Edward now had only a month left to find himself a house before his friends got back from Somalia, and the search had been tough going. House prices in Auckland rivalled Hong Kong and Sydney as some of the most expensive in the world, and any that had come within Edward's budget had sold at auction well outside it. The process was disheartening, and Edward had become increasingly despairing of finding anything in time.

Meanwhile, Mark had done nothing but whinge. And it had nothing to do with the weather. He was sulking. He knew it, and he suspected Edward knew it. Grace certainly fucking knew it.

He loved Edward's sister. They'd got on like a house on fire from the first time they'd met, when she and the rest of the Newton coven —as Mark liked to tease his sisters—had arrived the day after the shooting. Edward's parents had visited as well, but they'd merely provided the background harmony to the invasion, the logistical infantry. The sisters, on the other hand, had swept in like a synchro-nised swimming team, and Mark had lost Edward to a flail of arms, hair, tears, hugs, and kisses. Seeing his boyfriend the focus of such intense feminine concern and effervescent energy, he finally got it—got Edward's need for space, and got why his family meant the world to him.

But it had been a shock to Mark's system, watching those caring family dynamics so different from his own. His own father had greeted the news of Mark's case and the shooting with appropriate concern but nothing more. A few phone calls since to make sure he was okay, and that was it. Mark would take Edward to introduce them at some point, but he doubted his dad would ever be a force in their lives, not like this.

Mark had hovered on the fringes of the clan the entire first day, unsure how to break in and feeling more than a little sidelined. They'd come prepared and hauled their bags into Edward's house, making it clear where they were staying and leaving Mark unsure of his place. He and Edward had slept together the night of the shooting, wrapped in each other's arms, too tired to do more than hold on and be thankful. But when his family arrived the next day, Mark was left wondering where exactly he fit in. He didn't even know what Edward had told them about him.

Intending to leave them to catch up, he'd gathered his stuff and prepared to say his goodbyes. Edward had taken one look at the bag and ordered everyone except Mark from the room. Then he'd pulled Mark down on the couch alongside him and they quietly made out for a few minutes—about two hours too short for Mark's liking.

And that's as far as Mark had moved from Edward for the rest of that day. Edward had called his family back in and made it clear in no uncertain terms who Mark was, how important he was in Edward's life, and, with apologies to his parents—who simply looked amused by his hissy fit—Edward had told his sisters to back the fuck up and let Mark in.

The silence and dropped jaws had said it all, and shocked and disbelieving gazes flicked between Edward and Mark. That lasted about fifteen glorious seconds before the barrage of questions began and Mark found himself under the same intense sisterly scrutiny as Edward had been. Edward, the bastard, had simply watched the proceedings from the quiet comfort of his couch, an amused smile playing on his lips, and Mark briefly wondered if escaping to his apartment could still be a viable option.

That lasted until he curled around Edward's body that night—safe from prying eyes, thanks to a convenient lock on the door. In the dark, he thanked God for the gift of this man in his life. And when the cuddling turned to a set of spectacular mutual blow jobs that left both their hearts full and bodies glowing, well, he wasn't going to complain about that either. And in the warm space that enfolded them after, a space with room to breathe and hope, they'd finally had that conversation, a sharing of all those tender multisyllabic words that in the end had come down to one four-letter word in particular.

God knew, it was too soon. Sure as hell, Mark hadn't expected it. But damn if either of them could ignore it. They might have only had three days up close and personal, but it had been a three-month dance getting there, and Mark had to wonder if he hadn't been in love with Edward Newton before Edward even kissed him.

Of all the sisters, Grace was the one Mark had been drawn to most. She was witty, sassy, sharp as a tack, and feisty as hell. They sparked off each other and quickly became friends—much to Edward's horror, who saw endless teasing in his future. *Damn right.* Though, as Mark caught Grace's eye in the rear vision mirror for the second time, he knew Edward wasn't the only one in trouble.

"If the weather holds, we should try and go to that new listing in Westfern," she piped up, smothering a grin.

Mark glared at her. "No, we really shouldn't." The sooner Grace headed back to Christchurch the better. She'd taken on the house search like it was her God-ordained mission, and for the life of him Mark didn't get why Edward was letting her.

Edward sent him a hopeful look. "It might be a good idea. I mean, it has a pool, after all. And a huge yard for Tink."

Mark's heart filled at the reminder of the ridiculously huge dog that had taken up residence in his soul. Tink had needed three surgeries to fix the damage to her lungs and diaphragm from the bullet she'd taken, and she'd spent three weeks at the vet clinic—thank God for pet insurance—but she'd finally been allowed home and was on the mend.

Picking her up the day she was discharged had rated right up there in Mark's all-time favourite highlight reel, the tearful reunion between Edward and the mastiff a thing of beauty. Twice she'd saved them, and Mark would never be able to thank her enough for keeping Edward safe. To that end he'd moved her into their bedroom on her own hugely expensive inner-sprung dog bed, and she'd stayed there ever since.

They were having to work on her separation anxiety, a hangover from the stress and injury, but the last week she'd been getting better at letting Edward out of her sight, and the neighbours had stopped phoning about her wailing when she was left alone during the day. That could also be explained by the fact they'd stopped shutting her outside with her kennel and left her inside to drool where she chose. So there was that.

"You're surrounded by beaches. Why would you need a pool?" Mark snapped, then mentally slapped himself. He really needed to calm the fuck down.

It wasn't that he didn't want to be involved in the search. Hell, he wanted Edward to be happy, to find exactly what he needed. It was just that the closer they got to move day, the closer Mark got to moving back to his own apartment—a place that had become little more than a glorified wardrobe and storage unit for the last two months. Since the shooting, he hadn't slept a single night there. And far from getting on each other's nerves as Mark had fully expected, he and Edward had blended their lives surprisingly well.

When either of them felt tight in his own skin and needed space, they'd worked out a system of time-out chairs. If Mark was in the two-seater in the formal lounge, Edward knew to leave him to his thoughts, and vice versa if Edward took himself into the study. No hurt feelings, no forcing a conversation, no tantrums—well, not too many. After all, neither was great about sharing his thoughts, and sometimes a push was needed. But so far, they were making it work.

Or at least Mark thought they had been. Until Edward started his house search and there'd been no mention whatsoever of where Mark was to fit in with the new living arrangements. So, yeah, he might have been a bit pissy about that, even a bit hurt. And... yeah... had he mentioned pissy? *Dammit*. He should just bring it up and say how he felt, but that seemed a little... risky. If Edward wanted Mark to move with him, he would have said, right?

They pulled in outside the new address, and Mark decided to be a better boyfriend and plastered a more enthusiastic smile on his face as he opened the door for Edward to get out.

Edward rolled his eyes and pressed a kiss to his cheek. "Don't even," he said. "I know what you're thinking."

Mark arched a brow and put his lips against Edward's ear. "If you knew what I was thinking, Edward Remy Newton, you'd have dropped Grace at that mall and taken me home to your bed for a good fucking. That way I could scream your name without advertising to your sister just how much I fucking love your cock in my arse." He stepped back and eyed his gaping boyfriend.

Edward's eyes flashed with heat. "I... um... yeah, that would have been... crap... a good idea." His gaze flicked to Grace, who was eyeing them with suspicion. "Is it too la—"

"Yes," Mark huffed. "We're here, so let's get this over with. I know you love this house, but you also said it's more than you wanted to pay. Nothing like a bit of self-flagellation, I guess." He turned to Grace. "Come on, Broom-Hilda. Polish up that wand of yours."

Grace walked past and whacked Mark up the back of the head. "Such a funny guy."

Mark swept an arm for Edward to go ahead.

Edward hesitated and leaned in. "Can I, um... take a rain check on the whole fucked-and-screaming-my-name thing?"

Mark kissed him on the nose. "Our bedroom at nine. No dog, locks on, me naked in your bed, your sister be damned."

Edward's cheeks flushed. "That's... good, then. Great. I'll, um... look forward to it."

There were no two ways about it, the man was adorable. "You do that."

Mark knew why Edward loved this house. It was for the same reasons Mark did, and they'd talked about it well into the night after the first viewing. Though smaller than the others he'd considered—only three bedrooms, not the four Edward had been looking for, with his large family bound to visit—it had a cottagey feel, with a large garden and a lovely slice of view over the harbour from the living area that bumped the price up to compete with the larger properties. If Edward had asked, Mark might have considered going in with him to buy it, even if they *were* still quite new to the whole couple thing. But Edward hadn't asked, so yeah, there was that.

The real estate agent took herself outside, and Grace went wandering upstairs while Mark and Edward headed for the kitchen. Edward took some photos while Mark snooped in the cupboards. Pantries told you a lot about people. He was so focused, he didn't hear Edward slip up behind until a pair of arms circled his waist and drew him close.

He covered them with his own and leaned his head back. "You done torturing yourself?" he asked.

Edward's teeth found his shoulder. "Don't be mean."

Damn. Mark spun in Edward's arms and pulled him close. "I'm sorry. I know you love it. I wish—"

"That I could afford it?" Edward pouted.

Mark winced. "Yeah."

Edward wriggled up against him. "Well, um, since we might not be back here, maybe we could find a bit of privacy in the bathroom for a bit? I'm sure the agent won't miss us."

What? Mark rested a hand on Edward's forehead. "Nope. Doesn't feel hot."

"Come on." Edward's hand drifted down to cup Mark through his jeans. "You chicken?"

Mark was sure his eyes must have popped out of their damn sockets. "Um, Edward? What's this about? You know we can't—"

"Why?" Edward worked Mark with his hand while he nibbled at his jaw, making Mark wonder if they could in fact disappear... No.

"'Cause it's n-not our frickin' house, that's w-why—ugh, stop that."

Edward did in fact stop manhandling Mark's dick which was... a surprise.

He took a step away and fixed Mark with a smile. "But what if it was?"

Mark froze, the statement hanging between them. "Edward, what are you saying?"

Edward winked, took him by the hand, and led him through to the lounge and its beautiful view through a wall of glass doors to the harbour beyond. Not to mention four friends, one sister, and two large dogs lounging on the grass.

What the hell? "Edward?"

Edward turned and took both Mark's hands. "I bought it."

Mark couldn't have been more shocked. "You did what?"

"You heard me. I bought it."

"But you said it was too" He frowned. "But... you didn't tell me?"

Edward bit his bottom lip and hesitated for a second, then said, "The minute I saw this place, I knew it was meant for us."

Us? He said 'us.'

Edward read Mark's surprise and smiled, then kissed him firmly on the lips. "Yes, *us*, you ridiculous man. Did you really think I was going to let you go back to that damned apartment?"

Mark's mind blanked. "I, um... I didn't know. I didn't want to assume..." *He'd said 'us.'*

"I wanted to surprise you, which I clearly did. I thought for sure you'd guess. God, I'm sorry if I messed up."

Mark's eyes brimmed.

Edward saw, and his eyes blew wide. "Oh, shit. I didn't mean... I'm so sorry if I—"

Mark grabbed him by the shoulders and took his mouth in a punishing kiss. "No. Don't be sorry. I'm just so fucking relieved. I was worried you'd had second thoughts."

"Never." Edward's kiss this time was lingering, his tongue sweeping through Mark's mouth as if he had all the time in the world. Finally he pulled back.

"So, you'll come live here... with me?" he asked tentatively. "I mean, you know I love you, right? So damned much. And I know you love this house as much as I do. But I didn't want to just assume... you know? I didn't want to put you on the spot. I thought, this way, I could buy it and we could live here. And you could rent your apartment until... well, until you were ready, and then we'd just go and get the deed changed. I didn't want to... rush you."

His gaze searched Mark's for reassurance, and Mark gave it in an instant. "Yes. Yes, I want this. Yes, I want you. Yes, it was a great idea, and a wonderful surprise, even if I was about to hit you on the head and drag you off to my cave so you didn't kick me out. But if you think anything is gonna change my mind about us, you've got another think coming. You make me so happy. And maybe I won't sell my apartment." Edward frowned, and Mark tapped his nose. "Maybe I'll just rent my place out, and we can keep it as an investment. Together."

Edward's grin was of epic proportions. "Together. Yeah, I like the sound of that." He tugged Mark by the hand towards the glass coffee table. "And, on that note, I have a gift for you." He picked a small paper bag up from the table and handed it to Mark.

Mark eyed it dubiously.

"Open it."

Mark did and discovered a bright red... collar. *Huh.* He dangled it between them. "Is this a new kink you want to try, babe? 'Cause I have to say I didn't see it coming."

Edward laughed. "Arse. And no, not unless you're the one wearing it." He looked thoughtful. "Yeah, I could get into that."

Mark snorted. "Nuh-uh. Never gonna happen."

Edward shook his head. "Shame. But then we'll just have to use it for its intended purpose." He grabbed Mark's hand again and rapped on the huge glass slider.

At the sound, Cam waved, got to his feet, and headed up the drive. A few seconds later he returned, leading a large, shaggy, black-haired behemoth of a dog with a mouth to rival Tink's and a whole lot of trouble written all over it.

Mark rounded on his boyfriend. "Edward, what have you done?" But he could hardly keep the grin off his face.

Edward blushed beetroot. "She's a, um... Newfoundland. About eighteen months old. Her owners couldn't deal with her size when she grew and handed her back to her breeder. So she's ours, yours... if you want?"

"Mine?" Mark's head spun.

"If you want. I thought they'd be good together, and it might help with Tink's anxiety. Plus, I know how much you love Tink. But she is kind of fixated on me at the moment, so I thought... well, I wondered if... I just wanted you to have—"

"Yes." Mark grabbed Edward around the waist and lifted him off his feet, crushing him to his chest. "I love her. I love you. And yes, I want her." He returned Edward to the floor, and Edward tugged his T-shirt back into place.

"Right, then, that's... good. Right." Edward blew out a relieved sigh. "I would've taken her myself, anyway, I just—"

"Too late, she's mine." Mark hesitated. "But what if Tink doesn't—"

Edward's guilty gaze slid to the side. "They, um, met last week."

"Oh, did they now." Mark watched Tink, Paris, and the other dog playing silly buggers on the lawn.

"I needed to be sure they'd, um... get along." Edward stood alongside him. "And they do, as you can see."

"Does she come with a name?"

"They, her other owners, called her Doodles."

Mark gasped. "Who the hell calls their dog Doodles? All the other dogs will laugh at her in the park. We're not keeping it."

Edward breathed a sigh of relief and melted against Mark's side. "Well, I thought of one... if you like it?"

"Go on, spill." Mark kissed the top of his head.

Edward looked up through those long lashes—a guaranteed way to get Mark's heart to melt, and the bastard knew it.

"Nana."

"Nana? What the..."

Edward held up a hand. "As in Nana, the children's dog from *Peter Pan*. It's a big debate whether James Barrie meant for Nana to be a Newfoundland or a St Bernard. But I'll, um, understand if you think it's silly. She's your dog, after all."

Mark cradled Edward's face and held his eye. "I think it's perfect. Just like you. Now, can I go and meet the new member of our family?"

Edward drew a sharp, stuttered breath. "Our family?" He sighed. "Yeah, I like the sound of that."

They headed for the door and the round of applause that rose to meet them.

Mark threaded his fingers through Edward's and squeezed. "Just one thing. We don't have near enough furniture covers."

The End.

Thank you for taking the time to read

UP CLOSE AND PERSONAL
Auckland Med 3

If you enjoyed this book please consider doing a review in Amazon or your favourite review spot. I didn't realise until I was an author just how important reviews are for helping an author's sales and spreading the word. I thank you in advance.

Buy the next in the series

AGAINST THE GRAIN

Auckland Med 4

I don't like labels and I'm happy that way, but it's taken a long time to get here. A jerk of a father, too many bullies to name, and a string of dipshit boyfriends whose interest in me rarely made it past the skirts I sometimes wear. Suffice to say, my faith in men runs a little thin.

The last thing I need is a gruff, opinionated, fiery, closeted, Paralympian jock messing with my hard-won peace. Miller Harrison is a wrinkle in my life I could definitely do without. I have a job that I love at Auckland Med., a boss who understands me, and a group of friends who accept me as I am.

I should walk away.

But Miller knows a thing or two about living life against the grain, and that hope I thought I'd buried a long time ago, is threatening to surface.

AUTHOR'S NOTE

HAVE YOU READ JAY 'S
SOUTHERN LIGHTS SERIES?

POWDER AND PAVLOVA
by Jay Hogan

Southern Lights 1

ETHAN SHARPE is living every young Kiwi's dream—seeing the world for a couple of years while deciding what to do with his life. Then he gets a call.

Two days later he's back in New Zealand. Six months later his mother is dead, his fifteen-year-old brother is going off the rails and the café he's inherited is failing. His life is a hot mess and the last thing he needs is another complication—like the man who just walked into his café,
   a much older...
   sinfully hot...

EPIC complication.

TANNER CARPENTER's time in Queenstown has an expiration date. He has a new branch of his business to get up and running, exorcise a few personal demons while he's at it, and then head back to Auckland to get on with his life. He isn't looking for a relationship especially with someone fifteen years his junior, but Ethan is gorgeous, troubled and in need of a friend. Tanner could be that for Ethan, right? He could brighten Ethan's day for a while, help him out, maybe even offer some... stress relief, no strings attached.

It was a good plan, until it wasn't.

REVIEWS OF POWDER AND PAVLOVA

"Funny, sexy, sweet and touching. Powder and Pavlova made me smile, made me cry, and I was so captivated by it that I raced through it in a couple of sittings. Jay Hogan has earned a place on my list of 'must read' authors."
  —All About Romance Reviews

"The story had that warm and comforting feeling that you rarely find and that you can't quite describe or explain, but we get it here.... A spectacular read."
  —OMG Reads

POWDER AND PAVLOVA
CHAPTER ONE

Ethan stared slack-jawed at the cremated remains. *Goddammit.*

Lucy slotted alongside, her birdlike fingers threading with his. "We were too late."

A hand landed on his other shoulder and Adrian rumbled gruffly in his ear, "I had a bad feeling about today."

Ethan turned and rolled his eyes at his friend. "Jesus, Ads. You have a bad feeling about *every* day. The word pessimistic has nothing on you."

"Doesn't make it any less true."

"We should've checked sooner—" Ethan didn't finish the sentence because he was being an arsehole . . . again.

Lucy dropped his hand.

Yep, arsehole.

"We?" Her gaze narrowed. "*You* left them, Ethan."

"I had to take a call. You knew—"

"How? By osmosis? Stop being a prick—"

Yeah, about that.

"How were we to know the babies were too hot? The kitchen is *your* domain."

She was right, of course. Didn't stop the choking scent of money going up in smoke—money the café couldn't afford.

"Ten minutes. I was gone ten minutes, and this . . ." He snagged a small, blackened orange syrup cake, turned it over in his hand, and threw it in the bin along with its 149 brothers and sisters. It hit with a heavy thunk that pretty much said it all. If he included all the prep time, the ruined cakes represented close to a full day's work and way too much wasted money to think about. *Crap.*

The café bell saw Adrian spin on his heels and hightail it out of the kitchen like his arse was on fire, and Ethan didn't blame him. He turned to Lucy whose bumblebee tattoo on her neck was pulsing in annoyance. *Shit.*

"Look, Luce—"

"No, you look, Ethan Sharpe." She stabbed a finger at his chest. "We *did* check, with five minutes still left on the timer. That's how we knew they were toast." She eyed the bin and her expression softened. "Literally, as it turned out. And if they were that tricky, you shouldn't have left them unattended. You employed us to run the café, remember, not bake."

She was right. And that particular oven had been giving Ethan grief for weeks. There just wasn't any money to get it fixed. None of this was their fault. He was just mad at *himself* for answering the damn call in the first place. Getting hauled over the coals by his bank for being well over his line of credit wasn't anything he'd needed to be in a hurry to hear.

"You're right," he apologised. "It *is* on me."

"Damn right." Lucy eyeballed him a moment longer, then threw her arms around his neck.

He sank into the hug with a groan. "Jesus, Luce. What the fuck am I gonna do? We needed this order."

"I know." She popped a kiss on his cheek and stepped back. "When are they supposed to pick them up?"

"First thing tomorrow. They're for Milo's twenty-first."

She blinked slowly. "Okay, we do another batch. You got enough oranges?"

"Not even close." He frowned, shaking his head. "Besides, another batch will wipe out our profit."

"But it keeps a customer, right?" She arched a brow.

He blew out a sigh. "True. And I thought I was the optimist."

Lucy smiled. "We both are, at least compared to our resident grumpy barista."

She wasn't wrong. Adrian had a decidedly cynical and pessimistic view on life for a thirty-something, hellishly attractive gay man in the hospitality industry. Looking like he'd walked straight out of a South American drug cartel—handsome, dark, and dangerous, with sky-blue eyes, a selection of leather cuffs, and a wardrobe almost exclusively limited to black T-shirts and jeans, Adrian was the epitome of a secret squirrel.

Not the most retail-friendly of styles, but his talent behind an espresso machine was unparalleled in Queenstown, at least in

Ethan's opinion, and for that, he was prepared to forgive much. And on some days, there was much to forgive. Besides, he had a soft spot for odd ducks like Adrian, and he couldn't imagine letting him go for any reason—his grumpiness was part of his charm . . . mostly.

"Right . . ." Lucy whipped Ethan's apron off, spun him around, and gave him a shove toward the swing door through to the café. "Get a coffee down you before your lower lip hits the floor. I'll call Raul to send us more oranges."

Ethan glanced at the kitchen clock. "They have to boil for two hours and then cool before we even start on the cakes. It's nearly four already. You're off the clock in an hour. I'll just call Milo."

Lucy dismissed the idea with a wave of her hand. "These are Milo's favourites, right?"

He nodded.

She tied the apron around her waist. "I'll order pizza. We'll have a baking party. It'll be fun. Now get out of here."

He stared, so fucking thankful for this tiny whippet of a young woman who'd walked into his café only three months before and changed his life for the better. Fired from her receptionist job in an automotive repair shop for making out with the owner's twenty-something daughter in the mechanic's pit—the impossibly green-eyed, blonde, small-boned, denim-loving, and prettily inked girl had blundered into Ethan's café to mope over one of Adrian's excellent lattes.

Seeing her in tears, Ethan had grabbed a seat opposite to make sure she was okay. Twenty minutes later, he'd hired her. Best. Decision. Ever. Scary smart with numbers, she ran the café like her own personal war room. He'd be freaking lost without her.

He pulled her into a bone-crushing hug. "I do love you; you know that?"

She blushed brightly. "I do. It's a shame our respective girl and boy bits don't like each other, or we could've made magic together."

Ethan almost choked on his tongue. "Yeah, nah. Be like kissing my sister."

She elbowed him in the ribs. "Hey, you couldn't handle these lips. Now go ask grumpy pants out there to make you a coffee, and warn him he's leaving late."

"He won't want—"

"Of course he will." She shooed him out the door.

The café was quiet other than a few tourists enjoying a coffee whilst ogling the spectacular landscape beyond the glass. Lake Wakatipu was at its glittering cobalt best, framed on its far shore by the majesty of the aptly named Remarkables—one of the ranges that encircled the tourist mecca of Queenstown and its chocolate-box assortment of all-time favourite tourist hits—world-class ski fields, adventure tourism to die for, movie sets coming out its ears, and some of the most stunning hiking and scenery on the planet. Hence the three million or so annual visitors to a town sporting a live-in population of around 20,000.

In May, with the flame of autumn on the trees, the place lit up like a fiery halo, and not for the first time Ethan thanked his lucky stars for that one-in-a-million view. It was without doubt, singlehandedly keeping his struggling café from liquidation. That and the ever-increasing squeeze on local infrastructure forced tourist overflow out to fringe suburban cafés like his mother's, or his, rather. And just like that, the yawning pit in his stomach cracked a little wider, because however beautiful the view, it wasn't going to be enough to save them.

"Coffee, boss?" Adrian had his eye on the steam wand as he frothed a new jug of milk.

"When you're done with these guys." He nodded to the two customers in line.

The woman nodded her thanks.

The man grumbled, "I've been waiting ten minutes already."

Shit. Don't do it, Ads.

"A good coffee takes time." Adrian eyed the man. "You want fast? There's a fuel station down the road."

And there it was.

The man's cheeks blew red.

Ethan grabbed Adrian's arm. "It won't be long."

The customer looked Ethan up and down. "Don't tell me this is your joint?"

Ethan sighed. "Yes, I'm the owner."

The man snorted. "Jesus Christ, I'm in a fucking kindergarten."

Ethan struggled to keep his expression neutral. Looking younger than his twenty-three years was a blessing, or a curse, depending on who he was with. "Hurry up with the man's coffee, Ads."

"But—"

Ethan sharply tightened his grip.

"Fine."

"Last time I'm coming here," the man grumbled.

"Also fine," Adrian grunted.

Ethan booted Adrian under the counter. "Take a seat. We'll bring it over."

The woman customer turned and watched the man shuffle off. "You're right, he *is* an arsehole."

Adrian raised his hand and the woman high-fived it.

Oh, for fuck's sake. Ethan perched on the stool beside Adrian's five-headed behemoth of a coffee machine. He had teenage memories of it singing like a choir with all five heads in action. The last month or so, they barely had a duet, if they were lucky.

"We can't afford to lose customers, Ads."

"Sorry. He just pissed me off." He flicked a wary glance Ethan's way. "You okay . . . about the cake thing?"

Was he? Ethan gave a weak smile. "Not much I can do about it. I just . . . well, we needed that profit, yeah?" He tunnelled his fingers—still sticky with orange syrup—through his hair, catching a million floury knots already embedded there and ensuring a painful session with the comb later. "Lucy suggested we do another batch . . ."

"Tell her I'll have pepperoni."

"Already ordered, oh grouchy one." She appeared at Adrian's elbow.

"Excellent." He tamped down the next portafilter and twisted it into the head with a snap.

Lucy turned his way. "Raul's sending a box of oranges in ten minutes, so you better make that coffee quick. I'll get the rest ready to go." The door to the kitchen closed behind her with a soft whoosh.

Adrian leaned in. "You um, need me to take a pay cut? I know things are tight and I don't want to work anywhere else. You're um . . . not an arsehole. So . . . that's a bonus."

Ethan snorted softly. "Gee, thanks. But no, and I'm hoping it doesn't come to that."

Adrian nodded. "Well, the offer's there. It's not like I have mouths to feed or a partner to explain it to, right?"

Ethan actually had no idea about *either* of those. Adrian was pretty much a closed shop when it came to anything personal, but he nodded vaguely anyway and wondered yet again about his handsome barista's secretive life. Adrian never spoke of his family, and the one-time Ethan had asked, he'd been shut down fast. He didn't even know Adrian's romantic *preferences*. He'd once caught him observing a particularly sassy male customer in a manner that could only be described as blatantly checking the guy out.

Ethan was under the bench grabbing a container of milk to top up Adrian's froth jug when the café bell sounded again.

"I'm making yours first." Adrian accepted the milk.

"I can wait."

"*They* can wait," he said in a tone that brooked no argument.

Ethan sighed. "Fine, whatever. I'll get their order." He stepped around Adrian and . . . froze. *Holy crap. Him.*

Ethan swallowed hard. The attractive man had been in a few times over the last couple of weeks, always ordering a tray of coffees but never when Ethan was behind the register. That had left him no option but to stickybeak from the kitchen—not nearly good enough.

There was just something about him that snagged Ethan's attention and refused to let go. Whether it was the flecks of silver in the wash of dark hair that swept up from a small scar on the top of his forehead, or the sexy-as-shit closely trimmed beard that faded up into his hairline. Or maybe it was those fucking slate-grey eyes that had pinned Ethan to the spot the very first time they'd landed on him the week before, hesitating just a second before the bastard added a devastating smile on top. He wasn't quite silver-fox material, but he was cruising that direction in significant style.

So, yeah, Ethan was crushing hard. But he also wasn't silly. He was twenty-three and looked younger, whereas this guy had maturity and confidence painted all over him like a damn Tom Ford suit—and was in all likelihood straight. Dressed in a pair of snug black chinos that hugged his arse like they were glued in place, a crisp, white cotton shirt left loose overtop—two buttons undone to reveal a tempting peek of dark hair—a brushed titanium watch, and black loafers, the entire outfit screamed cool, chic, and successful.

Not that Ethan had noticed, of course. Nope, not him. Just like he hadn't noticed the slight limp he sported on colder days or the way his lips quirked up at the side when he saw something he liked on the menu. And all this spotted from the depths of the kitchen giving him a crick in his neck. Ethan cleared his throat and did his best not to look like a total fool.

"Hi," the guy said, looking faintly bemused—nothing to do with the fact that Ethan had been staring at him for about a year too long.

Ethan tried not to focus on that sinful mouth, but yeah . . . epic fail. *Goddammit.* Adrian's mocking eyes drilled into the back of his neck like laser headlights.

"Oh, right . . . um, hi," he flustered, his gaze stuck on those full lips as they stretched into a sexy grin. *And ugh, now he was getting hard.* He clenched his teeth and dragged his eyes back up to lock onto those gorgeous smiling eyes—smoky-grey and sharp as a tack. As if having that body wasn't enough. How was that even fair?

The toe of a boot landed on the back of his calf.

"You okay there, boss?" Adrian chuckled. *Bastard.*

Ethan threw Adrian a menacing, don't-you-fucking-dare scowl which earned him another chuckle. *Double bastard.*

"You want me to deliver this to our resident arsehole," Adrian commented dryly, "so he can get the fuck out of your café?"

Ethan winced and a shot a glance at the sexy man in front of him whose grin had just broadened. He was gonna kill Adrian, and then he was gonna fire him. "Just behave yourself," he warned. Then he turned and shrugged at the customer. "Good help is hard to find, right?"

The man studied him with a curious expression. "So you're the owner then?"

Ethan felt his cheeks heat. "Yeah. For my sins. Don't be fooled by this cultured air of sophistication—" He grinned wryly. "—I'm younger than I look."

The man snorted.

"So, can I get you a coffee?" Ethan's voice cracked a little and he coughed to cover it. "Sorry, flour caught in my throat," he explained. Not a damn thing to do with the mouth-watering slice of sex on a stick standing right in front of him, of course.

"Would seem like the thing to do," the guy answered, adding a sexy smile. "Getting a coffee, I mean."

He leaned in just a fraction and Ethan nearly swallowed his tongue.

"Unless you had something else in mind?" He hovered for a second, almost in licking distance—well, if Ethan climbed the counter and launched himself across it, he was. He leaned back. *Embarrassing crisis averted.*

Ethan stared, and a pair of smiling eyes danced back. *Holy shit.* Had the guy just flirted with him? In what universe was that even possible? It hadn't entered Ethan's head that the guy might be gay, or bi, or whatever. Bad enough he pressed every one of his buttons and a few he didn't even know he had, but to also walk Ethan's side of the street? *Well, shit. It was gonna suck not living up to that possibility.*

"Jesus," Adrian murmured under his breath. "Is it hot in here, or what?"

Ethan levelled a glare at his barista. *Definitely firing him.*

Adrian batted his eyes innocently.

Ethan turned his back and narrowed his gaze across the counter at his customer. "We make good coffees. How many?" he asked bluntly, as if it mattered neither one way nor the other, as if he was just another customer—one that didn't have Ethan juggling his balls with every deliciously heated gaze.

The guy smirked, not fooled for a minute. "Four, actually, to go. Two triple-shot lattes, one cappuccino, and a flat white. Oh, and a half-dozen of those delicious excuses for a heart attack in your cabinet." He pointed out the raspberry jam donuts made fresh daily by Ethan's business-neighbour-in-crime, Elle, the middle-aged, potty-mouthed darling who ran the Kiwi Collectibles shop next door.

He rang up the order, then grabbed a box for the donuts, and tucked six inside. "I'll need a signed indemnity form before you take them," he deadpanned and held the box out. "The café won't be held responsible for any adverse effects from said sugar and cream consumables. We at the Golden Spoon recommend moderation in all indulgences."

And . . . Oh. My. God. Had he really just said that?

The man beamed, and Ethan wanted to lick the smile right off his face.

"Is that so?" The look he levelled Ethan's way could have singed his eyebrows clean off. "In *all* indulgences, huh? Now that *would* be a crying shame, don't you think?"

Jesus. Ethan couldn't move, the innuendo cutting off all blood supply not directed to his balls and related appendages.

The man tugged gently at the box of donuts. "You, ah, wanna let go?" His smile drove a halo of warmth around Ethan that promised a whole lot of things Ethan had no right or time to explore. The guy smirked.

Bastard. He knew exactly what he'd done.

"Sorry, it's been a long day." Ethan blew out a shaky breath and stuck the coffee order on Adrian's machine. "Gotta check something out back. Coffees shouldn't be long." He hightailed it back to the kitchen, catching the hint of a chuckle as he left.

Safe from those heather-grey eyes, Ethan collapsed against the door jamb and tried to calm his thundering heart. What. The. Ever-loving. Fuck? He checked his forehead for the tell-tale loser sign he was sure he'd find carved there. Nope, just a shit-ton of nervous perspiration.

"Mister Hot and Heavy is in again, I take it?" Lucy smiled from the other side of the stainless prep bench, her hands white with flour.

"I have no idea who you're talking about." Ethan wiped his hands on his jeans and rearranged the order forms stacked on the desk.

She snorted in disgust. "You can't lie for shit Ethan; I don't know why you bother."

"You're being ridiculous," Ethan scoffed. "The guy's gotta be close to forty." *Just how I like them . . . apparently.*

She looked up from measuring the dry goods. "Well, he's damn hot."

"I hadn't noticed." He collated the pencils according to colour.

"Liar."

He threw the last of the pencils in the caddy and fell back against the wall. "That obvious, huh?"

Lucy's grin split her face. "Like a whore in a convent."

He snorted. "There's an image I didn't need."

Lucy reached for the huge sieve and worked her way through a second mound of flour. "So, what are you doing in here?"

"Hiding?"

"Well, get back out there, mister. He'll be gone in a minute. You wouldn't want to miss a final perv."

Ethan pushed off the wall. "I wasn't perving. I merely took his order."

Lucy's gaze dipped south of Ethan's belt. "Yeah, right. Tell it to your friend."

Ethan blushed furiously and crossed his legs.

"And I'll bet coffee's not the only order you'd like to take from him," she added with a wink.

A host of delightfully filthy images raced through Ethan's head and he groaned.

"And there it is." Lucy smiled knowingly.

"Oh. My. God. What is it with you lot?" Ethan grumbled, mortified at how badly he'd been caught out. He tugged his shirt a mite lower and flipped her off. "You're lucky I love you, bitch."

"You're lucky I let you, arsehole."

He pushed open the door and ambled back into the café. *Nothing to see here, folks.* His effort at nonchalance was ruined the second he laid eyes on mister tall, dark, and fucking combustible when he caught his foot in a stool and tripped. Arms windmilling, he stumbled almost to his knees at his feet. *Really Ethan? Really?* Not one of his better Kodak moments.

He glanced up in time to see the man bite back a laugh, but he refused to linger on that whole teeth-on-lip action. If there was a prize for most humiliating crush on an *almost* silver fox, he'd win it hands down.

A white cuffed hand appeared in front of his face to help him up. *Ugh.* Add gallant to the list and bury Ethan then and there. He had little choice than to accept the offer, totally unprepared for the reality of actually touching his crush for the first time.

Warm and dry, the sexy man's hand wrapped confidently around Ethan's, and he helped him to his feet, holding a little longer than Ethan thought was strictly necessary, but Ethan wasn't complaining. He wasn't thinking anything much at all, to be honest, lost in a buzz of sensation that centred primarily around his dick but with added notes of unexpected calm that completely threw him for a loop.

"Tanner," he said evenly.

Ethan stared like a fool. "Huh?" *Oh yeah, he was smooth.*

He arched a brow. "My name, it's Tanner."

Ethan's cheeks blazed. "Oh, right, Tanner. That's, ah . . . good.

Ethan . . . I'm Ethan." *Shit.* There was always the chance the café floor would do him a fucking favour and swallow him whole, but no— the universe clearly hated him. So be it. He tossed his head and met Tanner's steady gaze with one of his own. He could do this.

"Nice to meet you . . . Ethan." He offered his hand . . . again.

Ethan wiped his hand down his jeans before accepting and was once again swept away by Tanner's composure. This time the hand-shake *definitely* went beyond mere courtesy, Tanner's fingers trailing over Ethan's wrist, so unmistakably flirtatious that Ethan jerked back in surprise.

Tanner instantly dropped his hand and stepped back, a pink tinge to his cheeks. "Sorry. I thought you . . . never mind. I'm sorry."

It was the first time Tanner had looked anything but poised, and it had Ethan's butterfly stocks spiralling upwards. *You thought . . . what? That I was receptive to a little hand flirtation . . . gay even? Yes, you ridiculous, gorgeous man. Of course I'm gay. What do you think this damn hard-on is? Starch in my underwear? Get back here.*

But none of that came out of Ethan's mouth because he was . . . oh right, standing there like a fucking dipstick, his tongue hanging out on the floor.

"Your order." Ads pushed the carry crate of four coffees Tanner's way with an expression that clearly said he found the whole thing fucking hilarious.

Tanner took the carry crate and slid the box of donuts under-neath. "You make excellent coffee—" He peered at the name tag. "—Adrian. Best I've had."

Ethan swore Adrian sprouted three inches before his eyes. He'd have been amused if it wasn't for the wad of jealousy that *he* was at the receiving end of a Tanner-shaped compliment. Ridiculous meet pathetic. And, *oh shit*, he really needed to say something before Tanner left with entirely the wrong notion about Ethan, like he was straight, for example.

Tanner flicked his gaze Ethan's way again. "And it *was* nice to meet you. I'm sorry if I read things wrong—"

"You didn't." Ethan finally found some words that actually worked on his tongue. "I mean . . ." He glanced at Adrian, who was making a piss-poor attempt to hide that he was eavesdropping, then grabbed Tanner's free hand and tugged him out of hearing distance. *Real classy.* Tanner looked surprised but didn't fight him.

Safe from prying ears, Ethan took a deep breath. "I'm gay," he said with a dramatic gush of air, as if the announcement was about to herald world peace.

The pop of eyebrows and amused smile on Tanner's face said it all. "Oh."

Ethan's cheeks heated . . . again. "That is . . . if that was what you meant . . . when you thought you'd got it wrong . . . I mean . . . oh shit . . . I've cocked up again, right?" Mortified, he spun to leave, but a firm hand landed on his forearm.

"It was exactly what I meant," Tanner said, those fine lines in the corners of his eyes just begging for Ethan's fingers to dally over them a while. And, oh God, did he just use the word dally? What the fuck was wrong with him?

Tanner added, "Snap. I'm gay too. How about that? Shall we exchange the secret handshake?"

Ethan's brows dipped.

"Just kidding." Tanner laughed, and the sound washed over Ethan like a warm breeze. "Nice to meet you, Ethan who is gay."

Ethan's turn to smile. "Likewise. Nice to meet you, Tanner . . . ? Tanner who is also gay. Oh fuck, I sound like a total prat, don't I? If you run away now, I won't blame you, and I promise never to stalk you in my café or on any social media sites . . . except maybe Facebook, 'cause everyone has one of those, right? And it's not really stalking when you do it on Facebook. It's practically a sign of mental unbalance if you don't . . . um, don't you think?"

Ethan caught a choked laugh from the direction of the coffee machine and realised he'd said all of that in an outside voice. *Fuck.* A quick sweep of the café confirmed his fear that his verbal vomit had grabbed the attention of all the remaining customers—all six of them.

He bowed dramatically. "That's all folks. I'll be here all week."

When he turned back, he fully expected Tanner to have fled for the hills. Instead, he was regarding him as you would a fascinating puzzle that you simply knew you were never gonna find all the pieces to. Welcome to my life, Ethan thought. You ought to see it from this side.

"Sorry," he repeated.

"Nothing to be sorry for," Tanner said. "Looks like you've got your hands full." His gaze swept the café. "I noticed your name on the door the first time I came in. I just hadn't put two and two together until you said. I'm guessing that happens a lot. You look—"

"Young? Wow, first time I've heard that." Ethan sent him a thin smile. "I'm twenty-three."

"So, yes, young," Tanner teased with a smile.

Ethan was less than amused. "Not helpful. Or funny, actually. There's twenty-three, and then there's *twenty-three*, right? Depends on what you did with those years. I've known plenty of older men who needed to do a fair bit of growing up."

"Ouch." Tanner nodded. "But you're right. I didn't mean to offend."

Ethan shrugged. "You didn't, not really. I'm just kind of over it, I guess. People tell me when I get older, I'll appreciate the fact I look younger than I am, but right now, not so much." He eyeballed Tanner. "People tend to make . . . assumptions."

Tanner smiled and Ethan wished, really wished, he wouldn't. "Duly noted," he said. "So, your café then? A lot of hard work, I imagine?"

Ethan tried to keep the worry from his sigh. "It was my mother's originally, but yeah, I guess it's mine now."

Tanner's brow creased in concern. "You say that like it's a bad thing?"

And suddenly Ethan wanted to tell this man he hardly knew exactly how much of a total screw up his life really was. He didn't, because . . . well, because he had to bake orange cakes . . . and the guy was a customer . . . and oh, that bit about hardly knowing him. So yeah, there was that.

"Not a bad thing, exactly," he answered carefully, feeling suddenly very small alongside this man who wore success like a quality cologne—subtle, but you knew it was there. "Just . . . unexpected, I guess, and . . . a lot to think about."

Like being behind on his business loan, a truckload of baking to do, a house that needed looking after, and a brother . . . *Ugh*, Ethan didn't even want to think about that particular shitstorm. So yeah, it was time to head back to reality where men like Tanner didn't hit on guys like Ethan.

"You best get those coffees to their owners before they get cold," he said evenly and stepped away.

Tanner glanced down as if he'd entirely forgotten he even had them. "Right. Well, I'll see you next time, maybe?"

Ethan shrugged. "Unless the door is chained, I'll be here."

Tanner frowned again, then nodded and left. And Ethan absolutely did not watch that sexy arse swing all the way across the car park and up the street, not even for a second. Must have been someone else.

"Get your mind out of the gutter, bro." Ah, the aforementioned brother, Kurt.

Ethan swung around to face his pain-in-the-neck younger sibling. At sixteen and with an attitude that had Ethan rolling his eyes heavenward with thoughts of, *you're lucky I didn't bury your disrespectful arse yesterday*, Kurt was deep in the throes of teenage snark and soaring hormones. A merciless combination at the best of times, let alone added to everything the two of them had faced over the last year. Ethan nodded at the clock. "You were supposed to be here half an hour ago."

Kurt shrugged, threw his school bag under the nearest table, and parked himself in a chair. "Missed the bus."

That fucking snippy tone. How parents managed not to kill all their offspring before any of them reached eighteen, Ethan had no idea. He grabbed the school bag and dumped it on Kurt's lap. "Tables are for customers. I need you on the counter till four-thirty. Luce and I are out back redoing an order."

"Screw another one up, huh?" Kurt sneered, and it was all Ethan could do not to thump him one.

"Can it." The last thing Ethan needed was Kurt's sarcasm. None of this was how he'd imagined it in his head a year back, six months before their mother died. Back then, he thought they'd be in this together. Back then, they were so damned close they may as well have been glued at the hip.

Kurt's lip drew up in that familiar sneer Ethan hated. "I thought you were all about wanting me to talk and shit, but whatever. I'm happy to shut up. Guess I should give you this then, oh, parent one." He feigned a mocking bow and shoved a crumpled envelope Ethan's way before trudging his way to the till to take an order from the queue of one gathered there.

Ethan steeled himself as he turned the envelope over. Bearing the school's monogram, he'd bet a month's takings it didn't hold congratulations on how well Kurt was doing in class. *Fuck.* He glanced at Kurt and caught a hint of nervousness in the kid's expression before it was visibly schooled into a scowl, daring Ethan to say something about . . . whatever it was.

Not about to give Kurt the satisfaction of watching his reaction, Ethan headed for the kitchen, Kurt's damning gaze drilling holes in his back all the way. He swallowed hard and pushed all thought of his mother to the back of his mind. He didn't need that guilt on top of everything else.

MORE BY JAY HOGAN

AUCKLAND MED SERIES

First Impressions

Crossing the Touchline

Up Close and Personal

Against the Grain

You are Cordially Invited (2021)

SOUTHERN LIGHTS SERIES

Powder and Pavlova

Tamarillo Tart

Flat Whites and Chocolate Fish

Pinot and Pineapple Lumps

STANDALONE

Digging Deep
(2020 Lambda Literary Finalist)

Unguarded (May 2021)

(Written as part of Sarina Bowen's
True North—Vino & Veritas Series and published by Heart Eyes
Press)

PAINTED BAY SERIES

Off Balance

On Board (2021)

ABOUT THE AUTHOR

Jay is a 20202 Lambda Literary Award Finalist in gay romance.

She is a New Zealand author writing in MM romance and romantic suspense primarily set in New Zealand. She loves writing character driven romances with lots of humour, a good dose of reality and a splash of angst. She's travelled extensively, lived in many countries, and in a past life she was a critical care nurse and counsellor. Jay is owned by a huge Maine Coon cat and a gorgeous Cocker Spaniel.

Join Jay's reader's Group for updates, promotions, her current writing projects and special releases

www.facebook.com/groups/hoganshangout/

Sign up to her newsletter:

mailchi.mp/adco1f36b9b6/jayhoganauthor

Or visit her website:

www.jayhoganauthor.com